HARRY NAVINSKI

The Duty

A not so Scottish murder

Harry Navinski

First published by Harry Navinski Books 2021

First edition

This book was professionally typeset on Reedsy.
Find out more at reedsy.com

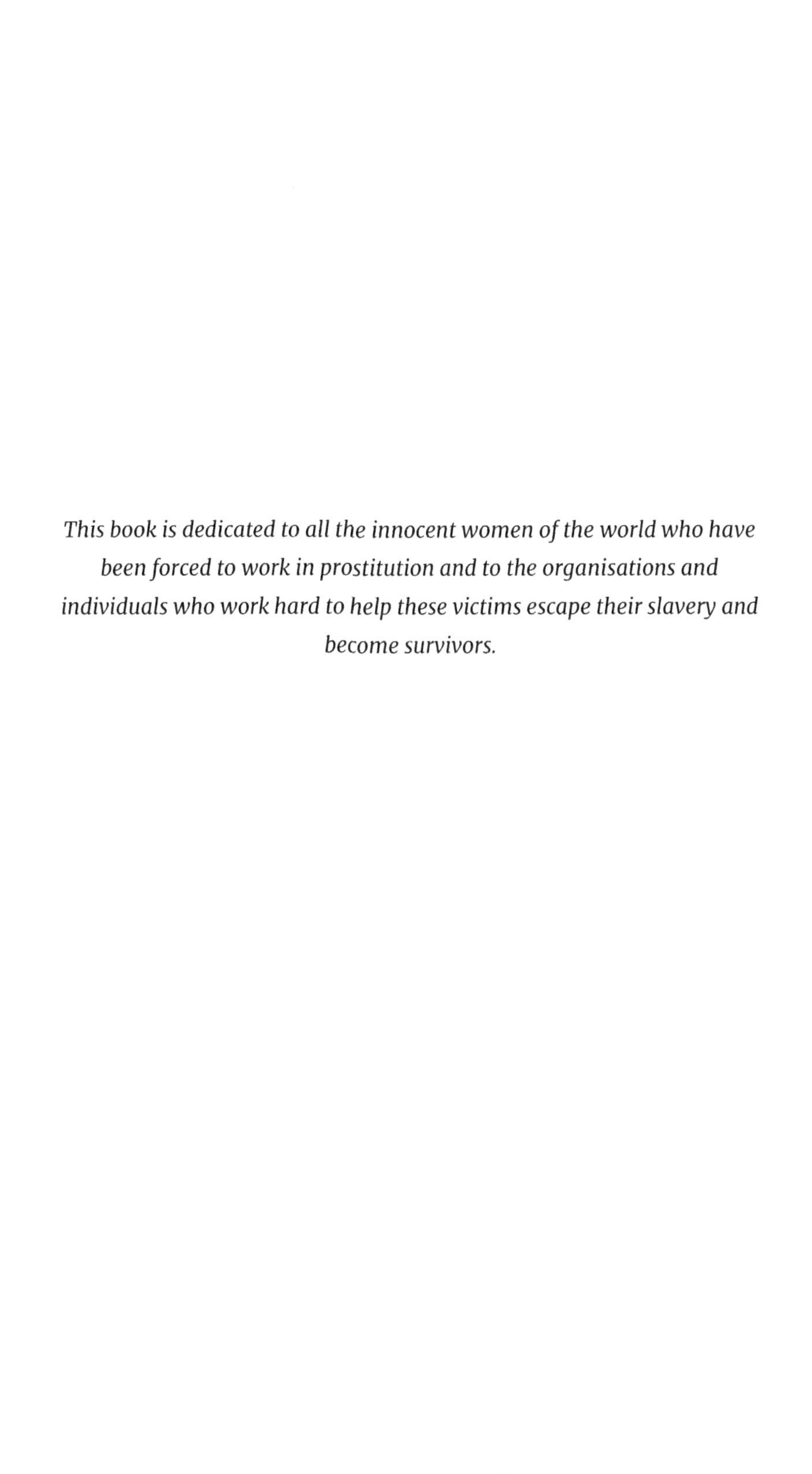

This book is dedicated to all the innocent women of the world who have been forced to work in prostitution and to the organisations and individuals who work hard to help these victims escape their slavery and become survivors.

Contents

Foreword

Much of this book is set in places far from Great Britain's shores, in countries where I have lived and worked, where memories, both good and bad, are powerful and fresh. As I wrote and edited this book, I shed many tears as memories returned, of innocence stolen, of suffering and pain but also heroic determination. This book is not merely a piece of imagination. It is based on the realities and situations of the people who live out their lives in tropical Bengal. Although the names of the people, what they say, and what they do are fictional, the story truly represents the struggles of the people on which it is based.

The Duty

A not so Scottish Murder

Second in the DCI Suzanna McLeod Murder Mystery Series.
By Harry Navinski

Chapter 1

Monday 16th February 2015

The woman regained consciousness as they rolled her out of the rug, the February night air chilling her head. The tears that had flowed earlier had crusted at the corners of her eyes, and she could feel mucous above her upper lip. She was still devoid of sensations below her neck, and couldn't raise a hand to attend to her face. It had been stuffy in the car boot, and she had drifted into unconsciousness shortly after they'd bundled her into that dark place. She recalled the recent past.

When she'd first regained consciousness after the fall, she could smell the mustiness of her mouldy damp cellar room – the room that had become her sleeping quarters since arriving in Scotland. But overpowering that aroma was the stench like that of a toilet where people had dirtied the walls and floors. She'd retched as the smell hit her nostrils and vomit had ejected from her mouth.

She had been upside down, unable to move, and had an excruciating headache but had felt no pain from her body. That's when she'd realised that the awful stink must have been from herself – the control of her bowel and bladder lost.

She'd heard voices above her and could tell the cellar door was open as light streamed down the precipitous brick stairs. The voices had descended and as they closed in, she could make out some words they'd spoken in her native language, mixed in with English. "What are you doing laying there?" Then "Disgusting." But she couldn't answer. The woman had touched her head and other words were heard: "broken neck, paralysed, illegal, and prison."

They'd dragged her up the steps by her ankles, as if a side of meat, and into the hallway. She'd tumbled over and over as they rolled a rug around her. When she was fully encased, her lips had touched the wool and fluff stuck to them when she'd tried to breathe. She had passed out again.

Her thoughts were interrupted as she heard them conversing. What were they saying? She heard the woman say 'identify', then she was looming over her, a large stone in her hand – her face evil, devoid of any emotion.

Chapter 2

Tuesday 17th

The five-inch knife plunged into the young woman's abdomen, glancing off her lower rib. Blood gushed from the wound as the attacker forcefully withdrew the knife, her body reluctant to release its grip on the blade. She screamed, then toppled sideways, her knees collapsing. She heard the crack of bone as her head struck a concrete block.

The man looked down at the woman who had tried to take his liberty, hatred in his face. He booted the hands that cradled her wounded belly as if trying to score a penalty. Someone stopped at the road's end and looked towards him, so he turned and ran.

Her cheek lay on the hard road, her nose sensing the odours of tyre rubber, old engine oil, and cement. Her hands felt smashed from the force of the kick and sticky from the blood. Bile rose in her throat, and she swallowed the disgusting acid, fighting the reflex to vomit her breakfast. As her consciousness faded, she looked at the row of garages, their aged paint dirty, peeling, scratched and graffitied. DI Una Wallace prayed that those ugly doors would not be the last thing she ever saw.

She had gone to the area because of a tip-off that a drug supplier was peddling smack to teenagers. It was a place that, although run down, could have a heart if only the junkies would let it. Dealers were in competition for territory. Fights, stabbings, and shootings had become regular occurrences. Smackheads broke into homes and mugged neighbours to fund their next fix. Una couldn't pass up the opportunity to take one down.

She'd stopped her car on the road and walked towards the temporary drug market. Her prey was in sight, and Una realised she should have brought one of the DCs with her. She tried calling for backup, but her radio had failed. 'Must be the battery again.' She'd thought about phoning the office and hanging off until someone arrived, but she wanted to make this bust, and time was pressing.

Una was ambitious and confident in her abilities. She hated the criminals who chose to take from others, to take what most people had worked hard to gain. They stole money, valuable objects, and lives. They injured and killed innocent people. It was her job to stop them, and she wouldn't back away from the challenge, even when it meant taking risks. This time, though, she'd made a mistake, driven by the determination to take out the scum, who, with his pals, had turned her parents' home area into a nightly no-go zone. It was personal.

A passer-by heard the scream and ran to her side as the hooded man ran away. Una's saviour dialled 999 on her mobile and spoke to the injured woman to reassure her. But Una had slipped into unconsciousness. As the rescuer answered the emergency service operator's questions, the blood flowed from Una's midriff, puddling on the concrete. Una never heard the soothing tone of the woman's voice, nor the reassuring words. She didn't see the woman remove her coat, bundle it, and press it against the oozing wound, in the hope it might stem the flow of her lifeblood.

Chapter 3

The two boys meandered their way along the riverbank, chatting inanely about their mums and school. They'd bunked off school again today. The morning had started damp and cold, but the sun had squeezed its way through the grey clouds and brightened the day, and the boys' spirits. They were almost skipping along, picking up flotsam – a pair of beachcombers looking for treasures.

They'd never found anything exciting or of value on these expeditions and didn't really expect to. But it was better than being in school. No stresses, no teachers pushing them to complete work, no bigger boys intimidating them. Fresh air and freedom. If they spotted a policeman, there would be the excitement of evading capture to spice up their jaunt – to get their hearts pounding; to feel alive and in control, clever, streetwise, confident.

"Hey, Aaron, what's that over there?"

"I don't see nothin, Robbie. Where do you mean?"

"Over *there,*" he said, pointing to the muddy bank where the salty smell of the estuary emanated. A rotten fence pole and rusty barbed wired stood above it.

"Don't know. Let's have a look," Aaron said, raising his voice over the sound of screeching gulls that circled overhead. The boys' feet crunched loudly as they walked more determinedly across the pebbly beach, stepping over driftwood and other discarded articles as they moved towards the shape. When they got closer, their progress slowed as suspicion demotivated them. The object was mostly dark brown but had cloth attached to its middle and upper part. They both stopped open-mouthed, one metre away, their curiosity over-satisfied.

The two lads looked at each other, then stepped closer. It was definitely a woman. Her dirty white bra had shifted, exposing one breast. It reminded Aaron of a large Tunnock's Tea Cake. Robbie immediately turned and ran off. Aaron moved aside the woman's long hair and saw her face. He retched at the sight, then ran after his pal. "Hey, wait up. I'm coming with yer."

The boys leapt back up the bank onto the concrete path that ran beside the beach, then ran off towards the shops. Robbie saw a man walking along the street and ran up to him. His Jack Russell wore a white-spotted red bandana, its lead taught from straining against the man's reluctant wandering. Unlike the old guy who held it back, the little dog had energy and a sense of purpose – to reach the next lamppost and sniff the scent of other dogs, before leaving his own mark.

"Hey, mister. We've found a dead body. You need to call the polis."

The man looked at the youngsters "Aye, sure you have." He walked off, led on by his dog, ignoring their pleas for help. They ran on until they reached a local shop, its yellow signs declaring it open all hours, and crashed through the door.

"There's a dead woman in the estuary. She's the same colour as you." Robbie said to the shopkeeper.

The man was shocked. "You'd better not be joking with me, lads."

"We're not," they chorused. "Call the polis."

He opened a door behind him and called up the stairs, "Ishraq. Come down and look after the shop. I have to go out."

Ishraq wondered why her husband needed to go out unplanned, with no notice. She would have to leave the ironing until later. Asim was becoming more erratic these days. But she knew better than to argue with him. It wasn't her place to challenge her man. "Okay," she said.

He turned back to the boys, who were waiting at the door. "Show me where this body is. You'd better not be wasting my time, lads."

The three left the shop, the boys running off towards the river and the man jogging behind, his large stomach jostling. The boys stopped on the banks and pointed to the body. Mr Salarzai couldn't be certain what it was when he first saw it, so jumped down and walked closer. Stood next to the body, he bent and felt the neck of the woman. She was cold, clammy and pulse-less, as expected. He looked at her face, then turned and cried. "My God. Who has done this dreadful thing to the poor woman?" His stomach tried to eject his lunch, but he clamped his lips closed and firmly cupped his mouth with his hand as he walked away.

He dialled 999, then explained what had been found and where. The first police car arrived ten minutes later, its sirens cutting through the peace. Two young female officers approached him. PC McPherson was the first to speak. "Mr Salarzai?"

"Yes, That's me. The body's over there," he pointed. The constable jumped down onto the beach, her short dark hair hardly moving as she landed, and strode across to where the body lay, leaving her colleague, PC Smith, to note Mr Salarzai's and the boys' details.

After seeing the body, she radioed in to confirm the discovery of a dead woman, returning to her partner, ashen-faced. Smith led Mr Salarzai and boys further away as she concluded taking their statements, then asked them to wait while she conferred with her colleague. The policewomen got together to exchange details. "It's horrible, Louise. Her face has been pulverised. She's a real mess. Nearly made me vomit."

Smith could see Kerrie was shaken by what she'd seen. Although both in the early twenties, they'd already seen a few dead bodies, so this one must have been awful. "She's Asian, right?"

"Aye. South Asian."

"What's the difference?"

"Asian could mean anything from Mongolian to Chinese. South Asia is the Indian sub-continent."

"Oh, I see!"

Another police car arrived, and two male officers got out. The four colleagues huddled to discuss the situation, then the two men retrieved some sticks and crime scene tape from their vehicle, to create a cordon.

Their sergeant arrived in another car a few minutes later. After speaking with the constables, he pulled out his phone and dialled.

* * *

Chief Superintendent Ewan Robertson strode into Suzanna's office without knocking His brow furrowed and his voice sounded stern as he spoke. "McLeod. Dreadful news!"

Suzanna looked up at the Chief Super, wondering whether he'd got to hear about her recent speeding offence and was about to suspend her. 'No, it couldn't be that – he looked sad, not angry.'

When he spoke again, his voice cracked: "It's DI Wallace... She's been stabbed and admitted to the hospital. She's in a bad way."

Suzanna's mouth opened in shock at the news. She was surprised to see the Chief Super emotional. She'd thought him to be a cold, pedantic, paper-pusher. His eyes looked like they were holding back tears. She stood, then asked, "What hospital, sir?"

"It's the Western General but there's no point going right now; she's in a critical condition. You won't get to see her until she comes out of theatre."

DS Caitlin Findlay marched to Suzanna's office, after taking a call about the River Forth body discovery. "Ma'am," she said, then noticed the Chief Super. "Sir. Just had word that the body of a woman has been found washed up on the banks of the Forth, near the bridge at Queensferry. Seems to be of Indian descent. Uniform are on scene, and they've informed the duty pathologist." Caitlin sensed that there was something else distracting the two senior officers from the news of the reported potential murder. She paused before continuing, wondering what it could be. "Who would you like to attend the scene?"

Recovering her composure, Suzanna responded. "You go, Caitlin. Take Murray or Owen with you. Report back when you've found out more, then we'll decide who should lead the investigation."

"OK, ma'am."

"Caitlin, before you go. You need to know that Una Wallace is in hospital – in critical condition. She's been stabbed. I'll let you know when I hear more."

Caitlin's eyes widened at the news. "Is she going to be all right?"

"We don't know yet. As I said, she's in critical condition. I intend to go to the hospital as soon as she's out of surgery. I'll update you when I hear anything. Spread the word around the team, please Caitlin."

"Right, ma'am. I'll tell the others, then speak with the pathologist and talk with the lads who found the body." She turned and strode away, the bun of her dark chocolate hair swaying with the motion of her walk.

"Keep me posted on this washed-up body and any news on Wallace." The Chief Super said, then strode away, holding back tears. When he'd shut the door to his office, the tears flowed. Una was a lovely lass. Young, ambitious, intelligent. She was so much like the daughter he'd lost. Taken from him by the inhuman, reckless use of a knife, by a mugger who'd tried to snatch her bag and she'd resisted. She'd been 22 at the time – her whole life ahead of her. The mugger had stolen her future and robbed her parents of a wonderful daughter. He prayed that Una would pull through, wiped his eyes with a handkerchief, then sat at his desk and resumed work.

* * *

"Guys," Caitlin said as she entered the main office. Owen, Murray, and Mairi turned. "Just heard from the Chief Super. Una's in hospital. She's been stabbed and is in surgery. She's in a critical condition."

"Bloody hell. How did that happen? She never let on where she was going when she walked out earlier," Owen stated.

Caitlin ignored his question. "We've got a dead body in Queensferry – on the banks of the Forth estuary. The boss has tasked me with taking over for the moment. Murray, you're with me."

"Right-o." He stood and grabbed his mobile and coat, then followed Caitlin out of the office, along the bland, grey corridor, down the lino-covered stairs, through the swing doors and out into the car park.

Chapter 4

As Caitlin drove along the seafront at Queensferry, her eyes were drawn upwards to the iconic nineteenth-century, cantilevered Forth Bridge looming above them. "I hear the railway bridge painters are employed all year round, starting at the beginning again once they'd got from one end to the other."

"No, that's not true anymore, Sarge. The last time it was painted, they used some fancy paint, like the stuff they use on oil rigs. They finished the job in 2011 and they said it would last 25 years."

Continuing along and under the more recently constructed Forth Road Bridge, they passed beneath the yet to be opened Queensferry Crossing bridge that would carry the M90 motorway, when it was finished.

"They've been building this new bridge for about six years now. Have you heard when it'll get finished?"

"Not sure. I think they said 2017. Hang on. Here we are. The CSI van is over there, and two police cars." Caitlin found somewhere to park, and they both walked across to the van.

"Hi chaps. DS Findlay. Is the pathologist here yet?"

"Hi, Sarge. Yeah. He arrived a few minutes ago."

"Do you know where he is?"

He pointed out towards the estuary. "He'll be in that tent, Sarge," the constable said sarcastically as if to say surely it's obvious.

Caitlin glared at the young PC. His smile shed from his face as he realised that he'd stepped over the line. But she said nothing. They walked away, leaving the constable to ponder on the wisdom of his impudence.

The young PC watched her stride towards the CSI tent, her pert bottom catching his eyes. He elbowed his colleague. "Fit, eh?" The other PC grinned back and nodded.

"Knock, knock," Caitlin said as she drew aside the tent flap.

The pathologist looked up. "Oh, hello Sergeant Findlay. I just got here. Too early to tell you anything yet, except the obvious."

Caitlin eyed the victim's scantily clad body. The mutilated face shocked her, but she didn't show any emotion. "Fair enough, Mr Whitaker. I'll talk with the CSI guys, and give you a while to do your preliminary checks."

"Great. I'll give you a shout when I'm done."

As she walked away, she noticed Murray hadn't followed her all the way to the tent but had already gone to speak with the CSI team. When she joined them, Murray turned to her, his spiky ginger hair unmoving despite the breeze off the river.

"Sarge. The team is still setting up, so it's probably best if we get out of their way for a while."

"Okay. Let's see if we can speak with the kids who found the body and the guy who called it in." They strode back to where the uniformed officers were standing. "Who was the first on scene?"

PC McPherson answered. "I was, Sarge. My colleague, PC Smith," she said indicating the female officer stood next to her, "took some details from the two boys and the man who'd called 999."

"These two clowns," McPherson said, looking at the two male PCs, "just turned up a few minutes ago. They know nothing. In fact they're pretty clueless, full stop!"

The young PCs glared at their colleague but refrained from a response, given that they'd already upset the DS. Caitlin glanced at the two male PCs, then returned her attention to the women officers and asked to see their notes from talking with the boys. Smith handed over her notebook and Caitlin scanned it. There were names and contact details, but little else. She photographed the pages, using her phone, then passed it back to Smith. "Thanks. Is that them over there?" She asked, looking towards where two boys and a man stood.

"Yes. They've been there a while and they're not really dressed for hanging around outside too long."

"I'll find somewhere warm we can take them to get their statements. If the pathologist emerges from his tent and seems to be looking for someone, please give me a shout, as I need to speak with him as soon as he's completed the preliminaries."

"Sure thing, Sarge," McPherson responded.

Caitlin strolled across to speak with the man and two boys. "Mr Salarzai?"

"Yes. That's me."

"I understand you reported finding the body?"

"Yes." Turning to look at the boys, he continued, "these two lads came running into my shop shouting they'd discovered it."

"I saw it first," Robbie volunteered, as Aaron stood quietly.

"Murray, you have a chat with Mr Salarzai. I'll talk with the boys." Turning back to the man, she spoke to Mr Salarzai again. "How far is your shop from here?"

He pointed down the road. "Just over there."

"Good. Can we go there to talk? You must be frozen."

"Yes. I *am* chilled. That would be good."

"Can we bring the boys, as well? Is there be somewhere we can speak with them separately?"

"The shop is too cluttered and there will be customers to overhear our conversation. But we could go upstairs to my flat. I have two rooms we could use. I hope this won't take long, as I have a business to run."

"Thanks, Mr Salarzai. We'll be as quick as we can. We'll need to get back to the scene soon, anyway." She turned and called by to the PCs. "We'll be in the shop, down the road." Smith gave her an acknowledging thumbs-up sign, so they walked off. "Come on, lads. Let's get you in out of the cold." The boys were shivering.

"Ishraq," Salarzai said on entering his shop.

"Ah! There you are. You've been gone so long."

"Please continue to look after the shop. These police officers need to speak with me and these two lads."

"Why are the police here? Why do they need to speak with you, and who are these boys?"

Mr Salarzai hadn't been exaggerating when he'd said the shop was cluttered. The aisles were narrow, and the shelves stacked high with as much as he could squeeze into the room. "We will use the sitting room and the kitchen. We won't be long," Mr Salarzai continued without answering his wife's queries.

Mrs Salarzai did not look happy. "You should have given me some warning. I haven't tidied yet."

"I didn't know these lads would find a dead woman on the estuary banks, my dear," he responded, looking annoyed that his wife was fussing at such a time. She went quiet and looked shocked by the revelation. They climbed the stairs, almost all of them creaking as they did. "This way, officer," Salarzai said to Murray as he walked into the kitchen. "You can use *this* room, sergeant," he said, pointing towards the living room.

The boys sat on the vinyl black and white sofa, and Caitlin sat opposite on a similarly untasteful chair. "Okay. So your name is Robbie?" she said, looking into the more outspoken boy's eyes before shifting her attention to the other. "And you're Aaron. Is that right?"

They both nodded in agreement, so Caitlin continued. "Robbie, you said you were the first to see the body. Tell me what you did and don't leave out any details." Robbie thought before answering. Caitlin noted down all he said, then asked Aaron for his version, which confirmed what his pal had said. "Lads. I'm wondering what the two of you were doing wandering along this bit of coastline on a school morning?"

Robbie went to speak, but Aaron jumped in first. "Please don't tell my mum. She'll go mental if she hears I've been bunking off again." Robbie had intended to give an excuse for their presence, but his pal had spoiled that. Now the copper knew they'd been playing truant.

"I've already got your addresses, but I need your parents' names and phone numbers, as well." She paused and waited. "Don't be shy, lads. Aaron: you first."

They both reluctantly provided the details. "And which school should you be at now?"

"Queensferry Primary," Aaron replied.

"How did you think you'd get away with not being at school today, lads?"

Robbie responded. "We're good at forging our mum's signatures. We'll write sick notes to take in tomorrow."

"You would have done. But now I will have to speak with your parents. I'll leave it with them to speak with the school."

"Aw! Miss. Please don't. We'll be in big trouble."

"Look, lads. I appreciate you reporting the dead body. If you'd not done that, the tide might have come in and taken it again. But I must contact your parents and school. They will be worried about you. And they'll need to know what you've just been through. It can be shocking to find a dead person.

"There's only our mums to tell. Neither of us has dads. Well, I do, but I've not seen him in years," Robbie offered.

Aaron added, "My mum said my dad died when I was a baby, so I've never known him."

"Sorry to hear that, lads. You just wait here, while I make some phone calls." She left them looking worried and called the mothers. They both responded in the same manner – were annoyed with their boys and said they'd get a clout when they got their hands on them. But neither agreed to leave work to collect them and take them home, claiming they wouldn't get paid if they did and they couldn't afford to lose any money.

Caitlin agreed to take the lads to school instead. When she shared this news with the boys, they seemed happier. Perhaps they were thinking their mums might have calmed down a bit by the end of the day. "Lads. I'm just wondering why you took the risk of bunking off school today, just to wander along the seafront. What's so wrong with the school that kept you from going?"

They looked timidly at each other, neither wanting to speak. Robbie was the first to open up. "There's a group of boys at school. Bigger than us. They've been pushing us around, and they said if we didn't give them our lunch money today, they'd beat us up." His head dropped onto his chest as he admitted he was scared.

"Right. Let's get you back to school. I'll speak with the headteacher. What's her name?"

"The head's a man. It's Mr Primrose. We reckon he's gay." The boys looked at each other and smirked.

"Just wait there, boys. I need to speak with my colleague." As she said that, Murray emerged from the kitchen with Mr Salarzai.

Chapter 5

They left the flat and shop, back into the cold again. Caitlin talked quietly with Murray. "You take the lads to their school. It's Queensferry Primary. Speak to Mr Primrose, the head-teacher. Tell him what the lads found and let him know they will need to keep an eye on them. This will have been traumatic and, although they seem to be handling it well, it could hit them later. Tell him I'll be in touch later to discuss the lads' absence from school. Okay?"

"Yes, Sarge... Lads. You come with me." He led them to the car as Caitlin headed back to where the uniformed officers stood. Despite him being the same age, Murray appeared to be younger than Caitlin – not by his looks but by the way he acted. The way he and Owen fooled around instead of focussing on policing. Even so, she liked Murray. He was a good officer, and one you could rely on.

The CSI team were scrutinising the banks of the estuary and had recruited the assistance of the two male officers. "Has the pathologist not left the tent yet?"

"Not that I've noticed, Sarge," McPherson replied.

Caitlin wandered over to the tent and drew back the flap, just as Justin Whitaker rose.

"Ah. Sergeant Findlay. Excellent timing. I've just finished my preliminary examination. The body will have to be moved to the mortuary now, so I can carry out a full autopsy.

He briefed Caitlin on what he'd found, then arranged for the body's transportation.

* * *

It took a while for Suzanna to find a parking space at the Western General. It was evident the complex had grown hugely over the time of its operation. The earliest architecture dated back to the Victorian era, but a multitude of buildings had been erected throughout the 20th century. For Suzanna, it was the ugly utilitarian blocks from the 50s that spoilt the site.

She tried three parking ticket machines before she found one that worked, so by the time she entered the reception, she was feeling frustrated that her time was being wasted. She held up her warrant card to the medical receptionist. "DCI McLeod. I'm here to talk with those providing care to my DI, Una Wallace. She was brought in a couple of hours ago with a critical stab wound."

"Just a minute." She picked up the phone and spoke to a colleague. "She's in recovery after surgery. Second floor, Ward 24. Take that corridor–"

Suzanna marched along the corridors and took the stairs two at a time, her heart rate rising with the exertion. The usual smells of disinfectant and stale air pervaded every room in the building. As she arrived at Ward 24, a man in blue scrubs emerged through double doors and caught sight of her. The doors creaked as they swung closed behind him and flapped twice before settling.

"Chief Inspector. Good to see you again. Just wish it weren't for the reason it is," the doctor said.

"Hello Luke. I agree with you there. It's always hard when it's one of your own who's been injured. How is she?"

"The knife went into her abdomen just below the ribcage on the left side."

Suzanna thought 'so a right-handed attacker.'

"It missed her stomach but cut into her large intestine and grazed her kidney. She's been lucky."

"Lucky! Taking a knife in the abdomen is hardly lucky!"

"Sorry, Suzanna. Being stabbed obviously isn't lucky, but at least the knife didn't seriously damage any vital organs. We've cleaned up the wound and sewn up the damage. She's also received a significant head wound. Her skull is fractured, and she's concussed. She'll be kept under sedation until tomorrow, at least, then we'll slowly let her come round."

"Thanks, Luke. Sorry I got uptight with you."

"It's understandable. I'm sure I'd have been sensitive if it were my colleague who'd just been stabbed. I know this might not be the best timing to ask, but if you're not busy at the weekend, might you like to come mountain biking?" He looked directly into her blue eyes. "A few of us are heading into the hills on Sunday. I know you're an adventurous type..."

"You're right. Not good timing. I do enjoy mountain biking, but I doubt I'll be available this weekend, what with Una's stabbing and possibly a new murder to investigate. Would I have been able to bring my man along?"

"Oh! Sorry. I thought you were single at the moment."

"So you were asking me on a date then?"

Luke looked sheepish. "Well, it would have been with a crowd but, yeah, I suppose it would have been a date. Would you have been tempted?"

"As I said, I like mountain biking, so would likely have said yes. Regarding the date... If I were not in a relationship," She smiled but said no more. "Look, I'd better go. I need to get up to speed with the potential murder investigation. See you around, Luke. And take care of my inspector."

* * *

Suzanna parked her car outside the cordon and walked to the crime scene. Recognising her, the constable lifted the tape for her to go through. A white tent indicated where the crime scene investigators were likely to be.

Opening the tent flap, she expected to see the body lying on the ground, but there was nothing. The tent was just being used to cover some equipment. She looked around and spotted her sergeant, waved to her and they both walked towards each other.

"Where's the body, Caitlin?"

"It's been moved already. The CSIs have taken loads of photos. They couldn't leave it where it had been found because it was discovered at low tide, and as you can see, the tide's come in."

"Ah! Of course. So the pathologist will have it back at the mortuary already?"

"Well, certainly on the way there. The CSIs are just wrapping up, because everything is under water and there's not much more they can do."

"Has anyone started the hunt for a dumping site?"

"Not sure, ma'am. You asked me to take control of things here but didn't know at the time who would be leading the investigation."

"True. Okay, thanks. I've been appointed Senior Investigating Officer, so once you've finished up here and written things up, you can hand over to me and Rab. As Rab is in Una's team, I can't have him investigating her stabbing, so I'll make him my deputy on this case. Angus will look into the assault."

Walking over to the water's edge, Suzanna looked out across the estuary. Whoever dumped her body would have found it difficult if the tide were out, so it would need to have happened at high tide or a couple of hours either side. If it had been as the tide was rising, the current would have taken the body upstream, so it would have been dumped east of where she stood. But if the body had entered the water at or after high tide, it would have drifted eastward, so would have been dropped in somewhere to the west. Looking up and down the coast, she tried to imagine where it might have happened, why, and who might have done it? If only the woman could speak.

* * *

The second time she'd woken, she found herself locked in a car boot. It smelled of tyre rubber and grease. As she laid there, her ears became colder. Her thoughts turned to when she'd first arrived in the UK.

The train leading away from the airport was modern, quiet, and fast, not like the trains in her home country. They had transferred to a huge rail station using underground trains. The tunnels were noisy, the walls mostly tiled but widely covered in large posters. She assumed they were advertising things but as she couldn't read English, she didn't know what.

Her saviour, because that is how she saw him, was kind to her throughout the long journey, explaining what she must do, where they were going and buying her food and drink. She felt so lucky to have escaped her previous captors and now have a good life ahead of her in this wonderful, rich country.

The train from London had sped its way to Edinburgh in just five hours, stopping occasionally at large cities along the way. The countryside had seemed beautiful: rolling hills, trees that she did not recognise, grasslands, and fields full of crops.

A taxi took them from the station to her new home; it was clean and quiet, and the traffic moved smoothly – amazingly obeying all the traffic signals. No one sounded their horns. It was tranquil compared with the roads back home.

Unlike the concrete boxes she was used to, the house where she was to live was large and had character. The luxury of the home's furnishings had awed her when she arrived and was greeted by the smiling woman of the house. She had felt so fortunate.

It had been a wonderful time initially, but after a while, the woman became resentful of her presence and mistreated her. Her saviour still expected her to provide services, but this was the least she could do for him, given what he had done for her.

Returning to the present time, she realised that promising start had turned sour beyond her imagination and now she was caged again and knew not what fate had in store for her. She cried herself back to sleep...

Chapter 6

Wednesday 18th

As she drove into the car park, Suzanna thought for the umpteenth time how the police HQ looked like it had been made with basic grey Lego building blocks. The architect certainly shouldn't win any prizes for its utilitarian blandness. She grabbed her bags and marched into the foyer, her mind still pondering the building. If it lasted as long as the other 1960s buildings, hopefully, they'd be tearing it down soon.

After settling in, Suzanna joined her team. "Okay, guys. Time for a brainstorm." She went through what was known so far before launching into the unknown. "So we need to know who the victim was," she started making a list on the board: "Where has she been living? What occupation might she have had? When and how did she die? Where was the murder carried out and where was the body dumped? Plus, what motives could there have been for killing her, and what type of person could be the murderer – who committed the crime? Obviously, it's too early to tie down some of these, but we can speculate and decide on what needs to be done next, to answer some of these questions."

Noticing the officers nodding their agreement, she continued. "Let's start with who she was. We know she had nothing on her to furnish an identity. We know she is of South Asian descent, and she likely dressed traditionally. That suggests she's an immigrant, rather than a young woman who had her childhood in the UK. Because, as we know," she said, looking at Zahir, "second or third-generation immigrants are more likely to adopt western dress."

Zahir spoke up: "Most do, ma'am, but many of my female cousins in the Muslim community dress traditionally when they become women – especially after they marry. It depends on how strict their parents and grandparents are. So she could be a Muslim woman who grew up in Scotland?"

"Thanks for your insight, Zahir. I hadn't realised that. So, either a Scottish born Muslim woman or perhaps a fresh immigrant." She looked around the room to check for any differing views but saw none, so wrote this on the board.

"Before we move on, I just want to reiterate the rules. We won't judge anyone's suggestions. I'll just note them. Then we can analyse the suggestions later after we've captured them. Okay?" She looked around the room for any dissenters. "Right. How can we find her identity?"

Owen raised his hand, as if still in school, his high forehead and receding hairline looking more prominent from where Suzanna stood. "We can trawl the DVLA database to look for a photo image match with the victim, check the criminal database, and the Home Office database."

She noted these on the board "Any other ideas?" Numerous ideas were suggested: checking with temples, mosques, schools, and colleges in the city, to see if anyone recognised her, having the woman's picture published in the newspapers. Suzanna posed another question, "Any thoughts on what job she might have been doing?"

"Anything, ma'am," Zahir said. "Being a young South Asian doesn't mean she'd have been more likely to be in one job more than another,"

"If she grew up in Scotland, I'd agree, although she'd be unlikely to be CEO of a blue-chip company. As a young woman of any racial background there are certain jobs that she's highly unlikely to have been doing and other occupations she would be more likely to have had. We need to think about gender employment demographics. If she was a recent immigrant, then the possibilities are more restricted... We'll leave that one for the moment. Next: How did she die?"

"On the face of it, drowning," Caitlin said, having seen the water-logged body before it was taken to the mortuary. "The pathologist checked the body for signs of blunt force trauma, knife or gun-shot wounds, bruising or strangulation. He said it's possible the attack on the woman's face was enough to kill her. But he couldn't be certain until he completed the autopsy."

"So why was she killed? Jealousy? Rage? Financial gain? Revenge?" Suzanna wrote as she spoke.

"An honour-killing, perhaps?" Murray suggested. Suzanna wrote it on the board.

"The damage to her face might suggest she refused to marry someone, so they disfigured her – like an acid attack – then killed her so no one else could marry her," Caitlin offered.

"But why disfigure her, *then* murder her?" Mairi asked.

"What if she'd fallen pregnant to a black man or a white European? Some Asians are more racially prejudiced than whites," Rab suggested.

Zahir jumped in. "Hang on. Just because she's South Asian, doesn't mean the motive is an honour killing or racial prejudice. She could have been killed for any of the reasons a white woman might have been killed. She might even have been the first victim of a serial killer."

"True. But these are all reasons she *might* have been murdered. Honour killings tend to be associated with the South Asian community. So it *is* fair to suggest them as possibilities. The racial prejudice suggestion is not too far-fetched, either. I recall a case where a

Pakistani woman was driven out of her family for falling pregnant to an Afro-Caribbean man."

"You're right, ma'am," Zahir conceded. "I've seen these prejudices at work. I would be allowed to marry a white, non-Muslim girl, although she'd be expected to take on our faith. My sister, on the other hand, could not marry a man, either white or black, from another faith. But would that be a motive for murder and disfigurement? I doubt it."

"Perhaps the disfiguring of the face was to hide the victim's identity, to make it difficult to trace her to the murderer. That would suggest a connection, rather than a stranger-killing. Next then: who might have murdered her?"

Suzanna wrote up their suggestions: her boyfriend, partner or husband, her mother, father, brother or sister, her employer, a stalker, or serial killer – a random psychopath.

"Another question in my mind, she was in under-clothes when she washed up, so where are her outer clothes. Why was she partly undressed – could there have been a sexual motive for the crime?" Suzanna said.

Zahir offered his thoughts. "You said she had on bangles and jewellery that suggested traditional dress. It's likely then that she had been wearing a sari when she was dumped. This is just a length of material wrapped around the body. It could have unravelled and washed away as she drifted in the current."

"Maybe she was raped, then murdered," Murray suggested. Mairi cringed at the mention of rape. Old memories resurfacing.

They discussed where she might have been murdered and agreed the priority was to identify where she had been dumped into the Forth and how she got to the site. Suzanna paused as she thought things through. "Rab. As soon as we have an approximate time of death, check out the Forth's tide table and marine charts to track back along the coast from where the body was washed up. Once you have a range of possible dumping sites, get out there with Mairi and get some uniformed assistance to find out where the dumping took place."

She paused again. "Murray. Owen. You two with me... Caitlin," Suzanna looked directly into her bronze eyes, "I need you to focus on helping Angus with the stabbing enquiry. Okay?" Caitlin nodded.

"Owen, check out the criminal database for any clues to who she might be. Murray, start trawling the DVLA database. I'll get on to forensics and get them looking for possible DNA matches for the victim. Zahir, I'd like you to visit all the mosques in the city and see if anyone recognises her. After that try Hindu temples, then community centres used predominantly by South Asians. If you draw a blank with those, colleges would be next on my list."

"Got it," he responded.

"Anything else on your minds before we split up and crack on?" She paused. "Okay. Let's get to it."

* * *

"Sorry I couldn't join you for the murder brainstorm, ma'am," Angus said as he stood in Suzanna's office doorway.

"No problem. I expect you to focus on the stabbing. Talking of which, how's it going?"

He combed his fingers through his spiky quiff before responding. "Nothing to report yet. We know she was working a drugs case at the time, and she was stabbed in an area where there's a lot of dealing. So a drug dealer would be the obvious suspect. But she didn't report where she was going or who she planned to meet. And I can't speak with her, so I'll need to go through the case files and talk with her team, to get started."

"Okay. Caitlin can assist you in tracking down Una's attacker. I've got Rab, Mairi and Zahir working on the murder case with me. I suggest you grab them straight away and get ideas from them before they head out on the murder investigation. I'll also hold on to Owen and Murray to help with the murder legwork."

Angus nodded in agreement. "Right, I'll get onto it, then."

As he turned away, Suzanna noticed his defined jawline and his dimpled chin, unmasked by the recent trimming of his beard. He was a good-looking young man and a good guy. If he'd been ten years older and if they'd not been colleagues, she could have fancied him.

Chapter 7

"Hi, guys. I just got back from the hospital. Una's still unconscious." Angus said as he settled in his chair. "They said she should have regained consciousness by now, so they're worried she's slipped into a coma. The head injury she sustained when she fell after the stabbing may have been more severe than they thought." Murray's jaw dropped open, and Owen's brow furrowed. "They'll be doing scans on her head to find out what's going on, but we can't expect to speak with her anytime soon."

"Bloody hell. She's worse than we thought then," Murray said.

"Look, were either of you in the office when Una went out the other day?"

"Aye. I was here," Owen confirmed.

"I need you to think back. Did anything happen just before she left?"

Owen's thin lips almost disappeared as he compressed them, deep in thought. "She took a phone call on her mobile."

"Did you see her speaking?"

"Aye. She seemed intense. It wasn't a long conversation. I remember her switching off the call, grabbing her bag and heading out the door."

"Did she say anything?"

"Err? Just, I'm off out, see you later."

"Did you hear any names in the conversation or places?"

"No. But I saw her write something on her pad."

Angus went straight to Una's desk and grabbed her pad. He inverted it and dabbed it on an ink stamp pad. Pulling it off he could immediately see, in relief, that she'd written down the location at which she'd been stabbed.

"Owen. I need an accurate time when she took the call."

"It would have been around 9 am. I can't be any more precise."

"This is important, Owen. Think, man."

"Hang on. An email had just come in and I had a notification flash up on my screen. I opened it straight away. It was just a routine chief constable's update newsletter. Just a minute." He turned to his computer and found the email. Here it is. It arrived at 8:46 am."

"Great, so, if I can get hold of her phone and find out who called her at that time, I'll have a good lead." He snatched his key bunch from the desktop and headed out, his face set in determination.

* * *

Angus marched into the grey hospital, that he'd left just an hour ago, along the bland corridors and straight into the room where Una laid. A nurse was checking the systems attached to his colleague. "Excuse me. I'm DI Watson. Can you tell me where Una Wallace's phone will be?"

"In her bedside locker, sir. All her personal possessions were placed in there."

"Angus tried the door, but it wouldn't open.

"It's locked, and the key is kept in the staff nurse's office."

"Can you get it for me, please?"

"Sorry, sir. I'm not allowed to let anyone have access to a patient's belongings without their permission."

"She's unconscious. She can't give permission," Angus said, looking dumbfounded by the nurse's statement.

"There's the problem. But it changes nothing."

"Look. I need to interrogate her phone to help me find who did this to her."

"Sorry, sir. It's against the rules. You'd need one of those warrant things before I could let you have it."

"Look, my colleague – my friend – is laying in a bed having been knifed in the gut by some low life scumbag. If you don't let me have the phone, you'll be letting him get away with his crime."

"I can't help that, officer. Rules are rules."

"Listen here. This is an active investigation into the attempted murder of a police officer. If you don't get that key right now, I'll arrest you for obstructing justice."

She turned and walked out of the room, returning two minutes later with the staff nurse – her lips puckered. "What's going on here. I'll not have you threatening my staff."

"So are you an uncaring jobs-worth as well? I can always arrest you both if you wish. Inspector Wallace has been stabbed. She could have died. We need to catch the bastard that did this to her before he stabs someone else and perhaps kills them. If that happens, you'd have that death on your conscience for life. Is that what you want?"

"No need to use bad language, officer... Susan, open the locker. Let him have *the* phone." She turned and walked away, huffing and muttering.

Angus took the phone, finding it was switched off – at least it should still have a charge. He turned it on and waited for the screen to illuminate. The phone played a tune, and animated images flashed across the screen as it booted up. He waited until the sequence ended and the phone requested a pin. What the hell could it be. He tried her day and month of birth, then month and year, then month and day. A message came up, saying he'd tried too many times and would have to wait thirty minutes before trying again. "Damn!"

Grabbing Una's handbag, he checked there was nothing else in the locker of interest, then closed it, locked it, and gave the key back to the nurse. "Thank you," he said, not really meaning it. Then left the hospital.

* * *

Rab and Mairi took charts and tide tables, leftover from a previous enquiry, into an interview room and laid them out on the table. They checked the date and time window that the pathologist had given them, for when the woman had been drowned – between 9:30 pm and 12 pm. They calculated from the tidal flows where the cadaver might have been dumped, considering speeds, slack tide, and currents. Timing of the dumping was crucial, as it hugely influenced the possibilities. They had to consider numerous scenarios and settled on a range of potential dumping sites on the southern banks of the river, concluding that they'd need to search the shoreline from Grangemouth right through to below the Queensferry Crossing bridge.

"Is it possible for the cadaver to have been dumped on the other side of the estuary?" Rab wondered.

"No. If you look at the flows shown on the chart, the body wouldn't have crossed the estuary. By the way, can we please stick to body? I hate that word – cadaver."

"Sure. No problem," Rab agreed, showing surprise at Mairi's request. "Another thought: could the body have been dumped by boat?" They poured over the charts again, to see what impact that option could have on travel and dumping sites. "The water flows faster in the centre of the estuary where it's deeper – up to three knots."

"That's fast. Just suppose the body was dumped off the bridge at Kincardine, at 11 pm, where would it have ended up?" Mairi asked.

"It would hang in the slack tide for a while, then drift off out to sea, accelerating as the tidal flow sped up. If we say it floats downstream for five hours, it could travel twelve miles, which would bring it to Queensferry. So a bridge-dumping is feasible, as well as a boat, from around that area. I think we should focus on the shoreline between Queensferry and Grangemouth first and see what we find. Although the bridge theory works fine for tidal flows, the reality is that no one could stop on the Kincardine Bridge, late evening without causing a traffic jam."

"What about the Clackmannanshire bridge?"

"It would be possible to pull off the road on that bridge and not hold up the traffic, but it would still be too busy and exposed to dump a body over the railings."

"Yeah. You're right. The southern shoreline it is. I'll keep my eye out for boats along the way that could have been used."

"You lead a team from the Grangemouth end, Mairi, and I'll take a team from Queensferry, and we'll meet in the middle."

"Deal."

Chapter 8

"What news, Rab?" Suzanna asked when he answered his phone.

"Nothing so far, ma'am. I've not heard from Mairi, so I assume she's also drawn a blank. She'd have called me for sure if she *had* found anything. Hang on a sec... She's just come into sight, so unless there's anything within the next few hundred yards, I reckon we'll have to look elsewhere. We're thinking the body could have been dumped from a boat further up the estuary, near Kincardine. So, that's where we're planning to head next."

"You'll soon be out of light, won't you?"

"Aye. The sun's going down, and people will be heading home for their tea, so, few around to ask about boats. Perhaps we should leave that until the morning. We could get out to Kincardine first thing."

"Sounds like a plan," Suzanna concurred. "Just a thought, though. Have you considered one of the jetties on the north shore by Kincardine? It would have a similar effect as dumping the body from a boat because it would drop straight into the flow?"

"Good point, ma'am. I'll check that out before knocking off. If we find nothing, we'll look at the boat option tomorrow."

"Okay. Let me know how it goes. I'm going to check in with the pathologist, to see what he might have for us."

* * *

"Hello, Mark. How are you?"

"Good thanks, Suzanna. I guess you're after an update on the body found at Queensferry yesterday?" the pathologist replied.

"You got it. What can you tell me?"

"Well, this is only my provisional findings. I've yet to open her up. As you know, the woman was in her early twenties. South Asian background. We've fed her DNA into the system and should be able to locate which part of the continent she originates from. The damage to her face is extensive. She must have taken numerous blows from a rough, heavy object – probably a rock or large stone. Minor fragments from the rock have been passed to Forensics for analysis. Once you have that, it could help locate the dumping site, but I wouldn't hang on that because it could be quite a wide range of locations."

"Thanks. I'll bear that in mind."

* * *

She watched as the grey rock rushed towards her, then smashed into her face. The pain was excruciating. She would have screamed, but the first blow smashed her jaw. Instead, the cry of fear and pain was just a whimper.

The rock hit again. Her nose and lips pulverised under its impact. Again. Her eyebrow split and cheek mashed. Again, again, again. She fainted with the agony. The woman had completed her task – satisfied she was unrecognisable.

* * *

"The most significant injury I found, after the obvious facial damage," Mark continued, "was a fracture to the C3 vertebrae, which crushed and partially cut the spinal column. It would have caused paralysis from the neck down. She had abrasions and bruising on her limbs. Her right arm had evidently scraped on a rough surface – possibly brick, with the scratches running vertically from her shoulder to her elbow. Both her patella were grazed, caused by a similar motion to that on the arm. Her skull had taken a blow to it, at the top of the perennial bone where it meets the frontal bone."

"Could you show me where that would be? I'm better with visuals than descriptions and not an expert on medical terms?"

"Why don't we continue this briefing beside the body?"

"That would be good. What was the cause of death, Mark?"

"Drowning." They walked through to the mortuary, their feet squeaking on the vinyl floor. The place smelled like a hospital, only the bleach smells were stronger. Mark uncovered the woman's body, indicating to Suzanna where the impact had taken place – on the top of her head.

"Here are the abrasions I mentioned." Mark showed her the woman's arms and knees.

"You said the grazing to her knees was from head-to-toe direction. But there appears to be scrapes and bruising on the underside of her patella as well?"

"True. I was going to mention that next. The injuries I've already described suggest that the woman fell down a set of stairs – probably brick, going by the fragments I found in the wounds. Damage to the lower part of her patella, and the bruising around her ankles, suggests she may have been dragged back up the steps by her attacker. The suspected brick dust has also been sent to Forensics for analysis."

"Thanks. I'll check with them later. What else did you find?"

"The scalp had bare patches, where the hair had been yanked out."

"Could the hair have been pulled out previously or would this have occurred around the time she was assaulted?"

"There's no regrowth, so the hair must have been wrenched from her head within a few hours of her death."

"Have you been able to tell when the broken neck occurred?

"It's not possible to be accurate, but my best estimate would be six to eight hours before she drowned."

"I hear that you've already informed my team, you believe she drowned late evening?"

"Yes, unlikely to have been earlier than 9:30 pm and probably no later than 12 am."

"The injuries to her face will have been made while she was still alive but paralysed?"

"Correct."

"Evil... Anything else of note, Mark?"

"Only that she had a tiger tattoo on her left buttock." Pulling back the coverings, he showed her the tiger. "I've taken pictures of everything. I'll send them through to you."

"Thanks, Mark. So, let me just talk this one through with you. From your estimates, the woman will have been assaulted late afternoon, where she will have lost some hair and sustained injuries from a fall down brick stairs, including a broken neck and paralysis. Later she was hauled up the stairs by her ankles. She was transported to the Forth estuary, her face was smashed with a rock, then she was dumped in the water and drowned, late evening."

"That about sums it up."

Chapter 9

She regained consciousness as they lifted her off the ground. Lapping water could be heard as it slopped against a structure, and she could smell the sea. Boards creaked as they stepped closer to where the gentle waves sloshed. Opening the only eye that was not encased by swollen flesh, she saw the man, his dyed black moustache, and the outline of his familiar face, a face she'd often seen from this angle - the face she'd once thought of as her saviour.

They laid her on the jetty, and she saw into his eyes, a hint of an apology in his features as he joined with the woman to roll her into the briny water. Drifting away with the current, miraculously facing the heavens and her mouth still able to breathe air, she tried to recall what had led to this end.

Her master had called her into his study, while his wife was out meeting other women for lunch at an expensive restaurant. The husband sought from her the sexual satisfaction that his wife rarely and only reluctantly provided.

She remembered the sound of the door opening as her master had called, "Yes, yes, oh my God...." Then came the shriek of the wife as she saw her husband in orgasm. Before she could raise herself from her knees, the wife had grabbed her by her long black hair and hauled her to her feet. The husband's organ was exposed as her lips were dragged away. One minute he was in ecstasy, the next shocked and humiliated, covering himself and yanking up his trousers.

Pulled from the room, she'd been hauled along the corridor. Then the wife had opened the cellar door and pushed her through, slamming the door after her, as she shouted "Nōnrā Bēśyā" – dirty slut. She remembered the fall and hitting her head at the bottom of the stairs, then nothing until the voices had woken her later.

As she drifted in the water's flow her body rotated, her sari unravelling – caught on something - murky, foul-tasting saltwater entered her mouth. She couldn't do anything about it and knew she was going to die. If only she'd been of the Hindu faith, like many of her friends in Kolkata, she could look forward to reincarnation and another chance at life. Her religion, however, taught Paradise as the next step but only for those who had strictly followed the faith's teachings. There was no hope for her...

* * *

"Any signs at all?" Rab asked Mairi as they met up at the end of their search.

"Nothing, really. We've bagged some items of clothing, although none of them looks like something our vic might have worn. We didn't come across any places that seemed like suitable dumping grounds. They'd have to carry the body a long way to get to most of the shore. Where there *was* vehicular access, there was either no way of getting to the water or if they had, they'd likely have been seen by people on the buildings overlooking them."

"Similar here. Let's let the uniformed guys go. We've one last place to try. The Chief suggested we check out the jetties at Kincardine because if the body had been dumped from a jetty into deep water, it would be like dumping it from a boat – into a fast-moving flow."

Clamping her lips together momentarily in thought, Mairi nodded. "I got one of the uniformed assistants to bring his car round to meet us. He should be here soon, so I'll get him to run me back to my car, which is parked at Grangemouth. I'll meet you at Kincardine. There's a car park near the largest of the jetties. I'll head there... Ah! Here he is."

"See you there, Mairi."

* * *

A triangular car parking area terminated the narrow, rutted lane leading to the jetty. Rab saw Mairi's silver Corsa standing just inside the car park, sensibly positioned away from the area adjacent to the structure.

Parking his Citroen next to her Vauxhall, he walked towards her, then spotted a thermos flask laying on the ground. He picked it up and opened it, wondering why it was there. Realising why it had been discarded, as soon as he noticed thin broken glass sloshing around within cold tea, he was annoyed that it hadn't been placed in the litter bin.

He looked ahead to the jetty and spotted a bin just before its entrance. The concrete jetty which had once channelled cooling water to the power station stretched out into the River Forth for a good fifty metres and at the end of its run, a cross piece completed it, like a very tall narrow T. Mairi had a long stick in her hand. She waved at him, then turned and reached over the railings.

Dropping the flask in the litter bin, he walked along the jetty to where Mairi still leant over the side, looking into the water. As he approached, she pulled back from the edge. "Got it!"

Lifting the stick, a sizeable lump of cloth followed it up the side of the jetty. He turned and went back to his car for a large evidence bag.

"Is that what I think it is, Mairi?"

"Yeah. I'm pretty sure it is."

Rab passed her the evidence bag then took out his phone to call for

Forensics' support.

As they walked back to their cars, Mairi spoke. "What was that I saw you picking up in the car park?"

"Oh. It was an old thermos flask. Sir James Dewar would be amazed to find out how his invention has become so popular around the World."

"Who's Sir James Dewar?"

"He invented the vacuum flask – back in the late 19th century. Kincardine was his home."

"Oh. I didn't know. You're full of useless information, aren't you?" she said with a grin.

Rab just ignored the jibe. Banter proved they had a good working relationship and added some fun to the day.

* * *

As Suzanna reached her car, her phone pinged. A text had arrived from Rab. *Sari found hooked on old power station jetty. CSIs on site. Will stay on here for a while. Brief you in the morning.*

"Good man." Looking forward to what leads the morning might bring, she got into her black BMW and headed home.

* * *

Sat on her sofa, a fizzy, orange vitamin drink in hand, her phone rang. It was the tenant of her house in Cockermouth.

"Hi, Gareth. What's up?"

"Hello, Suzanna. We've got a problem. There's water pouring through the ceiling in the kitchen."

"Have you turned the stopcock off?"

"No. Where's that?"

Suzanna rolled her eyes. She was sure he had been briefed where to find it when he moved in. "It's in the cupboard under the sink. Turn that off immediately, please."

"Just a minute." She could hear Gareth shuffling things around and some cursing. Then he came back on the phone. "It's jammed. I can't get it to turn."

Frustrated that she couldn't pop round the corner and solve the problem, Suzanna offered further advice. "Try turning the tap in the opposite direction first, then try turning it off again."

"Okay." More grunting and cursing could be heard from Gareth, then he spoke. "That's got it. It's off now."

"Has the flow from the ceiling slowed down yet?"

"Just a sec... It's slowed a little."

"I guess there's loads of water in the ceiling, so even if the leak has stopped, there'll still be water trickling for a while."

"Yeah. I suppose so." There was a pause. "I think it's slowed some more."

"Okay. Good. I'll get onto the maintenance company and try to get a plumber out to you as soon as possible."

"Please do. With the water off, I'm stymied. No drinking, flushing the loo or showering."

"Leave it with me, Gareth. I'll get back to you as soon as I've spoken with the maintenance company." She hung up, then went straight into her study to dig out the files. It took her another hour to get things sorted and let the tenant know when to expect the emergency plumber. Finally she settled down on the sofa again – this time with a mug of coffee. She could drink coffee just before bed and still get off to sleep with no problem.

When she'd bought the two-bedroomed terrace house five years back, she'd been thinking of moving to Cockermouth, so decided to get somewhere of her own and rent it out. She'd expected the rent to cover the running costs, but so far it had been a loss-making enterprise because the Victorian property had so many underlying problems that kept draining her reserves. The plumber should fix the leak, but there may well be damage in the bathroom and the kitchen ceiling would need repairing. She had insurance, but there was a £500 excess for water leaks, so that was useless.

As she prepared for bed around midnight, a text pinged on her phone. 'Plumber has fixed leak. It was cold pipe to bath. No damage in bathroom but ceiling is sopping wet and might collapse.'

'At least the leak was fixed,' she thought, 'but what repairs might now be required and how much would she have to pay out?' She lay, eyes closed for ages, her mind refusing to stop thinking about the house issue. It was 2 am before she finally drifted into sleep.

Chapter 10

Thursday 19th

When the alarm sounded, Suzanna was groggy – not yet ready to get up, but she forced herself to slip out of bed. As she ate her hearty muesli breakfast, she tuned into BBC Radio 4. Public sector sickness was reported as costing the taxpayer £150m per year. Two men had been given life sentences for stabbing a man, following a drug deal. A man had appeared in court for sex attacks on buses in Glasgow. He'd been charged with sexually assaulting five females at different times. "I wonder where the good news is," she thought out loud.

She fired up her laptop and researched builders in Cockermouth who might sort out the damaged ceiling, then sent off a couple of emails to them, to get the ball rolling.

Driving to work was as gloomy as the news. There was low cloud and drizzle. Something caught her eye as she emerged onto the main road and she slammed on her brakes as a car passed the junction. She'd not seen it until the last second. She shook herself before continuing. The lack of sleep must have affected her attentiveness.

At the morning catch-up meeting, Suzanna asked Rab for the latest on the potential dumping site. "The lump of cloth Mairi discovered wrapped around one of the jetty's uprights was, as expected, a sari.

That's with Forensics for analysis. We're hoping it will be a match for the victim. The CSIs collected other evidence from the site: cloth fibres from the jetty, images of mud tracks at the entrance to the jetty and tyre impressions in the grass just at the edge of the car parking area, where it seems a car manoeuvred before reversing up to the jetty. There are also some footprints. We've had no feedback yet, but we should have something by late morning, as Forensics are prioritising the work."

"Great. We'll just have to wait it out then. Chase them if you've heard nothing by eleven." Rab nodded.

"So we know where the body was found, and when and probably where it was dumped. We still don't know who the victim was or who ditched her into the river. Hopefully, the forensics evidence will help with that, so let's turn our attention back to finding out *who* she was." She thought for a few seconds before continuing. "Has anyone matching our victim's description been reported missing?"

"I checked yesterday, ma'am, and there was only one early twenties South Asian woman reported missing in the last six months," Owen said. "Do you want me to follow up with the parents to get a DNA sample if they have one?"

"Yes please, Owen." She paused, recalling who had been allocated which tasks, then turned to face Murray. "How did you get on with the criminal database search, yesterday?"

"There were hardly any young South Asian women on the database. Of those there were, it was for shoplifting or fighting, where they were both victim and attacker. It's difficult to say, given the only image we have, but I'd say none of them was our victim."

"Okay. Let's park that one. Did you find any matches on the DVLA database?"

"There were several hundred matches based on gender, age and ethnicity. By filtering to only those in Edinburgh, I got the list down to a couple of hundred. I started going through the images, one by one, comparing what I could make of the features from our vic to the database pictures, but, as Owen mentioned," Murray continued, "the image we have for comparison is dreadful. It would be easier to match snowflakes. I've eliminated half of them so far, so about 100 to go."

"Thanks. Keep at it, Murray, and let me know as soon as you've completed the task." Turning her head to look at Zahir, she opened her mouth to speak, but he beat her to it.

"I visited several mosques and showed the picture to imams, but none of them recognised her. There's about twenty mosques in the city, and I still have about twelve to visit. I was planning to get going on that as soon as the meeting's over."

"Good. Please do that. If we can find anyone who knew her, that would be a huge help in tracking down where she's been living. Based on your experience yesterday, how long do you think it will take to visit the rest of the mosques?"

"At best, I should get around them all by the end of today."

"Okay, so we need someone to approach Hindu places of worship and South Asian community centres. We could also try South Asian food shops, sari shops, and restaurants. Any other ideas, Zahir?"

"I'll think about it, but you've picked the best places to start with."

"Mairi and I could do that, ma'am," Rab suggested.

"Okay, so that's those lines of investigation covered." Suzanna looked at the board again, tucked a stray blonde-grey hair behind her petite ear, and considered what they'd captured so far. "I think we need to get onto Immigration. Perhaps she'd only recently entered the country. We'll need to contact the Home Office to get information on immigrants and visitors that might match with our victim. Since you're all busy, I'll do that – starting with Scottish airports."

Angus had sat at his desk quietly during the murder case investigation catch-up, but as it drew to its conclusion, turned his chair into the crowd.

"Look, I've got Una's phone, but I can't get into it. Does anyone know what pin she might be using?"

"Have you tried her shoulder number?"

"I've never seen her in uniform, and have no idea what it is."

"Hang on. I'll check." Mairi offered. She turned to her computer and a minute later turned back. "try 3697."

Angus typed it into the phone, but it didn't unlock. "That didn't work. Any other ideas?"

"I suppose you've tried her birthday?"

"Aye. That was the first thing I tried."

"Birth year?"

"Do you know which year she was born?"

"Erm... It'll be 1982."

Angus typed it in. "Yes! I'm in."

Suzanna returned to her office, making a mental note to speak with her team about communication security. Using a birth year for a PIN was far too obvious...

Interrogating her calls, Angus found one that had been made at the right time. He noted the number and name on a notepad, then dialled the number. Instead of the normal brr-brr, brr-brr sound, a hip-hop tune played down the line. Angus wished people would just leave their phone set to normal ring tones, instead of programming them to play tunes for callers.

"Hi. How're you doing, little missy?

"Hi, Calvin. This is Angus. I work with Una. She's been stabbed. I need your help."

"No way!"

"She's in hospital, in a critical condition."

"I canna help you, pal." The phone went dead.

"Damn it." He called again, but the phone didn't get answered.

"Blast it! Caitlin. I've got the number of the person Una spoke to just before she left the station. He'd told her where to go – to where she was found stabbed. So either he stabbed her, or he knows who did. But he's refusing to speak with me. Can you get onto the phone company and get a fix on that phone, we need to speak to that man?" He gave her the details.

"On it, boss."

Chapter 11

An email notification sounded on Suzanna's laptop. She opened an attachment sent by the Home Office. It contained a list of women of the right ethnicity and age, who had entered Scotland via Edinburgh and Glasgow airports in the last two years. There were over 1500.

'That's going to take a while to trawl through,' she thought. She looked at the other attachments. One was a list of women who had left Scotland over the same period and the third listed the women who had arrived but not subsequently left the country. There were 400 – more manageable, but still a large number. A thought entered her mind. She headed off down the corridor to another office.

"You caught me at a good time, Suzanna. I can spare you a couple of hours," Alistair offered after she'd briefed him on the task required. As ever, his centre-parted greying hair was immaculately groomed.

"Brilliant. I'll send you through the second half of my list. If I get to the end of mine, I'll check in with you again." On returning to her office, another email caught her attention. It was from Forensics. She opened it and noted that the ethnicity of the victim was given as Bengali. She opened the Home Office's data file and filtered on women from West Bengal and Bangladesh. Now it was down to less than a hundred.

She split the list, sending half to Alistair, and giving him the good news that the list was considerably smaller. Partway through the list, her phone rang. She considered hitting the red phone symbol to cut off the call. Taking personal calls in work's time was seen as inappropriate by some – especially the Chief Super – even though they often worked unpaid extra hours. Instead, Suzanna answered it. "James. How are you?"

"Good, thanks, Suzanna. It's been a while since we got together. I was beginning to wonder whether you were avoiding me."

"Sorry, James. I've got a murder investigation to run, so don't have much spare time for relationships. Even when I'm not at work, I'm thinking about the case, so wouldn't be much company."

James was quiet for a moment. "Is there any chance we could get together for a meal soon?"

"I'd love to, but really can't, James. Sorry. When this case is over or we run out of lines of enquiry, I'll call you. I can't say more than that. I'm as keen as you to spend time together, to relax or perhaps be energetic," she said with a smile in her voice.

"Alright, I'll let you get back to your case. But if I don't hear from you again in a few days, I *will* call."

"Okay, James. Speak soon." She hung up and went back to her list analysis.

* * *

By the end of the day, Suzanna and Alistair had reduced the list of possible immigrant victims to thirty. Now that *was* doable. The team was still scattered, completing their investigations, so she printed off a map of the area and plotted the locations of the people on her shortlist. She allocated each of her team a small cluster of potential victims to visit, then emailed them all their tasks for the next day and proposed a catch-up meeting at 13:30 hours.

Time to go home...

* * *

Having worked late, the drive home was easier than when she normally knocked off work. Most day-workers would already have been having dinner, perhaps in front of the TV watching a soap, or reading their kids' bedtime stories. Nonetheless, she crawled through the city's streets within the frustratingly slow 20 mph speed limit; she could cycle faster.

It had occurred to her to use her bike more often, but with the weather so unpredictable and the lack of cars in the police pool, she often needed to use her own. There were also times when her last job of the day was somewhere other than in the station and she'd go straight home. She'd just have to put up with the restrained progress.

As she parked her black soft-top, she wondered how long it would be until she could get the roof down again. February was not the best of months for that. She missed feeling the air tumbling around her as she drove, the connection with nature when she travelled outside the city, and the sun on her back when the skies were blue.

In contrast to the police station's ugliness, Suzanna loved looking at the building she called home – its Georgian architecture, black railings separating it from the pavement, stone steps leading to the double width entrance door, the tall windows. Everything said grand, tasteful, stylish, in contrast to the minimalist, featureless boxes built in the 1960s and 70s.

As she rustled up dinner, stir-frying vegetables and adding a curry sauce, the smell of the spices set off rumbling in her stomach. One of the great advantages of having so many South Asians in the UK was the proliferation of curry-houses and quality cooking sauces in the supermarkets. Apparently, there were now more Indian restaurants in the UK than any other type, and the UK's favourite meal was supposed to be Chicken Tikka Masala.

After spooning the meal onto her plate, Suzanna sprinkled on some toasted cashew nuts, then took her meal into the lounge. Sat at her mahogany antique dining table, she switched on the TV, selecting a travel programme showcasing winter holidays. Once this case was over, she'd take a week off work and go skiing. Perhaps James might go with her. She messaged him with the idea, then continued eating. The Jalfrezi sauce was delicious – coriander, turmeric, and cinnamon blending with the chunky onions, peppers, and chillies. Her phone pinged within thirty seconds and the message read 'absolutely. no probs getting time off. just give me dates when you can.'

She smiled. The idea of exhilarating skiing, vin chaud or perhaps gluhwein and maybe a log fire, warmed her heart. As she thought about this intended excursion, she realised how lucky she was to live a life of plenty, when so many around the world were still struggling to feed themselves, pay for medicines when they were unwell, or even have clean water to drink and sanitary toilets. She logged into the website of the charity she supported and messaged them to double her monthly Direct Debit. She'd hardly notice an extra £30 leaving her account each month.

It took her mind back to the dead woman. If she had recently entered the country, perhaps she was a victim of trafficking? She remembered her time in Kolkata, ten years back when she was on sabbatical. She'd worked with a social enterprise, helping women to exit the sex trade. There were thousands of them in the city – all *owned* by another person. Enslaved. Getting them released from slavery always presented the company with a challenge.

In her short time there, she remembered seeing a new intake of sewing trainees start their course. They'd looked timid, worried, out of place, like a flock of sheep in a butcher's shop. She'd been told they were under-confident, and many lacked basic skills, like using scissors. But by the time they'd completed their training they had been transformed into more assured, skilled women, ready to join the workforce. 'One day, I'll go back for a visit,' she thought.

Chapter 12

Friday 20th

Rab knocked on Suzanna's door frame and entered her office. "I've just heard from Forensics." Suzanna looked at him quizzically, waiting for the detail. "The sari had traces of the victim's DNA on it, so we've definitely found the dumping site."

"That's encouraging. We're actually getting somewhere."

"The tyre tracks they found at the scene are from a Pirelli P7 – most likely a 225/45 R17. They're commonly fitted to the E Class Mercedes, BMW 5 series and the Audi A5."

"Can you get someone onto CCTV scrutiny?"

"Already in progress, ma'am. The footage has just arrived and the Terrible Two are on it." Suzanna grinned at the term Rab used for Owen and Murray, her full lips tightening. They had been called the Likely Lads, the Comic Duo and the Two Comedians – the list of names was growing.

"There's not much CCTV in the Kincardine area, but there are cameras on the two bridges and the junction of the M867 and the M9, which should pick up any vehicle heading west. But if the murderer had approached the jetty from the north and east, we'll be lucky to pick them up. The nearest cameras are in Alloa, Solsgirth and Dunfermline.

So, at nearest, five miles away and at worst eleven."

"Hmm. I guess we'll have to check them all, but probably best we start with the bridges. I'd leave the motorway junction to last because they'd get picked up on bridge cameras anyway if they were heading to the motorway."

"Exactly my thought, ma'am."

She smiled, acknowledging that he was on top of it – informing her what was happening rather than seeking her direction.

"I'll get started on the camera footage from Alloa."

"I'm free for a while, so send me the Dunfermline footage."

* * *

By mid-afternoon, the team had trawled through the CCTV footage for the five closest locations and drawn up a list of vehicles that might match the tyre tracks at the jetty.

"Okay, so we have over 200 vehicles," Rab stated. "We need to get that list down to a more manageable size. I'm betting that some cars on the list aren't the right models. It's difficult to tell the difference between a 3-series BMW and a 5-series, from the front. Similarly, the C-class and E-class look much the same, as do the A4 and A5 Audis. Let's split that list and trawl through the DVLA database to eliminate the smaller cars, then get back together again to see where we are."

The team divided up the lists and went to work, with Suzanna returning to her office. As she sat down, the phone rang. "DCI McLeod, CID." She noticed the extension number was the communications officer.

"Hello, Suzanna. It's Steve Gibson. How's the washed-up woman case going?"

"Hi, Steve. You're sounding like a member of the press, with the 'washed up woman' headline."

"That's what one paper has named the case. I have to provide a press release today. Is there anything you can give me?"

"We're making good progress, but I have nothing specific that you can use to brief the media, I'm afraid. It's definitely a murder case but I can't release details of why we know that just yet. We still don't know who she is. She's not been reported missing and there was no identification on the body. Our focus has been on finding out who she was and where she was dumped into the estuary. There's not much more I can say, at the moment."

"Do you not have a picture we could put in the papers and ask if anyone knows her?"

"The only picture we have is the one of her in death and her face is so disfigured it looks like a child made it from papier mâché. I wouldn't want to scare the public by releasing it. The press would likely start speculating that it was such a brutal murder, perhaps this is the first of a forthcoming series of murders."

"Alright. I'll put something together from what you've told me, but I'm going to need more before long, or you'll start seeing derogatory headlines about police incompetence."

"Fair enough, Steve. As soon as we have something to report, I'll let you know."

She sat pondering for a while. Was there anything else they could be doing? They should get an artist's impression made of the victim's face as soon as the autopsy was complete to show how she might have looked before her face was disfigured by the attack?

"Ma'am," Rab said as he stood at her office door. "We've identified which vehicles on the CCTV were of the right models. We now have only nine that crossed the bridges at Kincardine, three in Alloa and five in Dunfermline."

"Do you have the list of owners?"

Rab stepped into her office. As ever, it was clean and tidy. The picture of her niece smiling up from the one framed photo on her desk, and the documents arranged in four trays, marked up, In, Too Difficult, Action and Out. He passed her the list, and she scanned down it.

"Okay. So we have seventeen drivers to question. Three live in Dunfermline, two in Falkirk, one in Alloa and the rest in Edinburgh. Can you get someone to visit the owners of the Falkirk, Alloa and Dunfermline vehicles – it could be done on one circular drive. And someone else can visit the ones in Edinburgh. We need to know why they were in that area at that time."

"Sure. No problem," Rab said, thinking 'that's exactly what I was planning.

"Get the team following up on the immigration list as well."

"I'll get Owen to visit the out-of-city car owners. Murray can do the city-located ones. That will leave me, Mairi and Zahir to follow up on the immigration list."

"Add me into that mix, Rab. We need to get cracking. Our team can focus on those women who were reported to be living in Edinburgh. Get some of the locals to call on houses in the locations outside of the city."

"I'll get that sorted and send you a list of women to visit."

* * *

Parking her car opposite the 1930s semi, with tile-fronted bow windows and an arched doorway, Suzanna approached via two sets of steps and some concrete paths. The original door with stained glass windows hadn't been replaced by bland white plastic ones, like many of the neighbour's houses, but it was tatty – paint peeling and rotten wood bordering the glass. After pressing the bell-push, she stood back and listened to the tinny, electronic tune playing an imitation of Big Ben's hourly chime.

The smell of curry spices wafted out when the door was opened by an elderly woman dressed in a green and yellow sari. “Yes?”

“Good morning. DCI McLeod, Edinburgh CID. I’m here to speak with Priya Kirtania.”

“Come in,” she responded and stepped aside. “Priya. There’s someone to see you,” she called.

Priya bounced down the stairs, happy that she had a visitor, but her face lost its brightness when she realised it was a forty-something white woman – probably an official of some sort. Suzanna could immediately see that the young lady was the one in the passport photo on her list. “Hello, Priya. Don’t worry, I just needed to confirm that you are living where you said you would be when you entered the country. Now I know you are, I’ll be on my way.”

Priya looked curious as Suzanna walked away, probably thinking the visit was to check on her for the immigration authorities. The next few visits went much the same, but on the sixth house call, the woman was no longer living at the address. Apparently, Riya Saha had married in September and moved in with her husband and his family in Galashiels.

“I’ll need the address and name of her husband, please.”

Mrs Roy looked flustered. After foraging around in the hall cupboard, then visiting the kitchen, she returned holding a paisley fabric-covered book. “Here it is,” she said, passing the open book to Suzanna, who noted the details and gave it back.

“Thanks for your help.” Just one more to go.

Chapter 13

"Boss. I've got it," Caitlin said. "The phone is stationary at an address in Restalrig. It's where the phone is registered." She grabbed her coat, bag, and car keys as they left.

* * *

After climbing the steps up to the 2nd floor, they found the door of Calvin Jones' flat. Angus knocked on the door: tap, tap... tap, tap, tap... tap, tap.

"Ah. The friendly knock!

As Calvin opened the door, Angus stepped straight in, followed by Caitlin.

"I'm Angus. We spoke earlier."

"Get out of my flat, man. I told yer before. I'm saying nothin'."

"Look, pal. You were the one who sent Inspector Wallace to the garage block where she was stabbed, and now she's in a coma from a head injury. Either you stabbed her, or you know who did. So if you don't want to be arrested for attempted murder, you'd better tell me who she went to meet."

"Hey, man, I ain't no murderer. You can't pin that on me."

"Watch me," Angus said, "taking out his cuffs. Turn around. You're coming to the station."

"No, no, no. I don't go near no polis stations. I'll tell yer what you want." He sat down on a hard dining chair with chrome legs, a circular Formica table next to him.

"Okay. Talk."

"I got word that Fraser was hanging around the garages again, selling smack to teenagers on their way to school. So I gave Una a call. She's a good woman. Heart in the right place. Never given me any hassle. I didn't know she was going to go there by herself – that was a crazy thing to do."

"I never said she'd gone by herself." Angus stared at him suspiciously. "How did you know she was alone unless you were there?"

"I just assumed. If she'd been with someone else, she'd likely not have been stabbed."

"Well, you assumed correctly, and the bastard stabbed her. So what's Fraser's full name?"

"He's Muir. Fraser Muir."

"Where does he live?"

"I dunno. He comes and goes. He's not from around here. I'll keep an eye out for him if you like?"

"You do that Calvin. But you can do more than that, you can describe the man to us first."

"I'm not much good with descriptions – I flunked English, but I'll try."

"Just do your best. As you said. Una's a good woman."

Despite Calvin's self-doubt, he gave a good description of Fraser Muir, prompted by Angus. Average height, slim, a scrawny face and almond-shaped head, thin lips, pig-like nose, mousey brown hair, a three-day beard, no moustache. They also found out Muir normally wore a tea cosy-like woollen hat and a hoodie, topped off by a puffer jacket when it was cold. When pressed, he recalled Muir wore white trainers, with a gold Nike tick.

"That's really helpful, Calvin. You're better than you think. That's the most detailed description I've been given in a long time. I'll let Una know, if she pulls through?"

"*If* she pulls through?"

"Yes. As I said, she's in a critical condition. That's why the charge is attempted murder. We hope we don't have to drop the 'attempted' from the charge."

"Me too, man; me too."

Leaving Calvin, they headed out of the block. "Let's check out this guy on the system," Angus said as they descended the stairs. "See if we can find out where he lives and put the word out to uniform to pick him up."

* * *

Angus dialled a number on his phone. "Bill, can you run a check on a name I've got," Angus asked the officer, as Caitlin drove away from the flats. "It's Fraser Muir." Bill asked him to hold on.

"Yeah. Got him. He's been brought in for questioning a couple of times, but the guys haven't had enough evidence to charge him. I'll give you his address." Angus noted it down.

"Do you want me to put the word out?"

"Yes, please Bill. We'll head straight to his home now, but he might be on the street."

"Okay. I'll do that."

Angus went to type the address into sat-nav, but Caitlin asked him what it was. Angus read her the address. "No problem. That's in Muirhouse. I know where that is. No need for the GPS." She took the next right turn, heading West.

* * *

Parking her Ford Fiesta on the road, Caitlin looked up at the block of council flats. The drab prefabricated concrete wall slabs had discoloured by dirty water running down them. The entrance was guarded by huge wheelie bins, but at least it didn't look totally neglected, like some she'd seen.

They entered and took the lift to the third floor, then strode along the corridor to Muir's flat. 'Strange that Fraser Muir lived in Muirhouse,' Caitlin thought. 'Perhaps they should rename the area Muirflat.'

Angus knocked on the door. Not a friendly knock this time, Caitlin noticed. As Angus focussed on the flat's door, Caitlin looked back up the corridor. A young guy, with a hoody, was heading down the stairs, so she jogged back to the stairwell. She shouted "Fraser Muir?" The guy looked back up at her, then turned and ran. "It's him," Caitlin shouted to Angus, then took off down the stairs.

Angus ran to the lift and punched the button, hoping it would still be on their floor, but it showed 5 on the panel, so he set off down the stairs as well. Emerging from the flats, Caitlin saw Muir running past the block of garages to her right, so ran off in pursuit. As Angus reached the exit, he saw Caitlin passing the garages and turning right, so took a right before the garage block to cut the corner.

Tyres screeched as a car slammed on its brakes to avoid hitting Muir as he ran in front of it. Caitlin was fifty metres behind him, but not closing the gap. Angus lost sight of Muir as he turned into a lane and sprinted away. Caitlin tried skipping through the traffic but hampered by a lack of recklessness lost ground on her prey. She sprinted along the lane but couldn't see Muir anywhere, continuing to run until the lane opened up and golf green flags could be seen scattered across the grassed area. He'd disappeared.

She turned back and met Angus, who was heading towards her. "He's given me the slip. Must have jumped the fence and headed off through those buildings." They both leapt over the railings and split up, aiming to go around different sides of the complex. Meeting at the other side, they looked at each other, Caitlin spreading her arms, turning her hands to the sky, and lifting them with a shrug of the shoulders. The guy had eluded them.

They searched around the buildings for hiding places. A group of skip-sized bins clustered in one corner. Angus opened and peered into each, the hinged lids creaking every time. The stench of rotting rubbish caused him to scrunch up his face as he tried to close his nostrils. They found nothing, so returned to the flats and the car, wondering where to look next.

Chapter 14

On returning to the station, Suzanna found she was last back, so called the team together to catch up. Five of the women on Rab's list were at the address visited. Two had married and moved away, so would need following up. One had been taken into custody by immigration officials for overstaying her visa. Apparently, she was awaiting expulsion. Three of those on Mairi's list had married and one had overstayed her visa. None of the women on Zahir's list had been in trouble with immigration, and only one married, but one was unaccounted for. She hadn't been reported missing yet, as it had only happened at the beginning of the week, and they thought she'd run away with a boy that the family had disapproved of.

"So this missing woman could be our victim, then." Suzanna surmised. "You'll need to follow that one up."

"Aye. I have the boyfriend's name, so visiting him is next on my list."

"As that's our only lead, so far, best you get onto that straight away." She paused. "Now, please Zahir."

"Sorry, ma'am. Will do." He grabbed his coat and the keys to his Honda, then left. He'd recently upgraded his car and welcomed the opportunity to drive his lime green, Type R Civic, with its rear spoiler and throaty exhaust.

Suzanna looked down as her mobile rang silently and saw the area code was Cockermouth's, so touched the red phone button. She'd deal with that later. Turning to look at Rab, she asked, "Have we heard from other stations about the women living in their towns?"

"Yes, ma'am. All accounted for, including the ones who had married. There were only two, and they both lived nearby the original addresses. Would you like me to follow up on the women from our lists that are still unaccounted for?"

Suzanna's mobile buzzed again. It was the same number. She switched off the phone again. "Sorry about that – a persistent caller. Yes. If they're in the city, get one of the team to visit. If they've moved out of the city, get the local force to call on them... Now, what about those cars seen on CCTV?"

Owen reported that at six of the houses he'd visited, the car was on the driveway or parked on the road out front, and fortunately, someone was in when he called. They all had perfectly good reasons to have been in the area, but he'd not yet had time to follow up on what they'd said. Of the other five, he'd found out where they worked and tracked down three of them. Again, good reasons to have been in Kincardine. He'd yet to speak with the last two owners. They were both more or less on his route home, so he was planning to call in again that evening.

Murray had similar success. Three of the six cars were owned by people of South Asian origin – all three middle-aged. Two were registered to white Scots – one a pensioner and the other in his thirties. One vehicle was owned by a young man from an Afro-Caribbean background. He had dreadlocks and his car was pimped-up with blacked-out windows and gold wheel hubs. He'd been suspicious initially, but it turned out that the driver was a vet, not a drug dealer. "Just goes to show that you can't always judge a book by its cover."

"I'm glad you learned that lesson, Murray. There've been too many reports in the press lately about police unfairly targeting black men in stop and searches," Suzanna commented. "Do any of your six need to be followed up?"

"Yes, just to confirm their stories. I was planning to do that after this meeting."

"Where are we then?... We have one missing female, who could be our victim. We've initially accounted for all the suspect cars but need to follow up on a few of those to prove the owners' stories." There were affirmative nods all around.

"Where next?" Suzanna had ideas but wanted the team to think for themselves instead of being directed all the time.

"We could knock on doors in the streets near the jetty and its approaches, and ask if anyone saw anything suspicious?" Mairi suggested.

"And ask whether they saw any of the vehicles on our list," Owen added.

There was another pause, then Rab spoke: "There could be private CCTV systems on some of those houses, so we'd need to ask for sight of their recordings for about the time the body was dumped."

"Agreed. I'll leave you to organise that, along with the married women follow-ups, Rab."

* * *

After returning to her office, Suzanna added to her report, noting the lines of enquiry followed and results so far. She flipped the lever on her chair, then pressed backwards, forcing it to recline, closing her eyes as she thought things through. What else could they be doing? What might they have missed? Was the tattoo relevant?

She sat up, her chair creaking as it hit its stops. The tattoo. Of course. It could be a brothel or a trafficker's brand. She pondered the idea, then opened up the crime database and searched for trafficker brands. There were multiple entries, mostly where the tattoo was the nickname of the trafficker or pimp, showing his ownership of the woman. The majority of women in the UK found to have branding tattoos were of Eastern European origin or African. There were very few from the Indian sub-continent and none of the brand tattoos on the system were of tigers.

But the tiger fitted well with where they believed the woman had come from. There had been cases of women brought into the UK from India and other countries in that region, as domestic slaves – an angle they'd not looked at yet. She fired off an email to Alistair, to update him on progress, and another to Steve in the communications department – just a holding statement.

On checking her phone, she saw there was a voicemail. "Hi. This is Paul from PB Builders in Cockermouth. I've been round to your house. There's about two square metres of ceiling board that will need replacing. I can do that for you. But someone had painted the ceiling with textured paint, and it might contain asbestos, so I'd need to get it sampled. Please let me know if you want me to go ahead with the test."

Oh, Great! she thought. If there was asbestos, she'd have to pay for a specialist company to remove it before she could get the ceiling repair carried out. Perhaps she'd better contact the insurers after all. She texted the builder. 'How much for the asbestos test?'

* * *

Rab popped in, dressed like a Michelin man, in his puffer jacket. "Just off out, ma'am. Zahir hasn't reported back yet about the missing girl and the boyfriend. Murray and Owen are following up on the drivers' reasons for being in the Kincardine area.

"What's Mairi doing?"

"She checked with the Home Office, who confirmed the visa overstay stories. They're both dead ends. She's heading out with me. Between us, we'll visit the registered owners of the last two cars that Owen didn't get hold of earlier. Then we'll follow up on the married and moved-away leads. One's in Dunbar, the other's in Peebles. And we'll check out your lead in Galashiels. We'll be heading home afterwards."

"Fine. What about door knocking and CCTV in Kincardine?"

"The Terrible Two have been allocated that task. If they have time tonight, they'll get some done. If not, they'll do that first thing tomorrow before coming into the station."

"Great. Good to hear it's all in hand. I'll see you in the morning then."

Rab headed off along the corridor, doing up his coat. Her phone pinged. '£75.'

She texted back. 'Please get it done.' If the test confirmed asbestos, she'd definitely have to claim off the insurance – more hassle, she could do without right now.

Chapter 15

"Mrs Basu?" Mairi asked as the middle-aged Indian woman opened her front door.

"Yes. And who might you be?"

Mairi and Rab held up their police ID cards. "Detective Constable Gordon. And this is Detective Sergeant Sinclair. We need to ask you some questions. Can we come in?"

"Well, it's not very convenient. I was just about to go out... Oh! Come in. I can spare five minutes," she said, checking her watch.

Moving into the sitting room, they all sat. The olive-green sofa had tassels hanging from the cushion corners. Glass cabinets housed small Hindu idols – Ganesh, Shiva and Durga.

"I would offer you tea, but, as I said, I'm short of time. What's this about?"

Rab spoke: "Your husband's car was spotted in the Kincardine area on Sunday night and there were two occupants. We need to ask why you were in that area at around 11 pm?"

"Goodness me. Why do you ask such a thing? Aren't we entitled to go anywhere in Scotland when we wish, without being spied on?"

"Of course, ma'am," Mairi responded. "It's just that a crime was committed near where you were seen and we just need to establish why you were there, to eliminate you and your husband from our enquiries."

"Oh! I see. We had been visiting my cousin. She lives in Clackmannan – the old part, not the tatty area near the Alloa road. We were on our way home after eating with her family."

"If you could let us have your cousin's name, address, and phone number, that would be helpful. As soon as we have confirmation that you were there, we can move onto the other people on our list," Rab said.

She looked at her watch. "I really need to go, or I will be late for my appointment."

"The details please, ma'am," Mairi said, passing her a notepad and pen to write with.

Mrs Basu shook her head from side to side and tightened her mouth, then took the offered pad, wrote the details, then passed it back to Mairi and stood. "Now, I really must go. Please leave."

* * *

Sat in the car outside the Basu's, Rab dialled the number on the pad. "Mrs Chakraborty?"

"Yes?"

"This is Detective Sergeant Sinclair. I'm running an investigation and just need to clarify some points about the location of various individuals. I'd be happy to call at your house to confirm my identity and ask you face to face, but it's just a minor thing to help us eliminate certain lines of enquiry. Could you tell me if you were at home on Sunday evening?"

There was a pause as the lady thought about the request. "Yes, I was at home. What is this about?"

"Did you have any guests that night?"

"Yes, yes. My cousin came for dinner. This is strange to be asked this."

"And your cousin's name, please?"

"Kakoli Basu. But I still don't know why you are asking me this."

"Please don't concern yourself, Mrs Chakraborty. If you could just tell me when Mrs Basu left, I shall trouble you no more."

"It was about ten-forty-five."

"Thank you, Mrs Chakraborty. You have been most helpful." He terminated the call. "That's confirmed Mrs Basu's story. Let's head to the Mukherjee's home now."

* * *

Mairi pulled up outside a large Victorian-era detached house, its double-height bay windows shrouded by intricately patterned net curtains. Rab rang the doorbell and waited, but no one came to the door. He banged on the door and rang the bell again but still there was no answer.

Mairi remained at the front door while Rab explored down the side of the house and into the rear garden. There was no car in the driveway, and when he peered through the rear garage window, he could see it was full of the usual stuff, but no car, so he guessed they were both out.

Nonetheless, he knocked on the back door, then tried the handle before looking through a large window. He could see straight through to the front of the house. The long lounge-diner, with a central archway, was neat and clean. The colours of the chairs and sofa were drab. Peacock images adorned the cushions that sat on the sofa. The 1970s teak dining table had a lacy runner down its length and a cut-glass vase with plastic flowers sat in its centre.

After returning to the front of the house, they both walked back to the car. "We'll have to try later."

On returning to the station, Mairi carried out a search on their system for Mr Mukherjee. "Hey, Sarge. Mukherjee's a doctor at that private hospital Murrayfield. We could try speaking with him there?"

"Good idea. Give the hospital a call first and see if he's in at work today."

Two minutes later Mairi called across to Rab. "Mukherjee's a surgeon. He does cosmetic breastwork – enhancements and reductions. He's in theatre at the moment. They said if we needed to speak with him, it would be best to call between 1 and 2 pm."

"Great. We'll do that. Best not let on to the others which department we're visiting or the Terrible Two will start jibing you about breastwork."

* * *

A middle-aged, overweight Indian-looking man, dressed in scrubs, a green hat on his head, walked towards Rab and Mairi. "Nurse tells me you wish to speak with me?"

"Yes, we do. I'm Sergeant Sinclair. This is Constable Gordon. Is there somewhere private we could go?"

"Yes. Come this way. My office is just down here," he said going ahead.

"What is this about, sergeant?" His eyes dropped to Mairi's breasts, perhaps checking out whether she needed any work.

His eyes returned to her face as she started speaking. "Just routine enquiries, sir. There was a crime committed on Sunday evening in Kincardine, so we're speaking with anyone who was in that area, in case they saw anything. Your car was spotted on CCTV, driving across the Kincardine Bridge at 11:12 pm. Would you have been the driver?"

"I see. Yes. My wife doesn't drive."

"Can I ask why you were in that area of the city at that time?"

"Of course. I had taken my wife to a restaurant for dinner. I normally take her out on Monday evenings to give her a rest from cooking."

"Oh. I'm surprised you found a place to eat on a Monday night. Most restaurants are closed on Mondays. Which restaurant would that have been?"

"The Royal Bengal Tiger, in Alloa. They're open seven days a week."

"And what time would you say you left there, sir?"

"It would have been about eleven o'clock."

Mairi asked the next question: "Does anyone else live with you and your wife, sir?"

"No, no. Why do you ask?"

"No matter."

"Thanks for your time, sir. We'll leave you to get back to your work."

Doctor Mukherjee looked at his watch. "Yes, I'd better get a move on. I need to eat my tiffin now, as I have consultancy work starting at 2 pm." He opened the door and stood back to let them out.

Outside the hospital, they strolled to Mairi's Corsa as they thought about what to do next. As Mairi drove off, Rab extracted his phone from his pocket, searched for the restaurant Doctor Mukherjee had named and called them. They confirmed they were open seven days a week and that the Mukherjees had been in on Monday night. The booking had been for 8:30 pm. "That's both suspects accounted for. Where next?" Rab thought out loud.

Chapter 16

As the working day came to a close, Suzanna reclined her chair again, her turned-up nose now pointing towards the ceiling. They had a couple of missing women who might be the victim, but they'd missed something...

She let tiger images flash through her mind. Where had she seen them? Tiger Balm. Esso petrol – put a tiger in your tank. Frosties cereal – Tony the tiger. Tiger Air. Tiger Air, that's a Singapore-based airline. 'Hmm! Ah!' A thought popped into her mind. They'd only looked at women who'd entered the country in Scotland. Many more women would have flown into London before travelling to Scotland. 'There's another job for tomorrow,' she thought, as she packed away her things to head home for the night.

She passed the Chief Superintendent's office and was glad it was empty. But as she turned the corner, heading for the stairwell, a familiar voice called out.

"Ah, McLeod. I need a word."

She rolled her eyes, then turned on her heels and returned to the office she'd just passed. "Sir?"

"What progress on this dead Indian woman case?"

"Sir. We don't know she's Indian. She could be Bangladeshi?"

"Same thing. Don't split hairs, McLeod. Have you found out who she is yet?"

"No, sir. She had nothing on her to provide an identity. All we know about her so far is she was of Bengali descent. She seems to have been traditionally dressed. So she was probably a recent immigrant or living in a family with stricter views on dress standards than most young South Asian women, who've been brought up in the UK. And she had a tattoo of a tiger on her left buttock."

"Any relevance to the tattoo?"

"Possibly a trafficking or brothel branding."

"Hmm. What other progress have you made?"

"We have a list of vehicles spotted in the area, that match with tyre tracks by the dumping site, we're following up on. We'll be doing door-knocking in Kincardine tomorrow and we're following up on recent arrivals of young women from Kolkata and Dhaka."

"Do you have any suggested motives for the murder?"

"As we know nothing about the woman, it's difficult to say. If she were a trafficking victim, perhaps her *owner* beat her too violently and destroyed his own *asset*," Suzanna said, cringing as she acknowledged someone could consider the young woman as property, rather than a fragile human being.

"Yes. Well, keep me informed. We'll need to hold a press conference on Monday, to keep the journalists happy. Any news on Una?"

"She remains in a coma, caused by the bang to her head when she fell. The doctors are hopeful she'll pull through. Angus and Caitlin are working the case." The Chief Super started packing his bag and reaching for his coat, so Suzanna left without another word. At least she'd not received another word-battering.

* * *

As Suzanna walked through her front door, she noticed the cloak cupboard door ajar. Her heart jumped a beat at the out-of-place door.

Despite her normal obsession for closing doors and drawers, just last month she'd left her apartment door unlocked, and an intruder had taken her magnifying glass – fortunately, and amazingly, nothing else. Suzanna definitely hadn't left the apartment door unlocked today though, so she was puzzled at how the cloak cupboard door was open. She gingerly walked into her living room, scanning for anything unusual, before moving into the other rooms. Everything seemed fine and her worries immediate faded away.

Returning to the hall, she hung up her coat, noticing a scarf belonging to her ex-husband hanging in the cupboard corner. Suzanna wasn't in the mood for cooking from scratch, so took a chilled vegetable curry from her fridge. A Naan bread was extracted from the freezer to thaw out and she withdrew a jar of brinjal pickle from the cupboard to add some extra flavour to the supermarket meal.

After changing into her running kit, she headed out for her four-times-a-week, three-mile run. She found running to be a good way to keep her heart and lungs fit, as well as ensuring she could chase after criminals when the occasion arose. During the run, her mind drifted off. Random thoughts popped into her head, were considered, then filed away. The exercise helped her to transition from work into leisure mode – to clear her mind of the investigation and turn her thoughts to her own life, the things she needed to do and to her relationships.

It was a Friday night, and she'd normally have a night out with friends, or a special friend. But tomorrow she had to be back at work, and she wanted to get to bed at a normal hour and sleep well, so her mind was fresh. It would be good to see James again soon, but not tonight. In fact, he'd not been in touch to suggest an evening together this weekend. Perhaps he was waiting for Suzanna to take that initiative – not wishing to be too pushy? She decided to leave it until tomorrow and contact him if she was in the mood for his company.

It was a dark night, but the street lights illuminated her way. She'd sensibly donned a Day-Glo yellow top and her running shoes had reflective strips built into the heel, so car drivers would see her when she was crossing roads. She'd seen too many runners and cyclists dressed inappropriately and dancing with death on the roads. Despite Edinburgh's low speed limits, pedestrians, and cyclists – particularly the latter – regularly ended up in hospital following a collision.

After her run, she showered, changed into comfortable clothes, heated her meal, then poured the one glass of wine she'd drink that night. She settled down on the sofa with some Hauser in the background. Cello was her go-to music when she wanted to chill out. She'd get an early night after reading a book for a while.

Feeling full from her meal, she rose and walked to her bay window. As she drew the curtains together, she noticed a man stood across the street speaking into his phone. She thought he'd been looking up at her. It was probably her imagination.

Chapter 17

Saturday 21st

Suzanna stopped in front of an open doorway. "Morning Alistair. What are you doing in on a Saturday?"

"Ah! Suzanna. Good morning to you too. I've only popped in for an hour or so, to progress a couple of admin matters, on my way to play golf – hence the casual attire," he said, sweeping his hands downwards and out from his body. "Thanks for the update yesterday evening. Seems like things are going as well as could be expected."

"Yes. I'm satisfied with the progress so far. We focused our efforts on the routes most likely to bring us success, but we now need to widen the search for the woman's identity. I'll get onto the Home Office this morning to obtain a list of all women in the age group that arrived in the UK via *any* port. We initially looked at only those entering the UK via Scottish airports."

"Right-o. That's the logical next move. Keep me posted."

"Will do. By the way, how's Helen? She not joining you for golf?"

"She's fine, thanks. Helen rarely plays golf with me nowadays. We both prefer to play with friends, as an activity that gets us out from under each other's feet. I might see her on the 19th green later though. She'll probably be there with her friends, drinking gin & tonics."

"You still play badminton together though, don't you?"

"Aye, we do like to do many things together, but it's good to have some activities where we do our own thing."

She acknowledged his statement with a nod, then said she hoped the weather held out for him, before continuing to her office. After settling in, she sent a request to the Home Office for information, before going for a coffee.

Suzanna took her coffee with her to the main office. "Morning Rab. Mairi. What news on the home visits yesterday?"

"Morning, boss," they chorused.

"The Dunbar lead was another dead end, boss. The woman was there, with her in-laws. Seemed happy enough."

"Another successful elimination, Mairi, not a dead end," Suzanna countered with a smile.

Mairi smiled back. "If you say so, ma'am."

"One of the two I dealt with was present and accounted for," Rab said. "The second one, in Galashiels, was not there. The family was very derogatory about their daughter-in-law, particularly the mother-in-law, who said she was a lazy, worthless girl. She left one day with her bag, and they've not heard from her since. She'd only lasted six months with them. The husband was in tears about it when I asked him if he missed her, but the mother stood in the door, arms belligerently crossed, looking like an angry Doberman. The father said nothing, but his face was firmly set, and seemingly supportive of his wife's rantings."

"Poor girl. Sounds like the mother-in-law was a dragon. We'll need to find her. She could be our victim. That's two runaways we've got now."

"On it. I'll let you know when we find them," Rab said.

"Oh! Did you ask the husband when his wife left and, importantly, if his wife had any tattoos?"

"Aye. Sorry. Forgot to mention. She left about ten days ago."

"So the timing could fit."

"Yes, but he said she didn't have any tats."

"Hmm. Okay. Pass that one to missing persons. The dead woman's tattoo wasn't new, so the Galashiels wife can't be the victim. Unless he's lying, of course?"

"True. We'll keep that one on the back-burner." Rab paused. "We've yet to track down the other missing woman."

"I see Murray and Owen haven't joined us yet."

"They reported in from Kincardine. They'll be along later. Zahir called in too. He visited the boyfriend yesterday, but there was no one with him. He was told the girl had left and gone back to her aunt and uncle."

"When did he say that happened?"

"Yesterday."

"So it could be the truth."

"Agreed. Zahir has gone to see her relatives this morning."

"I was just thinking that we could get someone to take the victim's sari – in an evidence bag of course – around the sari shops when they're visited. Oh! And the bangles."

"To see if any of them might have sold the sari, ma'am?"

"Exactly that, Mairi. And they might have ideas on where the bangles were sold."

"I'll add that to the list, then."

"When the others report in," she said, looking Rab in the eye, "let me know so we can get together for a chat. I've requested immigration data covering the whole of the UK, so we should have a huge list to go through today."

Rab's neck straightened, and his mouth opened slightly, surprised by the announcement. "I'll get onto the Terrible Two. If they have anything already, we could make a start on following up, while they continue their work. We'll need to have all hands on deck for the immigration data trawl."

"Agreed. Just one point, Rab," Suzanna gently implored, "please drop the Terrible Two nickname for Owen and Murray. The Likely Lads, the Two Comedians or the Comic Duo I could just about put up with, but I think it's unfair to use the term terrible, to describe them. They're both good detectives."

"Sorry, ma'am."

"It's Okay Rab. It's good to have a bit of fun within the team and nicknames are fine. Just not that one. I worry about what you might be calling me when I'm not in the room."

Rab went to speak, but Suzanna held up her hand. "I don't want to know. Let's just leave it there," she said, then returned to her office before another word could be spoken.

* * *

It was late morning by the time the team got together. Owen and Murray reported on their door-knocking session. They had checked out all the routes a car could take to reach the jetty and called on houses along those routes. Only two of those homes, both on Station Road, had cameras mounted outside. They were the type that are combined with bell pushes. So they only picked up images crossing in front of the doors, not coming towards, or moving away from the house – so no licence plates. The cameras hadn't picked up any BMWs or Audis around the time the body was dumped, but two Mercedes had passed by. They believed the Mercs could have been E Class models, gong by their outline and size – both heading away from the jetty. There were no Mercs captured heading towards the jetty earlier.

The occupants of houses on Station Road had noticed nothing unusual, but when pushed, one of them said that when he was walking his dog, he saw a car backed up to the jetty, and he could see some activity, but couldn't say more than that. This was around 11 pm.

It suggested the time of dumping was at the latter end of the window the pathologist had estimated. Suzanna tasked them with printing some still shots from the videos, as it might help prove the culprit's car had been there once the culprits were identified.

After they'd finished their reports, Suzanna asked. "What about the follow-up work you did yesterday on the car owners' stories for being near Kincardine?"

"Mine all checked out," Owen said. "Three had been at work and on their way home. Seven had been visiting friends or family. They were also corroborated by the people they'd been with. One couple had been for a meal. I checked with the restaurant, and they confirmed the couple had dined with them... Oh, by the way. I got a DNA sample for the only young South Asian woman who'd been reported missing and passed it to Forensics to compare with our vic. Hopefully, we'll get an answer on Monday."

Murray and Rab reported similar results, so Suzanna turned to Zahir for his report.

"As I mentioned to Rab, the boyfriend said she was no longer with him. He said she'd gone back to her relatives' house. But when I checked back with the family, she hadn't returned. So she's still missing. I asked the boyfriend about tattoos, and he said she had a hummingbird on her right shoulder, but no others. If he were telling the truth, she couldn't be the victim. If he'd murdered her, though, he'd lie about the tattoos, anyway."

Rab pulled out a picture of the victim and placed it on the table in front of them. It was a reminder of the brutality of the attack. Zahir laid the missing woman's picture next to it. "I know it's difficult to be sure because of the damage to our victim's face but looking at the bone structure and some features individually, I'd say these pictures are not of the same person."

"Agreed, but let's not rule out the possibility yet, Zahir. I'd like you to stick with this line of enquiry a *little* longer. Get the missing woman's picture circulated around the stations and ask all uniformed officers to keep a look out for her."

As Suzanna went to continue, Zahir interrupted. "Would you like me to revisit the relatives and probe them about her life with them, and other friends she may have? Who she could have gone to stay with?"

"No. We need you here. After you've got uniform looking for her, post her picture on the board. We'll need you to help with the data trawl. Another line I'd like us to look at is that she might be an illegal immigrant. She wouldn't show up on any government databases. The tiger tattoo on her buttock could be a trafficker or brothel brand." They all nodded agreement. "So how do we pursue that line of enquiry?"

"If she was a prostitute, perhaps some of her colleagues might recognise her," Mairi suggested.

Suzanna nodded. "Mairi. You head out and talk to prostitutes. But be careful, we've already got one team member in the hospital. The rest of us can focus on drilling into the data that the Home Office has promised me." Suzanna stood up, so Mairi grabbed her coat. The others wheeled their chairs back to their desks, and she returned to her office to check her emails. "Excellent." There was one from the Home Office.

Chapter 18

"Okay guys," she said, re-entering the main office and walking to the giant shared printer-copier in the corner, "the immigration data is here." She grabbed the pile of A4 sheets and returned to where they had gathered. "It's not as bad as it looks. There are five data sets in this stack. The last twelve months of young women entering the country where their initial port of departure was Dhaka or Kolkata. Then each year before that, going back five years in total. We'll concentrate on the most recent period first, then work our way back, if we have to."

She broke the wad of paper into yearly piles and placed four of them on the top of the filing cabinet, each pack criss-crossed with the other, then brought the last pile to the table, spreading it out, so they could all see the size of the task.

"We believe our victim to be in her early twenties, so this set of data is based on women in the age range 19-25. If we step back into the twelve months before this period, the age range is 18-24, and so on." The team gave an acknowledging nod, with some faces showing agreement with the logic of how the boss had requested the data.

"The list represents all entries into the UK, less any women who have subsequently left. That still leaves us with 2000 names. Mairi's out and about, so there's just the five of us. That would be four hundred names each. Still too much. Fortunately, another filter has been applied, so the list only includes those who subsequently flew to Scotland after entering the UK in London. There may be some women who travelled here by train, bus, or car, after landing in the south, but we'll concentrate on the fliers first. You'll be glad to hear that sees the list reduced to just 200 names, so forty each."

There was a communal sigh of relief. "That's still a heck-of-a-lot of addresses to visit. If we all walked the streets, it would likely take us four days to get around them," Murray said.

"What would you suggest, then?" Suzanna was fishing again, trying to encourage her team to work out their own solutions. She worked on the principle of training her successors, so when she moved on, people could step up into her shoes.

"We could recruit uniform to help?" Owen proposed.

"Absolutely, but how would you suggest we allocate the work?"

"If we correlate the data geographically," Rab suggested, "the clustered lists could be farmed out to uniform from adjacent stations."

"So our job today is to do that work. I've got hold of multiple packs of coloured map pins to plot the addresses." Suzanna laid out three maps covering Scotland's central belt, which would take in most locations. "Let's get stuck in."

Anyone would think she had announced the start of a fun board game. They all grabbed bags, tore them open and started writing.

* * *

Three hours later, having eaten their lunch on the hoof, the maps were covered in coloured pins, and they all sat back to peruse their work.

"Now for the next phase. We know where police stations are located. There will be ten within these areas, so on average, they'd get twenty visits to do each – not a huge ask. What I'd like *us* to do is pick a handful of women – five or six each – who gave addresses close to where we each live. We can call on those addresses before going home. That would be 25-30 fewer leads to follow up later." There were nods all around.

"We've been working nearly six days already, and I want you all to have Sunday with family, so you're fresh to start again on Monday. This isn't a sprint, but I hope it won't turn out to be a marathon. We need to pace ourselves accordingly, though."

They all noted down a few women to visit. "Rab, please make sure the rest of the list is allocated to appropriate stations and request they visit the women and report back to you on Monday."

* * *

Rab stayed back after his colleagues headed out to call at houses near their homes. He allocated clusters of individuals to police stations and wrote emails to colleagues in those stations asking for their support. It took him two hours to get the work done, so by the time he got home to his semi-detached house in Murrayfield, it was dark. His wife had parked her car on the drive, so he left his Citroen on the road out front.

He called out as he opened the front door. "Hi, Ainslie. I'm home." His son ran down the stairs, toothbrush in hand. "Hi, Hammy." He hugged his son, then asked if he'd like his dad to read his story to him when he was ready for bed. Hammy enthusiastically confirmed he would like that, then ran back upstairs to finish getting ready for bed. Rab wandered into the kitchen and found Ainslie at the sink, washing dishes. He put his arms around her waist and whispered into her ear. "How's my beautiful wife?"

"Better now you're home. I wish you didn't work such long hours. It's difficult for me holding down a full-time job and having to play mum all the time without a dad around to help."

Rab nuzzled her neck and gently kissed her cheek. "Once I've got Hammy in bed, do you fancy a film and a bottle of wine? Perhaps a romcom? Maybe we could get romantic later? ..."

"I wish you wouldn't call our son Hammy. He's not a hamster. What's wrong with using his full name? Hamilton's a lovely name."

"I agree. But everyone shortens names and often add a Y to the end: William to Billy, Charles to Charlie, Douglas to Dougie."

"Yes, but Dougie isn't the name of a small furry creature!"

"Okay. I take your point." He paused as he breathed in her perfume, then nibbled her ear.

Ainslie shuddered, then shrugged him off. "That's enough of that. You get Hamilton to bed, and I'll get our pizzas in the oven and open a bottle of wine."

Rab broke away, "Deal," and headed up the stairs, hopeful that he'd get some excitement later.

Chapter 19

Sunday 22nd

Suzanna parked her car in the lay-by off Braid Hills Drive, changed into her running shoes and headed off towards Braid Burn for her walk along to Agassiz Rock. It was a calm, bright day, dry and crisp. She loved these weekly early morning walks in the park, getting close to nature and clearing her mind. 'Waldeinsamkeit', she believed the Germans called it.

As she walked, her breath creating small short-lived clouds, her heart rate rose with the exertion of striding out. She climbed the hill, and dropped into the valley, her heart rate steady now at 101 beats per minute – the Fitbit watch indicated.

She started the running function on her Fitbit and upped her pace into a slow jog. Suzanna had been injured multiple times before from Judo and Squash, so had to be careful not to push out too fast, too quickly. The jog gradually increased into a steady run, probably doing about eight-minute miles. Suzanna kept this up for thirty minutes, before slowing again, back into a jog, then a walk for the last few minutes back to her car.

She wasn't as fit as she'd been in her prime, but was still good for her age and could out-perform many of her younger male colleagues.

She wasn't the size of a model – "was anybody in reality" she thought – and didn't want to be. In fact, she was a little overweight according to the medical guidance but if she'd been 'correct weight' she'd be gaunt and bony. She was content with her size, and most people liked her shapely figure.

As she approached the path alongside the road, a dog walker passed by. Her tiny companion, a border terrier, was extremely keen to make friends. The terrier's little legs angled at 45 degrees, and its paws scrabbled for a grip on the asphalt, as the owner held it back. Its sideways travelling reminded Suzanna of a plane coming into land in a crosswind. The dog had the determination of a much bigger animal – the spirit of a tiger.

The thought took her mind back to the dead woman's tattoo. It had to be a trafficker's or brothel's brand. Irrespective of whether any of the young women listed as entering the UK over the last year or more turned out to be missing, they still needed to know where she'd come from, who'd brought her into the country and why? There was only one way to find out.

* * *

Suzanna's mobile rang. She picked it up off the dining table. It was Callum!

"Hi Callum. Long time, no speak."

"Suzanna. Good to hear your voice. How are you?"

"Doing okay, thanks. Busy as ever."

"Look. I was wondering whether you would be free this evening. I was hoping to talk to you about the future. Could I take you to dinner? I've tentatively booked a table for two, but if you can't join me, I'll cancel."

Suzanna thought for a few seconds. She had nothing planned and she could do with a distraction. And sorting out their mutual parting of ways was overdue. "I'd love to. What time did you have in mind?"

"If I pick you up at seven, would that work?"

"Yes. Seven works for me. See you then." She ended the call and wondered again what had brought on this invitation. James popped into her mind, and she felt guilty at putting him off, then accepting a dinner date with her ex-husband. Well, soon to be ex- if they sorted out the divorce.

She picked up her phone and found Callum's number to call him back and cancel. But as she went to touch the green button, she changed her mind. It would be good to agree on the way forward, so she could draw a line under things. She went through to her bedroom to find some clothes and jewellery to wear, but Callum hadn't said what restaurant they'd be going to, so the task was impossible. She texted Callum. 'Where are we eating?' The phone pinged as she went to lay it down, and the message said. 'Secret. But dress posh.'

Callum did like to create intrigue. It was one of his good points. If she didn't know better, he was planning a romantic dinner to win her back. She put the idea out of her mind and hit the shower to wash away the saltiness of her earlier exertions.

* * *

Suzanna checked her appearance in the full-length hall mirror. The little black dress went well with her short, grey-flecked blonde hair. She'd enhanced her features with a little make-up – just enough. She didn't like to plaster on foundation, as it created an unnatural mask. Her diamond earrings and a diamanté necklace glittered as she moved. Before slipping into her black court shoes and grabbing her Ted Baker overcoat – bought when the sales were on – she opened her phone and texted Zahir. 'Are you fluent in Bangla?'

She knew Callum would arrive soon. Promptness was another of his qualities. Her phone pinged, and she looked, expecting to see a response from Zahir, but it was Callum. 'Don't tell me he's cancelled at the last minute,' she thought. The message read simply 'outside red Merc.' She glanced out the window and saw the car parked across the street. He waved at her, and she waved back.

Chapter 20

She closed the passenger door. "What's with the red coupe, Callum? A bit flash for you, isn't it?" He looked even more handsome than the last time she'd seen him. His neatly trimmed dark brown hair was greying at the temples. A small quiff rose above his forehead - a backward wave, held stiffly in place by hair gel. Callum's facial bone structure, unmasked by double chins, hinted at his fitness. She reminded her, not for the first time, of Pierce Brosnan – although his nose was broader and his eyes brown, not grey.

"I'm compensating for having switched to diesel. If it had been a petrol version, I'd likely have gone for navy blue but to balance out my responsible choice, I chose red," he said with a grin.

"What do you mean, responsible?"

He responded as he drove off. "The petrol version would likely have been as bad for the environment and my wallet as your BMW, but the diesel gives me over 45 mpg. So, much less costly to run and less carbon being pushed into the environment."

"But the diesel cars are sluggish, aren't they?"

"Not at all. Nought to sixty in seven seconds. Top speed 150 mph."

"Wow. That's as good as my 325i. But as impressive as it is, you can't match the gorgeous purr of my straight-six engine, can you?"

"I have to admit to that one."

"I doubt I'd get a diesel. Not just because of the lack of zoom-zoom sounds, but because they're dirty."

"What do you mean?"

"Clouds of smoke come from their exhaust when they're accelerating hard."

"I think that's only true of the older diesel engines and ones that aren't regularly serviced."

"I guess so."

The journey to the restaurant didn't take long, and Callum soon turned into the long driveway leading up to the converted manor house. It sat in secluded parkland to the south-west of Duddingston Loch. She knew of its existence but had never been before.

As they waited for their dinners to be served, they talked about how things had changed for them both since they'd split up. Suzanna had thrown herself into her role, even more than before, and had remodelled her apartment.

Callum had recently been made a partner in his firm and his income had stepped up accordingly. She asked where he was living now. "I recently bought a detached house on Napier Avenue in Merchiston."

"Wow! You have jumped up in the world. That's a lovely area of the city. But why a large house when there's just you. I thought you'd have bought a flat in the city centre."

The sound of sizzling accompanied smoke that emanated from the hot plate the waiter carried to their table. He placed it carefully in front of Callum, then served Suzanna's vegetable lasagne. She took a sip of wine, then tucked into her meal. Callum cut a slice off his meat and carefully placed it in his mouth.

"How's the fillet steak?"

"Superb," he said, after swallowing. "Tender, juicy and tasty. How's the lasagne?"

"Excellent. I hate the lasagnas served in most bars. They're usually just a sheet of flat pasta floating in a tomato sauce, topped with cheesy white sauce, and hardly a vegetable to be seen. But this one's firm, like a pasta and vegetable terrine... So why *did* you buy a large house?"

"Our split-up hit me like a baseball bat in the hands of a major league player. I rented a flat for a while, and after I got over the initial shock of being single again, started dating and getting involved in other circles. Our old friends ostracised me, so I had to build another network of friends." Suzanna looked sympathetically at her ex-, despite the fact he'd brought it upon himself by cheating on her.

"I grew up, Suzanna. I'm in my late forties. It was time I stopped playing the young man and settled down. Perhaps one day, I can fill my new home with a family?"

She smiled at him and reached across to touch his hand. Her initial anger two years ago had waned. Although he'd transgressed, deep down he was a decent man. "I hope you do, Callum. Despite you spoiling what we had, you deserve a good woman and a family." He looked back at her pleadingly, and she wondered why.

* * *

As they ate dessert and drank coffee, her phone pinged. It was Zahir responding to her earlier message. "Excuse me a minute. I must answer this." Zahir had confirmed his language skills. She texted back. 'Planning a trip to Dhaka and Kolkata for us. Be ready to roll when we get the go-ahead.' "Sorry, Callum. As I mentioned, we're in the middle of a murder case."

"No bother. I understand. Being married to you all those years, I got used to it."

She smiled. "Look. It's been a lovely evening. Thanks so much for bringing me here. It's been wonderful. It's really quite a special restaurant, isn't it? But I need to go home and prepare for tomorrow. I expect to be out of the country for a few days."

"That's a shame. I've so enjoyed your company. Like the old days before I became a stupid, weak-minded idiot." His smile was apologetic, acknowledging that he'd been the one to wreck their marriage. Despite having invited Suzanna to dinner to discuss their future, they'd not got around to talking about divorce.

As Callum drove her home, Suzanna wondered how things would have been if he'd not wrecked things. Despite what he'd done, she had missed him. Initially, her love had turned to hate, but the hate soon waned into mere annoyance and dislike of the man. But time had healed the emotional wounds and she no longer felt injured. She'd pulled through the early depression and was buoyant again. But if he'd not had sex with that woman, things would be so different now.

Chapter 21

Monday 23rd

Suzanna was buoyant the next morning. Well rested and a warm feeling in her soul. That soon changed when she got to the office.

"DCI McLeod. A word, please." The Chief Superintendent turned and walked up the corridor, away from her.

"Yes, sir." Suzanna followed him into her office, thinking 'what's he want *now*?' She closed the door behind her and remained standing, as was her boss.

"I've just been informed that you've requested flights for you and Usmani to Dhaka and Kolkata. Why do you need to go?" He said, like a headmaster talking to a naughty student. "Can't you just contact the police in each country and ask them to make enquiries?"

"Sir, the police forces in those countries are atrocious. There are thousands of reports of injustices because the police either can't be bothered to do a good job, they're incompetent or they take back-handers from the criminals."

"You can't go around making accusations like that about our South Asian colleagues, McLeod."

"Do you want this murder solved, or don't you?"

"Well, of course, I want it solved. It's just that I have to manage our expenditure on such things. If I allow officers to swan off around the world at a whim, there'd be nothing left for genuine expenses."

"Genuine expenses! Like driving to the golf club and the Masons for networking events?"

"How dare you, McLeod! My official functions are essential to maintain good ties with the community. I'll not have you questioning how I use my official car. Do I make myself clear?"

"Yes, sir." She stood, her face deadpan and her eyes staring into his.

"I don't see why you have to go as a pair. Can't you go alone and halve the cost?"

"I don't speak Bengali, sir. Zahir does."

"The Bengali officers will probably speak English."

"Yes, I'm certain they will. All middle-class people in those countries speak our language, but only when it suits them. If they were withholding information or discussing bribes with those being questioned, I'd never know. When I was in Kolkata, I learned a smidgeon of Bangla, but that was a long time ago, and I would never be able to follow a conversation."

"I didn't know you'd been to West Bengal before. Why were you there?"

"I took a sabbatical from policing and went travelling. Three months of my break were spent in Kolkata, assisting a social enterprise."

"But what could a police officer offer a business in India?"

"I helped some of their junior managers to develop their English, to improve communications with their customers in the West."

"I see. Well, if you can't speak the language, perhaps we'd better send Usmani by himself, then."

"Sir. He's just a DC with a couple of years' experience. You can't expect him to handle senior officers in those countries. It would be like sending in a dachshund to round up a flock of sheep, instead of a collie. Besides, this is a murder investigation, and it deserves the focus of a senior investigation officer. As that SIO, I need to go to find out who the victim was, and how she ended up dead in the Forth."

"Yes, but-"

"I can't believe that you're questioning the importance of this trip. You never queried the need for officers to travel to the USA when that yank was murdered two years ago... Ah! Perhaps that's because he was a white man, whereas this vic's a black woman?"

"McLeod. That's enough! Don't you dare suggest I'm racist! You can have your bloody flights and hotels – economy class only, though – but don't stay a day longer than necessary and don't come back empty-handed." He opened the door and marched out, face set and focussed on his route, probably wishing to avoid eye contact with other officers in the main office, in case they'd heard the exchange.

Suzanna mouthed, "thanks for nothing, boss." There'd not be much sleeping on the economy class flight. She sat at her desk, booted up the computer, then took a few deep breaths before checking her emails and commitments for the day, as she calmed herself down. She contacted the admin department and arranged the flights, then reviewed the case so far and where they needed to head next, before leaving her office and seeking Zahir.

* * *

Ewan Robertson sat in his executive leather office chair. His large mahogany desk, clear of paperwork, shined from a recent polish. Not a fingerprint could be seen. He glanced at the picture of himself with his wife and only daughter, Christine. He felt sad. McLeod infuriated him. She had no understanding of budgetary constraints. He didn't have a bottomless pit of funding. Last year the Chief Constable had chastised him for overspending on overtime pay and travel expenses. He was determined not to be humiliated again. He'd have to keep

McLeod in check, even if he didn't like confrontations with the strong-willed, tenacious officer. She was a damned good detective, but he'd not tell her so. She was already too self-assured.

* * *

Suzanna strode into the main office. "Zahir. Leave early today and pack your bags. Our trip to the home of the Bangla people is on."

"Why didn't you just say Bangladesh, ma'am? Did you know desh means home in Bangla?

"Yes. But we're going to West Bengal as well. Both states are home to Bengalis."

"True. How long do you expect we'll be away? My parents and fiancé will wish to know."

"Can't be certain. I'd pack for a week. We've two countries to visit. You'll know as well as I do that the Bengali culture requires time spent getting to know each other before getting down to business, and time-keeping isn't the top priority."

"Aye, you're right."

"I didn't know you were engaged, Zahir. When did that happen?"

"My parents have been trying to match me with good Bengali girls for years now, but I've been resisting. Finally, they introduced me to a girl who I found attractive, and enjoyed her company, so I said yes. The engagement party was last November."

"You kept that quiet. How come all your colleagues didn't get invited? I'm sure we'd all have loved to witness another way of celebrating."

"Sorry. My parents are old-fashioned. Only Bengali families received invitations. The boy and girl getting married don't get a say in who comes."

"When I was in Kolkata, I got invited to a wedding, along with everyone else who worked with the young lady getting married."

"But what religion were they? Christian, Hindu or Muslim?"

"Hindu."

"There you go then. Each religion has its own traditions."

Suzanna tipped her head and extended her lips. "We're booked on the 11:30 am flight from Edinburgh to London tomorrow. You're out Ratcliffe way, aren't you?"

"Yes, ma'am. Causewayside, near the BP garage."

"Can you get a taxi from there and pick me up en-route to the airport?"

"That'll be fine. What time do you want the taxi to get to you?"

"Let's say eight-thirty. We need to be at the airport about nine-thirty, but it shouldn't be too busy at that time of day."

"Okay, ma'am. I'll sort that. It is Drumsheugh Gardens, isn't it?"

"Yes, at the Rothsay Place end of the street."

* * *

Suzanna went to make a coffee and found Angus in the kitchenette chatting with Caitlin.

"How's it going, guys?"

"Annoyingly slow on capturing Una's attacker," Angus responded. "We're fairly sure we know who it is – a drug dealer by the name of Fraser Muir – but when we called at his flat, he did a runner. We've got uniform keeping an eye out for him. And the informant that told Una where he would be, has said he'd let us know if he sees him. We have a few other cases to keep us busy, but I'm frustrated that we haven't got the guy behind bars yet."

"Keep at it, guys. It's only a matter of time before he shows up. Just a thought: as he knows you're onto him, he may have left the city and gone to stay with someone in another town or city. Perhaps it would be worth circulating his details wider than Edinburgh?"

"Aye. We'll do that," Angus said, indicating to Caitlin that she should pick up on the suggestion.

Back in her office with a fresh coffee, Suzanna pondered how to conduct the investigation in the two Bengali countries. She suspected that outwardly the police forces would act like they were glad to help, but in practice wouldn't be cooperative. Suzanna knew Edinburgh had a significant Bangladeshi community and a West Bengali one. She was familiar with Kolkata, so if the Dhaka police were unhelpful, she'd concentrate on the place she knew best and hope it was the right decision.

She Googled *International Justice Task Force* (IJTF). The website declared, 'We locate enslaved young women and girls, and partner with police to rescue these victims of trafficking. We help survivors build a new life – one where dignity and respect are the norm and their self-worth is rekindled.' "The mission's unchanged then. Good."

She filled in the contact form and sent it off, hoping the organisation would help her if the police didn't. Next, she searched for *Justice Operations,* another non-government organisation with a similar mission to IJTF. Belt and braces, she thought – hopefully, one of the NGOs would help her.

Suzanna reclined her chair and reviewed arrangements she'd made, checking things off in her mind. Ten seconds later she sat up straight again, shocked by what she'd not yet done. She called up her favourite hotel search engine and entered dates and the destination.

Chapter 22

Mairi opened the door to the *Male Massage Parlour* and walked into its foyer. A late-30s blonde woman sat behind the counter, her skin aged from smoking and the smell of a dirty ashtray emanated from her clothes. Her eyes were heavily made up, and she'd tried to hide the blemishes on her face with thick layers of foundation. But it hadn't worked. She looked nearer fifty.

"Hello Rozalia, how's it going?" Mairi asked.

The room had bench seating around the dirty magnolia walls. Scattered around the room were cheaply framed photos of smiling young women in masseuse uniforms. The excessive skin on show hinted at the real service they provided.

"Detective Mairi. I hope your visit won't cause me problems."

"No, Rozalia. I'm not here to hassle you. I'd just like you to look at a picture and let me know if you recognise her." She offered her the photo of the dead woman.

Rozalia had seen many women after they'd been knocked around, but this beat them all. She was shocked.

The sound of a castrated, growling grizzly came from a room down the corridor as a customer reached the climax of his *massage*. Mairi tried to ignore the distraction and Rozalia let a diminutive, embarrassed smile flash before looking serious again. "She's taken a big beating. No?" She paused, looking for Mairi's acknowledgement of this statement. “I’ve never seen this poor girl.” She handed the picture back to Mairi.

“The beating was dished out just before she was murdered,” Mairi said.

Rozalia’s face changed to show a hint of sympathy. “Very sad. Let me see again.” She took the photo and studied it in more detail. “Like I said. I’ve not seen her. Is this the girl the papers have named ‘washed up woman’?” She handed the photo back to Mairi again.

“That’s the one. We need to find out who the woman was and who might have known her. Any ideas for me?”

“You know most of my girls are Eastern European. I’ve never had Indian women working here. I don’t know of any other parlours that have. But I do have many clients from that background.”

“I guessed you’d say that, but I had to ask... Perhaps she could have been working alone?”

“It is possible. As you know, not many girls stand on the streets now. But many advertise on websites as escorts. Have a look.”

“Thanks for the suggestion. That’s a good idea. You take care, Rozalia.”

“You too, detective.”

Mairi walked to the nearest coffee shop, just up from Haymarket Station, and bought herself a cappuccino. Sat in the window looking out at the travellers and traffic, she reflected on whether the dead woman might have been a prostitute. It was possible, of course, but as Rozalia had said, women from her background were uncommon in the trade.

She opened Google on her phone and typed in ‘escorts Edinburgh’. She was shocked when the images of young women appeared on her phone. There was no pretending they just wanted to provide good company for men. Most of the pictures showed the women in scant clothing and there were extremely explicit videos of women, legs open and all on display.

Mairi scanned the images and came across one woman who looked to be Indian. She clicked on the image and followed through to contact the woman but was taken to another page, showing multiple other women and a requirement to register as a client. She shelved that idea for the moment and finished her coffee before heading out to visit another couple of businesses.

* * *

Suzanna strolled to the main office and found the team chatting. "Rab. Have you had any returns from the stations yet?"

"Aye, I have. They're starting to come in. That's what we were discussing. Would you like a summary?"

"Yes, please." She grabbed a spare chair and sat with the group.

"Oh, before I forget, we had feedback from the Forensics Department that the DNA of the woman reported missing is not a match with our victim, so that's another door closed." Rab continued. "Getting back to the immigration checks, half of the stations have already completed the work, and we have their reports. Ninety percent of the women were found to be where they said they would be. Five women had moved to stay with other family members and were found at the new addresses. Six had married, four of whom were found at the new family's home. Four women were found to be in hospital. Two of those were the married women – they'd just had babies. The other two were in for other medical reasons, a serious illness and an accident."

"So far then, all women accounted for?"

"Aye."

"Zahir and I will be leaving early today, as we'll be flying out tomorrow morning. But we still have time for some investigative work. Have you come up with a plan?"

"Aye, we have. But before that, we haven't yet debriefed our findings from our visits on Saturday, have we?" One by one they shared about the visits they'd carried out. Murray and Owen both reported success at finding the women on their list. Zahir had to visit another home before he'd tracked down his five. Suzanna's five had all been found.

Rab was the exception. "Three of mine were home, no problem, but the fourth one I visited, they told me the woman had returned to West Bengal last week. I need to get onto immigration and find out how come she's still on my list if she *had* left the country. On the fifth visit, they said she'd married and gave me the address of the new family but when I called there, they said she had gone off on holiday with her husband, so I haven't tracked *her* down yet. Apparently, they went to Centre Parks, down near Penrith. I'll contact the company and see if they are there. But we'll need a physical check to be certain."

"Agreed. Once you've confirmed it, get the Penrith police to pay a visit.. Mairi. How did you get on with the prostitute angle?"

"I checked in with three massage parlours but none of the managers recognised our victim. In fact, they all said the same. None of them has ever had women from South Asian backgrounds working for them. It was suggested I try escort agencies, so I had a look at one and was shocked at the blatant sexual nature of the website. I was thinking we could try to find one or two women from a South Asian background, then arrange to meet them. But it would need to be an undercover operation, involving one of the men." She showed them the website she'd visited earlier, and the men's eyes became frog-like as they stared.

"Any volunteers, guys?" Suzanna asked. All four men opened their mouths to speak, but Suzanna continued. "Bear in mind that if you meet up with one of these escorts, and someone you know sees you with them, there's a possibility it could get back to your friends or family."

All their mouths closed again. Zahir was the first to break the silence. "Although I'm not married, my parents would kill me if they thought I'd been with a prostitute."

"And you don't have time to set this up, anyway, Zahir, with us leaving in the morning."

"My family's not in Edinburgh. I'm the least likely of us to get seen by someone who knows me, so I'll volunteer." Murray offered. "I take it, that if the Audra gets to hear about it, you'll back me up, boss?"

"Of course, Murray. Thanks for volunteering. I know your wife can be fiery. Her name means storm doesn't it?"

Murray nodded in acknowledgement. "Her best friend, from her home in Lithuania, seems to be equally excitable, and her name's Rami, which means calm one!" He turned back to his desk and started browsing escort websites.

"Rab, while waiting for the other stations to report back, what were you thinking the rest of the team could do?"

"We still haven't completed our visits to businesses and community organisations, so the plan is to split up and head off out. We've already listed the ones we think would be best to try, and I've split that into five groups."

"Great. I'll take one of those lists. You can stay here to correlate returns as they come in." Rab picked up the lists that had been geographically sorted and passed them out around the team.

Chapter 23

Owen parked his car on the street and strolled down the asphalted path towards the building's entrance door. It was a single storey wooden building that could at some time have been a scout hut. As he entered the Bangladeshi Community Centre, the hall hushed, the hubbub of voices silenced, and he faced a wall of staring eyes. The women looked shocked that a young white man had invaded their space. One woman stepped forward. "This is a ladies' group."

"Sorry to intrude. I'm Detective Constable Crawford. I don't wish to interrupt. But I'm hoping you can help me."

The woman looked displeased but responded positively. "Of course, Constable. What help do you need?"

"You may have heard that the body of a young South Asian woman was found on the banks of the Forth last week?" She nodded.

"I have a photo of the victim. I'm afraid it's rather gruesome, but I'd like you all to have a look and tell me if you recognise her." He offered the picture to the woman, who appeared to be the group's leader.

She took it and on seeing the dead woman's face, screwed up her own in revulsion. She handed it straight back to Owen. "Oh, my God. What has this poor woman suffered? I cannot bear to look at it."

"Sorry, ma'am. She had been beaten before she was drowned." He stepped away from her and passed it to another woman, who reacted similarly before passing it to her group neighbour. A wave of disgusted expressions followed the image's journey through the group. Owen made a note to bring this up at their next meeting.

The photo passed around all the women, then stalled at one, who studied more closely before passing it to the next lady. Owen stepped towards the elderly lady, who'd looked longer than the others. "Did you recognise the woman?

"No. It looked similar to a girl who lives next door to me, but it cannot be, because I only saw her yesterday."

"Oh. I see." He stepped back and looked to see where the picture had reached. The last lady passed it back to him. "Do none of you recognise the woman?"

They all shook their heads. "Sorry, Constable," their leader said. "This was a horrible crime. I wish we could have helped. I hope you find whoever did this to the poor woman. He must be a monster."

"Thank you, ladies," he said, scanning their eyes before he turned away. "I'll let you get back to your meeting."

"Just a minute, officer. We were about to have lunch. We have lots of food. Can I offer you a snack?" Owen hesitated. "Come this way, Constable." He followed her towards a door, which she opened and entered. She picked up a platter and turned back. It was piled high with samosas. His stomach rumbled at the sight and the smell of curry.

"Please help yourself. There is plenty to go around."

He took two, then thought and took a third. They were still hot and smelled delicious. "Thank you, so much. It's very kind of you. I'll eat them in my car."

"No, no. You must stay and eat. It's not good to rush your food. Come." She led the way back to the group, carrying the platter, which she passed around the ladies.

"Tell me, officer. Who do you think killed the young woman?"

He swallowed a mouthful of spicy vegetables and fried pastry before responding. "If I knew, I wouldn't be here asking you ladies. If we can find out who she is, that would help us find out who murdered her."

"I see. What a terrible business. Do you think someone is targeting South Asian women? Do we need to be especially careful?"

"There's no evidence that this was a racially motivated attack. We certainly hope there won't be another to prove us wrong. I doubt you have anything to worry about. The number of serial killings in the UK is tiny – extremely rare, despite how many there are in books and TV series. Most murders are committed by people who are known to the victim."

"That's good to know, officer. Do eat your samosas."

Owen munched on the tasty snacks, watched by the women, then reiterated his thanks and left. 'One down, four to go,' he thought as he climbed into his car.

* * *

The shop's door-mounted brass bell tinkled as Mairi entered. The shop stocked a little of everything, but that wasn't much, given its size. A blue-turban-headed man behind the counter, busily emptying coins into the till drawer, looked up as Mairi approached.

"Excuse me, sir. Detective Constable Gordon. Could you please take a look at this picture and tell me if you recognise the woman?" She held it up in front of his face before he had answered. The man's eyes widened in shock, and he gagged. His hand shot to his mouth, then he barged his way through the door behind him. She heard another door crash, then the sound of retching.

He emerged after his stomach had voided itself. "Very sorry, Constable. It was such a shock. The woman's face was so... so gruesome. Appalling. Why did you show me such a horrible picture?"

"My apologies, sir. I hadn't meant to upset you. We are trying to find someone who might know the woman. She was murdered last week."

"Oh! Is that the woman who was found drowned?"

"Yes. She'd been murdered," she repeated.

"Let me see the picture again." He took it from her and studied the woman's mangled features. "It's difficult to say. Her face has been so severely damaged. There is one possibility from my customers. A young woman, whose ears are similar. She lives on the next street. I haven't seen her in a week, which is unusual."

"Do you have a name, sir?"

"Yes. As I said, she is a regular here. Comes in, most days. Her name is Zurafa Ahuja."

"So, a Sikh woman?"

"Yes, yes. Many of my customers are Sikh."

"I doubt it will be her then, as we are looking for a Bengali woman. Is there anyone else you can think of?"

"Although she has a Sikh name, she could still be of Bengali descent. A Sikh man could have married a Bengali woman."

"Oh. I didn't realise. I thought Sikhs only married within the religion."

"No, no. It is allowed. Even Sikh women can marry non-Sikhs, although it does not happen much, in my experience."

Mairi wrote the woman's name in her notebook. "Zarufa's address please?"

The shopkeeper gave Mairi the address. "I hope you find who killed the woman. He must be an evil, god-less person."

"Thanks for your time, sir." She turned and left the shop. The woman's home was within walking distance of the shop, so she entered the address into her phone's mapping app, then strode off down the street.

Chapter 24

The team gathered again later in the day. They'd all had similar experiences. Shock and horror at the picture, but no-one had recognised her. Suzanna realised they couldn't continue using the death photo much longer, so tasked Rab with getting an artist's impression done as soon as possible, so they wouldn't unnecessarily shock others during their enquiries.

Mairi had tried sari shops, but no one had identified the victim or her sari. One shop owner said that most of the bangles were commonly available but had pointed out that one of them was unusual. He'd seen nothing like it, sold in the UK. Suzanna requested a picture of the bangle to take with her on the trip to Bangladesh and India.

Mairi acknowledged the request, then continued briefing about her enquiries. Another shopkeeper had suggested the sari would never have been sold in Edinburgh, as it was thin, cheap cotton, with a simple print. Purchasers in Scotland were only interested in better quality saris. This reinforced Suzanna's hypothesis that the wearer had been a recent immigrant, rather than a long-term immigrant or British-born woman.

"Oh, I forgot to say, I got a lead from a Sikh shopkeeper. He gave me the name and address of a woman who he thought looked similar to our victim, but when I called at her home, no one was in. I'll have to return another time to check that out." Mairi concluded.

Suzanna left them discussing the further returns they'd received from other stations and went off to meet with Steve from communications.

* * *

"Ladies and gentlemen," Steve Gibson announced. "Thank you for coming." The room went quiet.

"As you know, on Tuesday 17th February, the body of a young South Asian woman was found on the banks of the Forth, near Queensferry. The woman had been drowned, but we later found that she had sustained serious injuries before entering the water. We can now be certain that she was murdered and had been cruelly treated before being dumped into the estuary at Kincardine."

"A number of lines of enquiry are being followed, but we have yet to find out who the woman was, as she had no form of ID on her. No one has been reported missing that might fit her description. And her face had been badly disfigured before she was deposited in the water. Any questions?"

Hands went up around the room and many journalists shouted questions. Steve picked out a woman with mousey hair tied in a side ponytail. "Amanda Pleasant, The Herald. What can you tell us about the woman? We know she wasn't white. Which community was she from? And what are the police doing to find out who she was?"

Steve turned towards Suzanna, inviting her with his eyes to answer the question. "The dead woman was from a Bengali background. We have been engaging with the South Asian communities around the city and nearby towns in an attempt to identify her. We are also interrogating all government databases. I have a photo of the dead woman to show you."

"Why didn't you release the photo earlier, Chief Inspector," Malcolm Etheredge, from the Telegraph asked without being invited.

Steve put the picture up on the screen behind him as Suzanna responded. “As you can see, the woman’s face has been badly mutilated. It is difficult to identify the woman from this picture. We hadn’t wanted to show it to you before, as it’s a shocking image. But the time has come to seek your help and the help of all your readers. If we cannot identify the woman, finding her murderer will be so much harder – if not impossible.”

Several hands had covered mouths as they looked at the battered and bloated face on the screen. Steve quickly switched off the image. The idea had been to shock the press into helping, but they didn’t want the picture in the papers.

“The woman’s neck had been broken and she would have been paralysed from there down when the assault on her face took place. She was struck a number of times with a heavy object to disfigure her and hide her identity.”

“Would she have felt the assault?” Another journalist asked.

“Undoubtedly... That’s why we are keener than normal to find the murderer. The pathologist tells us the poor woman would have felt every crushing blow to her face and would likely have been conscious when she was dumped into the estuary to drown. This was a cruel murder by an evil person. He or she must be found, and we hope you will help us in this endeavour.

“Surely you don’t believe a woman could have done this,” the Herald journalist asked.

“We keep an open mind, Ms Pleasant. In my experience, women can be just as evil as men. Now I must get back to the job of finding that evil person. Steve Gibson will ensure you each get a description of the victim and we will issue an artist’s impression as soon as we have one. She turned and walked out, as further shouted questions came from the throng.

A reporter from one of the tabloid papers called out, "Was this racially motivated? Could the murder have been the start of a killing spree?"

She ignored him and the other speculative questions shouted to her departing back. They were always looking for a sensational headline. Next stop, the pathology department. Mark had texted her about a new finding.

* * *

As ever, the department was clinically clean and smelled of disinfectant. Its bland walls and stainless-steel tables hinted at open chest cavities, of blood and dissected organs. Suzanna disliked the place. Like butchers' shops, it was used for one purpose – to cut up dead bodies. Mark was sitting at his desk, typing into his computer. She tapped on his door and entered the office. Mark updated her on his latest finding.

"You've found traces of semen in the victim's throat. I'm surprised it wasn't washed away by the saltwater."

"It's sticky stuff, Suzanna. Has to be to do its job," Mark said, smiling. "there were more traces further down the gullet."

"Has it been DNA checked yet?"

"No, but I've sent samples to the lab. Not sure how long it will be until you get a result from them. I also found a tiny quantity of blue fibres in the lungs."

"Is there anything else of note from your examination of the corpse?"

Mark gave her a summary of what his report would say once he'd written it up – most of which she already knew. She thanked him and turned to leave, keen to chase Forensics about the sample. "Oh! Can our artist get access to the body now, to do an impression of her face?" Mark confirmed that would now be possible, so she turned and hastened away.

Chapter 25

As the woman walked through the double doors, Murray's jaw dropped. She wore a red sleeveless dress, trimmed with white, contrasting with her almond skin and black hair, drawing his eye to her face. The whites of her eyes similarly contrasted with the mahogany centres, sparkling. She noticed the single red rose on the table and walked towards him like a model along a catwalk. He was mesmerized as her hips swayed and breasts pushed towards him.

She bent and kissed him on the cheek as if they were already best of friends. "Hello, Murray." She picked up the rose. "For me. How kind."

Murray remained speechless, hypnotised by her beauty. The small slim nose, the red full lips, the prominent cheeks, and pretty ears framed by her hair gathered behind her head.

She smiled at him, reading his thoughts. She'd seen this reaction many times before, and it pleased her to be so appreciated. It made her work less painful. She knew most of the money given to her by the client would be stolen away by her man. Her controller.

"Er... Would you like a drink, Anika?"

"Yes please, Murray. A white wine spritzer."

He waved at a passing waiter and placed the order before turning back to her. Anika asked him what he did for a living, and he lied that he worked in a building society. He stuttered like a nervous teenager on a first date, as he told her how boring it could be.

Murray felt awkward. As he waited for the waiter to return, he glanced around the wine bar. It was eclectically decorated, with each wall a different colour: mauve behind the bar, purple on the adjacent wall by the entrance door, with the other two walls shades of heather and lilac. Black and white pictures of Old Town and New Town Edinburgh adorned the walls, framed in rugged recycled timber, or mass-produced frames, hand-painted to give them character. The bar was lit by chandeliers – each one different, their multitude of bulbs reflecting off the glass in the pictures.

After his escort's drink arrived, he snapped out of his dream world. "Look, Anika. I've not been entirely truthful with you. Actually, I need your help with something."

"Can't you get it up, Murray?" Anika whispered. "Don't worry. I'll soon have it working well again."

"No. No. That's not the issue. I don't have any problems like that." He whispered back, blushing, then pulled an envelope from his pocket and slid it across to her. She extracted the picture. Her face turned serious, wrinkles above her nose detracting from her beauty and her eyes lost their sparkle. "What is this? Why are you showing me this appalling picture? Is this some sort of threat? My minder is waiting nearby. He'll beat the crap out of you if you try anything."

"No. It's not like that, Anika. Sorry to shock you." He looked genuine as he spoke, and her face softened a little. "This is the woman who was found dead in the Forth last week. We think she might have been working as an escort and hoped you might recognise her." Murray made a mental note to chase the artist's impression of the victim. The picture *was* horrific.

"You're a policeman, then?"

"Yes... Can you help me? We believe she was wearing a sari when she was dumped in the water."

She passed the envelope back to Murray. "I've never seen her before, and I've never seen or heard of any escort dressing in such a traditional way when working. Where's my money? I must leave."

"Just a minute. I'll give you your fee, but you're supposed to keep me company all evening, so there's no rush."

She squeezed her lips and pouted unattractively, then relaxed again. "Okay. You're right. My fee does buy my time." She looked intently at Murray, deep into his hazel eyes, wondering whether she could trust him or whether he might try to trap her. He wore a branded polo shirt, lengthy ginger chest hairs peeking out from the triangular neck opening. His broad, rounded face and wide nose looked concerned. Perhaps honestly so?

A waiter delivered two plates of steaming pasta to the adjacent table, the smell of Bolognaise sauce wafting between them as Murray paused. He spoke quietly to Anika. "Look. This woman was likely beautiful until her attacker smashed up her face. That's why we wondered if she'd been working in your business. If we're to track down the person who did this to her, we need to find out what her name was, where she lived and who her friends and colleagues were."

"As I said. I've never seen her before. I can't help you."

"Do you have any idea, who might know her?"

She folded her arms. "No idea. I'd like to go now, please."

"Look, Anika, if she were working in your trade, her death could be someone targeting women like you. Have you heard of the Yorkshire Ripper? If you don't help us catch the culprit, perhaps you could become a victim."

"I already told you. I don't know who she is. Now I *must* go."

"Okay. Okay. Look, here's your fee," he said slipping her a small wad of banknotes. As their hands touched, he fleetingly wished he were single and could afford to spend the evening with this stunning woman. He'd never been with anyone who could compare with her looks. But then he remembered that her life might look glamorous and exciting and perhaps enjoyable at times, but she was likely a victim herself.

He held her hand as she went to take the money and looked into her eyes. Her hand was smooth and soft. "Anika. Are you afraid of your man? Does he beat the crap out of *you*?"

She tried to pull away, but he held onto her hand. "If you're trapped in a life, you don't want. There *are* options, you know. We *can* help you."

She harshly pulled her hand clear, banging her elbow on the chair back. She yelped as the pain shot up her arm, then tears wetted her eyes. "You can't help me. No one can." She stood, her chair scraping on the floor, and grabbed her coat.

Murray stood as well and passed her his card. "If you change your mind, and want our help, call me."

She slipped his card into her purse, met his eyes once more, then turned and walked away. Murray sat again, then watched her walk away, worried about what might become of her.

Chapter 26

"How long will you be gone, son?" Zahir's mother asked as he sat eating dinner.

"I don't know, Mum." She always fussed. "The DCI said perhaps one week. We have two countries to visit. She hasn't booked return flights, because we just don't know how long it will take to track down our victim."

"You say the poor girl was Bengali? That's terrible. Do you have any idea why she was killed or who killed her? Was it a racial attack?"

"Look, Mum. I can't talk about details of the case. It's confidential."

"I'm your mother. You shouldn't keep secrets from me. Besides, if it *was* a racially motivated attack, we need to know. Maybe your sisters are at risk?"

"Mum. I cannot share information about the investigation. But if we thought there was a risk to the Bengali community, there would have been a public announcement."

"So, if it wasn't racially motivated, why do *you* think she was killed?"

"How many times, Mum? I can't tell you. If details about the case became known to the public, it could jeopardise the investigation."

"Are you saying you don't trust me?"

"Mu'um. *None* of us are allowed to speak about the case to *anyone* else, no matter how trustworthy we might think they are."

Mrs Usmani crushed her lips together and shook her head at her son's intransigence, then took away his just-cleared dinner plate. The rest of the family would eat later. Zahir rose and gave his mum a peck on the cheek. "Love you, Mum." He left her in the kitchen and went to his room to pack and relax for a while before getting an early night.

* * *

Suzanna's phone rang, and she picked up.

"Hello, Suzanna. How's it going?"

"Good, thanks, Dad. How are you?"

"Doing well. Keeping busy. You know me."

"Yes. I bet you'd still say you're so busy, you don't know how you used to find time to go to work!"

"True. True. Did I tell you I've recently joined the parish council?"

"No! What brought that on?"

"Well, now that I've retired and we've decided to make our home in Wiltshire, I have an interest in the community. When I was in the R.A.F. there wasn't much point thinking about the environment in which we lived, as we knew we'd only be there a couple of years before we got moved on again."

"Yeah. I get that. I always missed the stability that most kids get. Being a *scaley brat* made me different from my schoolmates. I remember each time I met someone new, they'd say, 'where are you from?' I could never say because I didn't have a home town.

"Do you know where the term scaley brat came from?"

"No. I've just always known that's what R.A.F. kids were called."

"Well. In the 50s, the scale for furnishing airmen's married quarters was Scale E. So married airmen became known as Scale Es or Scaleys. Their children became Scaley Brats."

"You're full of useless knowledge, Dad."

"Yeah. I know. Interesting, though, isn't it?" He paused. "I suppose you found it difficult having no roots. What would you say now, if quizzed about where you're from?"

"From Edinburgh, I suppose. Having spent much of my life in Scotland, I feel Scottish, even if I don't have the accent. But I'm uncertain I'll stay here forever. It's a great city but I'm drawn to the Lakes. There's something about the place that just feels like home."

"It's nothing to do with little Athena then?"

"Well. I do love being with my niece, and it would be great to see more of her, but she's not the prime draw. It's the fells and the lakes, the gorgeous skies, the west coast sunsets, and the friendly people."

"I know what you mean. It's a wonderful place, isn't it? Your mum and I always enjoy our walking holidays there, when visiting your sister. Have you seen Charlotte lately, by the way?"

"I visited a couple of weeks ago. Charlie was fine – as ever. Still trying to get me back into church, though!"

"Good for her. You know how we feel about you going away from God!"

"Yes, Dad. I know. As I told you last time, I'm not an atheist but organised religion seems so hypocritical. It keeps me away. So do the monotonous, droning sermons, delivered by men in frocks, and the 300-year-old hymns. Did you know Google suggests sermons are *a long or tedious piece of admonition or reproof*? From what I heard over the years of forced attendance, they're right."

"Yeah, well, some vicars aren't gifted orators, and others hang on Old Testament damnation stuff. But they're not all like that. Just you keep an open mind, young lady. We want to see you back on the narrow road once again."

"Dad. I try to keep high moral standards and be nice to everyone – except the criminals, of course."

"You know it's more than that, don't you?"

"Yes, Dad. Anyway, I must go. Things to do. Give Mum my love."

"Will do. When might you come to visit? It's been a while?"

"Yes, it has. But I don't remember the last time you and Mum visited me in Edinburgh..."

"Hmm... Fair point. I'll have a chat with your mum. Call soon. Love you."

"Love you too, Dad."

Suzanna wished her parents and sister wouldn't keep pushing her about church. At least they weren't continuously asking when she was going to marry again and start a family, like a lot of parents.

* * *

Once she was fully prepared for her trip abroad, Suzanna went for a workout. The gym was buzzing when she entered. Exercise bikes, step machines and cross-trainers whirred away, their occupants sporting sweaty sports tops. The women had clingy Lycra leggings or shorts, whereas most men had loose, if rather short, shorts.

Her luck was in. A woman dismounted from a cross-trainer and wiped it down with cloth and spray, just as Suzanna arrived. After storing her drinks bottle in its receptacle, she connected her earbuds and started music going on her smartphone. Before long, she'd joined the sweaty brigade.

Her eyes took in the surrounding faces, all intent on a video screen, ear-pieces isolating them from their neighbours. Many of the faces were familiar to her. But couldn't say she knew any of them. She remembered her younger days when she played hockey. Team sports seemed to be much more beneficial than mere exercising in the gym. Sports were sociable, helped develop mutual support and cooperation, but this type of exercise only offered fitness and escape. She resolved to re-join the badminton club she used to attend when she was still with Callum. Her thoughts brought back memories of good times.

Suzanna filled the rest of her exercise hour by meandering around different options for her future. Her post-marriage independence, with the power to make her no-compromise decisions, had been good. But she recognised there was a gap in her life. She liked her own company but missed the interaction of sharing life with a man. Maybe she should change that..?

Chapter 27

Tuesday 24th

Suzanna looked out of her window. The park, sandwiched between the two rows of houses, still looked bare. The leafless trees, like skeletons, waited patiently for the warmth of spring, but snow drops and primulas were already flowering, their heads dotting the ground with whites and yellows. New life beginning. Another season. Should this be the start of a fresh season in her life and relationships? After the winter bareness, was it time for a new beginning – one that was richer, more colourful, although perhaps less certain and more complex? She saw a car draw up, then heard her phone ring. That would be Zahir.

She deposited her bag in the boot, then opened the car door. "Morning Zahir."

"Morning, ma'am."

"You all set then?"

The taxi drove off.

"Aye. I sure am. I've only been to Bangladesh once when I was a teenager, and I've never been to India before. So I'm looking forward to the trip. Have you been to Bangladesh before, ma'am?"

"Yes, briefly. I stayed with some acquaintances in the city for a couple of weeks while learning Bangla. Can't say I leant much, and

I've forgotten most of it. It will be great to visit both countries, but particularly Kolkata, as I still have friends there and it will be good to see the place again."

"My mum told me to visit my uncle while I'm in Dhaka. I told her I'll be there on police work and doubt I'll have time to do that, but she was adamant I must."

"If there *is* time, then you must do as your mother proposed, but I doubt we *will* have any spare." They sat in silence for the rest of the trip to the airport, looking out at what was happening around them. Suzanna's mind was rechecking that she'd packed everything. She looked for the fifth time in her handbag, ensuring her passport and flight tickets were there, and her purse with debit and credit cards. If she need to take out any cash, she'd use the credit card, as it was offering free withdrawals from foreign ATMs.

Check-in went smoothly and after a short spell in the departure lounge, boarding for their flight to Heathrow was announced. Her phone rang while the announcement was still in progress. The screen said PB Builders. She answered the phone but struggled to hear what was being said. It went quiet and Zahir stood as if to board. He looked at Suzanna, and she gave him a two-finger sign to say, give me a couple of minutes.

"Hi. Sorry! Can you say that again? There was a lot of background noise here."

"Yeah. I heard it. Are you at an airport?"

"Yes. I've got to board my flight in a minute. Did you get the asbestos report?"

"Yeah. Sorry to be a bringer of bad news, but they confirmed the paint has asbestos in it. Would you like me to arrange for its removal? It would be best if you did the whole kitchen rather than just a patch."

"Yes, please. But I'll need a quote for the work, then your repair afterwards. I'll contact the insurers and get a claim going. I'm going to be abroad for a few days, so if you can email me that would be best."

"Sure thing. I'll get the quotes sorted out as soon as I can."

She ended the call, grabbed her cabin baggage, and joined Zahir in the queue for boarding, checking again that she had her passport and boarding pass to hand.

* * *

It was not possible to talk about police business surrounded by other passengers, so Zahir pulled out a paperback from his bag to read. Going by the cover, Suzanna thought it was likely a thriller with ex-SAS black ops missions.

Suzanna tried to think about the case. Who would they be visiting and working with? What was the aim of the trip? What questions would they ask? More questions came to mind, and she noted them. Eventually, her mind drifted off. The last time she'd flown with British Airways down to London was 27 years ago. She was surprised it had been so long. She'd received a call on her eighteenth birthday from a firm of solicitors, who had informed her she was now eligible to take her great-great-uncle's test. Her father had told her about the test when she was in her mid-teens. He'd taken it when he was eighteen, but he hadn't found the right solution.

The firm had invited her to attend their offices in London and to pay for all her expenses - transport and hotel, on full board. She grabbed the chance. Even if it led nowhere, she'd enjoy a couple of days out in London and would get to learn more about her distant family. Apart from mentioning the test, her father had never spoken about his great-uncle. It seemed there were bad feelings between his grandfather and the younger brother.

The solicitors had instructed her to travel down and check into a hotel they'd booked for her, then report to their offices the following morning. Once she'd been introduced and read the terms and conditions, the firm passed her the test and informed her how long she would have to complete it. She would remain on the premises, utilising their conference room until she had written her response. She could only leave the room to use the toilet. Lunch would be brought to her. If she broke the rules, the test would be invalid, and she would lose the opportunity of the inheritance.

The test read like a short crime novel that kept her occupied through to lunch. After which she studied the appendices that accompanied it. These gave her details of evidence gathered by the consulting detective in the story. She was required to decide how the story would conclude and who the murderer was. Her response took a further two hours to complete.

She had left the offices and returned to her hotel, eating out alone that evening at a restaurant in Covent Garden. It was still too chilly to eat at tables outside the restaurant, but she could hear buskers entertaining the crowds. String quartets, dressed formally, played to their audience like professionals. An opera singer blasted out arias, accompanied by music from a CD player. She treated herself to three courses, as the firm was paying, and two glasses of white wine. She hadn't yet rejected meat and had enjoyed the beefy rich tomato, Bolognese sauce and spaghetti. After her meal she had wandered the West End's streets watching magicians, dance groups and circus performers entertain.

Suzanna had entered the Tube station and wandered onto the platform, catching the smell of hot brakes and grease. While waiting for the train, a man had grabbed her bag and pushed her. She'd almost fallen onto the tracks. He'd worn a dark hoody sweatshirt, jeans, and trainers. She'd only glimpsed his face momentarily, but Suzanna had seen drugged eyes, lost hope, and desperation. By the time she'd recovered, the man was out of sight. She'd cried for a while, her cultural experience shattered by the realities of life, by a man who took from others instead of contributing to society and the economy. But one who was himself, perhaps a victim.

A British Transport Police officer had taken her statement but gave her little confidence that her attacker would be caught. In the morning, Suzanna called the solicitors and explained her predicament. They arranged a taxi to collect her, which the firm paid for on arrival.

She was invited into the senior partner's office. "Suzanna. We have deliberated over your response to the test. As you will appreciate, it is not a simple right or wrong answer. Your great-great-uncle wanted to ensure that the person who inherited his estate would have a mind deserving of the reward. He wished the person to have similar abilities to himself. Simply stating that Person X had committed the murder would not be enough. Someone could merely have made a guess."

He paused. "He instructed this firm that the person must detail their analysis of the facts provided and their deductions. They must also arrive at the correct solution but must have shown how they reached that conclusion." He paused again. "Having considered your submission, in great depth and with much debate..."

Suzanna sat, tensed, waiting for a disappointing result to be announced.

"...the partners have concluded that you... have succeeded. And you *will* inherit his estate."

She had been astounded, her lips parting and her mouth hanging open for a while as she absorbed the fact. She couldn't believe it. Tears of joy had wet her eyes and trickled from the corners. No one had told her how much she might inherit, so she didn't at that time know whether this result would be life-changing.

The first thing she had been given was a cloth draw-string bag containing a heavy object and had been instructed that this was the only item that had been retained from her great-great-uncle's life and she was to look after it. As she took the magnifying glass from its pouch and twiddled it in the light, she had immediately thought of the fictional Sherlock Holmes. The Test had been written much like a Sherlock Holmes story, and she wondered if her distant relative could have been a detective, on which Sir Arthur Conan-Doyle had based his character?

As she thought about the event, she realised that day *had* been life-changing. She had been the victim of crime the night before, then affirmed as a talented detective the following day. This had been when her journey to becoming a professional police detective had begun.

Chapter 28

Murray hurried into the station, hiding from the cold drizzle. It was another grey day, but at least there was no frost. The bridge over the Forth had been clear this morning, so he was at work early for a change. But he was still not in a good mood. His wife had been unhappy that he'd stayed out all evening on police business instead of going home. He'd not told her what he'd been doing and hoped she didn't find out.

Rab was already in the office, staring at his computer screen. The immigration list enquiry results had been sent to him from the remaining police stations. He trawled through the lists, picking out the unconfirmed cases and checking the responses where they had been closed. As before, some women had already married, but most of them had been tracked to their new address. The women who had moved away from the district that the stations covered had been left open-ended. And if they could not confirm, for any reason, these had been highlighted.

The correlated list added up to eighteen women. His team would need to follow up on these. Rab passed the list to Mairi and asked her to split the list geographically and allocate a team member to each group. He turned and spoke to Murray. "How'd it go yesterday, with the escorts?"

"It depends on how you judge success. I met with three young women – all South Asian. They were all gorgeous. Just wished my missus looked as exotic and sexy."

Mairi caught what he'd said and turned towards him, with a look of a sister discovering her younger brother had been up to no good. Murray noticed the look and quickly continued before she had a chance to speak.

"Anyway. I asked them all if they'd seen our vic. Two of them said no, refused to talk with me further, and stormed off without taking their fee. The third woman also said she'd not seen her before. I persuaded her to answer some questions before leaving. She said that young South Asian girls wouldn't wear a sari on an escort assignment. They'd only wear one if attending a formal occasion, like a wedding. Otherwise, they'd dress like any Scots lass."

"So another dead end then!"

"Another possibility eliminated, Sarge" Mairi piped up, emulating the DCI's earlier positive spin, when *she'd* been negative. She smiled.

"Aye. Thanks for that, Mairi. You're right of course." Rab went back to his email responses – thanking each station for their valued assistance. As he hit send on the last one, Mairi caught his attention again.

"Sarge. I've finished the allocations. Shall I get the guys together?"

"Yes, please, Mairi, but I just want to grab a coffee. Let's say ten minutes."

The kettle was still hot, so he made his coffee and returned to the main office. The rest of the team had already gathered around and were looking at the documents that Mairi had handed out. She'd allocated six visits to Owen and Murray and three each to herself and Rab.

"Hey. How come my list is twice as long as yours," Owen asked, like a spoiled kid complaining that his brother had more baked beans than him.

"Because yours are all within a tight area, whereas Murray and I have got further to travel to get around ours," Mairi said, looking peeved at

Owen's challenge.

"This is our last chance to find out who our victim was," Rab said. "If we don't identify her from this work, I don't know where to turn next."

"We could try South Asian businesses and community centres in nearby towns and villages," Murray offered. "We've only visited locations within Edinburgh, so far."

"Good point."

"We haven't tried the charities that support domestic abuse victims yet," Murry added.

"Could you pick up on that line for us, Mairi? We've probably all heard of or dealt with one or more of them over the years, but it would be good if you could list them for us, with addresses and contact numbers. If you cover the whole central belt area, that will give us something to do next."

"Sure thing, Sarge."

"Oh, by the way, did you visit that Sikh woman's home again?"

"Yes. Sorry. I forgot to say. I spoke with a woman at the address I'd been given, but she was middle-aged. She said her daughter-in-law had gone to Birmingham to stay with her brother's family for two weeks."

"Did she say why?"

"The woman looked annoyed when I asked her. She said there had been a family disagreement, so it was decided it would be best to create some space, to let matters settle down. I asked if a divorce was likely? She was most put out when I suggested that, saying that Sikhs do not divorce. I got the feeling that the falling out had been with the mother-in-law, rather than the husband."

"Okay. But we still don't know whether the young woman is alive."

"No. I've requested West Midlands police to visit the brother's home and confirm she's there, safe and sound. It will likely be tomorrow or the next day before we hear from them."

"Okay. Fair enough. Thanks for the update."

* * *

Angus was at his desk, absorbed by his inbox. He scanned for emails that *weren't* informing him of policy changes, training sessions on offer or other routine administrative things. There were still no leads to where Fraser Muir might be hiding out.

They had returned to his flat and asked around his neighbours, but no one had seen him for a few days. They'd widened the net, asking police in nearby towns to look out for him, but no luck. The guy seemed to have gone to ground.

He checked his phone, but no texts had arrived since he'd last looked at it. He looked glum as he rose from his chair and headed out of the office. "Coffee, Caitlin?"

"Yes please, boss."

He returned a couple of minutes later and handed Caitlin her coffee. "I'm getting frustrated at our lack of progress in catching Una's attacker. Is there something else we could be doing? What do you think?"

Caitlin stared at the wall for a minute, silent. Thinking. "We've been putting our hopes on a sighting of Muir, but we haven't spoken with family or friends."

Angus looked astounded "I don't know why we haven't already done that. I can't believe we missed such an obvious line."

"I agree, boss, but we have been progressing multiple other cases. As the Chief says, we're only human!"

"Yes, but this is about finding the person who stabbed Una. We should have kept focussed on tracking him down and put more effort into it, even if that meant less effort on the other cases." Angus responded. “I tell you what. I’ll head out to Muir’s flat and try to speak to neighbours again, to see if I can get any leads on people he’s been seen with, and you find out where his relatives are, so we can pay them a visit.”

“All right, boss. Call me when you’re done at the flats. If you have any leads, perhaps I could join you. If I find any of Muir’s relatives, I’ll let you know. We can call on them together.” She turned to her computer screen and started tapping the keys as Angus grabbed his coat and headed out of the station.

* * *

Murray parked his car on a street in Falkirk, then climbed the steps and steep path leading to a stone-built Victorian house. It was an impressive home. He knocked on the door and rang the bell, then stood back and looked up at the house.

Unusually, the windows, in what were probably the living room and the master bedroom above, had triple groupings of narrow panes, separated by thin strips of stone. It reminded him of the split windscreen of his granddad’s 1950s Morris Minor.

No one answered the door, so he knocked and rang the bell again, then gave up after a couple of minutes. ‘One for later,’ he thought.

* * *

Mairi turned off the A908 in Sauchie. The road split two ways shortly afterwards, and the sat nav told her she had reached her destination. A pebble-dashed, brown-window-framed, semi-detached house was her destination. She parked the car and walked up the path, noticing that its entire front garden had been paved over, with not a green leaf or patch of earth in sight. On either side of the door, short rows of bricks stuck through the rendering – some sort of architectural feature, she guessed. Very odd!

She knocked on the door, having not seen any bell push. It was opened by a light-brown-skinned young woman, with long black hair hanging down to her hips. She was dressed in a light cotton blue kameez top, with a scarf draped over her shoulders and covering her chest. There seemed to be two layers of vests under the spotted top. She'd substituted jeans for the traditional cotton salwar pants – very sensible given the February temperatures.

"Good afternoon. I'm looking for Akula Mandal."

"That is me, aunty," the woman responded. "How can I help you?"

"I'm Detective Constable Gordon from Edinburgh CID. I'm just checking on the whereabouts of young women who entered the UK in the last year. Do you have any identification you could show me?"

The young woman's face dropped. She looked worried. "Yes. Yes, of course. Do come in out of the cold." She stood back and stepped aside for Mairi to enter. "Go through to the sitting room, on the right side... Please sit. I will fetch my passport."

The room smelled of cats, although she couldn't see any basket, scratch stand or toys to support her assumption. A minute later she was back carrying the black document with gold writing in Sanskrit and English, declaring the holder to be a member of the Republic of India. She passed Mairi the passport for scrutiny but remained stiffly standing as if a soldier on parade.

Mairi checked the details matched with that on her list and passed it back to Akula. "Thank you, Miss Mandal," she said. "Will you stay much longer in Scotland?"

"As long as your wonderful, but cold country, will allow me. I am staying with my aunt and uncle to improve my English."

"Your English is very good."

"Thank you, aunty."

Mairi smiled at the way the younger lady continued to address her as aunty. She stood and bid her well, then returned to her car and set up the sat nav for her next destination.

Chapter 29

"Right. Let's get the results on the board," Rab said when they gathered together again after their house calls. "Murray. You, first."

"I had six to call on. No one was in at the Falkirk address, so I'll have to try again later. Chances are they were at work. The Bonnybridge address turned out to be a flat over an Indian takeaway. The woman I was looking for was working in the takeaway when I called. So, from our point of view, she's been eliminated. But her visa was for visiting family and friends, so she shouldn't have been working. I passed on the info to the Home Office to look into. The other calls were straightforward. The young women were all at the listed addresses. So I've just the one to follow up."

Rab turned his eyes. "Owen?"

"As you know, I also had six visits to conduct. They were mostly in the east of the city. Five of them were easy. Three of the women actually answered the door – couldn't believe how simple that was. The other two were at home as well. The sixth was reported to be out somewhere with friends. I'll go back later."

"Okay... Mairi?"

"I just had the three. Mine were all north of the Forth. Dunfermline, Valleyfield and Sauchie. Similar to our first batch. I accounted for two, but one was reported to have married. I got the name of the new family and their address. It's in Dundee, so I'll get the local police to check that out, but if they aren't able to confirm, I could always take a drive up there one evening. I haven't seen my mum and dad for a while."

"Good thinking, Mairi. Two birds, one stone, eh?"

Mairi smiled and mouthed yes. Rab paused, looking strangely at Mairi. "What's that on your trousers?"

Mairi followed his eyes to the side of her right buttock. A pile of grey fluff was clinging to her bum cheek. She pulled it away, examined it, then threw it into the bin. She *had* smelt cats in the house she'd visited. "Cat hair," she declared to Rab.

"I didn't know you had a cat," Owen said.

"I don't. It came from one of the homes I visited. We can't have a cat because Brodie's allergic to them."

Rab cut short the conversation. "Of the three visits I made, one was reported to have left the family, but they didn't know where she'd gone or with whom. They told me they'd reported her missing but when I checked Missing Persons she wasn't listed, so that's suspicious and needs following up. One had married and the last one was reported to have returned to Bangladesh. That one will need to be followed up with Immigration." He paused for a few seconds. "So, that gives us seven to follow up. In the meantime, we should think about charities."

Mairi jumped in. "There's an organisation called BEMIS – Black Ethnic Minority Infrastructure in Scotland. It helps charities around the country that are focused on supporting the BAME communities. I found there are multiple charities operating in this field, but two of the biggest in this area are Scottish Women's Aid and Shakti Women's Aid. Shakti mentions on their website that they help women who are under threat of forced marriage or have actually been pressured into marriage to someone, and honour-based abuse issues. They both have offices in Edinburgh, so I thought they'd be good places to start."

"Great. Visit both charities tomorrow. We all need to follow up on missing women from our list, but for the moment, I think we should turn our attention to what Murray suggested earlier: identifying and visiting community centres in the surrounding towns and villages."

* * *

Angus knocked on Fraser Muir's neighbour's door, then waited. It was answered by a woman in her late twenties, a baby in her arms. "Yeah?" She looked belligerent. Her bleached blonde hair appeared unwashed and was tied back in a ponytail. She smelled of milk vomit.

"Detective Inspector Watson, Edinburgh CID. Have you seen anything of Fraser Muir, in the last day or so?"

"No. Not seen him at all. Nor heard him either, thankfully."

"What do you mean?"

"Well, he often plays loud music, the bass beat pounding through the walls. I've thumped on the walls but that's not changed anything, and I knocked on his door once, but he just told me to piss off and slammed the door in my face. The bastard even turned the music up, afterwards. I hope he doesn't come back."

"If he does, please let me know immediately, as he's a person of interest in an enquiry." He passed her his card. "I need to speak to him. But please don't let him know that you've seen him or confront him. He could be dangerous."

The woman looked worried when she heard that. She tucked Angus's card into the baby's leggings, as she couldn't find anywhere else to put it. A second child started crying, dragging the woman's attention back into the flat. She moved backwards and started closing the door, but Angus stopped her. "I have some other questions for you. Can I come in?"

"Aye, sure. Close the door after you," she said as she went to find out why the toddler was crying.

Angus followed her, stepping over the kids' toys, discarded baby blankets and dirty nappy bags. He waited whilst she dealt with her young daughter before speaking again. "Have you seen other people coming and going from Muir's flat?"

"Aye. Loads of people. Mostly other young men and teenagers. Some nights it's like a bloody nightclub. My kids get woken by the revelry."

"Do you know any of the people who call? Names or addresses?"

"I've seen a lot of them about in the area, but don't know any of their names or where they live. They'll be local lads and lasses, though."

"I'd really like to speak with one or more of those people, as they may be able to provide clues about where he's hiding. We believe he has committed a serious offence. If you want rid of him, anything you can tell me will be of benefit to you, as well."

She thought for a while. "He's got a girlfriend. She's often around here. I think she lives in the next block of flats. I'd say she was about sixteen or seventeen."

The toddler came up to Angus and invited him to pick her up. "Milly. Leave the man alone," her mum said.

"It's okay. She's alright." Angus picked her up and sat her on his lap before turning his attention back to the girl's mother.

"Can you tell me anything else about her? What she looks like: hair, build, face, clothes?"

"She usually wears one of those puffer jackets. A black one. And a short skirt. In the summer you can see her pants when she bends or lifts a leg, but at this time of year she wears her skirt over thick leggings or jeans."

She thought again. "Her face is spotty – like a lot of teenagers – and she has a ring in her lip and a stud in her tongue."

The blonde girl on Angus's lap felt warm and soft and smelled of soap. Maybe one day he'd have a wee girl of his own if he found the right woman. "What about hairstyle and colour?"

"She's got pink dyed shoulder-length hair. She often has it tied in pigtails."

"Which block did you say she lives in?"

"If you turn left out the front door, it's the tall one. You can't miss it."

"Thanks very much for your help, Mrs...?"

"It's Miss. Boyle. Charmaine Boyle."

"Thanks, Charmaine. Don't forget if he comes back, avoid him, but call me. Okay?" Angus noticed a strained expression on the little girl's face, then caught a whiff of baby poo.

"Sure. I'll do that."

Angus put the little girl onto the floor. "I think she needs a nappy change... I'll see myself out."

He closed the door behind him and headed out, extracting his phone as he went.

"Hi, boss. Did you get anywhere with the neighbours?" Caitlin asked after answering the call.

"As it happens, I did. There's a young single mum living next door. She's given me the description of Muir's girlfriend and the block of flats where she thinks she lives, so I'm heading there now. Did you track down his family?"

"Yeah. His parents live in Danderhall. He's also got a brother and a sister. It seems his brother lives in Hawick and his sister's in Glasgow. I thought I'd pay his parents a visit but ask the locals to call on his brother and sister."

"Sounds a good plan, Caitlin. Let's catch up tomorrow when we've both followed these leads."

* * *

Chief Superintendent Robertson turned off Fettes Avenue and drove into the HQ courtyard. As he turned to park in his assigned space, he saw a car and braked sharply to avoid hitting it. "Damn! Who the hell's parked in my slot?"

He had to drive to the undesignated parking area, to search for a place to leave his car, then marched into the station, fuming. "Sergeant Brunswick."

"Yes, sir," the desk sergeant replied.

"Find out who has parked in my slot and get the car moved immediately."

"Certainly, sir."

"And let me know whose car it is. If the culprit is in the Force, I'll be having a word with him... or her." He stormed off up the stairs to his office, his face set like an angry bulldog.

Pete Brunswick left his post and stepped outside, noting the car make and registration number, before returning to his desk. He checked on the computer and found out who owned the car, then called him.

"DI Watson, CID."

"Sir. It's Pete Brunswick. The Chief Super's fuming that your car is in his slot. You'd better move it sharpish."

"Bloody hell, I was only popping in for a few minutes and couldn't find a place to park when I arrived. I thought he'd left for the day. I'm on my way." He put down the phone, closed his computer, and rushed down the stairs. He may as well head home now, anyway.

As he was leaving, Pete shouted to him, "DI Watson. I'm under orders to inform the Chief Super who the culprit was."

Angus stopped in his tracks and returned to the sergeant's desk, and spoke quietly. "Can you cover for me, Sarge? I'm moving it now."

"More than my job's worth, Inspector."

"Come on Pete. Give me a break."

"You'll owe me a favour, sir..."

"Okay. Fine... Thanks, Pete." He turned and jogged out of the building.

Chapter 30

Wednesday 25th

By the time Suzanna and Zahir reached Bangladesh, they'd been travelling for about twenty hours. It was 10:30 am in Dhaka when they exited the airport terminal, but to their body clocks it was 5 am. As they emerged into the dry, dusty warm air, there was a hubbub from the crowd of people outside the terminal, waiting to meet family and friends off the inbound planes. Many shouted greetings as they spotted their loved ones. Drivers waiting to collect their pre-booked fares, stood to the side of the main group holding clients' name signs. Many passengers headed past the throng to the taxi rank.

They followed the crowd until Zahir spotted their driver. He waved to the man, then they walked directly towards where he stood. The driver motioned for them to head to their right as he walked to his left. He met them at the end of the barrier. "Come this way, please," the driver requested, before taking Suzanna's bag from her.

They followed the man across the dusty concrete concourse to where he'd parked the car. Suzanna noticed Zahir's normally well-groomed black hair had been messed up by the headphones he'd worn during the flight. It was sticking out around his ears. It was the first time Suzanna had seen him looking dishevelled. She probably didn't look too good herself!

The driver loaded her bag into the boot of his car, then took Zahir's from him and placed it beside Suzanna's before shutting the lid and opening a rear passenger door for Suzanna to enter. He took his own seat and waited for Zahir to get in and close his door before driving off.

As they drove away, Suzanna looked up at the huge Hazrat Shahjalal International Airport sign. When she'd last visited, the airport had been called the Zia International Airport. "Excuse me, driver, do you know why the airport's name was changed?"

The driver ignored the question, so Zahir repeated it in Bangla. This time he answered and Zahir translated for Suzanna. "The name was changed in 2010 to honour Shah Jalal, a Sufi saint. Hazrat is a term that denotes respect and reverence."

"Thank you, Zahir. It's interesting how some places around the world rename their airports after famous people, for instance, Paris, to the Charles de Gaulle Airport, the John F Kennedy, in New York, and the Liverpool John Lennon Airport."

They sat quietly as the driver navigated the roads. Dhaka had changed little since she'd last visited. The four-lane highway leading into the city was hectic, with vehicles competing for space. Unlike some countries she'd visited, amazingly, they actually obeyed the traffic lights here, without the need for stick-carrying traffic cops.

On the way to the Bangladesh Police Headquarters in the south of the city, they passed huge hoardings advertising everything from jewellery to helicopter charter companies. High-rise office buildings and blocks of flats lined the route. They drove by a park where the grass had lost any sign of greenness. As they passed a bus, Suzanna looked up, realising it was a red double-decker – a reminder of London. They went under a covered footbridge across the highway, looking from the distance like a windowless rail carriage.

As they reached central Dhaka, the roads choked up with traffic, reducing their speed. Sat at a set of traffic lights, she noticed a man walking along the road beside the lights was the same one they had seen at the last set. 'Worse than London,' she thought.

They passed bus pickup areas, where people – keen to beat each other onto the buses when they arrived – had spilled into the road, swallowing up the inside lane. The car emerged from the city's central area onto a raised section of road and the traffic started flowing well again.

As they left the centre behind them, lush green shrubs became the backdrop for the tall black and white painted kerb-stones. They turned off the highway into the Police Headquarters compound, passing through the already-open wrought-iron gates, bordered by dark red concrete pillars. Unlike government buildings in India, the dark red theme of the walls didn't extend to the buildings. These were all creamy, pale yellow painted.

"Ma'am." Zahir caught his boss's attention. "The driver said to leave our bags in the car. He will take them into the HQ for us. We're to go into the entrance and sign in at the security desk."

* * *

Superintendent Khondka welcomed them to the Bangladesh Police Headquarters "Good morning Chief Inspector McLeod. Welcome to Dhaka. Please join me in my office. We have cha and snacks for you."

"That's very kind, sir. Thank you for agreeing to help our investigation."

The Superintendent's office was spacious but bland. He sat behind his desk in a decades-old, solid hardwood carver dining chair. The other chairs lined up around the walls of his office, like a waiting room, were in a similar wood. But these were without arms and had imitation leather seats and wooden backs. There were no pictures or photographs but many framed certificates with awards the Superintendent had collected throughout his career.

The cha was creamy and teeth-rottingly sweet. It smelled over-brewed. Suzanna ignored the biscuits and snacks on offer, having already eaten breakfast on the plane. Zahir grabbed a samosa and bit into it. The pastry parcel was spicy but cold. He momentarily wondered whether it was safe to eat, but continued to munch it. His fingers soon became greasy, but he could see no serviettes on which to wipe his hands, so he dug in his pocket for a handkerchief.

Seeing Zahir devouring the samosa, Suzanna recalled a funny episode in Kolkata when she'd lived there for a while. She'd gone to the shop selling hot snacks but instead of using the Bangla word singara, she used the better known Hindi word. In Bangla, samosa means problems. So when she'd said, "samosa ache?" she'd been asking the storekeeper if he had any problems. He'd roared with laughter, and so had she when she realised why.

"Chief Inspector, please tell us how you think we can help you."

She placed her empty glass on the floor, then responded. "Sir, the body of a young Bengali woman was found a few days ago, just outside of Edinburgh at a place called Queensferry."

"Ah. Queensferry. That is where the iconic Forth Rail Bridge crosses the Firth I believe."

"You are well informed, sir."

"I visited your city some years back. My cousin is a doctor there."

Suzanna opened her mouth and expressed a silent Ah! before responding. "This woman had been assaulted. Her neck had been broken and while paralysed her face had been smashed with a rock to disfigure her before she was put into the water, still conscious we believe, where she drowned."

"A horrible crime, indeed."

"The woman had a tiger tattoo on the left cheek of her buttocks and our theory is that this is the brand of a trafficker or brothel owner, either in Bangladesh or West Bengal. I have brought a photograph of the tattoo. I'm hoping your officers can help me identify the brothel where she worked before going to the UK."

She passed the photograph around the room, the officers present each shaking their heads and passing it to the next man. There were no women officers.

"My hope is that we could visit the brothels and speak to those working there. If we can find someone who recognises the dead woman, perhaps they will provide clues to who took her to the UK."

Assistant Superintendent Chakladar spoke. "My officers have never seen this brand in Dhaka. But there's a large red-light district, Daulatdia, about 90 km west of here. It's estimated to have 1600 sex workers. Virtually the whole village is a huge brothel – well, multiple brothels, really. Perhaps the tiger brand is from one of those?"

"Would middle-class men from Dhaka travel to Daulatdia for sex?"

"Doubtful. It takes four hours to get there. Most of the customers are locals or truck drivers passing through."

"So, a Bangladeshi who lived in the UK but visiting Dhaka would be unlikely to go there?"

"I would say that is unlikely."

"But where would such men pay for sex?"

"There are brothels around Dhaka," Chakladar responded, "but no large red-light district. Prostitution is considered to be an immoral trade. From time-to-time raids are carried out on brothels in the city and sex workers thrown out onto the street."

"If you are certain that the woman has not come from a brothel in Dhaka, I *would* like to visit Daulatdia." She turned her eyes to the Superintendent again. "Can you facilitate that for us, sir?"

He looked towards his assistant superintendent. "Chakladar. I'm sure you can spare one man to accompany our British colleagues to the brothel village." It was a statement, not a request.

"Yes, of course, sir." He turned to one of the younger officers. "Detective Sub Inspector Begum will assist you." DSI Begum looked surprised and opened his mouth to speak, but thought better of it. Instead, he just nodded acceptance of the task. It would be good to get out of the city, anyway – a break from his nagging wife and screaming children. And the British detective was glamorous, after all.

"How soon can we leave for Daulatdia?" Suzanna asked.

Begum answered. "The journey, including the ferry crossing, will be three to four hours." He looked at his watch. "It will take a little time to organise the vehicle and accommodation. I suggest we stop at the Padma River View hotel overnight before returning in the morning. We could leave here about 1 pm."

Suzanna and Zahir checked their watches. "Fine," Suzanna responded. "Thank you so much for your support, Superintendent. Is there a desk I could sit at, to work from my laptop, so I can send reports to Edinburgh?"

"I'm sure we can find one for you and your constable." He looked again to Chakladar, who responded with an angular tilt of his head, before replying to the instruction.

"Of course. We will find you two desks. It would be good to have some lunch before leaving, as food along the way is not good quality and may be unsafe for your delicate stomachs. I can suggest somewhere local to eat if you like. But first, let us find you somewhere to work. Come this way Chief Inspector." He stood and moved to the door.

Suzanna stepped forward and shook the Superintendent's hand before following her Bangladeshi counterpart.

Chapter 31

Suzanna fired up her computer, then asked DSI Begum, "do you have Wi-Fi I could log into?"

Begum was busy booking their hotel for the night but heard the request and rotated his rickety office chair to face her. "I'm sorry, ma'am, for security reasons we don't have Wi-Fi. All our computers are on wired broadband."

Suzanna looked disappointed, so the inspector added. "But I have a 3G data package on my phone. You can hotspot from that."

Suzanna was relieved, having been concerned about the bill she would otherwise have racked up if she'd used the roaming data on her UK mobile. "Thank you. That would be most helpful. By the way, what is your first name?"

"It is Jadid, ma'am. Jadid Begum."

She connected to the Jadid's phone, contacted the Dhaka hotel she'd booked for the night, to slip the booking a day, then checked emails. The download speed was terribly slow, so she looked around as she waited for the download to finish. Jadid looked to be in his late 20s. Black-haired, of course, and clean-shaven. His nose was broad, eyebrows bushy, and his cheeks chubby. Jadid's belly gently pressed against his shirt, straining the buttons. Eventually, she had a full inbox, which would keep her busy for a while. Zahir was engrossed in his phone. She wasn't sure whether he was checking emails or playing a game.

She scanned the list of messages and prioritised them in her mind, before opening the one from the Superintendent. 'Hi, Suzanna. Hope all's going well out there. Are the Bangladeshi police being cooperative? Not much progress at this end. Any thoughts to help guide your team? Keep me posted. Alistair.'

In response, she wrote: 'Hi Alistair. The Bangladeshi police have been most accommodating. I'm borrowing one of their desks to check emails. They're adamant that the tattoo is not a Dhaka brothel brand but have suggested Daulatdia – a brothel village out of the city. We'll be heading there after lunch. Will send an update after the visit. Suzanna.'

She turned to Rab's email. There hadn't been a lot of progress. Murray had drawn a blank with the escorts. She settled her mind and focussed on the Edinburgh end of the investigation, recalling all they'd done so far. As she stepped through the investigation, she realised they'd missed something, so hit Reply and started typing.

Rab. Thanks for the update. Every dead end you hit is another road eliminated. You'll recall the dog walker saying there was activity near the jetty around 11 pm. That needs to be followed up.

I suggest that the list of cars caught on CCTV be reduced to only those captured after 11 pm and given the results with Kincardine door-knocking, only the Mercedes. Run background checks on those car owners and their partners if they have any and see if that highlights anything. Also, did the CCTV footage include traffic heading towards Kincardine, as well as away from it? If the vehicle came from outside Kincardine, we should see the vehicle arriving before it leaves, unless it was just passing through once.

She added in an update of her progress, then clicked Send.

* * *

"Chief Inspector... Ma'am," Jadid, tried again. Suzanna realised she was being addressed and turned to the inspector.

"If we are to eat lunch before leaving for Daulatdia, it would be best to leave now." She checked her watch – time had sped by – closed her laptop and bagged it, ready to go.

Assistant Superintendent Chakladar joined them, and they walked out of the headquarters, took a left then along the highway, before crossing over and heading down a side street. Further on, they entered a hotel and took the lift to the rooftop restaurant. From there they could see over the lower buildings and the surprising greenery in between, to other high-rise structures in the distance. They could also look down to the street where buses blocked the highway as they exchanged old for new customers near the market.

They ordered curry with rice and pakora, which was served within two minutes of the waiter leaving their table, and before their drinks had even arrived. "Is the service always this speedy?"

"Yes. The food is safe and tasty and the service fast, so it suits our brief lunchtime," Chakladar answered. "Tell me, Chief Inspector, how does Edinburgh compare with Dhaka. I have never travelled outside Bangladesh."

"Call me Suzanna. No need to be formal. Edinburgh is hundreds of years old, and many grand buildings remain from the earlier years. The streets in the central part of the city are lined by rows of large Georgian stone houses."

Chakladar looked puzzled. "Georgian houses. What is this meaning?"

"Sorry. The houses were built in the Georgian period – the late 1700s and early 1800s. They have a particular architectural style."

"But why would one hundred years be called Georgian, surely one king could not have lived that long?"

"No. You're right. Four kings reigned during that time, all of them George. George the first, second, third and fourth."

"Ah. I see. Thank you kindly for the explanation."

She opened her phone and Googled Georgian period architecture – sod the Chief Superintendent and his penny-pinching. On the first page was The Circus at Bath. Not Edinburgh perhaps, but a good example of Georgian architecture. "Here's an example," she said, showing the picture to him and then Jadid.

"Pride and Prejudice," Chakladar exclaimed. "It was set in this period, no?"

"Indeed it was."

"Jane Austen. She's a tremendously famous author, I think?" Jadid added.

"You are both knowledgeable about British history after all."

"You forget, Britain ruled India, including Bengal from the mid-1800s through to 1947, when it was portioned into India and Pakistan. Before these empire days, the East India Company was in control. So for perhaps 200 years, the lives of many Indians were affected by the British."

Suzanna looked embarrassed because she was ashamed of how the Brits of that era had taken huge areas of the world by force, oppressed their peoples and stole their natural resources. Best to move the subject on. "Tell me, Superintendent," he hadn't offered his first name, "have you been to Daulatdia recently?"

"It has been perhaps one year. Crime in Dhaka keeps me busy. We leave Daulatdia to the local police to deal with unless the crime has links to other parts of our nation, which requires a wider response." As he finished speaking, his phone rang, and he took the call without excusing himself, walking away from the table.

They chatted casually as they finished the food and washed it down with fresh lime sodas – the acidic fruity liquid refreshing their mouths. The assistant superintendent returned. "I have been called away. Pressing business. It has been a pleasure to meet you, Chief Inspector

McLeod. I hope your visit to Daulatdia is fruitful. I shall leave you in the hands of my sub-inspector." He shook her hand and departed.

"It is time that we were making tracks, also, ma'am," Jadid said.

"Yes. Will the waiter bring the bill, or should we go to the counter?"

"He will come." The inspector shouted at the waiter. "Bill deben" – *please give the bill.*

The cost of the food and drinks was a tiny sum compared to Scottish restaurant bills. Suzanna paid, as was expected, and they departed. On the journey back to the police HQ, undistracted by Chakladar's talking, she noticed her surroundings. The streets were dusty and littered. Tricycle rickshaws swarmed through the lanes and along the highway, sounding their horns and dodging the auto-rickshaws and buses, which belched black smoke. She turned to Jadid. "Are the auto-rickshaws working fixed routes?" In Kolkata, she knew they operated as micro-buses.

He thought for a minute. "Ah! You mean the CNGs. No. Each one is a taxi, taking customers wherever they wish."

"What does CNG stand for," Zahir asked.

"Compressed Natural Gas."

"So why do you call auto-rickshaws CNGs?"

"Because they must all run on CNG. Before the change in law came into use, they burnt petrol in two-stroke engines, and they were most polluting. When the change to CNG came in the late 1990s, people would ask for a CNG auto-rickshaw. This became shortened to just CNG, and everyone now knows them by that name."

"Fascinating," Suzanna said, "like we call vacuum cleaners Hoovers because that was the first brand of vacuum cleaner in the UK."

* * *

Jadid had arranged for a vehicle and driver to take them to Daulatdia.

As they drove west out of the city, Suzanna asked the sub-inspector why he wasn't driving them.

"Goodness me. It is not my job to drive, ma'am. If I were to do that, this chap would not have employment. Besides, it is better if we let the professionals take the risks in the traffic and leave us to think and plan."

"Interesting," Suzanna said. There were so many intriguing cultural differences in this part of the world.

The first part of the three-hour journey to the Padma River took them along the two-lane carriageways, with fields on both sides and occasional tin-roofed shacks at the roadside. Every now and again there would be shabby-looking venues serving drinks and snacks. It was surprisingly easy-going travel, just looking out at the rice-paddy landscape and observing the variety of vehicles that would never be allowed on the UK roads.

Tricycle van rickshaws crawled along the dual carriageway, their flatbed load areas piled high with precarious jumbles of mismatching items. They joined the N5 highway for the latter part of the journey – a road with no central reservation to keep the traffic separated. The vehicles passed at worrying speeds.

Before crossing the river, they checked into their hotel to ensure their rooms were an acceptable standard, with working showers and clean bedding. It was a seven-storey grey concrete block with air conditioning units scabbed onto the side. The reception area was bland but clean; they couldn't complain – they weren't on holiday, after all. Satisfied their rooms were okay, the driver took them to the terminal, and they boarded the next ferry across to Daulatdia.

Their car was surrounded by trucks and buses, so they left it and walked around the deck. Typically for February, it was a still day, the sun warming their faces. The motion of the boat created a pleasant airflow. At the rear of the ferry the slowly revolving engine loudly thudded, *donk, donk, donk, donk...*, its diesel fumes vortexing back and irritating Suzanna's nostrils.

She hastened away from the sound and air-polluting machine then stood at the side of the ferry. The view was hazy. No wildlife could be seen, but other vehicle and passenger ferries provided regular breaks to the otherwise boring view. The smooth leisurely river crossing took an hour and twenty minutes, the ferry tracking across the flow. As they drove back onto land, Suzanna wondered how they would be received in Daulatdia.

Chapter 32

Their driver parked the car on the highway adjacent to Daulatdia and said he would wait for them. Zahir and Jadid had spoken throughout the road trip, Zahir glad to practice his Bangla. They walked ahead of Suzanna, chatting as they approached the village. She felt excluded but didn't complain.

The houses of Daulatdia were plain, unpainted concrete with corrugated iron roofs. They were squashed close to each other with narrow walkways between. Multiple solid painted steel doors lined the alleys, enclosing windowless working rooms. One door stood open as she passed, exposing a tatty mattress that sat on a basic wooden frame, its sides butting up against the room's walls at both sides and its head. It looked dirty, and she sensed the aroma of sweat and sex.

Women huddled at junctions, smiling provocatively at potential customers, trying to entice them to go with them – life depended on it. Others grabbed men's arms and attempted to drag them to their rooms. The women all wore make-up, competing to look more attractive.

Despite the seediness of Daulatdia, Suzanna didn't feel threatened. The women smiled at her and spoke to her words she couldn't understand. Zahir was more of a draw for their attention.

The two men spoke with selected groups of women, showing the tiger tattoo photograph to them, and asking if they had seen this on any women in the village. Some women offered to show the men their own tattoos, twisting their bodies and exposing their upper buttock cheeks. The women laughed, some cackling as the men drew back, avoiding physical contact but curious to see the tattoos.

Being unable to communicate with the women, Suzanna felt unneeded, although she picked up a few words, she knew. Kemon acho? – how are you? bhalo – good. But she relished the opportunity to see how these women lived, to better understand their situation. It satisfied her curiosity and made her realise how lucky she was.

One group of women shook their heads when shown the photo but gesticulated along a lane, so the men followed the pointing hands. They stopped and talked many times, but each time the answer was the same, "Nah, nah," – no, no – and a shake of their heads.

They had been there half an hour before they were approached by two men. Both were dressed in shabby, unpressed, dusty trousers, their chests covered by soiled white singlets. Suzanna could see aggression in their faces and hear the sharp tone of their loud voices as they questioned Zahir and Jadid. The Bangladeshi officer pulled out his police ID card and showed it to the men, but this just created shouting The men waved their hands, presumably suggesting the officers should leave the village.

Jadid's face angered as one man got so close he could feel his breath. His arms rose and extended forward, then pushed the man away with force. He stumbled backwards and fell onto his posterior. The other man shouted more loudly as his colleague scrambled to his feet. A knife appeared in the hands of the man who had been pushed. He moved towards the officer, waving the knife. Other men were moving along the lane towards them, drawn by the commotion.

Suzanna stepped forward, separating the men, and raised her hand towards the face of the pimp, like a traffic cop signalling for cars to stop. The man was shocked. He stopped and pulled back from her, wondering why the white woman was intervening. "I think it's time we left the village, Zahir," she said without taking her eyes off the knife-man.

"Agreed, ma'am." He stepped forward beside his boss, and spoke in Bangla, in a calming voice as he removed his sunglasses so they could see his eyes. The men instantly calmed and backed off. Zahir explained why they were in the village and showed them the picture of the victim's tattoo. The men looked at each other, then back to Zahir, repeating what all the women had already told them. There was no brothel with that brand in Daulatdia.

Zahir maintained eye contact, thanked them for their help, and asked them to escort his group out of the village. The men had calmed and appeared to be happy with the suggestion. They walked on, indicating to those in front to move out of the way. The three officers looked at each other and agreed with their eyes that they should follow the men. They walked along the lane and turned into another, then one more. They weren't entirely sure whether they were being led out of the village or deeper into it, but now that the alleys were crowded with curious pimps, madams and sex workers, there was little choice.

On turning the next corner, there was an open space large enough to pitch a family tent. A fierce-looking man stood on one side of the dusty square, and the two men who'd challenged them went straight to him and spoke. Zahir whispered to Suzanna, "I don't like what they're saying. They seem to have led us to some mafia-type boss and they're telling him we're police trying to find evidence to arrest them."

"We could never have expected these people to be trustworthy," Suzanna whispered back. "Be ready to take defensive action if it escalates."

"Yes, ma'am."

The boss approached and spoke in English. "These men tell me you are British police?"

Suzanna responded. "I am Detective Chief Inspector McLeod from

Edinburgh in Scotland. Thank you for sparing the time to speak to us. Your English is very good," she complimented him. "We are not here to cause you any trouble." She paused, looking for and seeing a softening of his expression. "A Bengali woman has been murdered in our city, and it is our duty to find out where she came from, so we can trace her murderer. She had a tiger tattooed on one of her buttocks," she said, showing him the photo. "Perhaps she came from this village?"

He studied the picture, then pursed his lips, tilted his head, and gave the paper back to her. "This is not a mark I recognise, and I know all the marks in this village. You must go now. You are not welcome here. Daulatdia is not a place for foreign police officers or white women." He gesticulated the direction they should go, then stared at them.

Suzanna thanked the man again. As they moved off, led by Jadid. She noticed the boss return to the two men who had lied to him about their reasons for being there. He backhanded the main spokesman, who fell to the ground for the second time that day, then slapped the other across the face. The two men backed away from the boss and disappeared down another alleyway.

Zahir heard the words spoken during the disciplining of the pimps. "Ma'am. The mafia boss just chastised the two men for lying to him about our purpose here." Suzanna nodded to acknowledge Zahir's translation but kept walking while staying vigilant as they headed toward the edge of the village. Those following kept their distance and the people in front moved aside to let them pass. Eventually, they emerged into an open dusty space with the road a short walk away. They were about half a kilometre from where they had entered. They could just about make out their car parked further up the road, so turned and walked towards it.

As they crossed the open ground, Suzanna heard hasty feet, and she turned to see the original two challengers running towards them, both with knives in their hands. "Zahir! Knife!" He spun around and saw the threat.

Jadid also turned and put his hand inside his jacket to reach for a weapon. He drew his pistol, but Suzanna and Zahir were between him and the men. They were both red-faced, eyes popping out of their heads, angry at having been humiliated and wanting revenge.

As the first man leapt at Suzanna, she grabbed his knife hand, rolled onto her back, as her leg came up into his stomach, then extended. The man flew over her and landed with a crash behind her, the wind knocked out of him. She continued her backward roll, bouncing up to land on the man, wrenching the knife from his hand and spinning him onto his front, his face in the dirt. She knelt on his back, then looked to where Zahir had been before her manoeuvre.

The other attacker was face down, Zahir's foot on his left shoulder and the arm extended skywards, his wrist locked by Zahir. Jadid still had the gun in his hand and was attempting to call for help on his phone.

A crowd emerged from the village, women and men moving cautiously towards them. Men were shouting angrily at them. Big sticks appeared in their hands. Jadid put away his phone and stepped towards the crowd, his gun pointing in their direction. He shouted for them to get back, and seeing the weapon in his hand, they complied. But, like a herd of bullocks, every time Jadid dropped his eyes or turned away, the crowd moved forward.

Their driver pulled up on the road behind them, having noticed the disturbance. Zahir dragged his attacker to his feet, then pulled him backwards toward the car, his wrist still locked out, preventing the man from spinning towards him. Suzanna hauled her assailant off the ground and pushed him towards the vehicle, his hand firmly behind his back. Jadid covered their withdrawal. They bundled the two men in through the backdoor of the vehicle, pushing them face down on the floor, then Jadid clambered in and covered them with his weapon as the British officers mounted and they drove off.

Two hours later they exited the local police station, having explained what happened, made statements, and seen the men locked up. The head of the station had expressed annoyance with Jadid for coming onto his patch without informing him. But in the end, things were smoothed over and they'd departed on good terms.

As they approached their vehicle, Suzanna could see the rear door ajar and feet sticking out. She strode out towards the vehicle, worried about what might have happened to their driver.

Chapter 33

"Inspector Watson. My office. Now." He turned and walked away. Angus rose from his chair and followed the Chief Super to his office, knowing what was to come.

"Who the hell do you think you are parking your car in my designated slot yesterday? How dare you! I've worked long and hard to reach my position and I've earned the right to park without having the inconvenience of having to search for a place."

"Sorry-"

"Sorry doesn't work, Watson. You should not have parked there. It undermines my status. It borders on insubordination."

"Sir. I thought you'd-"

"I don't want your excuses, Watson. Just don't do it again. Now. Get out of my sight." The Chief Super sat and turned his attention to his computer – bollocking over.

Angus was exasperated at not having been listened to, so returned to the main office to continue work. After a few minutes of sitting at his desk, re-running the Chief Super's behaviour through his mind, he realised he'd not be able to concentrate on work, so went to the kitchenette to make a coffee. He returned to the main office and phoned Sergeant Brunswick. "Pete, it's Angus Watson. I thought you were going to cover for me?"

"Sorry, sir. I tried. I said I got held up by answering calls and by the time I went outside to check, the car had gone. But he'd already made a note of the make, model, and number. He ordered me to check whose it was, while he stood over me. I had to tell him it was your car. He'd have found out, anyway."

"Okay. Fair enough, Pete. Thanks for trying."

Angus was sitting, sipping his coffee when Caitlin arrived. "Morning, boss," she said on entering the office. She dropped her handbag on her desk, draped her coat over the chair, and headed off to the toilets.

On her return, Angus spoke. "How did you get on at Danderhall yesterday? As Muir's not in custody, I assume he wasn't at his parents' place?"

"I called at their home, a council-owned end-terraced house. It stood out from the neighbours' houses, which must have been bought by their occupants, because the Muir's garden was a mess, with rubbish piled up out front of the house, including a rotting old sofa and a dirty mattress. It's incredible how people take a pride in their home when they own it but rarely give a stuff about the place when it's rented."

"Depends on the person, Caitlin. I'm renting my flat, but I keep it clean and tidy."

"Aye, well. Suppose you're right. Anyway, when they answered the door, Mr Muir was antagonistic and uncooperative. He accused the police of hounding his family and trying to pin crimes on them. I asked him when he'd last seen his son, and he said he'd not seen him for weeks. When I said, 'so he's not here then,' he went off on one, saying I was accusing him of lying, then he slammed the door in my face. So, his son could be hiding out there but without a warrant, we'll never know."

"Hmm. I didn't have any better luck. I found out where Muir's girlfriend lives. Apparently, her first name is Blaire. She's still with her parents, but no one was home when I called, so I'll have to try again. Would you like to come with me this time?" Caitlin nodded as she took another slurp of her coffee.

* * *

"There it is," Mairi said to herself, as she pulled over and parked her Corsa on Albion Road, just around the corner from Hibernian Football Club's stadium. A black Porsche 911 shot past her and sounded its horn as if annoyed she had stopped. She guessed he'd not been paying attention and had to manoeuvre sharply to avoid a collision. 'Arrogant, overpaid footballer,' she thought. 'He probably gets five times my salary, just for kicking a ball around a pitch.'

Across the road stood a four-storey, stone-built, early twentieth-century office block surrounded by black wrought-iron railings and gates. She strolled across, keeping an eye out for any other speedy football stars on their way to or from the stadium.

Mairi was met at the entrance by Shakti's manager, Ankita Ghatak, who invited her in for tea. Some of the staff smiled and waved to her as she entered the open-plan main office. Others were on the phone or had eyes fixed on their computer screens. The furniture appeared to be good quality – made to last. Which was just as well, because it had probably been around for a decade or three. Mairi was surprised at the mix of staff ages and racial backgrounds.

She'd been expecting them all to be of South Asian origin, but it was evident from their skin tone, hair, and facial features that they or their families originated from many countries. She reckoned one must have been Somalian, or perhaps Ethiopian. Another probably West African (Nigerian perhaps), and there was definitely Southeast Asian influence in one of the staff – maybe Vietnamese? There were a number of South Asians and several white Europeans. It was difficult to tell, but some were likely Scots (particularly the woman with red hair and freckles), whereas others had more Eastern European features. None of them wore foreign-influenced clothes such as saris or salwar kameez. She guessed that many were second or third-generation immigrants.

"I understand you want us to look at a picture of someone who might have been an abuse victim, to see if we can identify her?"

"Yes. You may have read the newspapers reports about the woman washed up on the banks of the Forth." Several women looked up when they heard Mairi mention the woman who had been found dead at Queensferry. "We haven't yet got a picture that could be published in the newspapers. So, we thought it best to reach out directly to organisations that might have come across the victim." Mairi handed the manager the death image.

"I see." Ankita said, then looked down at the picture in her hands. As she studied the picture, tears formed in the corner of her eyes. This is most terrible. I have seen many abused women, but this is mutilation, not battering. She turned to her staff and held up the picture. "Has anyone seen this woman?"

Many shook their heads, but others came forward to look closer before concurring with their colleagues. "It is difficult to be sure from the photograph, given that her face has been damaged so badly and bloated by the water. If only you had a better picture," Ankita said.

"Unfortunately, that's all we have. You will appreciate," Mairi said, making eye contact with the staff nearest to her, in turn, "that this woman was subject to a severe attack by an evil person. We need to catch that person and see justice done. So please study the picture closely, and if anyone comes to mind, do get in touch. I'll leave my card with you, Mrs Ghatak, just in case." Mairi went to leave but turned back.

"By the way, ladies. Thank you for what you're doing, particularly those of you who are unpaid volunteers. I wish your roles and mine were unnecessary. But in the imperfect world that we live... Thank you, again."

The women smiled and nodded. Mairi shook the manager's hand and turned to leave for the second time. "Just a minute, officer." One lady had stood and was walking towards her. "Parvati Nag." She held out her hand and Mairi shook it – it was podgy, soft and a little damp. Parvati smelled powerfully of cheap perfume. "There was one client who is a possibility. Let me check the files."

Mairi waited as Parvati retrieved some documents from a filing cabinet, then waddled back towards her. "Here is the photograph we have on file." She passed it to Mairi, who looked closely at the woman's features and compared it to her photo of the dead woman.

"I see what you mean. There are *some* similarities. Have you had any contact with this woman recently?"

"The last time Isha visited us was perhaps four months ago." As she spoke, her head wobbled like a nodding toy dog on a car parcel shelf. "Would you like me to contact her?"

"Absolutely. Could you do that now?" Mairi was amazed at how people from the Indian sub-continent could move their heads fluidly – a smooth combination of nodding and rocking. She'd tried it once, as she looked at her reflection in a shop window, but realised she just looked like a humanoid robot that had a neck joint malfunction.

"Yes. Yes. No problem." She shuffled back to her desk, her thighs likely rubbing on every step, then picked up the phone. After letting it ring for over a minute, she gave up and turned back to Mairi. "Sorry, sorry. No answer."

"Please try again later. If you cannot reach her by phone. Would it be possible to visit her?"

"It would be too risky for us to call. The man who was abusing her might realise that she had complained to us. He might become angry. Then she would be at greater risk. We wouldn't want to make things difficult for her."

"I understand. I'll check with you later, or perhaps tomorrow morning. If you've not reached her, I'll need her name and address. I *will* ensure that, if we have to call, we'll find an excuse that would not raise the man's suspicions."

Parvati looked to Ankita for guidance. "Strictly by the rules, we cannot share this information, but in the circumstances, I think we must. You must understand, though, that if by doing so the woman suffers, we will never again trust the police on such matters."

"Of course, Mrs Ghatak. I'll check in with you in the morning if I've not heard anything. Thanks again Parvati." She shook hands one more time and left.

Chapter 34

"This is the block," Angus said.

"It's smarter looking than its neighbour where Muir lives."

"Aye. I think it's newer."

They entered the foyer, as another tenant was leaving, then caught the lift to the fifth floor. The door was opened by a woman who they both assumed was the girlfriend's mother. "Sorry to disturb you. I'm Detective Inspector Watson, from Edinburgh CID. Are you Blaire's mother?"

"What's she been up to now?" She turned and called back into the flat, "Blaire, get your arse out here."

"We don't believe Blaire has been up to anything illegal. We just need to talk with her about someone she knows."

"Oh. Okay! You'd best come in then." Blaire arrived, looking moody. She matched the description they'd been given. Her mother indicated she should go back into the living room, and they all followed her in, Caitlin closing the door behind her.

The room had two scruffy brown leather three-seater sofas, one of which was against the wall. The other split the room into two zones, and behind it stood a dusty and smeared cheap-looking pine dining table. The vinyl seat covers of the matching chairs were scratched and torn from wear.

A large flat-screened TV sat in the corner on a glass contraption, with piles of DVDs scattered on the shelf below. They were tumbling out onto the grey, swirly patterned nylon carpet. In the corner of the room, a Staffordshire Bull Terrier was curled up in a dog basket. It was mostly white but had black patches around its eyes like someone had thrown paint across its face. It growled at Angus but settled back down.

"So, what's this about, then?"

"As my colleague said, we need to speak with your daughter about someone she knows. For the record, could I have your name please?" Caitlin asked, still looking at the mother.

"It's Mrs Fraser."

Caitlin looked at Angus and their eyes met. They both were thinking the same thing: weird that Blaire Fraser was going out with a man called Fraser Muir from Muirhouse. If she'd married him and he'd changed his name – not that he would of course – he'd have become Fraser Fraser, Caitlin thought.

Caitlin turned to the girl. "Blaire. We understand your boyfriend is Fraser Muir. We just need to ask you some questions about him."

Blaire was slumped nonchalantly on the sofa by the wall, next to her mother, who was perched on the front of the sofa. Her mother turned to her daughter. "Who's this boyfriend? You've never mentioned him." Blaire just ignored her mum.

"How long have you known Fraser?"

"About two years, s'pose."

"Have you been his girlfriend all that time?"

"No. We only started going out last year."

"When was the last time you saw Fraser?"

"A few days ago."

"Do you know where he is now?"

Mrs Fraser was still scowling at her daughter.

"No. I haven't seen him. I texted him and he said he'd gone away for a few days. Don't know when he'll be back."

"Could you show me the text, please?"

"Why should I?"

"Because I asked you nicely, Blaire."

"Show the polis your phone, girl. You've no reason not to."

"I know my rights. You can't take my phone unless you've got a warrant."

Angus stepped in. "Perhaps you'd prefer to continue this conversation at the police station, Miss Fraser?"

"No way. I'm not going to no station. You'll have to arrest me."

"This is ridiculous. Give me that phone." Her mother tried to wrestle it away from her daughter, but it slipped from both their hands and landed on the floor by the dog basket.

Angus went to retrieve it, but the dog suddenly awakened, stood over the phone, and growled, baring its teeth aggressively. Angus withdrew his hand slowly and backed away.

Blaire pushed her mum away and grabbed her phone back, holding it close to her chest with both hands.

"Blaire. We need to see your phone," Caitlin said. "We can do this the easy way: you just let us have a look. Or we arrest you on suspicion of abetting a man wanted for attempted murder, and we'll lock you in the cells for a couple of days while we sort this out."

Both mother and daughter were flabbergasted by the accusation of attempted murder. Blaire threw her phone to Caitlin. "Here, have the phone, then."

Caitlin tried to catch it with her left hand, but it hit her fingers and bounced. Angus snatched it out of the air like a cricketer in the slips, saving it from crashing to the floor again.

"PIN code, please Blaire?"

"Two, eight, oh, three," she responded with a huff.

Angus typed it into the phone, then interrogated the texts. He found her messages to and from Fraser, confirming that he'd said he would be away for a while. He noted the phone number in his pad, then stood and passed it back to Blaire. "That wasn't so hard, was it?"

"Blaire. Your boyfriend is a suspect in an attempted murder case. If he returns to the area, please call us. For your own safety, don't go near him. We think he stabbed a woman – a police detective. A friend and colleague of ours."

"You hear what they're saying, girl. You stay away from that Fraser Muir."

"But I love him, Mum. He's been good to me. And he loves me too."

"Blaire," Caitlin said. "I understand you must have feelings for him. But he might have attempted to murder a woman. Please stay safe. After we've caught up with him, if it turns out he's not the one who stabbed our colleague, he'll be released. You could resume your relationship with him then. But if we're right, you could be putting your own life at risk if you go back to him."

Angus stood, and Caitlin followed his lead. "Thank you for your cooperation, Mrs Fraser, Miss Fraser. We'll get out of your hair."

Blaire ignored them and started playing with her phone.

Outside the flats, sat in Caitlin's car, Angus called the station to ask for assistance in tracking the phone. They'd just have to wait until they had the result. There was no point in calling the man and asking him to meet up.

* * *

The murder investigation team gathered again at the station. Rab asked Owen and Murray how they'd got on. Owen reported on his visit to the community centre, leaving out the part about stuffing his face with samosas. Murray reported on the three community centres he'd visited. Again, no leads had been forthcoming.

Mairi reported on her visit to Shakti Women's Aid. "At least there's one line to follow," Rab surmised. "I didn't have any luck with the charity I visited. No one recognised her, although they all said how upset they'd been when the news came out. They reckoned she'd be a victim of domestic abuse that had gone too far, with her abuser also her murderer. That sounds likely as the motive. Best one I've heard so far, anyway."

Mairi asked if the artist had yet provided an impression they could use. Rab went red, swore internally at himself for not having chased the artist. "No. I left a message for the artist we normally use, but she hasn't got back to me yet. I'll get onto that again after this meeting.

"By the way, Sarge, West Midlands police got back to me," Mairi reported. "The Sikh woman was found to be at her brother's, as we'd been told. I also heard from the Dundee police. The woman who married and moved to the city was accounted for, so that's another two women eliminated."

"Okay. Thanks." Rab stood and went to the board. "You'll see we have five names on the board, of people who might be our victim. We'll need to visit their homes and check. Murray, you take this one at the top of the list. Owen, the next two – their homes are in the same district of the city. Mairi, if you take the fourth, I'll pick up on the last one. If there's nothing else, let's get on it straight away."

Chapter 35

Suzanna washed away the dust of the journey and the dirt from combat. She smiled when she remembered finding that the reason their driver's feet had been hanging outside of the vehicle at Daulatdia, was because he'd taken a nap, not been assaulted. The hotel's shower was weak and barely adequate. She missed the rain-head shower in her apartment at home that cascaded water over her entire body. The shower she'd taken after Callum had left on Sunday night came to her mind. She had been glowing inside from the sensations and emotions of their time together. Her thoughts went back to that night, reliving it in her mind.

After their meal together, he'd taken her home. As she went to get out, the realisation came that she'd forgotten to bring something with her earlier. "Wait here, Callum. It just occurred to me that one of your scarves is still hanging on a hook in my cloak cupboard. I'll fetch it.

"I may as well come up, to save you coming out again on this chilly night."

They'd walked up the stairs, and Suzanna opened the entrance door to her apartment. She stepped inside and went straight to the cloak cupboard to get Callum's scarf. As she'd turned, they bumped into each other. Suzanna had lost her balance and Callum had grabbed hold of her to stop her from stumbling away. "Sorry. I should have waited by the door."

Their faces had been close enough to kiss, but she'd pulled back. "That's okay, Callum, I shouldn't have spun around so fast. Look, as you're here, would you like to see what I've done with the apartment?"

"Absolutely. Your description of the changes sounded great, but no verbal depiction can fully substitute for seeing something with your own eyes."

She'd taken off her coat and hung it in the cupboard. "Would you like a coffee?"

"Most certainly," he'd said, passing her his coat and closing the outer door.

Suzanna had led the way into the living room and walked around the kitchen island to put the kettle on.

"Wow! The open plan living works really well, doesn't it?"

"Aha."

"I like the way you changed around the sofa and sideboard. The new orientation works so well. It doesn't look like the same place I lived in two years ago." He'd sauntered further into the room and had taken a seat on the sofa.

Kettle boiled and coffee in the cafetiere, Suzanna had joined him on the sofa, perching on the edge at an angle to face him. They'd chatted naturally as if they were best friends, not husband and wife considering their divorce.

"I was dreading this evening, truth be told." He'd paused as he thought of his next line, and Suzanna had tilted her head attentively, wondering what was coming next.

"It's been wonderful spending time with you again. I'd forgotten how good it had been before my foolishness. You do know that time you caught me in bed with the other woman was a one-off. Honestly. It had never happened before with her or any woman."

Suzanna had sat silently looking into his eyes. She had felt a reconnection with him that evening. If he hadn't betrayed her, they would still have been together, in love and enjoying being a couple.

"I never really said I was sorry. Properly." He'd pause. "The split, after you rightly kicked me out, devastated me. I was still madly in love with

you and distraught that I'd hurt you. I never meant to do that. It must have been some sort of mid-life crisis – my weak ego needing to know I was still attractive to the opposite sex and easily flattered by a younger woman."

"I was shattered as well, you know," Suzanna had said, gently.

He reached forward and took her hand. "I was a bloody idiot. Pathetic. Will you forgive me?"

She'd nodded, her face showing understanding. Their blue eyes had locked on each other, and their faces had drawn together as if their mouths were magnetic. Their lips had touched, brushing feather-like, then firmly sealed in a passionate embrace.

Suzanna had felt the stir of excitement run through her like tingling electricity, making her squirm. They'd drawn closer together, their arms holding each other, his around her neck, squeezing her lips into his, as their excitement took hold. He'd kissed her neck and nibbled her ears, then touched her in a way that only he could know. That's when she'd known where it would end...

The reunion of their bodies had been wonderful. Exciting, passionate. They seemed so perfectly matched, and surely would never have split, if it hadn't been for his infidelity. There had been a rekindling of love in both their hearts.

* * *

She finished showering and dried herself with the thin towel that felt like it was made from straw, then dressed for dinner. They gathered in the hotel's restaurant and ordered food – no alcohol, as expenses wouldn't pay for that. The driver was staying in a cheaper hotel nearby, sleeping rough, as his allowances wouldn't cover the cost of their hotel, and he was forbidden to mix with the officers.

They reviewed the events of the day, discussed their good fortune that there hadn't been a larger group of attackers and that Jadid had not needed to discharge his firearm. "I shall write my report about what happened today," Suzanna informed him. "Would you like a copy?"

"That would be most efficacious, ma'am. I would not need to duplicate your work."

"Great, I'll do that, then. What's your email address?"

He reached into his pocket and pulled out a business card, handing it to her after changing the phone number. "I cannot get another batch of cards printed until the end of the year," he explained. "Changing my phone number does not warrant such an expense."

"Fine. No problem." She popped the card into her phone wallet, for later. "And now I will bid you goodnight. I will write up my report before sleeping. She stood, thanked Jadid again for his assistance, then departed, leaving the two men to chat.

* * *

Back in her hotel room, Suzanna opened her laptop and checked for work emails. Most of it was circular emails, keeping everyone informed about upcoming events, points to note, the chief constable's emphasis on policing at that time and changes to policies. She scanned it quickly to clear it down, then opened Rab's email. He updated her on the progress made in tracking down missing women. Still no strong leads, but a few possibilities.

Her phone beeped, and she noticed a WhatsApp message had arrived from Angus. 'Just had word from Hawick and Glasgow police. Fraser Muir not hiding out with sister or brother.' Frustrating progress. She replied: 'Never mind. Keep at it.'

Her attention returned to her emails, this time her personal account. There was one from Callum. She'd been wondering when he might next contact her. Further down the inbox, there was a message from

James. She guiltily ignored that for the moment and opened Callum's email – it was short but lovely to read.

'Hi Suzanna. Sunday night was fantastic. I had a wonderful time – not just the incredible sex! I'm over the moon that you've forgiven me and we've re-bonded. Hope we can meet again soon after your return to Edinburgh. Love Callum.'

After her recall of their experience whilst in the shower earlier, the message was welcome. It reiterated her feelings of love for Callum – or was it just lust?

She hesitantly opened James's email. 'Hello, gorgeous. I've missed you so much and worried that something is amiss, as we've not spoken for days now. Have I done something wrong? I know you're not in the country and busy with the case, but please let me know if we're still okay? I hope you're not going to break my heart. Love you, James.'

Feelings of shame overwhelmed her. What the hell was she doing? By sleeping with her estranged husband, now *she* had betrayed James, just as Callum had done to her. Her eyes welled up and tears flowed as she condemned herself for her actions, for having let her desires take control of her body. Now she was in love with *two* men.

An hour had passed of remonstrating and sobbing before she pulled herself together and wrote up her report. She emailed it to Jadid, as promised, as well as to Alistair back in Edinburgh. Sleep evaded her for some time...

Chapter 36

Thursday 26th

They emerged from Kolkata's Netaji Subhas Chandra Bose International Airport into mid-day sunshine. Crowds stood with their trolley bags, looking for their rides home. Battered old yellow cabs lined up by the pre-paid taxi kiosk. It was pleasantly warm and dry – so different from when she'd last visited. The new airport building was air-conditioned, clean, and functional.

On her previous visit to Kolkata, the old building had served as the air gateway to West Bengal. It had been a disorganised dilapidated building. Cats had climbed over luggage, sniffing for any food that might be around. Money changers lined the periphery of the baggage hall and people fought for space by the luggage carousels. She'd ordered a pre-paid taxi to avoid being ripped off by the taxi touts. It had felt like walking into a fan oven when she had walked outside into 38 degrees Celsius and 97% humidity. Her thin cotton top had been turned into a wet rag within ten minutes of leaving the airport in the non-air-conditioned taxi. The Austin Ambassador cabs were based on the 1950s Morris Oxford, and they had changed little, if at all, over the five decades since their introduction.

Zahir grabbed her attention and led the way to a man holding a cardboard sign with their names on it. Uber and Ola cars swarmed through the pickup area, called by their customers' apps. It was still chaos, but at least it was air-conditioned chaos and fixed prices.

Their ride to the central Kolkata hotel had changed little since Suzanna's last visit. The roads were still heavily congested. Everyone used their horns frequently and there was no lane discipline. Every gap between vehicles stopped at intersections would get filled by something – a motorbike, rickshaw or even another small car.

The buses were exactly the same. They hadn't been replaced by modern buses and most relied on open windows for conditioning the passengers' air. It worked okay when the bus was moving, but as soon as they stopped and there was no airflow, the passengers' sweat would run. But one big change was the reduction in yellow cabs. There'd been a multiplication of white smartphone-ordered cars and individually owned vehicles. And en-route, she saw signs for shopping malls that hadn't existed at all when she'd last been there. These were signs of increased wealth – of a growing middle class.

They arrived at the Lalit Great Eastern hotel, checked in, and went to their rooms to freshen up. They met twenty minutes later for their journey to the headquarters of Kolkata's police force in Lal Bazar. It was the first time that she'd stayed in a five-star hotel – gleaming marble lining the walls and floors. Her room was luxurious, but she didn't expect to spend much time in it.

When last in Kolkata, she'd stayed at the Baptist Mission Society guesthouse on AJC Bose Road. Although she'd already lost her faith in God by that time, it had been recommended to her by her parents as a cheap and safe place to stay.

The guesthouse had been an oasis of calm in the middle of pandemonium – where the sounds of the street were held back by eight-foot-high brickwork. The loudest sounds inside the compound walls were the squawking crows – especially at dawn.

***

Suzanna would have preferred to walk in the 22 degrees warmth – to take in the sights and smells of the city and to stretch her legs for the ten minutes it would have taken but the driver was adamant he must drive them the half-mile from the hotel to his headquarters. Honoured guests from the British police had to be treated with reverence. Diplomacy was important if she were to get their cooperation, so she went along with the driver's wishes.

The headquarters had been a grand building, back in the days of British rule, with the typical deep rusty pink brickwork, contrasted by cream window surrounds and cream corbels. On arrival, they signed in at reception, then lingered in the entrance foyer. The internal walls were painted in the same colours as outside, with the archways in cream and the floors stone-flagged.

They waited longer than one might expect for *honoured* guests. But Suzanna was conscious of the cultural complexities of India. Although she and Zahir were on time for their booked appointment with the Commissioner, promptness wasn't as important outside of Europe and North America – relationships were given priority. Eventually, they were summoned to his office. The Commissioner gave them five minutes of his time to welcome them to his city, then passed them over to the care of a superintendent.

"Chief Inspector. Welcome to Kolkata. Is this your first time?" the Superintendent asked.

"No. I spent three months here about ten years ago. It's great to return. The city is a wonderful place."

"And this must be Constable Usmani," he said, turning to Zahir, nodding to him. He didn't smile or pay much attention to the young officer, as his status didn't afford it. "Come this way, Chief Inspector." He led the way to his office, where other officers sat chatting.

The room was basic. No pictures, no comfortable seats and little technology. The computer was an old PC. The superintendent introduced them to Assistant Superintendent Banerjee and Sub-Inspector Anand, then laid out the rules under which they must adhere, as foreigners. They would be accompanied at all times by a Bengali police officer when carrying out investigations in the city. They should ask questions through their escorting officers, who would act as interpreters.

He reiterated his welcome and promised cooperation in seeking the identity of the murdered woman, then handed them on to their liaison officers – shaking Suzanna's hand but ignoring Zahir.

Zahir wasn't surprised by the senior officers ignoring him. He knew that status played a huge part in South Asian culture. Within uniformed forces, lower ranks were expected to do their superior's bidding without question. Age was also a significant factor, with elders lording over anyone younger than themselves, except if the elder was of lower caste.

Although illegal, the caste system still operated in these countries. Zahir had seen it even within his own community, in Scotland, although less so there. He was still upset that his father hadn't acknowledged his success at joining the police and becoming a detective. The old man was still annoyed that his son had not joined the professional classes.

"Come this way, Chief Inspector," her Kolkatan counterpart invited. Like the Commissioner and the Superintendent, Banerjee had a full moustache – a sign that they were all Hindus. Muslims tended to have beards or be clean-shaven but rarely had a moustache. Christians were a tiny minority in this Indian state, despite Kolkata's fame for being home to Mother Teresa. Suzanna followed him down the corridor and into another office, where more moustachioed officers sat.

"Please use my first name: Suzanna. It will be much easier to communicate."

Banerjee nodded but didn't offer his own first name in return. "Please sit." He pulled some documents into the centre of his sparse desk and selected an image of the tattoo found on the dead woman's buttock. "I understand you believe this tattoo might be a brothel branding?"

"Yes. I know it's normal practice for brothels to tattoo their girls, to indicate ownership. We know the dead woman is Bengali and we have already been to Dhaka, but the police didn't recognise the brand."

"I'm sorry to inform you that your journey has been wasted. This is not a Kolkatan brothel brand, either."

Suzanna considered his statement before responding in a non-challenging tone: "How can you be certain that the brand is not from a Kolkatan brothel?"

"We know all the brothels in the city. None of them has that tattoo as their brand."

She sat staring into the eyes of the Assistant Superintendent, assessing whether she should believe him. He looked away, unable to hold the connection, and busied himself with tidying his desk. "I think it would be best if I called the driver, to return you to your hotel?"

"No, please don't... I have to accept that you know your city well and that the tattoo is not a brand known to you, but I have come a long way and the woman had come from Bengal, so I'd like to ask around, anyway. Perhaps someone will recognise the mark or her picture?"

"I really can't afford the manpower to escort you on a wild goose chase. It would be a waste of time."

"If I don't at least try to identify the woman, this trip will have been a waste of my time and my Chief Superintendent will chastise me for unnecessarily spending the department's money. I'm sure you can appreciate that it's not good to upset your boss."

"Yes. Yes. I understand, but what can I do?"

"Just let us have Sub-Inspector Anand for a day or two. If we don't get anywhere, I'll go home."

Banerjee pursed his lips and his brows squeezed together as he thought. "I will let you borrow Anand, but only for today. I must have him back on Kolkatan police work tomorrow."

"Okay. Deal." She rose and shook Banerjee's hand before he could change his mind. "Lead the way, Sub-Inspector."

Anand stood, looked for the nod from his boss, then left the office with the two British officers. They entered a larger room with several officers sat around talking and working on the computers, bashing away at their keyboards.

"The Assistant Superintendent is right. It's not a brand we recognise. But maybe there's a brothel we haven't raided yet. I can take Constable Usmani into the red-light districts and ask around, but it would be unwise for you to come with us because you would stick out too much – being a tall blonde, white woman."

"Understood and accepted. Zahir, are you fine with this arrangement?"

"Yes, ma'am." His face brightened at the prospect of being allowed to progress the investigation without his boss. He'd be able to ask the questions, rather than just take notes.

"Tumi ki bēṅgāli kathā balō?" Anand said, looking at Zahir.

Zahir feigned ignorance, given the rules they'd be under. "Sorry. What did you say?"

Anand smiled. "I just asked if you spoke Bengali. Clearly, you don't. Going by your name I thought your parents must be Bengalis, and you'd speak the language."

"They are Bengalis. Originally from Bangladesh. But unusually, they wished to cut ties with the homeland and have me brought up as a Scot." He exaggerated his accent to emphasise the point, as he lied about his language abilities. "I know a few words but couldn't hold a conversation."

"No problem. I will be your translator, anyway," he said, whilst wobbling his head in the uniquely Indian way.

"Thank you, sub-Inspector. I'll just need a few minutes with Constable Usmani, then I'll leave him with you." They chatted about how Zahir was to conduct himself and what questions to ask. She encouraged him to keep at it as long as he could because this might be a one-off opportunity. He would phone with a progress report later in the day and they'd meet for dinner in the hotel that evening. Anand arranged for a colleague to escort Suzanna out of the building. She hoped Zahir's visit to Sonagachi would be successful.

Chapter 37

It was late morning when the phone rang and Mairi picked up. It was the Shakti manager. "Good morning Mrs Ghatak. Any word on the woman Parvati mentioned?"

"No. That is why I'm phoning. Parvati has called her number many times, but she is not answering the phone. Do you have a pen and paper handy? I'll give you her details."

Mairi noted the name and address of the woman, thanked Mrs Ghatak, then wrote a note for Rab to let him know where she was heading.

* * *

Mairi turned into the narrow street in the Abbeyhill district. One side of the road was lined with cars, leaving just enough room for vehicles to pass through. She drove to the other end, without finding space to park, then found it was a dead end. There was no way to turn around, so she had to back the car all the way along the road and out onto the main street again. 'What a pain' she thought.

She turned left, then past some industrial-sized waste bins. They seemed to favour the huge bins in this section of the city, instead of individual wheelie bins for each house, as several more took up parking spaces along the street. She eventually found somewhere to leave her car and walked back to the road.

The houses were all stone-built, of course, and there was a third floor in the roof space of every building. Long flights of steps led upwards, directly from the pavement, to the entrance doors of all the properties along the left side of the street. On the right, paths led to doors on the ground floor. It seemed strange initially, but Mairi soon realised the ground floor entrances to the houses on the left side were accessed from the street behind. They were all flats. She found the address she needed halfway down on the right, took the path to the door, and knocked.

A skinny white guy opened the door, a straggly beard thinly covering his bony chin and a ring hanging from his left earlobe. He had a tooth missing, and the others were stained yellow. He stunk of smoke and had a roll-your-own cigarette hanging from his left hand. It could have been a spliff, Mairi thought. "Whaddya want, bitch?" the man slurred, slumping against the door frame.

"I'm Constable Crawford. There've been reports from your neighbours of shouting and screaming. We suspect someone might have been injured." She moved forward and gently shoved him into the house.

He stumbled backwards and almost fell. "Hey, you canna come in here. You need a warrant."

"I have reason to believe a crime has been committed and a person could be in danger. I don't need a warrant... Hello. Is anyone here?" she called out. The front room was sparsely furnished with well-worn chairs and a sofa. A small rickety table sat in the corner, with two equally unstable chairs at its side.

She heard a whimper from the back of the flat, so strode forward through the door into the kitchen. On the floor, at the end of the room, a young woman sat with her hands around her legs and head resting on her knees. She looked up as Mairi asked her if she was hurt.

Her black hair was a mess. It straggled across her face, screening her features. Mairi checked behind her, but the man was nowhere in sight. She crouched down beside the woman and tenderly moved her hair aside. Her face was swollen and reddened – her lips split. Tears had washed her eye makeup down her cheeks in dark rivulets over her chestnut-coloured skin.

"Did he do this to you?" The victim nodded. "Okay. You just stay there a minute." She stood and took her phone out, then called for uniformed officers and an ambulance.

As she turned, the runt of a man who had beaten his partner entered the room. With his long face and large ears, he looked like an anorexic hyena. He had a knife in his hand. "I want you oot of me hoose. NOW! Go on, get oot. You've no right to interfere. She's *my* woman. She brought it on herself, the selfish bitch. She should have done as she was told."

Mairi was cornered in the kitchen, with no way to get past the man and his knife. She felt great anger towards this controlling, violent male, remembering having to fight off an older boy who'd wanted to have sex with her when she was an unwilling teen.

She welcomed the confrontation but recognised that she really should cool the situation, to avoid injury. "What's your name, sir?" She looked him in the eye unflinchingly, her peripheral vision keeping his knife hand in sight.

"I'm no telling you my name, bitch. Get oot of me hoose, I said." He stepped towards her, leading with his left hand. He waved the knife towards her face. "Get oot, or I'll cut yer."

He didn't see the movement until it was too late. Mairi had picked up the wooden, racket-shaped breadboard from the kitchen worktop. She smashed it against his wrist, knocking the knife from his hand. He pulled his arm in towards his body, gripping it in pain. Disarmed now, he was little threat. She stepped forward, grabbed him by his hair, and dragged him forward and down to the floor. His face thudded as it hit the lino, his arms trapped under him, and he cried out.

Mairi smiled momentarily, happy to have inflicted some pain – a little retribution for his victim. As she moved forward, reaching for the handcuffs she heard motion behind her and turned to see the woman. She had stood and was now swinging a coffee mug towards her head. She ducked – too late.

"Leave my man alone," she shrieked. The mug caught Mairi across the side of her head, smashing, and the sharp edge carved a furrow down her left ear. She lifted the remains of the mug to strike a second time.

The sharp pain to her head mobilised Mairi. She stood, blocked the woman's attacking hand, grabbed her wrist and pulled her forward, then twisted. The mug fell from her fingers and landed on the man's head as he started to rise from the floor.

Mairi pulled the woman down on top of the man, then pinned her there, securing them both by kneeling on her back. She waited as the siren got louder, then uniformed officers charged into the house. She handed over to the two male officers, instructing them to arrest both for assaulting a police officer, but whispered to the officer taking control of the woman to go easy on her.

An ambulance turned up as the officers were leading their charges from the house. The paramedic looked at them and demanded they both go to the hospital to have their injuries treated.

* * *

Suzanna exited the Kolkata Police HQ into a pleasant warmth, glad to have escaped the chill of the air-conditioned offices and the senior officer's smiling uncooperation. Her phone pinged. It was a message from Callum. 'The other night was wonderful. I still love you. Please let's get back together.'

She closed the screen and tried to ignore the message, but her memories of making love with him and snuggling up afterwards reminded her of all the good times they'd shared. He'd admitted to having been a fool and understanding her reaction to his infidelity. He seemed genuinely repentant. Maybe, just maybe, it *would* work?

Her phoned pinged again – this time an email from James. "Damn! I should have responded to his text, yesterday." She opened the email and noted that he was wondering what he'd done wrong – why she was ignoring him. She replied immediately. 'Sorry. Nothing you have done. Still on the murder case. Out of the country. Will get back to you soon. Suzanna.' She pressed send.

"Am I in love with two men?" she asked herself as she set off down the street towards her hotel. She ordered a coffee, then took a seat in the reception hall. It was opulent beyond anything she'd yet encountered. A walnut veneered grand piano sat next to the opposite wall, and to its right three giant pottery urns stood tall like soldiers on guard, in front of a bowed archway. The chair was soft leather and there was near silence in the room – such a contrast from the bustle of the streets.

She spent an hour dealing with insurers, starting the water damage claim on her Cockermouth house, then found the contact details of IJTF's Kolkata office and dialled the number provided.

* * *

Angus answered his phone, giving his name, then listened. "You've not been able to trace it because the phone is switched off. Okay. I understand that, but even if you can't give me its current location, surely you can tell me roughly where it was when it was last used, and when it went off the air?"

He listened to the response, then concluded. "Look, this is important. It's not some routine enquiry. We're trying to trace a man who attempted to murder a police officer... Okay. Thank you." He replaced the phone on its base and turned to Caitlin. "We asked for this information yesterday and they've only just got back to us to say they can't find out where Muir's phone is. Ridiculous!"

"So, did they agree with your suggestion?"

"Aye. Hopefully, we'll get an answer within the hour, now I've explained the urgency." He stood. "Coffee?"

"Yes. I'll come with you."

When they returned to the office, the phone was ringing. Angus placed his coffee mug on his desk, sloshing a little over the side in his haste. "DI Watson." He turned to face Caitlin and smiled, then put his thumb up. "Okay. So the phone was last used yesterday afternoon. And the time?" He wrote the answer on his pad. "And the location when last used? Danderhall, you say. Can you give me a rough location within Danderhall?... Okay. Great. Thanks very much. That's brilliant." He turned to Caitlin.

"I bet the last time the phone was used was receiving a call about the time we left Blaire Fraser?" She said, tilting her head to the side.

"You got it, Caitlin. That little madam must have called to warn him we had his number. That's likely why he switched it off. You'll have heard the last known location was Danderhall. They said it was at the southern end of the village, near the Co-op store. Guess which road leads down to that shop? Yep. Newton Church Road, where the Muirs live."

"I'll get a warrant then," Caitlin said, turning to start the process.

Chapter 38

"Welcome, Suzanna. You found us OK, then. I'm Michael," the head of IJTF's West Bengal operations said, holding out his hand.

"Yes. No problem." She shook his hand and looked into his smiling face. The expression seemed genuine, unlike the forced smiles some of the police officers had put on for her.

"Come this way." They settled themselves in Mr D'Souza's office and he introduced her to the other IJTF team members, already in his office – David and Priya. The rooms were smart, and the paintwork unblemished, unlike the walls of the police station she'd been in earlier. The glass windows to the outside, and those separating the offices, were clean. Posters lined many of the walls, declaring their mission statement, highlighting their successes, and graphs indicated previous and current statistics. It all looked very efficient.

"So, I understand that a Bengali woman has been found murdered in Edinburgh. You want to identify her and try to find out how she ended up in the UK?"

"Yes. We know she's from this region of the continent by a DNA check we ran, but her face was damaged by her attacker, and it has not been possible, yet, to match her to any known immigrants. We don't know her name, when she entered the country, or where she's been living."

"I see. But she has a tattoo that you think might be a brothel brand.

Do you have an image of the tattoo with you?"

Suzanna handed Michael an A4 print-out. He studied the tiger image, then passed it to his colleagues. David nodded to affirm recognition. "This might be a Sonagachi brothel brand. Have you heard of this district?"

"Yes. I used to work in the DigniTees factory on the edge of the district about ten years back, so I'm well aware of the infamous red-light area – still possibly one of the biggest in the world."

"Yes, the last estimate suggested there were 10,000 sex workers operating in Sonagachi. Similar to Mumbai's largest area: Kamathipura," Michael confirmed. "What else do you have that might help identify the dead woman?"

"I have a photo of her. Obviously, the disfigured features will make it difficult for anyone to recognise her."

Michael frowned deeply as he looked at the image, then gave the picture to his colleagues to peruse. They had also seen badly beaten women – it came with the job. "Yes. The photo will not be a good resource for identifying the woman."

Suzanna continued: "she was also wearing this bangle – it looks unusual." She offered a picture of the bangle to Michael, but Priya leaned forward and took the paper.

"Yes. It is an unusual design. The red and gold colouring is common, but these patterns could denote something special. The leaves on either side of the small flower are pretty. But it's these diagonal profiled finger ring shapes I've not seen before. Perhaps someone will recognise it?"

"As you know, we're an NGO and rely on donations to fund our work. We'll happily help you with this if it might bring about justice for the poor woman, but it would be diverting us from our normal business that's funded by our donors."

"I appreciate your cooperation, Michael. I'd be happy to make a donation to IJTF to compensate for the distraction. Having spent time with DigniTees, and been briefed on IJTF's work, I'm fully supportive of what the organisation has achieved and continues to do. My time is limited, so when might it be possible to visit Sonagachi?"

"I'm sure you'll understand, Suzanna, that a tall white woman would stand out in Sonagachi, like a giraffe in a heard of zebras. And if you accompanied our field workers, it would identify them as officials, rather than potential customers. We try to keep a low profile. So, you'll have to leave it with us."

"Fair enough. I suspected you'd say that. But when might your staff be able to ask questions in the district?"

"Tomorrow should be possible," David said.

"I have a colleague with me, whose parents are Bengali's. Could you take him in with you?"

David looked towards Michael, who tipped his head. "Yes. We could do that. You'll appreciate that most of the trade occurs during the hours of darkness, so tomorrow evening would be best. If we give you a location near Sonagachi and a time, can you get him to meet us there?"

"Certainly." She ensured David had her phone number, then thanked them again for their cooperation before calling another Ola car to return her to the hotel. While she waited, they fed her coffee from their capsule-operated machine – so much nicer than the instant powder coffee often offered in West Bengal. A plate of biscuits was laid on the table in front of her. She thanked them, sipped her coffee, and ignored the biscuits – probably wouldn't be worth the calories, she thought.

Her phone pinged – a message from her sister Charlotte. 'Hi Suz, tried to call for a chat but went to voicemail. Call me when you can.' Suzanna replied. 'Sorry Charlie. In India on duty. Will call on my return.'

Her phone pinged within seconds of her responding. 'India. Wow. You get around a bit. What are you doing there?' Suzanna responded, 'Following up on a murder you might have heard about – washed-up woman.'

Another ping sounded. 'Yes, I heard about that. Call me for a chat when you get home xxx.'

Chapter 39

Suzanna was tired from not sleeping well on the plane and the time difference. When she got back to her room, she took a two-hour nap, luxuriating in the comfy bed, then showered, dressed, and went to the restaurant, as arranged. It was a spacious facility adorned with large ornaments drawn from the heritage section of the newly refurbished and extended hotel. She sat on the plush fabric-covered dining chair opposite Zahir, the material soft to the touch.

"How'd it go Zahir?"

"Waste of time, ma'am. They took me into Sonagachi, and we wandered around the streets. It was an eye-opener for me, I have to say. It was teeming with people. They were all ages: school kids to grannies. There were shops and food stalls, markets selling fresh produce and jewellery shops. Not what I was expecting at all. I thought it would just be full of bars and brothels. Even in the afternoon, there were women lining some of the lanes, smiling at potential customers. But the officer just chatted to a few women and asked them if they knew anyone with a tiger tattoo. Most said no, but even when one of them indicated recognition, the Anand just ignored her, and he pretended she'd said no. It was obvious they were only paying lip service to the agreement to help us. Just as well that I didn't let on about speaking Bangla."

"Yes. Well done on that account, Zahir. Sharp thinking. While you were walking the streets, I met with IJTF, one of the charities I mentioned the other day, and they believe the tiger *is* likely a brothel brand. They've agreed to take you in again tomorrow evening. There will be more women on the street to talk to. We'll get a location and meet time from them later. Take a copy of the bangle picture with you, as IJTF reckon it's quite unusual and might be recognised. Let's hope you will find someone who might know our victim."

Zahir smiled at the prospect of more undercover investigative work. "What would you suggest we do with our spare time during the daytime tomorrow?"

"You catch up on some sleep. Have a lay in, a late breakfast and prepare yourself for the evening's adventures. I'll spend the morning dealing with emails and after lunch, once the team is back at work, I'll call Superintendent Milne and Angus, to see how things are going. Let's meet for an early dinner."

Zahir waited for his boss to continue. "My thoughts are that IJTF will want to go in after 7 pm. That's when most of the office workers finish work and stop off for a bit of fun, before going home," she said, giving the quote sign with her fingers as she said the word fun. Suzanna's phone pinged just as she finished speaking, and she read the message. "That's confirmed, then: 7:30 pm outside the north-west exit of Girish Park metro station."

Zahir looked impressed at his boss's accurate time estimate for the meeting with IJTF. "Sounds good. Shall we eat?" he said, looking down at the extensive menu. Suzanna's stomach rumbled when she caught a whiff of food sizzling as it was taken past their table by a waiter heading towards other customers. If she was not mistaken, it was halloumi cheese on the hotplate. She knew what she'd be ordering.

* * *

After dinner, Suzanna returned to her room and fired up her laptop. There was an email from Rab.

Hi ma'am.

We followed your advice and focussed on Mercedes cars leaving Kincardine after 11 pm. Five cars shortlisted. We did background checks on all five, plus family members. No criminal records. A couple of speeding offences, that's all. Nothing to raise our suspicions. The South Asian men originated in West Bengal. They are both senior doctors - consultants. We will visit neighbours of the five and see if anything comes up.

We've had no luck identifying the woman at this end, yet.

Hope all's going well in Bangladesh. Stay safe.

Rab.

She WhatsApped Angus. "Any progress on tracking down Una's killer?"

A minute later, WhatsApp told her she had a message, and she saw Angus had replied already. "Just had word from the phone company that the suspect last used his phone in Danderhall. His parents are from there. Next stop Danderhall, with a warrant to search."

* * *

Caitlin turned onto Old Dalkeith Road and followed the road south. Glancing to her left as they crossed a junction in Newington, she glimpsed Arthur's Seat in Holyrood Park. She'd not been in the park for quite a while. The Old Dalkeith Road took them all the way to Danderhall. She turned into the Co-op car park, where they'd agreed to meet uniform colleagues, then parked her car close to the marked police vehicle. They chatted with the officers then drove out of the car park, stopping again outside the Muir's home.

One of the police officers was deployed to watch the back of the house and the rest went to the Front door. Angus thumped on the door, then stood back a step. The door was opened by Fraser's mother. "What do you lot want? You was just here the other day."

"We have a warrant to search these premises." Angus held the paper up for her to see, but she just backed up and attempted to close the door. Angus stepped forward quickly, jamming his shoe in the doorway, then pushed it open and entered.

They searched the house but found no sign of Fraser. The uniformed officer assisting with the search found a number of DVD players and laptop computers stacked up in a bedroom. "I suspect these will have been stolen. Would you like me to check?"

"Aye. You do that. Look, we're on an attempted murder case at the moment, so don't want to get bogged down in house-break-ins right now. Can we leave you to follow this one through?"

"Certainly, sir. It will be my pleasure. There has been a spate of break-ins lately around here. I'm sure my boss will be happy that we've stumbled across the evidence."

"Great. It's no wonder the Muirs were so keen to keep us out of their house. We'll be off then."

Outside, they walked back to Caitlin's car. "Another dead end. Where's the bugger gone now?" Angus asked, not seeking an answer.

"Who knows, boss? Who knows?"

Chapter 40

Friday 27th

Suzanna rose refreshed, washed in the walk-in rain-shower cubicle, dressed, and took breakfast in the hotel restaurant before returning to her room to check her inbox. James deserved a follow-up to her holding response, but she didn't want to say anything about Callum, yet. Suzanna felt like a teenage girl with two boys vying for her attention, but she felt guilty. What would she say to James? What were the options?

Thanks for the good times, James, but I'm going back to my husband; or sorry, I slept with my ex-, do you still want to go out with me? Neither of those scenarios was good. She wrote a quick email to James, explaining she had been in Bangladesh and was now in West Bengal. Uncertain when she'd be back yet. She'd be in touch once the flights were booked. But until the murder was solved, she'd have little or no time to get together. Hopefully, that would give her space to consider her future.

She noted an email from Angus and quickly scanned it. The suspect appeared to have been hiding at his parents' house in Danderhall, but when they searched the house, he wasn't there. The parents were uncooperative. He'd mentioned the suspected stolen property found in their house. Angus suspected the girlfriend had warned Fraser about having his phone number. Una's condition was unchanged.

She finished dealing with her inbox and had time to spare, so went for a walk. The hotel was close to Newmarket, so she headed there first. The area, behind Esplanade, was virtually shoulder-to-shoulder with shoppers and traders (and no doubt pick-pockets). She kept her bag close, as she couldn't afford to lose her purse and phone. She remembered when she'd last been in Kolkata. One of her DigniTees colleagues had his iPhone stolen from his pocket in this area.

There were shops lining every street, selling leather goods, shoes, men's clothes, backpacks, and shopping bags. She wondered who paid tailors to make business suits, as she'd never seen anyone in the city wear one – it was normally far too hot and humid for that. There were jewellers, rug sellers, sari, salwar kameez and children's clothes shops, and others that had shelves laden with scarves, shawls, and pashminas. Suzanna was tempted to add to her collection.

She entered the rabbit-warren-like bazaar. As she passed a shop selling kitchen goods, three touts latched onto her. These 50-60-year-old *Basket Boys* wanted to show her around, acting as guide and picking up a commission from the storekeepers. But Suzanna just wanted to wander by herself, browsing at stores along the way and haggling with traders to get the best deal - without hangers-on.

She politely told them to leave her alone, as she didn't need their help, and they eventually got the message. But as she rounded the next corner, another man came alongside her and attempted to persuade her to visit his emporium. She agreed but was then shown a load of goods that she had no interest in. She left the bazaar and headed off towards the BMS Guesthouse to see if it was still the oasis she recalled.

As she neared the end of Sudder Street, she heard a bell ringing, like the type still used in some pubs at closing time, only larger – and it seemed to be getting closer. Trumpton's fictional Fire Engine came to mind, and she soon realised her thought had been a good one. An old red fire truck, with a long wooden ladder on top, came along the road at 15 mph, rushing as best it could to an incident somewhere in the city.

She turned onto Rippon Street. It should have been called Rickshaw Road or Trishaw Terrace or perhaps Bike Boulevard. It was teeming with pedestrians and all those means of transport. Even more chaotic than she remembered.

Young, lean, muscular men pedalled the single-geared three-wheel rickshaws. The hand-drawn rickshaw pullers, however, were mostly middle-aged or old, and scrawny - a dying breed, she guessed. The motorcyclists were mainly young guys in their twenties, riding as fast as the conditions allowed. They wore no helmets, as that was uncool – both aesthetically and heat-wise. These young men wove in and out of the pedestrians and vehicles, using both sides of the road and beeping their horns. They even squeezed between vehicles coming towards them, and the near-side kerb.

Unlike the occasional old codger, who goes down the wrong side of the motorway in the UK, these guys were doing it on purpose. But it was accepted and expected, so a relatively safe practice.

Chapter 41

Street-dwellers still camped on the pavements near the guesthouse entrance, hoping that the visiting Christians would be generous towards their predicament. They looked up, sad-eyed, as they held out their hands, but went back to what they had been doing as soon as she had passed.

Suzanna had always struggled with what to do about people begging in the streets. She remembered a verse in the Bible that said, 'If you have two shirts, give one to the poor. If you have food, share it with those who are hungry.' But when she'd arrived in Kolkata last time and volunteered with Mother Teresa's *Sisters of Mercy*, they had advised them all not to give to beggars, as it perpetuated their begging and fed their drug habits. Instead, they should give to charities who would feed them and take them into their hostels when they were ill or dying. Suzanna chose to follow the advice she'd been given, although she occasionally gave beggars food – but never money.

Suzanna knocked on the steel gate of BMS and it was opened by the guard, who seeing her colour immediately assumed she had a right to be there and let her into the grounds. She walked around the corner of the guesthouse building and was shocked to see a large accommodation block that had not been there on her last visit. The lawn still looked inviting and, as before, crows perched in the palm trees. She entered the office and asked about the new accommodation.

They informed her that the rooms in the new block were all air-conditioned. When she'd stayed, there were just ceiling fans stirring the hot, damp air – no air con.

Reminiscing over, she headed up Elliot Road. The pavements had been dug up to lay pipes or cables and roughly filled in with dirt and rubble. No attempt had been made to restore the original surface, so she had to walk head down most of the time to avoid tripping. She took a shortcut through side streets to reach Park Street, passing vegetable stalls, laid out on sheets of thick, dirty cloth.

Many people had been living on the streets in central Kolkata in the noughties, and that hadn't changed. There were many signs of a growing middle-class, but the wealth hadn't filtered down to the poor. She emerged from the lanes by the Assemblies of God church. The last time she'd been here it had amazed her when she heard of the hundreds of street people the church fed every day.

She walked along Park Street and saw babies sleeping flat out on bits of cotton and cardboard, their mothers nearby. Shoe repairers crouched with their hammers and irons at the ready, and shoe-shine men looked around hopefully for a customer, occasionally banging on their shoe step to catch the attention of passers-by.

As she waited for the traffic lights to go red, she watched a mass of vehicles speed away from one of the other roads connecting to Park Street, as if unleashed and competing for pole position on a racetrack. The motorbikes inevitably were first out in front, their engines revving hard as they accelerated. In the still February conditions, the air was choked with particulates from oil-burning petrol engines, smoking diesels, and coal-fired stoves that heated cha or cooked chapattis. It was difficult to breathe in these conditions.

A young man greeted her as she walked past. "Hello. Are you enjoying our lovely city?" He spoke very good English – sounding well educated. Suzanna said she was, thanks, and he started walking alongside her, chatting. A friendly young man, perhaps interested to meet a foreign woman? The conversation soon turned into a sob story of how he'd come to Kolkata for work but was sleeping rough as he couldn't get employment. He explained he could get a security job, but he had to provide a photo for his security pass and asked whether Suzanna could help him.

She was sceptical about the request but wondered whether she could help the young man. Just a couple of hundred rupees should pay for his photo and that might get him into work. Prior to handing over cash, though, she wanted to know more. Before she could ask her questions, a white man in his thirties turned up and asked the guy why he was not working. Apparently, the other man had paid for him to have photos taken two days before. Suzanna was sad that the guy was trying to con her, slipped away as the conversation between the two men got more heated, and entered a restaurant.

As the door closed behind her, Suzanna took a deep breath of the filtered air and smelled cooking onions. She remembered the bistro from her time here before. It had changed little. Even the menu listed similar meals. But that was fine with her, as she enjoyed most of the food on offer. She ordered a vegetable fricassee with garlic bread. It was cheesily delicious.

After lunch, she took a taxi back to the hotel, but to complete her sightseeing she got the driver to go via the Victoria Memorial. The incredible, intricately carved stone building, from the days of the British Empire in India, stood tall and proud, displaying its grandeur. The Memorial could be seen from all around, being surrounded by expansive gardens - now not as glorious or tidy as they would have been in the early years. Nonetheless, it was impressive, although not quite as inspiring as the Taj Mahal.

Victoria Memorial was a tourist pull, and the road leading to the entranceway was populated by stallholders selling snacks and drinks.

Most notably, dozens of horse-drawn carriages plied for trade, their bodywork adorned with silver coloured intricately designed panels, like something from a fairy tale. But when looking closer, she could see they were tatty, and the horses' ribs stood out like the ridges on a draining board.

Suzanna was looking to her left at the distant Eden Gardens stadium, where international cricket matches are held, when the driver slammed on his brakes and the car skidded, its tyres squealing. Having no seat belt on, she was thrown forward, her face thumping into the front seat headrest. The car shook, and she heard a metal-on-metal bang as the taxi stopped – a motorbike hitting it from the right side. The driver flew over the car, landing on the road. Horns sounded all around them as other vehicles stopped abruptly. The driver forced his buckled door open, shoving the twisted motorbike out of the way, then rounded his car to where the motorcyclist lay.

Many drivers and pedestrians gathered around as the taxi driver argued with the injured rider over who was to blame for the collision. Fortunately, the rider had been wearing a helmet. The two men faced up, the rider removing his helmet, and they shouted into each other's faces.

Suzanna put her hand to her mouth. Her lips felt swollen from the seat collision. It was time to get out and walk away before the situation escalated.

Chapter 42

After taking a swim in the hotel pool, Suzanna returned to her room and called Zahir. He was happy to take up her suggestion that they go to Girish Park and eat there while waiting to meet with the IJTF field worker. Suzanna also briefed him on another idea she'd had. They would visit the social enterprise she'd worked with when in the city ten years before. It was close to where they would be meeting IJTF and perhaps the DigniTees staff could assist the investigation.

Before leaving, she quickly checked her emails and noticed one from the builder, with quotes for asbestos removal and ceiling restoration. She forwarded the quotes to the insurers and asked for approval to proceed.

The weather was still pleasant, so Suzanna and Zahir walked to the Chandni Chowk metro station. It wasn't one of Kolkata's finest. A squeaking escalator took them down to the dirty central platform. Although the rush hour was still a couple of hours away, there were masses of people waiting for the next train. A ceiling-mounted TV showed advertisements and occasionally reminded passengers about safety issues.

A gust of wind rustled their hair as the approaching train pushed into the station, the carriages a piston in a large cylinder. The mob moved towards the doors as the train came to a rest, making a human barrier across each exit. As the doors opened, passengers tried to board the train before those needing to exit it could get off. Human traffic jams at each door resulted from this amazing behaviour. Exiting passengers had to force their way through, creating the space that was needed for those entering. Suzanna watched the activity with a smile on her face – nothing changes. After the mob had boarded, she and Zahir stepped into the carriage, its doors closed, and the train departed.

Three stops later they exited the train, and Suzanna trod a familiar route out of the station, taking the escalator and emerging just before the Liberty Cinema. She'd never been in the grubby building but heard they showed porn movies. That would certainly fit with her observations – she'd only ever seen men queuing to see films there.

They turned left off Chittaranjan Avenue, onto a narrow lane. Huge lengths of bamboo were soaking in the water, running from a standpipe on the street corner that continuously channelled the unfiltered Hooghly River water. Incredible life-sized objects were being modelled from the split bamboo. Men pasted wastepaper onto these skeletons, and others painted those already completed. When last here, she'd seen model trucks, cars, camels, elephants, giant vases, ancient Roman buildings, and globes being created on the streets around this area of the city. In one lean-to, Zahir spotted a finished ten-foot-high giraffe – a cartoon version of the animal. "Wow. Look at that, ma'am. Amazing!"

"Yeah. They're brilliant, talented artisans, aren't they? It's a year-round industry here, with one festival giving way to the next a few weeks or months apart. By the way, when we're not in a formal situation, call me by my first name."

"Okay, ma'am."

She smiled at his response. Difficult to shake the habit, she supposed.

As they passed DigniTees' smaller, original manufacturing unit, where they still made t-shirts, she noticed the usual pile of garbage on the corner of the narrow lane. She recalled watching this pile continually grow all day, as the locals deposited their rubbish onto it, but also shrink back as the dogs, crows, cats, and rats ate any discarded food. Each morning, the consumables in the remaining pile would be set on fire, belching acrid smoke into the surrounding buildings, and a man would come with his boxy rickety wheelbarrow, and shovel up what was left to take to the local collection point.

They entered the DigniTees factory gates, left open because of the coming and going of staff between their two buildings on either side of the street. Rolls of jute and cotton lined the long room ahead, and workers were busy at the cutting table. She turned right into the open courtyard, where the kids from their crèche sometimes played, and looked up at the four floors above her. The sound of sewing machine motors could be heard, and the smell of warm machine oil drifted down to her.

Zahir's eyes followed hers. Used saris hung from ropes strung between balustrades on the second floor, drying after being laundered. These multicoloured vertical banners lined the courtyard, leading the eye upwards to the hazy blue sky above. Cardboard cartons were stacked to their left, full of goods bound for the USA, New Zealand, and the UK. A kiwi accented voice called down to her.

"Is that really Suzanna McLeod I see?"

She looked up and smiled at the big man, his beard now shaggy and greying. "Yees." She responded, mimicking the Kiwi accent. He looked much older than she remembered, but his eyes still sparkled, and he still wore a black DigniTees t-shirt – his no-need-to-iron casual uniform.

"Come on up, Suzanna."

He met her at the top of the stairs and hugged her. Zahir held back, embarrassed to witness this intimacy. "Wow! You're even more beautiful than when I last saw you."

She took the compliment. "Good to see you, Matt. How're you

doing?"

"Great, great. Come through to the kitchen. Would you like a coffee?" He paused and turned his attention to Zahir. "And who's this you have with you?"

"This is my colleague, Zahir – a Bangladeshi-Scot."

"Welcome to DigniTees, Zahir." He shook his hand, then turned and led the way into the family's kitchen/living room. Coffee was served as Suzanna and Matt caught up on developments in each other's lives and his business.

"So what brought you back to Kolkata, Suzanna – and with a young man in tow?"

"We're in the city on official business. Zahir is a detective constable on my team. A woman of Bengali descent was murdered in Edinburgh last week and we believe she may have been trafficked into the UK from Kolkata. There's evidence of sexual activity prior to her death and she has a tattoo on her buttock. I can't go into the details, but my thinking is she might have been a sex worker in Kolkata before being taken to Scotland. So, I'm here to identify her and hopefully find a link between her and the trafficker."

"You think the tattoo is a brand, then?"

"Yes," she said, reverting to the British version of the affirmative. "I was wondering whether any of the ladies working here might recognise the tattoo?"

"Possibly. Do you have an image with you?"

Suzanna pulled out the sheet of paper from her bag and passed it to Matt. He didn't appear to have seen the tattoo before, but that was unsurprising given its location on the woman's body. He stood and walked out, returning a couple of minutes later with one of the older ladies. Suzanna recognised her. She put her hands together and spoke to her. "Namaskar, didi. Kemon achen?" *Greetings, older sister. How are you?*

"Bhalo, bhalo," came the response. *Good, good.*

"This is Aashi," Matt said, for the benefit of Zahir. "She's been with us from the beginning but doesn't work in the factory nowadays. She's our field worker, meeting women in the community and letting them know that there are other ways to earn a living if they want to leave the sex trade. The name means smile, but you'll note she doesn't do that very often."

Zahir spoke up: "You said there was other work for sex workers *if* they wanted to leave the trade. Don't they *all* want to leave?"

"It's complicated. In the early months or even years, most women would gladly leave the trade given the opportunity, but eventually their trade becomes normalised in their life. It's what they do, and they see no possibility of doing anything else. Their owners wouldn't let them go because they've bought them from a trafficker – they are possessions. It's business and they need to get a return on their investment. If they tried to leave, they'd likely get beaten badly."

Matt had a tear roll from the corner of one eye as he mentioned the beatings. "But once women age, they become less attractive to many of their customers and the price for their services diminishes – supply and demand at work. The brothel madams will all have been sex workers before they became managers. The longer a woman has been in the trade, the more likely the owners are to let her go."

Matt took a swig of his coffee, then continued. "You'll see for yourself if you look around the sewing rooms that the average age of our workers is probably over forty, but we do have some youngsters here. We've been able to give work to daughters from Sonagachi, catching them before they get dragged into the trade. When we do that, I'm a happy man," he said, his face brightening again.

"How do you employ girls before they're forced into the trade? Surely the pimps and madams would do that soon after they reach puberty?" Zahir asked.

"Good point. Being a Fairtrade employer, we can't take the girls on until they're of working age. So, we work with the mothers and other NGOs to get the girls places in hostels elsewhere in the city, or beyond, where they can be safe and continue their schooling until they're old enough to employ."

Zahir silently indicated his understanding and respect for what this social enterprise was doing.

Matt passed the tattoo picture to Aashi and asked her if she knew any brothel that used this brand. She hadn't seen it before, but stood and left the room. She'll ask around the women. Perhaps one of them will have seen the tattoo.

"Would you like a tour whilst you're here, Zahir? Can we sell you some t-shirts, perhaps?" Matt offered.

"That'd be grand." Zahir stood, and Matt took him out into the factory to hand him over to another member of staff.

Chapter 43

Matt returned a few minutes later and sat again. "It's strange hearing an Indian talking with a broad Scottish accent. I'm so used to the Indian lilt."

"I hear it every day, back home in Edinburgh, but I still find it odd, having been so used to the Indian accent. His parents will still sound Indian, well Bangladeshi because they'll have been brought up outside of the UK."

"Seems like a nice young man. Is he good at his job?"

"Yes. Loads of enthusiasm. Intelligent and ambitious. He'll definitely make sergeant and who knows after that."

"And what rank do you hold now, Suzanna?"

"Chief Inspector."

"Like DCI Barnaby?"

"Hardly! I always laugh at those TV detective series, where sleepy villages have multiple interconnecting murders and complex plots. Real life's not like that. Most murders are carried out by spouses, partners, or close friends. Although there is a growing trend of stabbings and shootings related to the drugs industry. But rarely is the Lord of the Manor poisoned, or a murder made to look like a suicide, with the door somehow locked from the inside."

"Now, now. Don't spoil things for me. I enjoy a good British crime series. I like New Tricks, Morse, and Lewis. Oh! And Vera, of course. I love cranky Vera."

Aashi returned with another woman, and Matt spoke with them both before reporting to Suzanna. "They say the tattoo is definitely a brothel brand." He spoke with the women again, then fetched a map of the area. He pointed to a place on the map. "They say it's close to this junction. The women from that brothel hang around that corner but they're not sure which building they operate from."

Suzanna turned to the women. "Dhonobaad." She smiled at them to emphasize her thanks. "That's really helpful, Matt. Zahir will be going undercover with IJTF this evening, so they can focus on that corner. Should speed up the work significantly – knowing where to start."

"Look. Glad we could help. Trafficking and slavery are evil crimes, taking advantage of the most vulnerable in society. If you need any more assistance with your investigation, just ask."

"I'd better let you get back to business. We need to get Zahir fed before he meets with IJTF. He might not finish his work until late."

"Sweet as!"

She smiled at Matt's use of the Kiwi dialect for fine or all's good.

"You'll probably find Zahir in the shop, just off the packing area in the courtyard. Great to see you again. And good luck." He stood and hugged Suzanna again.

* * *

Suzanna and Zahir ate in a family vegetarian restaurant near the metro station. The menu was extensive and cheap. "The Chief Super should be happy with our claims for food," Suzanna suggested after ordering her meal.

"Aye. But will he be happy about the five-star hotel bill?"

"Don't worry, Zahir. The cost of our hotel is about the same as a

B&B in Edinburgh."

Zahir squeezed his lips together and pouted. His eyebrows rose. "Amazing!"

Their meals arrived, Suzanna's a paneer tikka butter masala with rice. She breathed in the aroma of garlic, ginger, chilli and garam masala spices. She hadn't noticed what Zahir had ordered, so was surprised to see a pizza in front of her colleague. "Zahir! You're in West Bengal and you're ordering pizza! That's like going to an ice-cream parlour and ordering a pasty. Are you mad?"

"I get Bengali food every day at home. It's good to get something different when I'm away."

The meal was tremendous, and they left just before 7:30 pm to meet with David.

Suzanna informed Zahir and David of the approximate location of women with the tiger branding that she'd learned from the DigniTees employee. She asked them to find out which building the brothel operated from and, if possible, to seek identification of the dead woman.

"It will not be easy, with her face so mashed and puffed. But we will try," David confirmed. "But maybe the unusual bangle will also help us find out who she was." He led Zahir away.

Suzanna was annoyed that she didn't have an artist's impression to show and made a note to chase Rab later. She couldn't think why it was taking so long. On returning to the hotel, she checked her emails, then sent one off to Rab.

* * *

"Be careful not to say anything that might offend anyone," David advised. "They can be a fiery lot. Let me do most of the talking. We can't go flashing that picture around in public. We'll have to wait until we're in a room with one of them. You do have the cash to pay for a woman, don't you?"

"How much will I need?" Zahir asked.

"It depends. The younger, prettier women might cost up to 500 rupees."

"Just five quid?" He was astounded at the cheapness.

"But the older, less attractive ones are probably available for about two hundred. It won't look right if you go off with someone old enough to be your mother, so you'll need to choose a good-looking youngster. I'll pretend I'm your oldest brother. I'll pick an older woman. That way, we'll have a mix of backgrounds and more chance that one of them might know your victim."

"Won't the others notice if we're out on the street again quickly?"

"Don't just show her the picture and leave as soon as she gives you an answer. Chat to her first. Explain why you want to know. You'll need to anyway because when she sees the picture, it will be obvious the woman is dead. The timing will be fine. They're not expecting to have long sessions of lovemaking. You'll be paying for a quickie."

"Okay."

"I'll see you back on the street corner where we find the women, within ten minutes. Don't go off by yourself. You might get mugged."

"Got it."

They walked into Sonagachi, ignoring the pimps that tried to get them to go off to their brothel. There were hordes of people milling about the narrow lanes, and lines of women stood along the edges. Most were chatting but immediately curtailed their discussions and smiled enticingly at the men. Some tried to grab their arms and lead them away, but David gently shrugged them off. He didn't want to disrespect them. He knew what they had gone through and how every day was a struggle, like animals in a jungle competing to live.

Food stalls frequented most corners, with steaming, fragrant mustard oil gently bubbling in the concave circular hotplates surrounded by already cooked pastry parcels, waiting to be sold. Concrete buildings rose upwards on each side, and constricted staircases led to the upper floors, where many girls leaned over the balconies, watching the throng.

David slowed as they reached a corner and spoke with a small group of women. Zahir joined him and listened in to the conversation. The IJTF man negotiated a suitable price with his woman of choice, and one for Zahir. He made out that his younger brother was a virgin, looking to lose his innocence. Zahir played the younger, naïve brother, saying little. The women led them away to where they could have privacy.

* * *

The young woman might have been gorgeous had she not plastered her face with make-up, and her clothes spoke prostitute. Zahir didn't find her attractive, but could easily have given in to her physical advances if he'd not been on the job and *was* a virgin. As soon as the door closed behind them, she pulled him close and felt for his penis, stroking him through his jeans – his manhood rising to the stimulation. She unzipped his fly, but he pulled back and took her hand away, then sat on the mattress. Her skin was soft to his touch.

"You want me to dance for you first?" she asked in Bangla. She gyrated, her hips swinging, her face fixed in his directions as she swung in front of his face. She lifted her cotton top to expose her pert breasts and stroked them, pinching her nipples, then thrust them towards his lips. Zahir couldn't help but get harder.

Minutes later, the brothel madam was pleased to hear the sounds of a man in the throes of orgasm. When Zahir and the girl emerged from the room, they were both smiling at each other. The young man had a huge grin. The madam was pleased. Her recent acquisition was proving to be a valuable asset – good at satisfying the clients. The girl said goodbye and went straight to the madam to hand over the cash.

Chapter 44

The two men emerged from Sonagachi and headed for the metro. "Any luck, David?"

"None. The woman I went with said the face was unrecognisable. Even if she had been a brothel sister, she would never have known by the picture. She thought she'd seen the bangle before, but could not remember who might have worn it. What about you?"

"Same as you. Nada. She'd only been in the brothel for six months, so she'd probably never seen the victim, anyway. But it was a scary situation for me."

"Why do you say that?"

He explained the girl's seductive techniques. "I had to stop her, then spoke to her gently, holding her eyes with mine. I asked her to sit and told her I did not wish to have sex with her. She'd looked offended. I told her she was beautiful and sexy, but I needed to ask her some questions about someone who may have worked there but had left - that the woman had been murdered and we needed to find out who killed her."

"She instantly transformed from a mature, sexy feline into a frightened kitten. She explained that, in her little time in Sonagachi, she had noticed several girls disappear and had worried about them, and what might become of *her* if she disobeyed her masters. I explained what we wanted to know and showed her the pictures. After she'd responded to my questions, she insisted I make noises like I was in orgasm, as her madam would be listening. It was really embarrassing, but I did as she asked."

"What a story. I've never been asked to do that. Did you pay her the fee?"

"Yes. And I gave her 500 rupees extra for herself."

"Good man. Oh well! At least we know where the brothel is located now. I'll get onto the State police and see if we can organise a raid, so we can interview more women from the brothel. It might take a day or two to organise, though. I'll get in touch with you and Suzanna again once I've set things up."

Zahir said thanks and cheerio to David, then boarded the next train heading south. Despite it still being rush hour, the train was less crowded because it was heading towards the business district, rather than away to the suburbs.

* * *

On his return, Zahir called Suzanna's room, and they met in the hotel bar. He reported on his visit to Sonagachi. Suzanna was disappointed. "David said if we stayed around and tried to go off with other women from the same brothel, they'd have been suspicious and we'd likely have got driven out of the area, minus our wallets, and perhaps with a few bruises."

"Understood."

"He'll speak with the State Police. They're more likely to act than the Kolkata Police. Rumour has it the local police take back-handers from the pimps and madams to turn a blind eye to illegal activity. But the State Police don't have the day-to-day connections. They work on intelligence and raid brothels when they hear of something worthy of the effort – perhaps underage girls."

"But that might take a while to organise?"

"Aye. He said probably a day or two, but when they receive intelligence they try to act fast, otherwise, they might miss the opportunity. If the community suspects something might be about to happen, they'll move the girl to another location."

"Okay. We'll just have to hope it's sooner than later. We can't sit around here for days on end waiting." Suzanna briefed Zahir on her communications with the team at home, and they agreed to meet up for breakfast the next day.

* * *

"Hello. Mrs Ghatak. Its Detective Constable Mairi Gordon, Edinburgh CID. I thought you'd like some feedback on my visit to Isha."

"Oh, yes. Thank you for calling. What has happened to Isha?"

"She's in custody, on suspicion of assaulting a police officer."

"Oh my God. How can that be?"

Mairi explained what had happened yesterday. "But the way I see it, she's the victim and I won't be pressing charges. Her partner *will* be charged and probably remanded. Isha will need support."

"Indeed. Indeed. Can Parvati come to the police station to meet with her?"

"Yes. As soon as she is here, I'll arrange for Isha to be released. Let's hope you can help her get over this traumatic period of her life and get her back on track."

"Yes, yes. I will dispatch Parvati forthwith."

"Thank you, Mrs Ghatak.

Chapter 45

Saturday 28th

After Zahir had eaten breakfast, Suzanna brought him up to date. "Rab finally found an artist to do an impression of the victim's face. Apparently, the two artists we usually use were unavailable, and he had trouble finding a replacement. He got the artist to work late last night, and it was in my inbox this morning." She passed a paper to him.

"Wow! The image is amazing. It definitely looks like our vic, but the artist has brought her to life again."

"Yeah. We should get better results with this image. I've already passed it onto Michael at IJTF. He says they've had some luck with the State police. He explained the situation to them, and they've agreed to raid the brothel this morning, on the pretext of there being reports of an underage girl. The raid should be going ahead soon."

"Incredible. I thought the Indian police were slovenly. Just goes to show, how wrong you can be."

"IJTF will call me once the raid has gone ahead. The State police have agreed to us observing the interviews, through one-way windows. They don't want them knowing who's behind the raid, and if any of the women see you, they might connect you with David, and his cover will be blown."

* * *

The call came two hours later, and they travelled in an Ola car to the headquarters in the city's Alipore suburb. The car took them through the Maidan – Kolkata's green zone on a wide, two-lane highway. Grand buildings, Army barracks, sports pitches, and tennis clubs were passed on their way.

Suzanna had checked Google Maps whilst waiting for the Ola car to arrive and it had suggested thirteen minutes for the 5 km drive. But the app hadn't properly accounted for Kolkata's traffic. Forty minutes later they arrived at the Directorate headquarters.

They registered at reception and were soon met by an officer in plain clothes. "Chief Inspector McLeod?"

"Yes. That's me." She held out her hand, and he shook it with vigour.

"Assistant Superintendent Das, at your service. Good to have you here, detective. Shame we didn't know you were coming to West Bengal earlier. I understand you got little help from the city police?"

"That's right. I'm surprised you hadn't been informed of our investigation. We booked the trip through Interpol. I guess they just went straight to the Kolkata Police, as that was our target."

"No problem. They have jurisdiction within the city. We deal with state-wide policing matters. Come on through." He led the way into a large office with numerous desks, computers, and phones lining it. Two officers were busy on the computers. "We've got ten women in custody, including the brothel madam, and one man. He's their babu or pimp. My team has carried out initial interviews, noting identities and asking them about reports of an underage girl. They've all denied that, of course. They would even if it *were* true! If you can let me have a copy of the victim's face, we can ask them individually whether they know her."

Suzanna passed him two pieces of paper: the original photo of the dead woman and the artist's impression. Das looked at both before responding. "I see why you've had the artist's impression done."

"The victim was thrown down a set of stairs, which fractured her neck, paralysing her. The damage to the woman's face was done when she was alive before she was dumped into the water, where she drowned. She must have seen every stroke of the weapon and felt the pain but been unable to even fight her attacker off. We've found no record of her in our immigration system yet, although that may change, now we have the artist's impression. We need to identify her and find out how she entered the UK, so we can track down her killer." Das passed the pictures to one of his staff, who left the room, presumably to make copies.

"Superintendent. If the copies don't come out well, I could email you the originals to print."

"Thank you, didi. We'll see how they come out."

"Okay, dada."

Das smiled at Suzanna's use of the older brother term, then twisted around as his subordinate returned to the office with photocopies. "These look fine." He gave Suzanna back the ones she'd brought with her. "Mandal, distribute these to the team and get them to start asking questions. Didi, come with me. We'll go into one of the observation rooms. Your man – sorry, I didn't get your name – can go with Mandal, here."

"It's Detective Constable Usmani, sir."

"Ah. Muslim. But not a common name in India. Which country are your parents from?"

"Bangladesh, sir."

"So, you speak Bangla then?"

"Hā," he said, with a momentary tilt of his head, forward and to the side. He didn't feel the need to hide his abilities from *this* team. The assistant superintendent smiled, then led Suzanna away. Zahir broke into conversation with the other detective constable, who took him to another observation room.

Two hours elapsed whilst questions were asked. No one admitted to recognising the victim. "Either they're exceptional liars, or they genuinely don't know the woman. Perhaps the tattoo was done elsewhere. There are many women trafficked from West Bengal to other cities, especially Mumbai and Dubai. She could have been branded in one of those cities."

"Yes, I accept that is a possibility and we may have to widen our net, but I was informed by a contact, through friends of mine who operates on the fringe of the district, that the brand *is* used in Sonagachi. However, if we are unsuccessful in Kolkata, would it be possible to gain the cooperation of other police forces within India to repeat this operation? If we can't identify her and where she was trafficked from, finding her killer will be much more difficult."

"Leave it with me. I'll get onto colleagues in Mumbai initially – as that's the second most likely place she would have been – and see if I can persuade them to investigate. The woman will most likely be an Indian national, so we owe it to her and her family to investigate."

She thanked the assistant superintendent and left by Ola car again. "Another waste of time, ma'am!"

"Not really, Zahir. By elimination, we're getting closer to finding out who she was. Let's just hope the Maharashtra state police are as helpful as this team has been. Just a minute." Suzanna typed something into her Ola app and the driver's phone pinged, notifying him of the change in destination.

Chapter 46

"Good to see you again, but what brings you back so soon, Suzanna?" DigniTees' CEO asked.

"Sorry to trouble you again, Matt, but we've drawn a blank on tracking down the murdered woman to Sonagachi. Yesterday when I visited, I only had a photo of a savagely beaten, disfigured face. I now have an artist's impression of what the victim most likely looked like before the attack. Can we ask the women again if anyone knew her? If the answer's no, we'll just have to return to the UK."

She passed him the new image. "Sure thing. Give me a few minutes." He walked off with purpose.

Suzanna looked around the building. It had changed little in ten years. A fresh coat of paint on the concrete walls was already showing signs of wear. Their huge generator still sat in the courtyard's corner, waiting to be fired up if the power failed. Power cuts used to be a regular occurrence when she was last in the city, but Kolkata's infrastructure had improved significantly since then, so she suspected it might not be utilised as often nowadays. Workers scurried around the building, carrying armfuls of jute bag components, up the stairs from the cutting section, and finished products back down to the packing department. There was a hubbub of chatter from the rooms – women engaged in sharing about life with their co-workers.

Stood in the courtyard, and looking up to the top floor, the logistics manager shouted someone's name. A man, Suzanna thought, as he'd added Da to the end of his name. After a short pause, a man responded, hanging over a balcony and shouting back down. The manager seemed satisfied with the response and went back to talking with one of his packers. There was no need for an intercom system, Suzanna thought.

Five minutes later, Matt returned. "The picture is being passed around all departments. Give us another ten to fifteen minutes... Coffee?"

"Wonderful."

She was halfway through her black coffee when Aashi entered the room with another woman, who was distraught. Aashi spoke to Matt, who turned to Suzanna. "This woman, Rachika, recognises the picture. She used to work in the same brothel. The woman's working name is, sorry was, Kittu – meaning Lovable in English. But she thinks her real name was Aaheli."

"Can she tell us anything else about her?"

Matt spoke to the woman again, his face showing understanding of Rachika's feelings, then translated the tearful reply. "She believes her family name might be Lohani. She came from a village in Murshidabad District – that's about 200 Ks north of here. If she's right, we should be able to help you track down the family as we have a manufacturing unit in Sherpur, which is close to the woman's home village."

"That's fantastic news," Suzanna commented, not showing any elation, given the grief being shown by the victim's friend. "Can you spare anyone to escort us north?"

Matt spoke with Aashi again, then returned his focus to Suzanna. "Aashi has other commitments, but perhaps one of our women from Sherpur could take you into the village where Aaheli comes from?"

"Thanks; that would be great."

"Have you heard of Justice Operations?"

"Yes. They do a similar job to IJTF, don't they?"

"Yees. Well, they have a team in Murshidabad. We're working with them on spreading awareness of trafficking in the district. If you like, I could ask *them* to assist you?"

"Yes please, Matt."

"If you want to go tomorrow, you're highly unlikely to get train tickets, so you'd need to hire a car and driver. I wouldn't recommend renting a self-drive car, given the road conditions and the unusual, unpredictable driving behaviours. I would normally suggest leaving at 5 am to clear the city before the rush starts, but as it's a Sunday, you'll probably be okay to leave at seven or perhaps eight. Would it help if I booked the vehicle for you – it would be about three thousand rupees a day, plus the driver's food and accommodation expenses?"

"That would be brilliant." She passed Matt her phone number, and he agreed to text her when he'd confirmed the booking.

* * *

Back at the hotel, Suzanna sat at the desk in her room. It had built-in power sockets for all types of plugs, plus an internet broadband connection and USB sockets for charge devices. The sumptuous chair seat was chestnut coloured leather, on a hardwood frame. It was dark, but she didn't recognise the type of wood. She'd heard most wood in this part of India came from Malaysia, as West Bengal didn't have forests.

She connected to the broadband, then checked her emails. Rab and the team had called on neighbours and work colleagues of the five shortlisted cars. They had asked general questions about the character of the car owners and whether any young South Asian women had been seen coming and going.

Two of the Simmonds' neighbours said he never spoke or even

acknowledged his neighbours. His wife seemed to be nice but just waved. She never spoke, either. No one had seen any young Indian-looking women going to or coming from the house. They found out he worked at Edinburgh Airport as a Logistics Manager. His colleagues had said he only ever spoke to them when he wanted to complain about their mistakes. Never a good word had been heard from his mouth. Suzanna formed the opinion that he was not a well-liked man but recognised that alone wouldn't make him a murderer.

McFarlane was reported to be courteous and well-liked. He often stopped for a chat if seen in the street. One neighbour had noticed a young, brown-skinned woman going to the house – usually on Thursday mornings for about two hours. They had questioned the McFarlanes and obtained the name of their cleaner. She was contacted and confirmed she was there every Thursday. She also agreed with the neighbours that her employers were good people. They were always respectful, friendly, and paid her cash each week. They had also checked with people where he worked – he was a senior manager with the City Council. The two they'd spoken with said he was a great boss. There were no weird personality traits or anything to suggest he might have been involved in the murder.

Richards lived in a rural location and had no nearby neighbours, but they'd asked in the nearest village and the response had been positive. Friendly chap. Happy to buy the bar staff a drink when he was in the pub. He and his wife were regular churchgoers at the local Kirk. Murray had spoken with the minister who praised the Richards' contribution to the church and community. He was reported to be a farmer and they couldn't find any work colleagues or employees to question.

Doctor Mukherjee was highly respected by his colleagues and staff at the hospital. Neighbours said they saw little of them, and they didn't join in any local events. The wife appeared not to work but was regularly heading off by herself in taxis – normally dressed smartly.

Again, Indian families had been seen visiting occasionally but no young single women. The neighbours had not noticed any regular visits by people who might be cleaners. But one said they'd often seen a young woman at the windows as she cleaned them. Mairi had spoken with Mrs Mukherjee. She said she had a cleaner come in every week. Perhaps the neighbours just hadn't noticed.

Doctor Basu was found to be well respected at work. His neighbours all thought he and his wife were good people. Never any trouble. They had a lady clean twice weekly, Tuesdays and Fridays, but she was probably mid-thirties. Certainly not early twenties. Other South Asian people were seen coming and going occasionally, but normally in families.

Suzanna sat back and reviewed the briefing. There wasn't much to throw suspicion on any of them, really.

She re-checked the reports made by Owen and Murray. Both home CCTV images had come from the same street. There was more than one way to access the jetty. She should have spotted that before. They'd focused on Mercedes owners, but a BMW or Audi could have approached from one of the other streets. They'd have to open the investigation out again.

Suzanna opened up Google Maps and pondered on what other routes could have been used. The car could have entered from the north-west of Kincardine through the roads that fed the old power station. If so, that would explain the lack of sightings in Kincardine. She wrote an email to Rab requesting he widen the investigation to include private CCTV systems on houses in Tulliallan and its golf club.

The communications officer had asked for an update, so she emailed Steve, providing him with a copy of the artist's impression, and asking him to circulate it to the press.

Another thought popped into her mind: car tyres. She emailed Rab again to seek further action.

Chapter 47

Sunday 1st March

Suzanna met Zahir in the hotel foyer at 7:30 the next morning; both of them had grabbed a quick breakfast, to keep them going for their journey north. Ten minutes later, a cream-coloured Jeep-type vehicle pulled up outside, so they grabbed their bags and exited the hotel. As Suzanna emerged, the driver approached. "Detective McLeod?"

"Yes. That's me."

"Come this way, ma'am." The driver had a swelling midriff and chubby face. He was likely in his late twenties. Typically, he had a moustache and straight black hair. He opened the rear door for them to deposit their overnight bags, then closed and locked it. "Best to be safe, ma'am. You wouldn't want your bag stolen at traffic lights. Would you like to sit in the front?"

"No thanks. I'll sit in the back. Zahir. Would you like to sit upfront?"

"Thanks. I'll get to see more from there."

They passed Hindu shrines perched in the centre of the two-lane road. Multiple families who slept on the pavements were going about their daily ablutions – washing under the ever-flowing standpipes. Being before 10 am, most of the shops were closed, but produce markets were already open, their make-shift counters overflowing with fruit and vegetables. They never got close enough to smell the meat and fish, but she remembered the unpleasant stench from when she'd last ventured into the market near DigniTees.

They exited the city about an hour later, the traffic having been relatively light. For the first part of the journey, they travelled along a dual carriageway, with a good road surface. They sped along at around 60 mph for a while, but the road turned into a single carriageway soon after leaving the city and the road surface became harsher.

After the change, the driver couldn't hold the vehicle in a straight line for over ten metres. He swung the steering wheel back and forth as he dodged the potholes and other vehicles on the road. In the villages, people just walked across the highway without looking, as if it were their right to do so and the driver's duty was to avoid them. No wonder the rate of death on the roads was so high in India, Suzanna thought.

The countryside turned greener as they moved further north. Field after field of crops stretched to the horizon in all directions, predominantly fresh green rice shoots glistened in the morning sun. Ducks frequented the multiple ponds that were scattered across the landscape. Buffaloes relaxed in some of these man-made pools and boys swam and splashed with their friends and brothers. Girls and women crouched at the pond-sides washing the dishes from breakfast or doing the laundry – the clothes being raised and pounded onto large wet stones many times before being rinsed and wrung out.

Further along, men and youths turned the soil in their fields, their old ploughs drawn by buffaloes. Nets covered some ponds, keeping the birds off to protect their small fish farms. Palm trees shaded the banks of these ponds, creating a superb tropical scene for Suzanna's camera to capture. After two hours they stopped at a roadside restaurant for a break and toilet stop. Suzanna suspected the WC would be grim, so she wasn't disappointed when her expectations were met.

The driver bought them all tiny cups of cha, and they gratefully accepted them. Despite having eaten at 7 am, the enticing smells tempted Suzanna into purchasing two samosas for each of them. Most travel advice was to avoid street food in India, but she'd always found that if the food had been freshly cooked in front of you, it was safe to eat. The fried pastry was crisp and the warm, spicy vegetables a delight. Replenished, they soon set off again.

* * *

They arrived in Berhampore around 1 pm, having stopped a second time for another toilet break and more cha. The driver had to ask several people before he finally found the Justice Operations offices. It was on the bottom floor of a three-story building that was split into flats. Typical for the area, all verandas and doorways had wrought-iron barriers to keep out monkeys and thieves. Drying clothes hung in some verandas and on most rooftops. The lane was unmetalled, dusty and uneven. The vehicle bounced from side to side as their driver navigated it, then swung the vehicle off the lane into a field and parked. He blew his horn twice and stepped out, stretching his legs. A man came into view. He raised his hand in greeting, then opened the iron gate and walked towards them, smiling, followed by a young woman.

"You found us alright, then?"

"Yes, eventually. You're rather hidden away here, aren't you? Hi. I'm Suzanna. This is Zahir."

"Welcome to Berhampore, Suzanna; Zahir. I'm John. This is Alisha."

They shook hands, then entered the Justice Operations offices. The driver returned to his vehicle and laid across the bench seat for a rest. The meeting room was basic, having just a plastic dining table and four ill-matching chairs. They drank tea and chatted.

"So, what's your reason for being based here?" Suzanna asked.

John responded: "We have a three-year programme to raise awareness about trafficking and general human rights training. We also train other NGOs in these matters, enabling them to continue the work once our programme terminates. The idea is to inform and inspire ongoing work in the district."

"I guess that's really necessary for this area of the state?"

"Yes. Murshidabad District has a high prevalence of trafficking young women into the sex trade, as well as bonded labour problems, mostly in the brick factories. There are, of course, sex workers within the district as well. Berhampore has a community of them near the centre of the city and we're aware of a small brothel area in Domkal, a small town to the east, near the Bangladeshi border. But the district's biggest red-light area is in Dhulian, about three hours' drive north of here. There's a large brothel area of shacks perched on the banks of the River Ganges."

"Do you work there as well?"

"We travel up there once a month to meet with women from the brothels. DigniTees have a manufacturing unit there, as well. They provide sewing work for women who want to leave the trade like they've been doing in Kolkata all these years. The Dhulian factory has only been open about a year, so they have just a handful of women."

As he finished speaking, a deafening air horn sounded and continued for over twenty seconds. They turned towards the source of the sound and noticed a train travelling along its tracks, just behind the houses. The conversation was paused, as it was impossible to be heard.

"That was incredible," Zahir commented. "Why do they sound the horn for so long?"

Alisha responded, "people sit on the rails to chat and walk along the tracks, so the drivers have to sound their horns to clear the way, or there'd be more fatalities."

"It's so different in the UK. No one's allowed anywhere near the rail tracks. You can get fined for trespassing if you do." Zahir's stomach rumbled. "Is there anywhere we can get some lunch around here," he asked.

"There are no decent eating places in this suburb, but we could drive into Gora Bazar and get some food there?" John suggested. "But we need to get a move on if you wish to get to Sherpur today. It's about thirty kilometres away but takes about an hour to get there."

"Could we pick something up on route, to eat in the car?" Suzanna asked.

"Yes. There's a restaurant near the Mohan Cinema that does excellent egg rolls and noodles. Lets' go there."

* * *

The journey took them alongside Chaltia Bil, an oxbow lake – the remnants of the Ganges when it had snaked through the area many years before. The surface was mirror-like, and its banks were covered in lush green plants and palm trees. Suzanna commented on its beauty.

"You should see it at sunset," John responded. "We get incredible orange-red skies above the trees and reflected in the lake." Suzanna was impressed with the photos he showed her on his phone.

Mohan Cinema, opposite the food stall, was a shabby-looking establishment, but its Art Déco styling hinted at a more glorious past. They watched as the cook made them egg rolls, breaking an egg onto the concave, oiled hot plate, then dumping a chapatti directly onto it. He let it cook for a minute, then turned it over, the egg now firmly attached to the flatbread. He flipped it over one more time, then added shredded vegetables and the juice of a lemon, before turning up the bottom and rolling it, leaving it open at the top. Wrapped in paper, he handed out the egg rolls one at a time. They gave the first one off the hot plate to the driver, so he could eat, then drive.

"Mmm!" Suzanna expressed as she bit into her first mouthful. After swallowing, "it's been years since I had one of these. I'd forgotten how tasty they are." They each took an egg roll, returned to the car, and drove off towards Sherpur.

Chapter 48

The drive took them over the Hooghly River, the bridge an ugly concrete structure with a crumbling road surface. This main highway to Dhulian was packed with buses and slow-moving trucks in both directions. A mile up the road, they turned onto a minor road, heading towards Sherpur.

There were many smaller bridges along the way, crossing streams and minor rivers. At each one, the driver slowed to a walking pace to avoid the jolt that would have come from a faster approach to these badly surfaced structures. Wherever the road met a bridge, there was a ridge offering to test the suspension of passing vehicles.

They travelled through many villages. The roads were lined by mud-walled, thatched dwellings, most with just one or two rooms within. Other, more substantial houses had corrugated iron roofs in a unique style, all four surfaces having convex curves. The shops beside the road were mostly ugly concrete buildings. Clearly, no architect lived in this area. They were entirely utilitarian, making East Berlin's Soviet-era concrete edifices seem like works of art. Sides of buildings were mostly painted in yellows and reds, with cement brands advertised. The hoardings beside the road promoted steel rods, used in concrete construction, with Bengali action film stars showing their muscles and smiling.

In each community, animals wandered the roads: goats, sheep, cows, and chickens. Tiny bare-bottomed children roamed unsupervised as the driver sped past. An old man on a bicycle emerged from a dirt track on the right and without looking joined the road, riding down the wrong side. As their vehicle approached, with not so much as a glance over his shoulder, the grey-bearded, scrawny grandfather swerved across the road. The driver stamped on his brakes and the vehicle squealed to a halt, missing the old guy by an inch. He continued cycling as if nothing had happened.

"I can't believe that old chap did that. He must be deaf and stupid," Zahir exclaimed, his voice heightened by the adrenalin.

"That's a bit judgemental, Zahir," Suzanna chastised, whilst actually agreeing with him.

The driver swore in Bangla, then drove off again, sounding his horn continuously as the vehicle passed the cyclist. The man seemed to be oblivious to how close he'd been to death.

As they crossed a long bridge, Suzanna looked off to her right, noticing a steep bank where workers were stacking huge rocks with the aid of a JCB. "This whole area will be underwater, come the monsoon," John informed them. "The river you see trickling along the dry bed will rise and flood all these fields, turning it into one huge lake. Some villages will be cut off by the floodwater, for weeks. I've seen people wading through the waters on foot and even on bicycles, where it is the shallowest. And boats suddenly appear, providing ferry services. It's quite a transformation."

Suzanna tried to picture the scene described. "What's happening here then?"

"That bank is protecting the village just beyond the river from the flooding. Each year the banks get washed away, threatening collapse, so they're lining the bank with rocks to protect it from the flow."

Eventually, they came to Sherpur. The State Highway, through this large market hub, was the worst Suzanna had ever seen. There was no asphalt left and the entire length was just a deep-rutted dirt track. Buses parked in unsuitable places, ignoring all around them and choking the traffic flow. Single-cylinder van rickshaws, overflowing with cross-legged and over-hanging passengers, putt-putted their way along, belching black smoke. Traders sat alongside and almost on the road, selling their vegetables, and chickens clucked in the cages, waiting to have their heads chopped off when the next customer was ready to buy.

The DigniTees factory was unseen from the road when they parked up. At ground level the building looked like a third world shopping mall, its rooms filled by traders, selling fruit, rice, mobile phones and cha and biscuits. As they stood around the vehicle, John pointed up to the large corrugated-iron-roofed, concrete warehouse. "It used to be a cinema, but the business collapsed a few years ago and it sat idle until DigniTees rented it and converted it into a weaving factory. Let's go in."

Someone waved from the factory's balcony as they walked towards the entrance. John reached through the wrought-iron gate and pressed the doorbell. But as he did, a gaunt-faced woman came down the stairs with keys in her hand. "Namaskar, dada, kèmon achen?"

John responded to the welcome as the anorexically skinny woman unlocked the gate. At the top of the stairs, the party was greeted by a Brit. "Welcome to DigniTees Sherpur. I'm Phil."

They entered the factory and had a quick tour, learning about the handloom weaving process. Suzanna was fascinated and would like to have stayed longer, but time was pressing.

"Matt tells me you want to visit a family in Valkundi. It's less than a mile up the road. One of our ladies comes from that village, so will come with you and lead you to the home."

"That's so helpful, Phil. Is she ready to leave now, as it's getting late already?" Phil turned and looked as if he were about to shout the woman's name when he saw Jamia standing behind him. She smiled at Phil's reaction.

"Phil. Do you live in this village?"

"No, I travel every day from Berhampore. I've got a wee house near to the Justice Ops office."

"Are you a Scot?"

"No. I just picked up a bit of the lingo when I lived in the Highlands, during the 80s."

"Look. We're staying at the Fame Hotel, near the railway station. Would you like to join us for dinner tonight – my treat?"

"That'd be great. Can I bring my wife?"

"Absolutely! Shall we say 7:30?"

"It's a date. See you there."

* * *

The driver took the vehicle as far as he could, parking at the end of a track. Suzanna, Zahir and John followed their escort, Jamia, for the last half kilometre to the family home. She led them into a dirt courtyard, surrounded by mud huts, speckled with rough discs, embedded with handprints, like a grid of brown checkers. She spoke to the elderly skeletal man squatting in the weak sunlight, his aged, dark brown skin hanging off his frame. Jamia spoke to John, confirming this was Aaheli's grandfather.

The old man indicated they should sit and, as they looked around for somewhere to do that, a woman emerged from a hut with rugs, which she laid on the dirt. The Bengalis moved to sit on the mats, so Suzanna and Zahir followed their lead. They sat cross-legged as John spoke with the man, suggesting he bring the family together, as they had important news for them.

An older woman busied herself making cha as the word went out into the surrounding huts and fields. John leaned towards the old man and passed him the artist's impression Suzanna had brought with her and asked him if he recognised her.

He said it was a good picture and wondered how this portrait of his granddaughter had come into their possession. John didn't answer but waited until the family had gathered. Suzanna leaned closer to John and asked about the stack of discs near to what appeared to be a clay oven.

"The villagers collect cow dung and mould it into balls with their hands, then slap them onto the sides of buildings and trees. When the discs have dried, they scrape them off and burn them to provide heat for cooking." Suzanna hoped they washed their hand thoroughly afterwards.

The woman served them cha, then joined her family on the mat. John spoke to the father, mother, and grandfather, his eyes flitting between the three elders. "I have sad news for you." The grandfather passed the picture to his son, who looked at his daughter's image and passed it to his wife. She connected the image and the hint of bad news, and at once started crying.

The grandfather spoke. "Young Aaheli left here many years ago to work in the city and send money home to support us. But some months back the money stopped coming, and we have been going without rice on many days, since. Don't tell me she has fallen ill?"

"This woman," John indicated Suzanna, "has come all the way from the United Kingdom to tell us about Aaheli." He turned to Suzanna. "Please speak and I will translate."

"It would seem that your granddaughter, Aaheli, came to Scotland. We think to work in a family home," John translated.

"I have travelled here to ask what you can tell me about when Aaheli left your home and went to Kolkata because we need to identify her movements." After translation, they looked at her curiously.

"The reason I ask for this information is, sadly, a young woman matching Aaheli's description, as you can see in the image, is dead." The mother stood, then howled, throwing herself around in grief. Tears formed in the men's eyes as they tried to maintain masculine dignity.

Aaheli's grandfather spoke, and John translated. "How did my granddaughter die?"

"We cannot be certain that it is Aaheli until we have matched DNA, but we believe she was murdered." The grandfather's tears flowed as he understood that his little girl's life had been ended early. "She appears to have travelled to the UK on a false passport, as no one with your granddaughter's name was registered entering the country legally."

"But how did she die?"

"She drowned. But it was no accident. She had been beaten before she was placed in the water." Aaheli's brother broke down when he heard this news. Even the father, who had arranged for his daughter to go into servitude, now wept.

The grandfather spoke again, addressing Aaheli's father. "Who was that man you brought to this house five years ago, when Aaheli was just fifteen? He was supposed to be taking her to live with a good family, to be their housemaid. He said they would look after her, feed and clothe her and pay for medicines. Why would she have gone to the UK and not told us?" The old man picked up his stick and struck his son on the shoulder. "Speak. Who was the man? Do not lie to me." The scraggy family goat jumped, then trotted away from the disturbance, droppings falling to the ground from its rear as it moved.

"I didn't know him. He was introduced to me in the market. I was told he was an agent looking for a girl for housework in Kolkata." The old man looked angrily at his son. "I knew we needed money to survive. Our fields did not provide sufficient food for us all. And my son," he said looking at the young man at his side, "had a wife and child to support. I couldn't let him go to the city. Who would work our fields when I become too old, like you?"

"You let your daughter go to the city with a stranger? How could you?"

"But I trusted the man who introduced him to me. He is a successful businessman in Sherpur."

"Which man, do you talk of?"

"Talat Ahmed. The hardware shop owner."

"Sir. Please spread the word in this village and the surrounding villages, to be careful not to let young women go to the city for work. The men and women who take them there are deceivers. They compel them to do *bad* work," John pleaded.

The grandfather responded: "What bad work are they forced to do? Don't tell me my granddaughter became a prostitute?" He looked sad as he asked as if he already knew the answer.

John nodded his head. "I am sorry. But that is what Aaheli had been doing in Kolkata."

The grandfather hit his son on the head. Aaheli's father ducked with the blow and rolled away, out of reach of the stick. "Don't hit me, father, I didn't know." He fell on his knees, his face in the dirt, and howled. The whole family broke down, even the children who were too young to have known their aunt.

"Two last requests before we leave you. Do you have a photograph of Aaheli, to help us with identification?" Suzanna asked. "And can we please take a DNA sample from the father?"

The mother went into a room and emerged a minute later, passing a small photograph to Suzanna. She spoke to John, "this is the only photo we have of our daughter. Please, return it to me?" On hearing the request, Suzanna took a photo of the picture with her phone and gave it back. The mother held it to her breast and started crying again.

CHAPTER 48

Zahir used his swab kit to take a DNA sample from Aaheli's father. There was little doubt the dead woman was Aaheli, but they had to be certain.

Chapter 49

"This way," the father said, as they left the vehicle outside the central area of Sherpur. He led them to a store selling construction materials and tools. There were rooms stacked with pipes, steel rods, and piles of cement. Behind the counter, rows of metal racking stored bolts, nails, brackets, and other minor items. "That is the man," he said to John. "He is Talat Ahmed."

John stepped forward and spoke with Ahmed. "This man and his family tell me you introduced them to a man from Kolkata five years ago, and his daughter Aaheli went with this man to the city. When she reached the city, she was forced into bad work. You must tell us the name of this man."

"I don't remember this event or any man from Kolkata. I cannot remember what I did five days ago, let alone five years! There is nothing I can tell you." He turned away as if that was the end of the matter.

"If you do not give us a name, I will inform the State Police and they will be the next people to call on you. Come on, man. We need to find this person who took his daughter away."

Ahmed considered the threat of state police and decided to talk. "Sorry, sorry. I remember now. Yes, yes, the man was recruiting for girls to do housework in rich homes. But I don't recall his name.

"I will return with the police and see if they can jog your memory, with their sticks." John turned as if to walk away.

"That will not be necessary. My old mind has, after all, recalled the man's name. The person you seek is called Amit Gupta, from Kolkata. That is all I know."

"I am glad that your memory recovered. We will go to Kolkata. If we cannot find Gupta because you have warned him, I will return with the police. Do you understand?" John looked straight into the man's eyes as if peering into his mind.

"Yes. Yes. I no longer have any contact with the man. Do not worry."

John noticed an old Nokia mobile phone on the counter, so grabbed it and immediately scanned the phone records. The name was there, and it had been only four months since they had last spoken. "You lied to me. You will regret that." He turned and walked away, carrying the man's phone.

"You cannot take my phone. On whose authority do you do such a thing? All my customers' numbers are there. How can I conduct my business without it?" His voice rose in pitch and volume as they walked away.

John just ignored him and hastened away. The others followed. "We need to get back to the car and leave before this man calls his friends. They may come after us." He sent Aaheli's father back to his village and got into the car. As the driver pulled away, three men came running carrying large sticks – hunters after their prey. They stood in front of the vehicle, demanding they get out. The driver tried to move his vehicle forward, but they beat the bonnet and raised their sticks as if to smash the windscreen.

The driver got out and shouted at the men to leave his car alone and get out of the way. One man hit him across the upper arm with his stick and the driver fell to the ground. The three men moved around the vehicle towards the fallen diver. Suzanna could tell what would happen unless someone acted. She opened her door and stepped out.

She was four inches taller than the men and more muscular. But there were three of them and only one woman.

Zahir got out and stood beside his boss, swaying the odds a little, but neither he nor Suzanna had sticks. The men turned their attention away from the driver to the new targets. One man raised his stick and stepped forward directly towards Suzanna, his face squeezed and focussed on her. He was surprised when she didn't step back and cower. Instead, she stepped forward.

While his stick was still in the air, she grabbed his coat, closed the gap, pushed a leg between his and behind one, hooking him, then pushed him backwards onto the ground. He fell hard, banging his head on the dust-covered solid earth. Another of the three men went on the attack, but Zahir took on the challenge, grabbing the arm that held the stick. He twisted it, driving his assailant sideways and onto the floor. The third man turned and ran. Zahir took away the two fallen sticks, and they got back into the vehicle. The fallen attackers rose to their feet and followed the other man back into the village.

"Turn the vehicle around and leave the village in the other direction. There may be more men with sticks heading this way soon," John commanded. The driver did as he was instructed and drove off fast, holding his sore arm. Scared!

* * *

Five Years Earlier

She danced and twirled, leapt, then crouched as the music played. The men ogled her body as they drank their whiskey and gradually became aroused. The young woman was shapely and naturally sexy, her lips and breasts plump, her eyes mahogany brown, the whites clear and bright. Her cheekbones stood proud, and her ears needed no decoration to be beautiful – so wonderfully had nature sculptured them. Her skin was the colour of caramelised sugar. She'd not chosen to be a dancer; indeed this was only part of her job – more intimate work would follow later.

* * *

At the age of fifteen, in a village surrounded by fields of the fresh green stems of fresh rice plants, she had sat with her parents and a man she had not met before.

"Aaheli," her father had said, "You know your brother has a family here and he must work the land to provide food for us all?"

"Yes, father," she'd replied.

"Good," he'd responded. "You know our fields do not produce sufficient rice to feed the whole family. Already we regularly go hungry, and as your brother's wife has children, more food will be necessary. We need you to provide for this family by earning money, so we may eat and buy medicines. And you know there is no paid work for women near here."

"Yes, father."

"Therefore, you must go to the city and earn money to send to us. Uncle, here," indicating the unknown man, "will take you to Kolkata. There is a woman he knows who will give you work, a room to sleep in, and rice to eat. This must happen if the family is to survive."

"I understand, father. Many of the boys in our neighbour's families have already gone to the city for work and some girls. It is my duty. I will do this," she'd replied, with tears wetting her eyes. But she had not known what the work would be.

* * *

Aaheli completed her dance with a flurry, dropping to the floor as the music reached its crescendo, holding a pose and smiling invitingly at the men – at least one of whom would likely now pay for extra private services. This was Aaheli's life now and would likely be so until she got too old and unattractive. What would happen to her then, she didn't know? Maybe someone would look after her in her old age? Maybe she would become a madam and control young women?

She hated this work, but she had no choice. There was no alternative, as far as she knew. She had been broken when she arrived in Kolkata. Locked into a windowless room, stripped, beaten and raped multiple times by her owners. Then sold to customers who liked to rape beautiful teenage girls. They had forced her to take on a new name, Kittu.

She'd given into it, eventually. Now she was condemned to satisfy men several times every day, so she could survive and send money home to her family in Murshidabad. The beatings, when she didn't do precisely as ordered, had become normal. She lived every day in pain: physical and emotional. She felt dirty and worthless as she danced for these disgusting men, who stunk of old sweat, tobacco, and whiskey. But she couldn't let them see how she felt – she had customers to entice, and money to earn. Survival relied upon it.

Chapter 50

As they drove away from the village, John offered Ahmed's phone to Suzanna. "You know I can't take that, as it's been obtained illegally."

"Yes, of course. Sorry." He noted the name of the trafficker and his phone number, then passed it to Suzanna. "I'll give this phone to a reliable contact I have in the Berhampore police and explain how I came about it. They'll likely want to speak to its owner and warn him about future contact with Amit Gupta or any other *agents* from Kolkata."

"Are you confident, you'll not get into trouble with the police?"

"It shouldn't be a problem. I work with them regularly. My contact is a friend as well as a colleague. I suggest you pass the trafficker's details to Assistant Superintendent Das, in the State police. You can say the number was obtained by a reliable contact in Murshidabad. I'm sure he'll want to act on the information and help you interview the man."

"Thanks, John. I've already met Superintendent Das. He seems a decent chap. I'll go with that. There's no other option if I'm to find the woman's killer." Suzanna sat contemplating the way forward as they travelled back to Murshidabad's administrative capital, re-joining the main Dhulian-Berhampore highway.

The police had turned one carriageway into a lorry park, like the British Operation Stack in Kent, when there are problems with the

English Channel crossings. Despite this police action, the journey to Berhampore by this longer route took over two hours, with traffic queued for over a mile to cross the Hooghly River bridge. They finally reached the hotel at 7:40 pm. Phil was sitting in the foyer, waiting for them with his wife. He waved and stood. Suzanna walked across the polished marble floor towards them as Zahir headed to the reception desk.

"Sorry, Phil. We're running late. I'll tell you more later. If you'd like to go through to the restaurant, we'll join you after we've checked in and freshened up."

"No problem. This is Cath, by the way."

Suzanna stepped forward and shook Cath's hand. "Good to meet you. We'll hopefully join you shortly." She smiled and went to the counter where Zahir was already sorting out their check-in. The room didn't live up to expectations, but it was clean and functional. At least it had hot water.

* * *

Twenty minutes later, a freshly showered Suzanna joined the rest of the group, who were drinking beer and eating spiced French fries. They ordered a variety of curry dishes, rice, Naan bread and more local beers, then chatted while waiting to be served.

"So, what brought you and Cath to Murshidabad?" Suzanna asked.

"Do you want the long story or the shortened version?"

"We've all evening, so don't condense it too much."

"The very short answer for why I'm here is because I received a calling from God." He responded. Suzanna looked curiously at Phil, inviting him to continue.

"I wasn't brought up as a Christian. My parents only went to church for weddings, christenings, and funerals, and I didn't know any

Christians. Certainly, none of my school friends admitted to believing or attending church. My view of religious people got tainted by all the bad press in the news and by the way, they were portrayed in movies and TV series. I began to see Christians as hypocrites and self-righteous busy-bodies, or weirdos who wore socks with their sandals." Suzanna laughed.

"I had been agnostic, I suppose, because I wasn't religious, but I didn't actually disbelieve in God. But later, as I saw all the suffering in the world and the violence carried out in the name of religion, my thinking shifted. I became an out-and-out atheist for several years of my life."

"So what changed?"

"Cath and I had started socialising with two couples who lived nearby. We were all in a similar stage in our lives: children, well-paid jobs, dinner parties, decent cars, and holidays. Life was good. Then I found out both couples regularly went to church. I was amazed. These weren't weirdos! I respected them. They were intelligent, well educated. They were like us – normal people. I reasoned that if they were believers, perhaps there was something in it after all."

"Then what happened?"

"Well, I shared my wonder that they were Christians and told them why I thought so. I'd drunk a few shandies that night! Anyway, they suggested I do an Alpha Course. I'd never heard of it. But they said it was a great course and it could change my life. They helped me find an Alpha to attend, and Cath and I both went on it. We became Christians on that course. I'd highly recommend it."

"Not you as well. My sister's been banging on at me about attending an Alpha course for years now, but I'm not interested in religion."

"Me neither. I don't do religion, but I try to live as a disciple."

"What do you mean: you don't do religion? You go to church and practise Christianity, don't you?"

Phil smiled. "True. I do go to church. And yes, I follow the Bible's teachings, but what I don't do is blindly follow tradition or strict rules and rituals, as many people do in the older established churches. One reason I'd stayed away from church most of my life was because of the religiosity I'd seen when I'd been forced to attend church. It all just seemed so irrelevant and restrictive. Talking about irrelevance, in the first session of the Alpha Course – the introduction – Alpha's leader, Nicky Gumbel, says about how he used to see Christianity as 'boring, irrelevant and untrue.' He has an amazing testimony of how he transitioned from atheistic barrister to a vicar in the Church of England."

"If you don't follow the rules of Christianity, how can you call yourself a Christian?"

"The churches I've attended since becoming a Christian don't follow the traditions and rituals. They allow space for people to engage meaningfully, rather than merely reacting to the vicar's pre-set prayers with specified responses. In some of the traditional churches I've been into, there's hardly a word said that isn't read from a piece of paper or projector screen."

"Do you not follow the Ten Commandments?"

"When Jesus came, it was to fulfil the prophecies in Scripture – the Old Testament – but he brought us the New Testament. We're not bound to follow the letter of the laws and be condemned by them for failing when we don't. Instead, we try to live as Jesus would wish us to, by his example, by service and sacrifice, given willingly rather than out of mere duty."

The food arrived, and they all tucked in. Suzanna spooned some Kadai vegetable curry onto her plate and ate it with garlic Naan, savouring the bell peppers and onions, in a coriander, cumin, and cardamom-spiced sauce. Zahir chose the traditional Bengali fish curry. After swallowing her first mouthful, she turned again to Phil. "You've told me how you became a Christian, but not how you came to be here."

"Aye, I know. That's the first part of the story. We started going to church, and through reading the Bible and listening to brilliant preachers and teachers, we both felt driven to help people less privileged than ourselves. Jumping forward a bit, we came on a trip to West Bengal and felt that God wanted us to come and serve him here. I thought all missionaries set up schools and churches and preached the gospel, but neither of us was like that. We both had skills in administration and management, so we wanted to put those skills to use, but we didn't know whether there was any call for our skills."

Suzanna noticed Zahir listening to the conversation – his curiosity piqued.

"Cath discovered DigniTees by accident and mentioned it to me. It just felt right. We spent three months working on projects with DigniTees and got caught by the vision to start businesses in Murshidabad. So here we are."

"Interesting story, Phil."

"I know you came here to speak with a family in Valkundi today, but why come all this way to do that?" Suzanna explained the reason behind the trip and what happened in Valkundi, then in Sherpur.

"We always knew there was trafficking going on in this part of Murshidabad. That's why we set up the factory in Sherpur. By providing training and work for women who've been assessed as most at risk of being trafficked, they can earn the money so desperately needed by them and their families, countering the draw of jobs in the city. It doesn't stop girls being abducted on their way home from school, though!"

"I understand you'd prefer to stop all trafficking but, apart from raising awareness of the risk, there's nothing DigniTees, Justice Operations or you could do about girls being stolen off the streets. What you are doing here is amazing, Phil. Good on you for giving up your career to come here and do this."

Phil nodded acceptance. "Living and working here has its challenges and rewards. You've seen some of the challenges today – the traffic jams and dangerous driving, the threat of malaria and dengue fever, and the climate, to name just a few. But knowing we've likely saved our women from being forced into sexual slavery makes it worthwhile. And the women gain in other ways. We provide counselling, trauma workshops, classes to improve the women's education, such as reading and writing, and simple maths. And for those with more promise, computer skills training and English language. Justice Operations also does training sessions on human rights. It's transformative working for DigniTees. The women have all learned new skills and gained self-confidence. They hold their heads high, instead of bowing to their male masters and feeling like second-class citizens. They're now the breadwinners in their households and have earned their family's respect."

"How long will you be here for Phil?"

"I don't know. We returned for six months initially and now we've been here for over two years. The factory is just getting going and we're continuing to take on more women, build more looms and make more scarves for sale around the world.

Suzanna chatted with Cath for a while about living in rural Murshidabad District and its administrative capital. Cath enthusiastically told her about the opening of Berhampore's first supermarket – well mini market. She sounded excited about being able to walk around a store and place items into a shopping basket. Normally she would have to stand in front of a counter, peering into the deep, dimly lit shops to see what was hiding on their shelves. Buying vegetables meant having to crouch or bend over to reach the produce scattered on the ground.

Suzanna was amazed that a city of 100,000 people had only one mini-market. She checked her watch, then spoke to Phil, Cath, and

Zahir. "I'm going to call it a night, as we're on the early train in the morning, and I need to check my emails first."

"What's happened to your driver?" Phil enquired.

"We sent him on his way, with a tip. I didn't fancy spending another five hours on the road tomorrow, and the hotel bought us seats on the train – the Bhagirathi Express, I believe it's called."

"That's the one. Leaves at 6:30 in the morning. You were extremely fortunate to get train tickets so close to the date. There must have been some cancellations. You'll certainly need to get to bed early."

Suzanna thanked John and the Justice Operations team again for enabling the success of their visit to Sherpur before heading to her room. The mattress was thin and hard, causing her body to ache as she laid, trying to relax. It had been a busy and eventful day. Sleep did not come easy.

Chapter 51

Monday 2nd

It was misty and cold at 6:15 am, as a tired and achy Suzanna stepped out of the hotel car that had delivered them to the station. Crowds of people swarmed around the station's forecourt. A large queue extended from the ticket office, where poor people were buying tickets for the third-class carriages.

Numerous kiosks surrounded a patch to the side of the station, apparently all selling the same packed savoury snacks and biscuits. She couldn't see anywhere to buy some decent food. Unlike other stations she'd seen in India, Berhampore Court had no fruit sellers. She couldn't think why this would be.

They carried their overnight bags, rejecting the offer of assistance from the porters, and followed the flow of passengers onto Platform 1, then over the footbridge to Platform 2. Suzanna asked a man where she should stand to board the air-conditioned chair class carriage. She'd chosen well because the man was booked on the same carriage. As they waited, porters carried huge boxes, cases, and bags of goods across the track, stacking them on the platform. They cleared the rails when they heard the approaching engine's horn.

When the train stopped, only a few minutes behind schedule, there was a mad dash to board it, with people pushing the backs of other passengers to force them to move into the carriage. She thought this was strange behaviour but realised why they had done so when the whistle blew and the train started pulling away, while passengers were still trying to board. It took a few minutes for them to find their seats and when they did, someone else was sitting there. Zahir spoke to the man occupying his seat, and the man vacated it, sitting himself down in another empty chair.

The seats were fairly comfortable, had reclining capability and sufficient legroom. She had hoped that the carriage would be warmer, but the air conditioning seemed to be running at maximum flow, pumping in cold air, so she kept her coat on.

No sooner had the passengers settled in their seats than hawkers entered the carriage selling cha and snacks. She asked the cha wallah if he had coffee and the man wobbled his head to indicate that he had. He tipped a little coffee powder into a tiny paper cup then added hot milky water from his huge kettle, before pouring the drink into a second cup, then back again, the gap between the two cups growing each time he poured – higher and higher. By the time he finished, the coffee had a froth on the top and he smiled at his creation. She expected him to say: "Cappuccino for the lady." But he just passed the drink to her and took the twenty rupees offered.

Suzanna was hungry, so was happy to see another hawker enter their carriage. "Buttered toast. Toast carbin," he called. When he came close, she held up a hand to show she was interested in buying some toast. The man took a tiny loaf that had been split in two and toasted earlier, then spread butter on two sides. As he went to dump them face down into a container of sugar, Suzanna grabbed his attention. "Nā. Chini Chara – *No, without sugar.*"

He smiled at her and asked, "Salt and Pepper?"

"Hā," she replied. Even all these years later, she still remembered a *little* Bangla.

Zahir went for the sweet option. Suzanna's savoury toast took away her hunger. After eating, she pulled out her laptop, switched on her phone's hotspot and the laptop soon connected. After downloading her emails, she switched off the hotspot to minimise expensive roaming charges, then started scanning through them. There wasn't anything from her team in Edinburgh. She assumed they'd taken Sunday off – fair enough.

Suzanna started scanning through the junk mail and deleting them. As she went to click on the next email, the person in front reclined their chair, almost knocking her laptop onto the floor. She looked behind to check the way was clear before reclining her seat to make room for her to operate, but still found it difficult to use her computer, laid back as she was, and the device perched on her lap, rather than the seat table. She closed her laptop, put it back in its bag, then relaxed back into her seat.

"Excuse me," a middle-aged chubby man sat across the aisle, said. "Is this your first visit to Murshidabad? Have you been to see Hazarduari Palace?"

Suzanna turned towards him and replied. "Yes, it's my first time, but I'm not here on holiday and I haven't had time to view any sights."

"You must visit the palace if you come again. Its name means one thousand doors. It was built in the 19th century by the British architect Duncan MacLeod. Perhaps you've heard the name. People travel from all over India to visit the palace. It is most wonderful."

"I've not heard of the architect, but I know many McLeods." Callum was also in that profession, and she wondered if there was any family connection. "It is a common name in Scotland. If I ever visit Murshidabad again, I will try to visit Hazarduari. Thank you for telling me about it."

"What business brings you to Murshidabad?"

Suzanna considered how to answer the question before speaking. She couldn't give away details, and she wondered whether it would be wise to let on that she was a British police officer. She decided honesty would be the best way, as it would raise awareness of human trafficking from the district. "I'm a police officer. We're trying to track down the trafficker of a Bengali woman who ended up dead in Scotland. She had been tricked into going to Kolkata for work but was forced into the sex trade."

The man looked shocked at the revelation. "Oh my goodness. That is dreadful. You have come a long way to fulfil your duty. I wish you success in your mission. Human trafficking is a terrible business."

"Yes. And it's prevalent in Murshidabad. Many of the women working in Kolkata's red-light areas come from this district." Suzanna noticed many of the surrounding passengers were now listening.

The conversation was interrupted as the carriage door opened and the stench of the toilets wafted through as the railway official entered. "Tickets please," he called, in English. Almost everyone in this carriage would speak English, as well as Bangla and Hindi. Her fellow travellers would be from the middle classes: teachers, doctors, policemen, government employees and business owners. Suzanna handed the official the A4 sheet of paper that the hotel had given her, with both their names listed. He looked and gave it back before turning to the opposite seats.

Halfway through the journey a man entered the carriage, put down his bag and started talking loudly in Bangla. Suzanna couldn't follow what he was saying, but it appeared he was an entertainer of some type. It soon became obvious what his act was when he called 'abracadabra' and pulled some artificial flowers from a coke bottle. She went back to reading a book on her phone as he continued his performance for several minutes more, then held out a cup as he wandered up and down the aisle collecting tips from those who had found him entertaining.

On arrival at Sealdah Railway Station, in Kolkata, they joined the throng of travellers exiting the station. It reminded her of the crowds outside football stadiums in the UK, only these masses were moving fast instead of milling around. Porters shouted for people to get out of the way as they pushed the steel-wheeled hand carts down the platform, loaded with baggage. It was like someone had disturbed an ants' nest. They grabbed a yellow cab and went straight to the State Police HQ.

Chapter 52

Assistant Superintendent Das met them at reception and escorted them to his office.

"So what news from Murshidabad, didi?"

Suzanna brought him up to speed and gave him the name of the trafficker, informing him that the family would testify against the man if he were charged with trafficking.

Das recognised the name, Amit Gupta, and immediately sent a team into Sonagachi to arrest him. Whilst waiting for Gupta to be brought in, Suzanna and Zahir left the HQ and went for lunch in a nearby restaurant. They received a call just as they were finishing their meal, informing them that Gupta was in custody and that questioning would soon begin.

They returned to the HQ and listened in to the interrogation. "Look Gupta, it's no good you denying it. We have witnesses from Murshid-abad who will give evidence against you. You took their girl on the pretext of placing her in work as a housemaid with a good family, but instead, you sold her into a Sonagachi brothel."

He sat, blank-faced, saying nothing. One officer slapped him around the back of his head. "We will not spend all day waiting for you to talk. We'll beat it out of you if you like. You will be charged anyway, and you will go to prison. Tell us who you sold the girl to." He told them where to go in colourful language, so the officer slapped him again.

"We're just trying to find out where the girl lived in Sonagachi because she's been found murdered. Finding her killer is more important to us than jailing you. If you give us a name, we will drop the charges, and let you go." He looked interested in the proposal. "Or my colleague here will fetch his stick."

Suzanna was not comfortable watching their interrogation techniques. This type of treatment had been outlawed in the UK decades ago. It was not her place to intervene, though, so she stood quietly, listening in. The approach taken by the Bengali police seemed to be effective.

"I'm not admitting anything. But if I had brought her to the city, I would have passed her to Paavani di – Paavani Haldar."

Das recognised the name as that of the madam they had recently brought in for questioning. "Very sensible, Amit. We shall follow this line of investigation, and if we can find out what happened to the girl, we will let you go." He turned to the other officer and said, "Lock him up," then left the interview room.

"Suzanna di," Das said as he opened the door to the viewing room, "Let's talk about the next steps."

They returned to his office and debated the best way forward. "Just let me be clear. We *will* be charging the trafficker, irrespective of where the investigation takes us. With the family to identify him, we have a good chance of success in the court."

"Glad to hear that. The man is a parasite. He needs to be locked up, so he can't trick any more families."

Das continued. "We could arrest the madam and bring her in for questioning, but I'm not certain that will result in the outcome you're looking for. We will arrest her for human trafficking offences, but I think, before we do that, you should try a different approach?" Suzanna tilted her head and looked at Das in anticipation.

"If you can get IJTF to go in undercover again and ask the girls from the brothel what they know. Perhaps this time they'll provide some useful information. If that doesn't work, then we'll go in hard and put Paavani under pressure."

"I'm happy to give that a try. Let me call IJTF and see if they're willing to help again."

Das left the room, and she called IJTF. "Michael. It's Suzanna McLeod. How are you?

"Good thanks, Suzanna. What can I do for you?"

"I'm wondering whether your team can help me again. We now have a strong lead. We know with some certainty which brothel the girl was sold into, and we want to go in again to ask more questions. If we can do this without police involvement, they might be more willing to talk. If that doesn't work, the State Police will go in and make arrests."

"Hmm... Just a minute." The phone went quiet, and Suzanna waited.

"I've just spoken to David. He can't go in again so soon and start asking questions. It would blow his cover entirely. I don't have anyone else who could assist – sorry."

"Okay. I understand. You have to take the long view, or your work will be jeopardised."

"Yes. Exactly right."

Suzanna thanked Michael for his organisation's support, then ended the call. She dialled another number and when it was answered spoke: "Hi. It's Suzanna. I need your assistance again..."

Chapter 53

"Hello, Rohan. Good to meet you. I understand from John that you're willing to assist us?"

"Yes. Happy to help Suzanna. We're in the same business, really – seeking justice – just in different ways. I've been talking with colleagues, and we've formulated a different approach to seeking the information you require."

"Tell me more."

"Rather than use my undercover field workers, I shall go into Sonagachi and ask direct questions of the women from the brothel. I'll explain why we want to know – that we're trying to find out what happened to a fellow sister who has been murdered after leaving their community. I will appeal to their better nature and show that I am no threat to their livelihood or freedom."

"Interesting. Perhaps it might work. If not, as I said on the phone, the State Police will make arrests. In fact, they intend to, anyway. The community is bound to connect your questioning of them with the good news

later arrest of the madam, so I assume it would become too difficult for you to enter the district again."

"Yes, you're probably correct. But I believe this is the right thing to do. Our mission is to bring about justice, so I will do the needful. Besides, I have just received the good news that I will soon be promoted to Justice Operations' Country Director and will move to Delhi, next month," he said with a smile.

Suzanna smiled back. "Fair enough, and congratulations."

* * *

Rohan and Zahir left Suzanna at the Sovabazar metro station, so she took a walk up the road to one of the chain coffee shops that had multiplied across the city since her last visit – another sign of growing wealth. She ordered her cappuccino and took a seat. She was the only customer at the time and there were three members of staff, but it was fifteen minutes before her coffee was delivered. They'd never hold down a job in Costa, she thought to herself, as she smiled a thank you.

Now she just had to wait...

* * *

Suzanna received a call forty minutes later. "Ma'am. Rohan's approach has worked. A girl we spoke to told us that Aaheli, known as Kittu, was sold to another brothel. We've been asking the wrong people. She's told us the name of a woman from this other brothel who she believes might have been a friend of Kittu's. We're going to where she normally operates from, now."

"Where are you heading, Zahir?"

"She normally stands at the edge of the district, on Central Avenue, opposite a small park and a bank. I think the bank has yellow hoardings. Just a sec... It's called the Bank of Baroda."

"I'll meet you there. I want to be there when you question her." She ended the call, grabbed her bag, and set off back the way she had come, waving goodbye to the staff as she left.

* * *

They crossed Central Avenue together and walked casually towards the corner with Durgacharan Mitra Street. As they walked, Michael made a call to his driver and told him where to wait for them. A group of men stood at the junction, looking up the road towards them. When a taxi pulled up nearby, they all crowded around as the occupants alighted. One man guided the newcomers into Sonagachi. The others regrouped and looked for the next taxi.

They passed the men, and just beyond the car battery shop, saw a large double metal gate. Next to this blank metal barrier stood a woman, her make-up over-done, her sari bright green and with gold bangles. Her black hair was tied up in a loose bun behind her head, and she was on the phone. As the call finished, Rohan approached. "Hanisha di?"

The woman looked at him, not recognising his face and curious why he knew her name. She nodded noncommittally.

"I would like to speak with you for a few minutes. I will pay you for your time." She showed no sign of whether she would cooperate. Rohan showed her the photograph on his phone, obtained from Aaheli's family. "I believe you were friends with this woman. What can you tell us about her?"

"Sir. I do know her, but I cannot tell you anything. It is too risky for me to speak with people about such matters." Her eyes furtively glanced at the crowd of men at the junction.

"Kittu left Kolkata last year, and we believe went to work for someone. We need to find the person she went with."

"You had better go. If my babu sees me talking to you, he will be suspicious." She glanced again over Suzanna's shoulder, her face showing the worry she felt.

"Can you tell me about Kittu?"

"I would like to, sir," she said, turning to look at Rohan again, "but whatever you paid me would not be enough."

"Do you like the work that you do in Sonagachi?"

The woman screwed up her face. "Do you think any of the women here like to service several strangers every day to earn a living? To have their bodies invaded by dirty men, looking for cheap thrills? Of course, I don't *like* it."

"What if I could get you out and help you start a new life?"

"How can I believe you could do this or *would* do this?"

"I work for an NGO that exists to bring justice to the oppressed. We can help you. We have a safe hostel and can train you in other work. My colleagues could help you return to your village if that is what you wanted."

She looked again towards the corner. "Please go. Babu will soon come, and you will be in trouble." But Rohan could see she was tempted.

"If you can help us identify who Kittu went with, we will help you escape this nightmare. Come with us, to freedom." He indicated she should walk with them. "I have a car close by."

Suzanna smiled at her, trying to show that they had her best interests at heart. The woman hesitated, then followed Rohan, and the two British officers followed. They'd walked twenty paces when a shout sounded. "Hanisha. Come back here. Now."

They kept walking, not looking back, but Hanisha looked nervous. They quickened their pace, with Rohan opening the car door as soon as they reached their vehicle. Feet could be heard running towards them, and men were shouting. Hanisha got into the car, and Rohan followed her in. Zahir had opened the front passenger door and Suzanna had gone to the offside rear door. As she opened it, the men caught up to them. They were red-faced, shouting the woman's name. She saw the glint of shiny steel protruding from the hand of the most vocal man –

Hanisha's pimp, she assumed.

A man pushed Zahir back into the open door. Another grabbed at the handle of Rohan's door, but it was locked. "Get in, Suzanna. Quick," Rohan called. But the pimp stepped towards Suzanna, the knife now in his hand, and pointed towards her. If she tried to get into the car, the man would stick her with the knife. She could end up another statistic.

Suzanna grabbed the man's knife hand at the wrist, lifted it above his head as she stepped forward and dropped low. She spun underneath his arm, taking it back with her, and twisted it sharply. The knife fell to the ground, and she thrust the man's arm up his back. He screamed in pain.

Zahir recovered from his push to the chest and kicked out at the aggressor, knocking him backwards into the man behind him. They tumbled to the floor. Zahir glanced across at Suzanna before entering the car and closing his door – setting the lock immediately. Suzanna turned the man away from the car and pushed him harshly away from her. He fell to the ground, his nose smacking into the asphalt and the skin on his face grazing as it rubbed along the ground. She jumped into the rear seat, slammed the door, and shouted: "GO".

The driver wasted no time pulling away rapidly and sounded his horn loudly as he forced his way into the Central Avenue traffic. A bus slammed on its brakes to avoid hitting their car. The driver shouted at them. Zahir looked back to where they had come and saw the three men getting into one of the yellow cabs that were parked at the junction. It immediately pulled out and joined the traffic. "The men are following us in a taxi."

Suzanna looked over her shoulder and the driver checked his mirror but couldn't see anything, because of the density of traffic. "Keep an eye on the taxi, if you can, Zahir." They turned right at the next traffic lights, which fortunately had turned green as they arrived. The cab followed them. A short distance up the road, they stopped in a queue for the next junction's traffic lights, outside the coffee shop where Suzanna had recently drunk her cappuccino.

"Two men have left the cab and they're running up the road towards us," Zahir informed them, the pitch of his voice rising. As the men reached their car, the lights changed and the vehicles in front started moving. The man nearest Suzanna had a wrench in his hand and swung his arm backwards, preparing to strike the window. Suzanna unlocked her door and swung it open harshly, smashing it into the pursuer's legs. He cried out like a distressed donkey and fell to the ground in front of a passing motorbike. It collided with him, the rider falling to the ground on top of the pimp. The second man tried the door handle on the near side but let go as the car drove away and went to his friend's aid.

They turned right at the lights, then left onto a back street, then right, then left again, before emerging on another highway, where they joined with the traffic. It seemed they had evaded their pursuers, but they would have to keep watch for the taxi in case it caught up with them again.

With the immediate threat diminished, Suzanna looked at Hanisha. Under the make-up, she could see old bruising. She met eyes with the woman and peered into them – into her tarnished soul. There was a dark depression beneath. Hanisha's liberally applied cheap perfume permeated the entire car. But Suzanna could sense the muskiness of sex beneath the powerful flower smell. She opened her window to gain relief from the scent, but it was replaced by traffic fumes and now car horns invaded their thoughts.

"Rohan. Why is it that drivers all sound their horns so much in West Bengal?" Suzanna asked.

"Ah! It is not safe to remain quiet when driving. No one looks in their mirrors, even if they have them, so each much inform the other drivers of their presence. Without the horns, there would be many more accidents."

Suzanna pondered on what he'd said. If they'd just use their mirrors, the place could be much quieter. Her mind returned to Hanisha. She reached out and took the woman's hand, then smiled as she turned towards her again, to reassure her. Hanisha's soft, damp hand gripped Suzanna's fingers for the rest of the journey as if Suzanna promised freedom, and she didn't want to let go for fear the opportunity would fly away.

Chapter 54

After driving for over thirty minutes, looking over their shoulders, the car pulled into an underground car park before the gate lowered again, securing them. The driver parked the car, and they walked up into the Justice Operations offices. Hanisha started crying again. Anxiety had set off the tears, but now she feared what the future might hold. There was no going back.

"Suzanna, you're bleeding," Rohan said.

She had extracted a few tissues from her bag and held them against the wound by her wrist, but the blood had soaked the tissues. "Yes. It's just a minor cut but I could do with something to clean it and dress it."

Rohan handed Hanisha to another member of staff, then went off in search of the first aid kit. He returned quickly, taking Suzanna's hand in his now-gloved hands. He removed the tissues and disposed of them before cleaning the wound with antiseptic lotion. "It's about one inch long but quite shallow. I doubt it would warrant stitches."

Suzanna glanced at the cut. "It'll be fine if we just cover it to keep the germs out."

"It's clean now, so I'll wrap it for you."

Suzanna was impressed with the neat way Rohan dressed her wrist and thanked him – she imagined him as a young boy, wearing a grey cape and a beret, with the St John's Ambulance Brigade badge. "Do you think Hanisha will have had sufficient time to get over the fright?"

"Hopefully. Let's ask her a few questions and see how it goes."

They went through to where Hanisha had been resting, and Rohan spoke to her in Bengali, translating her responses each time for Suzanna. "Hanisha di, thank you for being brave and agreeing to come with us. I promise we will look after you. You will not regret coming with us." She smiled weakly, still unconvinced she'd made the right move.

"You said Kittu had gone with a man, a regular customer?"

"Yes. He had been visiting her for three years or more. He used to come a few times, then she wouldn't see him for many months. She thought he must live in another city."

"What can you tell us about this man?" Rohan asked, his face indicating the importance of the question.

"He looked high caste. I think she said he was a doctor. He was old, perhaps fifty."

"And his features?"

"A black moustache. Black hair. Thinning on top. He had a swollen belly and bloated face, and would be about your height."

"If I showed you a picture of him, would you recognise the man?"

"Yes. Most definitely – as sure as a mother would recognise her own child."

Rohan briefed Suzanna on what had been said so far. "I'll get one of my colleagues in Edinburgh to send us photos of our current suspects. Perhaps she will recognise one."

Rohan turned back to Hanisha. "We will find a bed for you tonight and provide your meals. Tomorrow, we hope to have some photos for you to look at. But before we leave here, I have a few more questions. Did Kittu mention the man's name?"

"She called him dada. I don't recall her using his name."

"Did she ever mention where the man came from?"

"She always wondered which city he lived in, but he never told her. Not until he asked her to go with him. He promised her a job as a housemaid. He said he lived in the UK."

"Did he say where in the UK?"

"I think she said that it was a city in Scotland?"

"Edinburgh?" Zahir asked.

Hanisha looked deep in thought. She answered. "I do not know. I cannot recall what city he was from."

"Okay. We're on the right track, here," Suzanna whispered to her colleague.

"Some months before Kittu left, the man took her photograph. She told me it was for her passport. One day, we were standing in our normal place when a car stopped, and the door was opened. She approached as if to enquire what service he wished, then she got in, closed the door and the car sped off. Our babu was furious. He beat me for letting her get in the car and for not shouting to him that she was escaping. He wouldn't let me stand on Central Avenue for about three months afterwards as he was afraid I would also run away."

"I am glad he changed his mind and let you return to the avenue. Now you are free from him." Hanisha started crying again. Relief and uncertainty driving the tears.

* * *

Suzanna and Zahir left Hanisha with Justice Operations and returned to their hotel. She checked emails, then called the Superintendent to update him on progress. Alistair was pleased with her report and agreed to get photos of the suspects sent to her without delay.

"How's Una doing? Is she still in a coma?

"I'm afraid so, Suzanna. The scans they did on her head showed significant trauma. They say it will take some time for her brain to heal and she'll likely remain in a coma until it does. Hopefully, there hasn't been permanent damage, and she'll fully recover. Then she will confirm who attacked her. Angus has the name of a suspect and is trying to track him down, but no proof that he committed the assault. But I don't want you to worry about that. We need you to remain focussed on the murder case."

"I've got a picture of our victim from her family. It's similar to the artist's impression and, although taken when she was fifteen, would still be useful for asking questions. I'll send it to Rab and ask him to show it to the suspect's neighbours to see if anyone recognises her."

"Sounds like a good idea. I'll let him know to expect the image and to get things set up for the house calls."

Suzanna sent off an email to Rab, with Aaheli's picture, then ordered a glass of red wine from room service. She wasn't quite ready for sleep. As the computer did its send/receive, an email popped into her inbox from Rab.

Hi ma'am. We rechecked the tyre type against other makes and models, as you requested. The size and brand is in use widely across a range of makes from Alpha Romeo to Volvo but when we drilled deeper, we found the Run Flat version, which has small differences to the standard tyre, is only used on the three cars we identified, plus the Mini Clubman, and two Cadillac models: the ATS and CT4. These are both rare on Scottish roads.

We rechecked the CCTV and found no Cadillacs had passed the cameras. Two minis had. They're not spacious vehicles but we checked them out, anyway. We spoke with the owners to ascertain their reasons for being in the area and carried out background checks on them. There was nothing of note from the background checks, and the reasons given for being near Kincardine seemed sound. But we did some more digging, anyway.

One owner, Mrs Gillian Todd, has her own company employing cleaners. We obtained copies of her records, and we're still trawling through them. Most of her workers were not born in the UK. I'll let you know how we get on with this investigation, in my next update.

The other Mini owner is Mr Raj Patel. He's about 30. His car was seen crossing Kincardine Bridge around 9:30 pm with a woman passenger, then returning around 11:15 pm with no passenger. He said the woman was his girlfriend, and he dropped her home in Dunfermline. He's from Bannockburn. We will check with the girlfriend ASAP and inform you of the outcome.

As you'd suggested, we called on properties in Tulliallan and got some footage of vehicles passing along the A977. But the road is distant from the cameras, so it provided no more clues. We still don't have any strong leads. Attached are pictures of the two men that we know are originally from Kolkata, plus one of Mr Patel. Good luck.

Rab

Suzanna replied with a quick thanks for the good work. She switched her focus to booking flights home. There wasn't a lot more they could do in Kolkata after they'd shown Hanisha the suspects' pictures. She texted Zahir, to say 'bring your bag in the morning, we'll be checking out.

Another email caught her attention. The insurers had authorised the work on her house in Cockermouth, so she notified the builder. At least that was sorted now. She could leave it with the builder to arrange. She pondered the idea of selling the house. It hadn't increased in value since she'd owned it, and it was just a distraction. If she did eventually move to Cockermouth, she'd probably not want to live in that house, anyway. It no longer seemed it would meet her needs and was tainted by having become a burden. Her mind involuntarily wandered around the subject, withholding the rest of sleep.

* * *

Chapter 55

Tuesday 3rd

The next morning, Suzanna woke feeling weary. As she cleaned her teeth, looking at her dark-rimmed eyes in the mirror, she made up her mind about the Cockermouth house. It had caused too many interrupted night's sleep. It had to go.

* * *

"Hanisha di. I have photographs of three men. I'd like you to tell me if you recognise any of them," Rohan said, having met with Suzanna before visiting the halfway house. The nondescript concrete building was on the edge of Kolkata, bordering fields, and off the beaten track. Unfortunately, its location meant that Suzanna and Zahir had taken over an hour to reach it. But it was quiet and safe from prying eyes.

He passed the photos to her, and she dropped her eyes to look at them. She shook her head and passed one back to Rohan, then looked at the second image. She gave that back as well. "Too young." Then she looked at the third photo. "This is the man who took Kittu," she responded, no doubt in her voice.

"Are you certain?"

"Yes. Completely. I have seen him many times. There is no doubt."

"Thank you, Hanisha di." He turned to Suzanna and Zahir, smiling. "A result! I think that's how you say it in the police?"

"Yes. Definitely a result... Hanisha di. Thank you. Dhonobaad," Suzanna said, looking the woman in the eyes and clamping her hands together as if in prayer. She smiled back at Suzanna, then tilted her head to the side before dropping her eyes.

"Hanisha di." Rohan said. She looked up again. "How are you? Are you feeling good about leaving Sonagachi?"

She paused, thinking, before responding. "Yes, dada, but I am also sad. I had many friends there, and now I have none. I am lonely." Hanisha looked like she felt – sad.

"You will make new friends. Do not worry. The future will be better for you now. Later today a nurse will come, and she will examine you. If you have any health problems, she will arrange for treatment."

"Thank you, dada." This time she didn't lower her head but stood and walked to the window to peer through the banana palm trees, across the sunlit countryside. Suzanna sensed the woman's spirit lift, as she looked out into the open space and bright light – symbols of a new freedom.

They left Hanisha to her thoughts. "So, what now, Suzanna?"

"We will need her testimony to help convict the man. We don't know yet whether he was her killer but certainly, it seems he helped her to enter the UK illegally. If we can prove slavery, he could also be charged with human trafficking." Suzanna paused.

"You will need official evidence of Hanisha's identity, I assume?

"Yes. Do you know if she has any?"

"I doubt it but we'll check. Survivors rarely have any formal documents. One of the first things we do is obtain an Aadha Card for them – sorry, their Indian identity cards. The card is necessary to obtain access to Government schemes and benefits."

"We'll also need a signed statement from her and to support that, it would be best to video an interview with her. Once you obtain documentary evidence of her identity, we should have credible evidence that our suspect was the man who took her to the UK. Hopefully, this will suffice, without the need to bring her to the UK."

"We don't have a video camera here, but I think there is a small tripod for mounting mobile phones onto. Perhaps you could video your interview by smartphone?"

"Yes, that should work."

It was too early in Scotland to call the station with the news, so she texted Rab to let him know and emailed the Superintendent, copied to Rab, just to be sure. Her boss was bound to check his emails as soon as he settled behind his desk in the morning. She added that there was now no need to follow up on the Mini Clubman owners or show Aaheli's picture to neighbours.

* * *

It was late morning by the time they finished taking her statement and had the videoed interview sorted. "Thanks so much for your invaluable assistance, Rohan. I'm now much more hopeful that we'll see justice done."

"It has been my pleasure."

"What will happen to Hanisha now?"

"She will stay here for some time, to give her the opportunity to break from her old life and to receive trauma counselling. After that, I'm not yet certain. If she could return to her family, that might be best – assuming we can find them. But it is difficult because she would be another mouth to feed and there will be no work for her in her village. It would be problematic for her to marry someone, having been away from her village for so long. Her purity will be in doubt. Hence, a return home might *not* be possible."

"So, will she stay here?" Suzanna scanned her surroundings. It was bare, basic accommodation. Not homely.

"No. This is just a halfway house. We have a hostel in the south of the city, near to a small manufacturing unit run by a church. She could move there, learn new skills and be employed in production if she can't return to her family."

"Oh! I didn't know that was a possibility. It's good that you can find her somewhere to live and work if she can't go back to her village... There's no more we can do here now, so we'll let you get on with your work, but please let me know how things go for Hanisha. Here's my card," Suzanna said. "Before we leave, I just need to make a phone call."

* * *

"Hello?" a confused, sleepy voice said.

"Rab. It's DCI McLeod. Did I wake you?"

"What time is it?"

"By my calculations, it should be 6 am."

Rab sat up, shook his head, rubbed his eyes, and looked at his bedside clock. "Aye. That's about right. My alarm was due to go off at half-past. Why are you ringing so early, ma'am?"

"Our witness has confirmed it was one of our suspects who had been seeing the murdered woman and took her from Sonagachi. I've put the details in an email I've sent you. It should give you a date window to focus on for her entry into the UK. Now we know who she came in with and have a picture of her, finding proof from the immigration department should be easier. This is what I need you to do..."

Chapter 56

Rab ascended the path and steps leading up to the stone-built detached house in Falkirk. He thumped loudly on the hardwood door and rang the bell. It was 7:15 on a misty Edinburgh morning. He'd roused himself after the DCI's call from Kolkata and phoned in to the station to rustle up support. Mairi was with him and a uniformed constable. He banged again on the door and held his finger on the bell push until the door was opened.

"Stop that, the woman shouted at Rab. What's the matter with you? There's no need for all this noise. What time is this to call on us?"

"Where is your husband, Mrs Mukherjee?"

She turned and shouted up the stairs, "Jeetu. The police are here, asking for you." She turned back to them. "You'd better come in. I don't want the neighbours seeing this unnecessary commotion."

She led them into the living room and offered them seats, but they stayed standing. "He'll just be a minute." She left them and ascended the stairs, calling again for her husband.

Two minutes later, Doctor Mukherjee entered the room. "Sorry to keep you, officers. I was undressed. What brings you here so early?"

"A serious matter, sir. I require you to accompany me to the station for formal questioning regarding the death of a young Bengali woman."

The doctor looked shocked, his jaw falling open and his eyebrows rising. Mrs Mukherjee returned, having quickly changed from her dressing gown into a sari, her hair still hanging loosely down her back.

"What are they saying, Jeetu? A murder. Why would they need to speak with you about a murder?"

"I do not know, my sweet."

"We need you to attend the station as well, Mrs Mukherjee."

"I couldn't possibly go to the police station with you. I haven't taken my bath yet. Ask your questions here."

"No, ma'am. You must come with us. If you refuse, I shall have to arrest you both on suspicion of murder."

"Me? Murder? No, no, no. We will come with you. No need to arrest us. The neighbours will think we are criminals." Doctor Mukherjee also agreed, then phoned the hospital to leave a message for his staff that he might be late today.

* * *

The Mukherjees were placed in separate interview rooms and left to stew for a while. Rab arranged for the husband's DNA sample to be taken, then popped in to see the Superintendent. "Sir, we have the Mukherjees in for interviewing. The DCI said you might want to send a press release through to Steve Gibson, to let them know the victim has been identified and we have two people helping us with enquiries."

"Good morning, Rab. I got an email from her earlier, so I've already drafted the release. I was just waiting for confirmation that you had brought them in. So that's great." He turned to his computer and started typing.

"I'll let you know how the interviews go, later on." Rab turned and walked away.

The Superintendent sent off the press release and copied it to the Chief Super, to keep him up to date with progress.

* * *

Seated in separate rooms, the interviews began. Rab borrowed Owen to sit in, and Mairi recruited Murray's assistance. Doctor Mukherjee looked uncomfortable, and so he should do.

"Mr Mukherjee..."

"Doctor. It's doctor, not mister."

Rab ignored his response. "Records tell us you regularly return to Kolkata and spend three to four weeks in the city, twice-yearly?"

"Yes. That is my routine."

"Why do you visit the city so often?"

"I have family in Kolkata but also a hospital there requires my consultancy. I regularly train surgeons on the best practices and techniques that we use in the UK."

"According to my records, you were in Kolkata between 20th September and 6th October 2014. Is that correct?"

"I cannot deny it."

"Whilst there, you visited an area near to the Sovabazar metro station?"

Mukherjee looked like a rat caught in torchlight. "How could you know this? Have you been spying on me? Am I a terrorist? Is that it? Just because I'm an Asian, you think I'm a threat to this country. This is racism."

"Calm down, Mr Mukherjee," Rab said. Mukherjee scowled. "We have not been spying on you, and you are not listed as a potential terrorist threat. But we know you were in this area of the city. Care to tell us why you were there?"

"No." He sat back and folded his arms.

"Do you deny being in that part of the city during your last visit?" Mukherjee sat stony-faced and said nothing. "You neither confirm nor deny being in Sonagachi?"

"Sonagachi? I would never visit such a place."

"We have a witness who saw you in Sonagachi. Not once but many times over three years."

"They must be mistaken. I have not been to that place. It disgusts me."

"This witness is not mistaken. She is definite that it was you."

"Then she is lying. I've never been to that district. I wouldn't dare. I have my reputation to think of, and it is full of dirty women and thieves."

"So, you are denying having any contact with a woman known as Aaheli?" Silence followed. "What about Kittu?" There was a glimmer of recognition in the doctor's eyes.

He recrossed his arms. "I want a lawyer. I will not answer any more of your accusations."

Chapter 57

Mrs Mukherjee looked defiant. Her lips pursed and faced firmly fixed. Mairi introduced her colleague, Detective Constable Docherty, then opened the questioning. "So, Mrs Mukherjee, how long have you known that your husband has been paying women for sex?"

She sat back in her chair, her head straightening. "What? What did you say? How dare you accuse my husband of paying for sex. You insult me. Don't you think I can keep him satisfied? Have you not heard of the Kama Sutra? Ridiculous!"

Mairi was pleased that she'd got Mrs Mukherjee off balance, where she wanted her. "Did you accompany your husband on his trips to Kolkata?"

"Not in recent years," she replied, relaxing a little. "My parents are dead and my brothers and sisters and cousins, all live in the UK or Canada. Besides, my back gives me too much trouble nowadays. The economy seats on Air India are so uncomfortable."

"As a surgeon, I would have thought your husband could afford business class seats?"

Her head wobbled before she responded. "My husband wouldn't pay for them. He said they cost four times more than economy seats, so we could not return to India as often. Jeetu still sends money home to his family – after all these years. We're not as wealthy as you might think."

"Would he not pay for a maid, either? Did you have to do all the cleaning and cooking?"

"No, no. Of course not. There are plenty of young women who will do the menial work for a little money."

"So, when did you get your live-in maid?"

Mrs Mukherjee paused before answering – always a good sign that they were trying to think how not to incriminate themselves. "I've always had cleaners come in. Twice a week is enough. We're not messy people."

"What's the name of your current cleaner? We'll need to talk with her."

She hadn't prepared herself for that line of questioning. "Oh! I can't remember. She comes in when I'm out shopping and having lunch with my friends. She has a key, and I leave her money on the kitchen worktop."

Sounded feasible, Mairi thought. "How long has she been working for you?"

"Three months, now. Yes, three months."

"Surely you didn't give the key to your home to a complete stranger, without first vetting her?"

"No, no. A friend recommended her."

"But you must have made a note of her name? Surely you must have her address and phone number – in case things changed, and you needed her to clean on a different day, for instance?"

"Well, yes, but I don't know what I did with the details."

"Which friend recommended her to you?"

She thought before answering. "It will have been Mrs Ganguly. Yes. It must have been her."

The name reminded Murray of sitting around a campfire with fellow scouts, singing 'ging gang gooley, gooley, gooley, gooley, watcha,' ... "We'll need this woman's contact details," he said, passing her a piece of paper and a pen.

"I cannot recall her phone number."

"Her address, then?" Murray responded. Mrs Mukherjee reluctantly wrote an address on the paper and passed it back to Murray. "Please show me your mobile phone."

She took the phone from her bag and showed him but didn't offer to let him hold it.

"As she is a respected friend, you will, of course, have Mrs Ganguly's telephone number on your phone. Please look it up. The sooner we can call her and verify what you told us, the sooner we can conclude our investigations." She couldn't really pretend that she didn't have the number, so reluctantly searched for it, and showed it to Murray. He noted it on the paper and left the room.

"Mrs Mukherjee." Mairi continued. "When your husband was in Kolkata, we know that he often visited a prostitute."

"How could you know this? I don't believe you. He's a good man. Jeetu wouldn't go with those dirty women. He wouldn't betray me."

"We have a reliable witness who has made a statement identifying your husband as being the regular customer of a young woman in Sonagachi."

"How could anyone who lives in that sewer be considered reliable? Those people are all criminals. They will say anything if they think they might gain from it. No, no. I don't accept what you're saying."

"We have a name for the prostitute he visited. She was known as Kittu." Mrs Mukherjee kept a straight face, but Mairi thought she saw a flicker of acknowledgement.

"Our witness said that your husband visited Kittu several times, then he would not be seen for many months. Each time he returned to the city, he would visit often. There appeared to be a six-month cycle to these visits." As she absorbed these facts, Mairi thought she could see her thinking that her husband had been betraying her over a long time, after all. She sat glum and silent, looking at the grey wall behind Mairi, avoiding eye contact.

"When was the last time your husband visited his family?"

"Last year. Err... September, I think. Yes, September. He always goes for the Durga Puja and returns just after the festival is finished. He is due to go again next month."

"That fits. Our witness told us that Kittu left Sonagachi with your husband in October last year." Mairi could see Mrs Mukherjee processing this information. She sensed that the woman was beginning to accept they would soon prove the young woman had travelled to the UK with her husband and had lived with them. That was almost certainly what had happened. They just needed to prove it.

Murray returned and sat down next to Mairi. "Mrs Mukherjee. I just spoke with Mrs Ganguly, and she has no recollection of recommending a cleaner for you. In fact, she was certain that you had a live-in maid. You've been lying to us."

"No, no. She is mistaken. She did recommend the mai... cleaner. I've never had a live-in maid."

"I see no point continuing with these questions if you're going to lie to us," Mairi said, then stood, the chair legs scraping across the floor, and walked out of the room with Murray. As she closed the door, she glanced at Mrs Mukherjee. She looked like a woman whose future was flowing away with every minute.

Chapter 58

The duty lawyer sat next to Doctor Mukherjee, who had worry written over his face.

"To recap, Mr Mukherjee..." Rab purposely antagonised him.

"Doctor. I've told you before, I am a doctor, not just a mister. You must call me doctor."

Rab ignored his mini-rant. "Let us return to our previous questions. We have a witness who says you regularly visited her friend, Aaheli or Kittu, and paid for sex." The doctor sat, arms folded again, looking cross. "She has made a sworn statement to this fact. The visits were cyclic – happening six-monthly. This fits in with the pattern of your visits to Kolkata." Still no response from Mukherjee. "Furthermore, she tells us that in October last year, you took Kittu away in a car, and she has never been seen again. What did you do with this beautiful young woman?"

"I don't know what you are talking about. Who is this witness? A friend of this prostitute that you say I visited. Who is she to be believed? I tell you I never visited Kittu and did not take her from Sonagachi."

"The name Kittu tripped off your tongue with much familiarity, doctor... You make out that, because you are a doctor and the witness a prostitute, your word is better than hers. But what does she have to gain from lying to us?"

"I don't know. But lying, she most certainly is. I am a respectable man."

Sergeant Findlay entered the room and passed some documents to Owen, who mouthed "thanks Sarge," before handing them to his colleague. Rab studied the documents before continuing with the questions.

"On 5th October 2014, you returned to the UK, clearing customs at Heathrow. We have images of you travelling with a young lady." He passed the images across the desk. The woman's face could not be seen. "You escorted this young lady through immigration." He showed him another image. He said nothing, but Rab could see from his expression that he was becoming concerned as the evidence mounted. "We checked with immigration, and they gave us details of the passport for this young lady." He slid another piece of paper across the desk with a copy of the passport. "Who is this young lady that you escorted into the UK?" He was unresponsive for a minute and Rab just let the silence hang as he stared at him, willing him to answer.

"It's my niece, on my sister's side."

"Why were you bringing her into the country and where is she now?"

"She needed some work and wanted to learn English, so we agreed she could live with us, without paying rent, if she did some housework."

"But where is she now?" Rab asked.

"Within three months of moving into our home, she ran off with a boyfriend. We haven't seen her since."

"Does your sister know her daughter has done this?"

"Yes. We told her when it happened, and she was furious. But what could we do? We couldn't keep her locked up all day. When she left, we didn't know where she had gone."

"Okay. So, you admit that a young lady *was* living in your house, and she was doing maid work for you. So why did you lie to us before? Why would you need to hide this from us?"

“I felt ashamed that we had failed to look after my niece. I didn’t want to admit this.”

“Mr Mukherjee. I don’t believe you. I think this young woman was not your niece, but Aaheli Lohani from Sonagachi – known to you as Kittu – travelling on a false passport. I think you brought her into this country to act as a domestic slave and to continue providing sexual services to you.”

“No. no. That’s not true. It was my niece.” He folded his arms again, fuming that the policeman continued to call him mister, then looked at the solicitor, who indicated that he should say no more.

Rab passed another paper across the desk. A picture of Aaheli. He shifted the passport copy to sit next to the picture so they could be seen side by side. “This photo is of Aaheli Lohani. You must agree these two pictures are of the same woman.”

Mukherjee shrugged, and his solicitor spoke. “I think I had better have some time with my client, given the evidence that you’ve just produced.”

“Fine. Interview adjourned. But I will need details of this niece you claim to have brought into the UK. I already have her name from the passport, but you must provide her address.”

“I don’t remember the address,” he replied, refusing to take the paper.

“Not even the street or district?” He pushed the paper closer to Mukherjee. This time Mukherjee wrote on it and forcefully shoved it back.

Directly after leaving the interview room, Rab sent a WhatsApp message to Suzanna. ‘Mukherjee admitted bringing a woman into the UK. Says it is his niece, Malabika Ghosh, as shown on the passport used. Email to follow.’ He sat at his computer and fired off an email, giving details and attaching a copy of the woman’s passport.

Chapter 59

They stood across the dusty road from a four-storey concrete town-house with a flat roof in Kolkata's suburbs. It had been painted white at one time but was now dull and dirty. The doors and shutters were all painted in milk chocolate brown, but many were peeling.

"Assistant Superintendent Das. Good to see you again."

"Good to see you too, Suzanna di."

"You know, I still find it quaint how Bengali's add on the shortened version of didi, older sister, and dada, older brother, to denote respect whilst still using someone's first name. In the UK, we're either formal or informal, but the Bengali way is in between."

"It's been that way for many, many years. But it *is* changing. Fewer people use di and da. Mostly it is used when someone is older or might be older."

"Are you saying I look old?"

Das smiled. "Suzanna di, you have greying hair. In India, anyone with grey in their hair would be addressed with respect. The truth is that most Bengalis dye their hair black until they are ancient and can't be bothered or perhaps, they're widowed."

"Thanks for clarifying that," she said with a chuckle. "Shall we speak with Doctor Mukherjee's sister now?" She walked across the road, then pressed the bell-push. The door was opened by a short, dumpy woman. She looked to be several years younger than her brother. Das introduced himself and the British officers in Bengali, then asked in English if they could speak with her family. She stood back and invited them in, shouting into the house to inform them they had visitors. They sat in the sitting room, while Mrs Ghosh put water onto boil and instructed her daughter-in-law to make cha. Mr Ghosh came down the stairs, straightening his shirt.

"Mr Ghosh." Das nodded to the head of the household. "We need to ask some questions about your daughter, Malabika."

"Oh, my God." Mrs Ghosh looked like she'd seen a ghost. "What has happened to her? I only spoke with her this morning. Has she been knocked down by a bus?"

"No, Mrs Ghosh. Do not trouble yourself. We do not believe any calamity has befallen her."

"Why are you enquiring about our daughter, then?" Mr Ghosh asked.

"A young woman entered the UK several months ago, using a passport that had your daughter's name and date of birth. We checked the address given when the passport had been applied for and it was this house." He showed her a copy of the passport.

"That's not my daughter! What is this? It must be a fraud. I am sure my daughter has never applied for a passport. She's never left the country. But how could they use these details?"

"Where is your daughter, now, Mr Ghosh?"

"She married last year. She is living with her husband and his family, here in Kolkata... You will need her address." He rose and retrieved an address book, then showed the relevant page to the police officer.

"Thank you, dada. We will visit your daughter forthwith. But first, I must ask about your brother, Mrs Ghosh."

"Which one?"

"Jeetu. Doctor Jeetu Mukherjee," Suzanna said.

The Ghoshes turned to face the British detective, who had until then been quiet.

"What about Jeetu?" Mrs Ghosh asked, looking concerned.

"I understand he is a regular visitor to Kolkata. Do you know where he stays when he visits the city?"

"He stays with us. He comes twice yearly."

"And he was here for Durga Puja, last year?"

"Yes, yes. He never misses the puja. It is the biggest festival in West Bengal."

"I know. I visited many pandals when I was last in Kolkata – pandal-hopping, I think you call it? Some of them are incredible."

"Yes, yes. They are wonderful, aren't they? I'm on the committee that organises the pandal near here, and all the celebrations." Cha was served to the guests, and biscuits were offered. Superintendent Das and Zahir accepted, but Suzanna declined the biscuits.

"So, your brother was definitely here in September-October 2014?"

"Yes. I just said so. Why do you ask this?"

Suzanna ignored the question. "Do you know anything about your brother's movements in the city when he visited you? He would stay for three weeks, I believe. That's a long time."

"Jeetu has many friends in Kolkata. He would meet with them regularly, but I don't know where he went. I only saw him when he was home with us."

"Did he leave on foot or by taxi?" Suzanna said, then sipped her cha.

"If he were going to the local club, he would walk, but otherwise a car would come to our door. Uber or Ola, not the yellow taxis, because you have to walk to the main road and try to hail one."

"Did your brother spend much time at home?"

"He would breakfast with us and would be here for dinner each night but most days he would be away from the house during the daytime. I still don't understand why you are asking about Jeetu. He is a good man. He is always kind to everyone."

Suzanna finished her cha and looked at her colleagues, who had also finished their drinks and biscuits. She looked at them quizzically, asking with her eyes whether they had any questions. "Mrs Ghosh," Das said, "You will have your brother's Indian phone number?"

She retrieved her phone from the next room. She looked up her brother's number and read it out to the officer, who noted it in his book. "Thank you for your time, Mr Ghosh, Mrs Ghosh. And thank you for the refreshments. We must go to visit your daughter now, to check some details with her."

"Just a minute, inspector. I'll call to see if she's in. She may have gone to the market." She called her daughter, then reported that Malabika was home.

Outside the house, Suzanna said, "If you check with Uber or Ola, they should have records of journeys that he made, which could tie in with his trips to Sonagachi."

"Exactly my thinking, didi. That's why I obtained his phone number. I'll get my team onto that now and we'll pass the information to you as soon as we have it."

"Excellent."

Chapter 60

They visited Malabika, now Mrs Debnath, and she confirmed she had never applied for a passport. She was about the same age and height as the murdered woman. There were even some similarities in her features. Aaheli, however, had been slim and attractive whereas Malabika was not as pretty and had already begun her journey to married chubbiness, having lost some of her youthful good looks. Das dropped Suzanna and Zahir at the airport. He reiterated that he would get information to her about Mukherjee's travels as soon as he had it, then shook her hand. "A pleasure working with you, didi."

"You too, dada. Thanks so much for your assistance."

They checked in and went through security and immigration to international departures. She looked up at the departures board and noted that their 19:10 flight was reported to be on schedule. The departures area was disappointing – just a few shops and no proper coffee shop. There were a couple of places serving instant coffee and clingfilm wrapped sandwiches and muffins, which Suzanna immediately rejected. They found a café that served proper coffee but in paper cups and when she drank it, found it to be bitter. She could see through to the Domestic Departures area and noted it had a comfortable-looking coffee shop – The Coffee Bean and Tea Leaf. She was envious of the domestic travellers.

As they waited to board their flight home, Suzanna scanned her official emails, then messaged Alistair and her team about progress made, before checking her personal inbox. James had responded to her last email, saying he understood that a murder investigation must need her undivided attention. Nonetheless, he still wished she could find a little more time to communicate with him. He was feeling shunned. He finished his email by saying he loved her and hoped to hear from her soon. Suzanna felt embarrassed that she'd not spoken with him recently and had parked his email, but she was still in two minds about what to do. Perhaps she should be open and honest with both men and say it would be best if they took a break. With time, if the bond between either of the men and her was strong enough, perhaps they would get back together. She drafted an email to James.

Hi James.

I'm sat in Kolkata's international airport waiting to board my flight back to the UK. The investigation has gone well, and we will probably soon be making arrests. Please keep this to yourself for the moment, as this is not yet known outside the police.

Sorry for having been uncommunicative recently. You're right that I have to focus my mind on the murder investigation and that focus has been productive. I could, though, have found the time to write to you if I'd tried. But something happened just before I left Edinburgh that has shaken me and left me wondering about our future. It's nothing you have done. This is about me and my feelings.

It wouldn't be right to tell you now in a cold email. You deserve to hear it from me, face to face. I'm sorry for dropping this vague, perhaps worrying information on you, but feel that I can no longer leave you hanging, thinking it's just the work that has kept us apart. It isn't.

I'll get in touch as soon as I'm back in Edinburgh and have some free time.

I am very fond of you, James.

Suzanna

Suzanna pondered whether to send it or review it before doing so. There came an announcement that her flight was ready for boarding. She clicked send.

* * *

Chapter 61

Wednesday 4th

Their plane landed at Edinburgh airport mid-morning the next day. Having already cleared immigration and customs at Heathrow, Suzanna and Zahir were soon out of the airport and grabbed a taxi to the police HQ at Fettes Avenue. Suzanna sent Zahir home to get some rest. The team would have to cope without him until tomorrow. But Suzanna went straight into work.

"DCI McLeod," came the call as she passed the Chief Superintendent's office. She backtracked and put her head around the door, hoping he might congratulate her on finding out who the victim was and the man who had brought her into the UK. She was disappointed.

"McLeod. You know my views on officers not abiding by the rules of our roads, don't you?" Suzanna nodded, realising she was in for a bollocking.

"Well, I've just had word that you were caught speeding three weeks ago on the A702. You were going nearly 30 mph over the speed limit. Two miles an hour faster and you'd have been banned from driving."

Suzanna's shoulders slumped. So much for being buoyant and motivated to do her job, instead of going straight home... "It's not good enough McLeod. I expect senior officers to set a better example.

If your team gets to hear about this, what sort of standard do you think that will set?"

"I'm sorry, sir. It was a one-off event. I'd just overtaken a long lorry and hadn't noticed my speed climb. I was still speeding when the constable caught me with his radar gun. It won't happen again."

"It had better not. And why, pray, were you away in India so long? How long does it take to track down a prostitute?" He said in a tone, perhaps suggesting the woman was of low value.

Suzanna sighed. "Sir, I could not have been quicker. I went to Dhaka first and drew a blank, then Kolkata. The city police were friendly but actually uncooperative. I had to seek help from two NGOs that I know work in anti-human trafficking and the State Police. We had to visit the victim's family to ascertain who trafficked her into Kolkata, so we could find out where she went in the red-light district."

"Even so. Surely you could have been back yesterday. How long can it take to track down someone?"

"Kolkata has over *fifteen million* residents and the largest red-light district, Sonagachi, has an estimated *10,000* sex workers. Flight times between Scotland and Bengal are twenty hours plus. Do the maths!"

"Don't get stroppy with me, McLeod. I didn't know it was that big. At least you didn't come back empty-handed, even if you did take your time." He harrumphed and went back to what he was doing. Suzanna rolled her eyes as she continued on her way to the main office to catch up with the team. She'd be glad when he moved on from his job into retirement. He may have been an asset to the Force some years before, but he seemed to have become a burden in recent times, hampering and demotivating his staff.

* * *

Suzanna logged onto her computer and scanned the emails. She opened the one from Kolkata. Das had the records from Ola, proving that Mukherjee had travelled to and from Sonagachi on many occasions, including on the day and time of Kittu's disappearance. She marched into the main office and addressed the team. "Hi, folks."

"Welcome back boss," Rab responded.

"Right. I want us to speed things up now. We have proof that Doctor Mukherjee brought the dead woman into the country, using a passport in his niece's name. So far, he's only admitted to bringing his niece into the country and says that she ran off with a boyfriend. What we don't have yet is evidence that the victim lived with the Mukherjees. So, we need to do that next. Rab. You arrange a warrant..." She saw his face. "You've already done it, haven't you?"

He nodded and mouthed "Aye."

"Well done, Rab. What will the search concentrate on?"

"As you said, boss, evidence that the victim lived with them. I've arranged for Forensic Services to attend and look for DNA matching the vic. We'll also be looking for any signs of the attack on the woman – damage to furniture or fittings and bodily fluids, for example."

"Do you have the warrant yet?"

"Yes, boss; and the CSIs will be ready to roll at 1 pm."

"Great stuff, Rab. I'll come with you to the house."

Chapter 62

An overpowering smell of bleach hit Suzanna's nostrils as she opened the cellar door, dressed in a white suit and overshoes. Underneath the chlorine stench, the whiff of faeces and urine mixed with cheap perfume hung in the air. This is where the woman will have fallen to her pre-murder paralysis, her neck broken by the dive, down the precipitous brick stairs.

The poor woman. She must have laid at the bottom of these stairs, unable to move, smelling her own bodily fluids and knowing she was at the mercy of her attacker. From what the forensics department had reported, she was still alive when her face was pulverised and when she was dumped in the water. It didn't bear thinking about...

* * *

As the water filled her lungs, Aaheli felt sad that she'd not lived long. She hadn't experienced real joy since she was thirteen years old when a boy that she fancied had smiled at her. She'd skipped along the mud track to her thatched home, happy to have been noticed. But when her brother reported this to his father, he had slapped her across the face, for having unworthy thoughts. He'd reminded her that only he would select whom she would marry. She must never think she could choose her own partner. Could never have a boyfriend.

Aaheli had cried for ages after that event – an incident that changed her outlook on life. No longer carefree, she'd become depressed, realising that she had no power over her future. She would never love and marry as they did in the Bollywood movies. She would have to do as her father ordered.

Her heart hadn't been in her schoolwork after that. There seemed little point. She would just be assigned to another man. To be his slave, to bear his children, to cook and clean. She'd seen it in her own mother. Married to her father when she was just fifteen and having never met him before the wedding. He was a man thirteen years her senior. He'd treated her like dirt; as a servant or slave. It dawned on Aaheli that day that her life was not her own. She would be owned and controlled by a man, and she didn't know who that would be.

Two years later, the unknown uncle had come to her family home, and she had been called to a meeting around the cooking fire. By then, she'd come to accept that she would do whatever her father directed. She accepted the need to go to the city to work to provide for her family. She couldn't have known what would happen to her in Kolkata.

The journey had been exciting. First the bus to Berhampore – a journey she had only done twice before, escorting her mother to the hospital to visit a gynaecologist and then for treatment. The train station had been teaming with men and women, the queue for tickets stretching back along the road. Uncle had bought her cha, and she'd drunk the sweet, milky tea with pleasure.

They'd been jammed into the rail carriage like cigarettes in a packet, hardly room to move their arms and nowhere to sit for the five-hour journey. Even without the space for passengers to move, hawkers still squashed their way into the carriages and forced their way through, selling their wares. Musicians and magicians boarded the train but only plied the first- and second-class carriages, where they had more room to operate and greater wealth to draw on for their income.

She had been bursting for a pee by the time they'd reached Sealdah railway station, but 'uncle' wouldn't let go. Instead, he led her out of the station and onto the first bus that was heading up the wide highway, running past the station. They left the bus a few minutes later and boarded a tuk-tuk which took them past markets and more shops than she'd ever seen in her fifteen years.

Finally, they'd walked into a teeming area of the city just beyond the Girish Park metro station. When they arrived at her new home, the kindly looking fat woman had shown her to a toilet where she'd relieved herself. Then the nightmare had begun...

After Aaheli had used the bathroom and eaten, she had been locked into a windowless room. When Aunty returned, a man was with her – a man as old as her father, his belly hanging over his trouser waistband. His white sleeveless vest had been grubby and wet with sweat. Black curly hair clung to his exposed chest, and his head hair had been a matted mess. He'd looked like the villain she'd seen in a movie on a neighbour's TV.

They'd ordered her to strip off all her clothes. She had refused, but they had torn the clothes from her body, leaving her naked. She'd curled herself into a ball, trying to cover her intimate parts, as the man stared at her, smirking, before he and Aunty left. Aaheli had been scared, embarrassed, shocked by this treatment. She had wept and called for her mum, but no one came.

Later they had returned. She'd tried to fight them off, but the man had slapped her, then punched and kicked her. Aunty had held her over a bench while he forced himself into her from behind like she'd seen dogs do it. She screamed as he ripped away her virginity, the pain and humiliation causing her blossoming womanhood to wither like a flower under a harsh drought. He was to be her babu - the man who would control her, bring her customers, rape her occasionally and beat her often.

The sex didn't last long – probably just two minutes, but it had been the worst two minutes of her life. Afterwards, she cried and cried until she ran out of tears. She'd sobbed as she called for her mum to comfort her. She'd cursed her father for sending her with the man who came to their home in Murshidabad. And Aaheli had lost all hope in the future.

* * *

"Guys, Suzanna called out," and when Rab and the CSIs arrived: "I want you to focus on this area first."

"Why's that, boss?"

"Can't you smell it? The bleach, suggesting a clean-up operation. And underneath that the aroma of a toilet, no doubt left from when the victim's bowel and bladder had voided after she broke her neck." Rab sniffed the air again, but could only smell the bleach. The female forensics officer started gathering evidence in the cellar.

"We believe there may have been a physical altercation leading to the victim becoming paralysed," Suzanna said to the other forensics man. "We need evidence of that: DNA, damaged furniture, doors, etc. You know the sort of thing." He nodded and wandered off to look around.

Chapter 63

"Mrs Mukherjee, I'm Detective Chief Inspector McLeod. I'm leading the investigation into the death of the young Indian woman, who was found on the banks of the Forth. Having read the transcripts of your initial interview and I have more questions for you. You will appreciate that aiding the trafficking of an illegal immigrant is a serious offence, likely to result in a prison sentence."

Mrs Mukherjee had defiance written across her face. "I told your constable before. We have no live-in maid, just a cleaner who has been coming in twice weekly."

"Which days of the week does this cleaner work for you, Mrs Mukherjee?"

She thought before answering. "Tuesdays and Fridays."

"There are three things that cause me to doubt the truth of what you've told us. First: we spoke with the lady that you suggested had recommended the cleaner, and she says she never suggested one. Second: you can't even recall the cleaner's name. And third: we've spoken to neighbours, and they have confirmed they regularly saw a young woman at the windows of your house – not just on Tuesdays and Fridays. You are lying to us, Mrs Mukherjee."

She looked flustered. "I couldn't remember the cleaner's name, but I do now. It's Kittu. It must have been another friend who recommended her. She doesn't always come on the same days each week. Sometimes she comes on other days, but normally it's the days I told you. I'm not lying." Suzanna smiled internally as she heard the name of the supposed cleaner.

"I've just returned from Kolkata, Mrs Mukherjee, and we now have significant evidence that your husband fraudulently obtained a passport, using Kittu's picture and his niece's details. Based on this evidence, we obtained a warrant to search your home and we have found evidence that a woman has been living in your cellar. I think it's time that you admitted Kittu has been living with you."

She re-crossed her arms tightly, her plump breasts bulging upwards. "I shall speak no more until I have a solicitor to advise me..."

Chapter 64

Thursday 5th

"Mr Mukherjee, I am..."

"Not you as well. How many times do I have to tell you people? I am *Doctor* Mukherjee – not *mister*. You must show me the proper respect.

Suzanna stared at him. "Respect is not something that goes with a title. It has to be earned and can be lost. In your case, you do not deserve the respect that goes with the title. Do you believe that a man who cheats on his wife with prostitutes regularly for many years deserves respect? Do you believe that a man who commits fraud and traffics a woman into this country deserves respect? Perhaps you might believe that even though you used this woman as your slave, for your sexual pleasure, you still deserve respect. Even if *you* do, no-one can believe you merit respect, having taken her life."

"No. These things are not true. I did not murder Kittu."

"So, you admit you brought Miss Lohani into the UK on a false passport and kept her in your home?"

He sighed and slumped back in his chair. It creaked under his weight. "Look. I admit I brought Kittu into the UK. She was trapped in slavery, having to service several strangers every day and was regularly beaten by the brothel madam and her babu. I wanted to help her get away from this slavery and give her a better life here in Scotland. I know it was wrong, technically, but I did it for her good. She was to live with us in return for domestic work."

"Are you trying to tell me that although you paid Kittu for sexual services multiple times over 3-4 years, once you had her in your own home, you did not expect exclusive services from her?"

"I just wanted to help her," he said, his eyes welling up like a little boy who'd been caught stealing.

"It is unbelievable that you would not have received sexual services from your resident prostitute, and a jury will certainly see through your lies. Let's not waste any more time, *Mr* Mukherjee. Tell us the truth."

He leant forward, placing his arms on the table, and looked straight at his interviewer, seething. "*Doctor* Mukherjee."

He sat back, and his solicitor whispered in his ear. He nodded his head but paused before speaking. "Very well. I brought Kittu into my home as a humanitarian act, to help her escape the sex trade. Although I had paid her for sex, I felt compassion for the young woman, so offered her domestic work. I went to great expense to bring her to Edinburgh and gave her a place to sleep and food in her belly. All we asked was that she would keep the house clean and do the laundry. But she was with us for just two months when she ran away. We haven't seen her since December."

"Lies. More lies. I cannot bring myself to call you doctor. And when you are in prison, you will be called Mukherjee, not even Mister Mukherjee. Mukherjee, do this. Mukherjee, go there. Mukherjee, get back to your cell. You are a *trafficker* and a *murderer*." Suzanna turned away from the man, paused, then faced him again.

"Let's go back to the night that you dumped Aaheli or Kittu into the Forth. You said you had been to a restaurant in Alloa. We confirmed this with the restaurant staff. You were booked in at 8:30 pm. The staff couldn't remember exactly what time you left. So, we had nothing to dispute your assertions that you left at 11 pm. But we now have evidence to the contrary." She laid two photos from CCTV on the table. "Here is the picture of you and your wife in the car crossing Kincardine bridge at 11:12 pm."

Mukherjee looked at the image but just shrugged his shoulders. Suzanna laid another image on the table, turning it so he could see. "This one was from a camera in Alloa. You will note the date and time logged on the image."

Mukherjee saw the time and Suzanna could tell his mind was trying to work out an answer to the question she was about to ask. "So, as you left Alloa at 10:38, not 11 pm, as you told us before, you would have reached Kincardine around 10:50. So what were you doing in the spare twenty minutes, Mr Mukherjee?"

The doctor slouched back into the chair. Mairi opened the door and passed Suzanna some documents. She sat and scanned their content, while the accused sat waiting. "I now have the forensics analysis results of evidence removed from your home, your car, and from the victim's body. We know that shortly before her death, Aaheli pleasured you, Mukherjee. We have a DNA match to you; from semen taken from the woman's throat."

The solicitor looked shocked and peered sideways at his client. "It's pointless denying it. She lived in your home until the day she breathed her last breath, as the water filled her lungs. And, as I suggested, you had been using her as a sex slave. You will be convicted of trafficking and slavery under the Modern Slavery Act."

Suzanna re-read one of the documents, then continued. "So, there is no doubt you trafficked the woman and used her as a sex slave. Worse still, you murdered her. We have evidence that her paralysed body lay in your car boot just before she was tipped into the water – fibres from the carpeting were in her lungs and her blood was in the car."

She paused before continuing. "She must have laid in the car boot all that time while you and your wife were eating in the restaurant – paralysed, unable to move or speak, while you and your wife chatted and enjoyed the good food. *How cold can you get*? You had broken her neck, then smashed in her face with a rock before dumping her in the Forth estuary, to drown."

He jumped up. "No, it wasn't like that. I didn't kill her. My wife caught Kittu giving me pleasure. She dragged her by her hair and threw her down the stairs into the cellar where her room was located. We had a huge argument, but my wife forgave me. She doesn't like sex with me anymore, so really it didn't matter. I wasn't having sex with both women. Only one."

"When Rashmika went to speak with Kittu, she found her at the bottom of the stairs, her neck broken and paralysed. We didn't know what to do. We were scared. Rashmika said that if we called the ambulance, the authorities would find out what I had done, and I would go to jail. She convinced me we had to dispose of her." He broke down, sobbing. "I did not want this to happen. Kittu was my little flower. Like her name, she was lovable. She brought joy to my life, but my wife destroyed that when she pushed her down the stairs. That was what killed her. Even if we had called for an ambulance, she would have been a vegetable for the rest of her life. What sort of life is that? Better that she move on and be reincarnated. That was much more humane."

"What you did to young Aaheli was an act of inhumanity, not for the good of the woman. You pummelled her face with a piece of rock, while she was alive and could feel the pain. How dare you suggest this was a humane act!"

"No, no. I did *not* do that. My wife picked up the rock, sat astride her and destroyed her face. I cried when she did it. I didn't want to go ahead with our plan. But there was no going back... I'm sorry..." He broke down again, sobbing. Suzanna stood and instructed her team to lock him up, and walked out of the room. Next, the wife.

She returned to her office and closed the door. Sitting in her chair, she pondered her next move, satisfied that Doctor Mukherjee had now confessed, but now she needed his wife to do the same.

Chapter 65

"Right, Mrs Mukherjee. This won't take long."

Mrs Mukherjee's face brightened, like a child who'd just been handed a present. "You will be releasing me?"

"Most definitely not. We will be charging you with serious offences. You will transfer from here to a woman's jail pending trial on modern slavery offences and murder." The smile left her face, and her complexion paled as the blood drained from it. She wilted into her chair.

"We have proof that your husband brought the young woman into the UK under a false passport in the name of his niece. We know Kittu lived in the cellar of your house until the day she died. We have forensic evidence that the young woman plunged down the stairs, having been shoved through the door by your hand, and at the base of the stairs broke her neck, leaving her paralysed. We also have evidence that she was transported to her death in the boot of your husband's car, proof of the car's presence at the dumping site, and proof that you were with him at the time that you dumped her into the Forth."

"What proof? This isn't true."

"The hair you ripped from Kittu's head as you dragged her to the cellar was found in clumps in your husband's study, and by the cellar door and some of this hair was also found on one of your cardigans. Skin fragments and blood left marks on the cellar walls and stairs. The mud on your shoes matches the soil at the dumping site. Need I go on?"

"I don't know what you mean. Why would I drag her from my husband's study to the cellar?"

"Because you caught Kittu kneeling in front of your husband, as he orgasmed into her mouth. We found his semen in her throat." Mrs Mukherjee cringed, probably embarrassed to hear such things talked about openly. Suzanna paused, giving time for the accused to assimilate the facts. "Your husband has already confessed, Mrs Mukherjee. To make life easier for us all, why don't you tell us what happened. Your sentence will be shorter if you plead guilty." The solicitor asked for sight of the forensics reports, scanned them, then whispered to his client.

"It is true. I found my husband with that young slut. His trousers at his ankles and ecstasy on his face. I was outraged. Yes, I grabbed her and escorted her to the cellar stairs. I let her go and ordered her to her room. I didn't throw her down the stairs, she must have stumbled and fell."

"Rashmika. It means ray of light, doesn't it Mrs Mukherjee?" The woman nodded in confirmation. "I think you are *no* ray of light but a bringer of darkness. Given your history of lies, I don't believe that Kittu stumbled and fell. I think you pushed the girl down those hard, steep stairs, meaning to harm her." She paused, then softened her tone as she continued. "But let's just suppose that to be the truth... What happened next?"

Mrs Mukherjee took a minute to recover from Suzanna's accusations before answering. "I argued with my husband for a long time, but I forgave him in the end... He is a weak man. He cannot control his urges, and I didn't want him pawing over me anyway – at my age." She paused again. "Later, I went to speak with the girl, but she was lying crumpled at the bottom of the stairs, unmoving. She was stinking of toilet smells. My God! I had to clean it up after we moved her." She seemed to relive that disgusting moment. Lowering herself to cleaning up the woman's excrement and urine.

"She was as good as dead. No one could have saved her. It was an accident. But we had to take her away from our house to let her pass on, and her soul to find a new home. She would have been trapped in a useless body for many years if we had reported the accident. Better that she be given another chance in a new body – samsara."

"Samsara?"

"Reincarnation. It is a major tenet of our faith."

"But the woman was Muslim, not Hindu!"

"No. My husband would never have taken a Muslim woman for sex. Her name was Kittu. She must have been Hindu."

"I met with her family in Murshidabad District. I can assure you they are Muslims, and the woman you murdered is named Aaheli. Kittu was her working name in Sonagachi."

"Oh my God. Oh my God." She started howling, "What have I done?"

Suzanna allowed her time to settle before asking the next question, softly, as if sympathising with her predicament. "What were you thinking when you had Kittu by the water? ...Kittu had brought the situation on herself by engaging in sex with your husband, then falling down the stairs. If she were found, and the face matched with immigration records, they would lead back to your house, and your life would be wrecked. Was that it?"

Mrs Mukherjee sobbed. It had caught up with her. Everything she had worked for. She had married well, lived a respectable life. She'd done charitable works, but because of her husband's weakness and this slut's willingness to serve him, her life was in tatters.

"So you grabbed the rock and smashed the woman's face so she would not be easily recognised?" Mrs Mukherjee nodded. "For the record, the accused has nodded, acknowledging that she used the rock to disfigure the victim's face before dumping her in the water. That is correct, is it not, Mrs Mukherjee?"

"Yes... For God's sake, just leave me alone. I did it. I did it. I didn't know what else to do. It was so unfair. My husband is to blame. He caused this situation by bringing that dirty whore into our home."

"Interview adjourned." Suzanna switched off the recording. She stood, then leant on the table, staring down at Mrs Mukherjee.

"That dirty whore of whom you speak was an innocent girl from Murshidabad District. She was from an extremely poor family that was tricked into letting their daughter go to Kolkata to be a maid and send money home to feed the family. But when she got to Kolkata, she was stripped, beaten, locked away in a windowless room and raped multiple times until she gave in to her fate."

She paused. "She was no whore... She was a victim, and *your* husband was one of the many thousands of men who feed that evil industry and encourage traffickers to take more girls and degrade them and steal their lives from them. You and your kind, with your undeserved attitude of superiority, *disgust me.*" She walked away, leaving Mrs Mukherjee sobbing.

Chapter 66

Suzanna felt satisfied, proud of her work in identifying the victim, the traffickers, and the murderers. It was this feeling that made detective work so worthwhile – knowing she was doing good, knowing she was taking criminals off the street, knowing she was gaining justice for the victims. She couldn't bring the young woman back to life, but at least she could ensure the people who mistreated her got what they deserved.

"Alistair," Suzanna said as she tapped on his open office door. "We've got confessions from both of the Mukherjees, now. The woman was the one who caused the original injury and paralysis, and she was the instigator of disposing of the woman and the one who disfigured her face before they dumped her in the Forth. But they're both guilty of her murder."

"Sterling work, Suzanna. Well done. You'll be due a couple of days off once you've written up your reports."

"Yes. I'm thinking of taking a week off, anyway. I'm due some leave."

"You do that," Alistair said as he stood. "I have a meeting with the Chief Super. Budgets!" Suzanna rolled her eyes, turned, and went off to grab a mug of coffee and find Angus.

"Hi, guv. I hear you've had a result with the murder case."

"Yes. Husband and wife, both guilty of murder. I think the case against them is solid. So, happy with that. How are you getting on with catching Una's attacker?"

"The little weasel keeps giving us the slip and going to ground. We're certain he had gone to his parents' house in Danderhall, but when we went to arrest him, he'd already left. We're not sure where he is now, but every officer in Scotland has been passed his details and should be looking out for him."

"*Just* Scotland?"

"Aye. As far as we can tell he doesn't like to go far, so we're assuming he's within Scotland."

"There's a saying my dad used to remind me of regularly. It came from his aircraft engineering days: Don't assume; check."

"But we have to make assumptions, at least initially... Okay, point taken. As we still haven't found him, we should open out the search and ask the forces in England to look out for him."

"Sounds like a sensible next move. Good luck with that Angus. Keep me posted." She returned to her office and picked up the phone... "Steve. It's Suzanna. I have an update for you on the 'Washed-up Woman' case..."

Chapter 67

Friday 6th

"Morning, Guv," Angus said as Suzanna entered the kitchenette. She noted Murray was dressed in a polo shirt and jeans. "I see you've still not entered into the spirit of dress-down Fridays, then!"

"Don't be cheeky, Angus," she retorted. "You know very well that I believe jogging bottoms and sweatshirts are for the leisure time only, not the office. Actually, you're well out-of-order given your well-pressed chinos and smart shirt. What's gotten into you?"

"Good point, Guv, but I have a reason. I'm meeting someone straight after work today – assuming we get off at the planned time," he said, hopefully, with an expectant grin on his face.

"I reckon he's on a promise, tonight," chimed in Murray.

"Well, you never know your luck. She certainly seemed keen last time we met. I've been a perfect gentleman both times we've been together. I've not attempted to grope her and haven't passed wind in her presence yet," Angus said, smiling.

"Too much detail, Angus," Suzanna said as she turned and wandered back to her office.

"I should hope not, boss," added Owen, raising his voice as she walked away, "especially if you'd drunk any beer the night before or had beans for lunch. Did you hear that factoid on Radio 2 the other day? Apparently, the average human farts fourteen times a day!"

Suzanna just ignored them and kept walking. She had to put up with a bit of crudeness in this job. It was still predominantly a male-dominated environment and, like the Army, when men got together having been through dangerous or stressful situations, their camaraderie bloomed and their language blued.

* * *

Caitlin sat, sipping her second coffee of the morning. She'd overheard the lads talking about farting and was glad she'd not been trapped in the room with them. It was Friday, and unless anything urgent came up today, she'd get out for an evening with her pals. It was her best friend's hen party tonight, and she'd hate to miss out on the pre-wedding fun. She'd already picked out the clothes and jewellery she was planning to wear. A night on the town was well overdue. The phone rang. "Sergeant Findlay, Edinburgh CID." She listened for a minute, then turned to Angus. "Boss. How do you fancy a trip to Carlisle?"

"No thanks. Why do you ask?"

"They've got Muir in custody."

"Bloody hell. That's brilliant. Tell them we're on the way."

Caitlin ended the call and grabbed her things. "Your car or mine?"

"Let's take a fleet car. I don't want to put the miles on mine, and your Fiesta's a bit noisy at motorway speeds."

"Fair enough." She booked out an unmarked police car, then met Angus in the car park. They drove off smiling, but also both apprehensive that this development might interfere with their evening plans.

* * *

Just over two hours later, Caitlin turned off the M6 motorway and followed sat nav directions into the outskirts of Carlisle. Fortunately, they didn't have to go into the city centre, as that would have added at least an hour onto their return journey. They turned off into an industrial estate and followed the road to its end, passing multiple warehouses and workshops before they came to the police HQ.

Angus approached the desk. "Detective Inspector Watson from Edinburgh, he said, showing the desk sergeant his warrant card. This is Detective Sergeant Findlay. We're here to interview Fraser Muir. I understand he was brought in last night?"

"Welcome to England, sir. If you could just take a seat, I'll fetch DS Graham." Angus and Caitlin sat on the hard bench seat opposite the desk and waited. Angus wondered whether the DS was Robert Graham.

"Angus Watson, me old pal."

"Bob Graham," Angus said, standing. "I wondered if it was you when the deskie said he'd gone to fetch you."

"It's been a while, hasn't it?"

"Must be five years, pal."

"And it took the stabbing of your colleague to get us together again... " His voice quietened. "Sorry about that, by the way. How is Inspector Wallace?"

"She's still in a coma. The knife was six inches and sliced through her intestines and nicked her kidney. She's lucky to be alive."

"Shocking. Shocking." He turned to Caitlin. "Sorry, lass. Bob Graham. And you are?"

Caitlin shook his hand. "DS Caitlin Findlay. So how far back do you two go?"

"We were constables at the same time. I started my career in Glasgow." He paused. "You'd best come on through. I've something you're gonna be pleased to see." They followed Bob through into his office and he pulled an evidence bag out of a draw. "Would that be about the right sized knife?"

"It certainly would."

"He had it on him when we picked him up. Let's not waste any more time. I know you've over two hours to drive back once he's handed over to you. I'll get him out of the cells. Just give us a minute." He walked off, leaving them in the office, so they sat and waited for his return.

Chapter 68

Bob popped his head around the door five minutes later. "He's in Interview Room 1." He held the door open and they followed him down the corridor. As Angus entered the room, he saw Muir's mouth silently say, 'Oh fuck,' to himself, and he dropped his head into his chest.

"Finally, Fraser Muir, I get the opportunity to speak with you. Why have you run off every time you saw me? Am I that ugly, pal, or were you just in a hurry to be with someone else?" Angus said casually.

"Aye. Something like that. I did'nae even know who you were."

"So why would you run from someone unless you thought they were a threat to you? Do I look like I'm from a rival drugs gang?"

Muir laughed at the suggestion. "No. Yer must be pissed if you think yer look like anything other than polis."

Angus was pleased that Muir had not denied being involved in drugs. "Well then, Fraser. Why did you run from the polis?" He didn't answer immediately, but they let the question hang, waiting for Muir to fill the silence.

"I was worried you'd try to pin something on me."

"Now, why would we want to do that?" Caitlin said.

"I don't know. You lot just grab anyone who fits the bill and fit them up."

"You've been watching too many police dramas on the TV, Fraser.

It doesn't work like that in real life. Nor do we beat the shit out of you until you gab." Angus paused again. "Now that we're finally together, I'm sure you'd be happy to answer a few questions. You being innocent of any crimes..." Muir didn't respond. He just waited for the question that would follow.

"I'd like to take you back to Tuesday the 9th. That was before you ran away, Fraser. Can you remember that far back?"

"Course I can. I'm no stupid."

"Tell me about that day."

"Well. It was just an ordinary day. Went to work, earned a crust, shagged me girlfriend, then slumped in front of the TV."

"And what work is it you do Fraser. Who's your employer?"

"I don't have an employer, I'm self-employed. You know. Sole trader."

"What's your trade, Fraser? Builder, Plumber, Scaffolder, Freelance Journalist?"

Muir smirked at the idea of him being a journalist – he flunked English at school. "I'm a trader. I buy things and sell things. Make a profit, you know."

"Give me an example of the things you trade, Fraser."

"Just things. Whatever I come across that seems cheap, and I can make a couple of pounds on."

"So, you don't trade in women then – you know, human trafficking?"

He sat up, his shoulders moving swiftly back. "No way, pal. I'd never do that stuff. Slavery's not my thing. Those traffickers are bastards."

"What about drug dealers, then? Aren't they bastards too?"

"They're just supplying a product. It's nae different to selling beer or whisky. Supply and demand. That's capitalism, ain't it. Someone wants something, you supply it and make a profit. That's how the world goes around."

"Let's move away from philosophy and back to reality. As a trader. If someone threatens to take your product away from you, you defend yourself; right?"

"Of course you do. If someone steals from your shop, you don't just watch them walk out the door and run away, do yer?"

"None of us would do that, would we? Unless we were cowards. And you're no coward, are you, Fraser? When you run, it's not because you're afraid – afraid to fight that is? You just don't want your product or livelihood taken from you. That's right, isn't it?"

"Aye. That's right. I'm no coward. I'll stick anyone who tries to steal my stuff."

"And is this what you use to stick them with, Fraser," Angus said placing the large knife on the table. "That *is* your knife, isn't it?"

"There's no point in me denying it. Cause this lot took it from my pocket. But I've never actually cut anyone with it. It's just for show, to ward off the guys who would stick me, to take my stuff. Check it. It will be clean."

"Oh, we *will* check it, don't you worry. And if there's the tiniest trace of blood on it, then we'll know you've been lying, won't we." Muir sat quietly, a worried look on his face.

"Let's go back to Tuesday the 9th again. We have a witness who says they saw you trading near a set of garages in Restalrig, about 9 am. The witness told us you were selling your product to school kids... What was it you were selling to these children, Fraser?"

He smirked before answering. "Just sweeties, Inspector. Sweeties. You know gummy bears, sherbet fizz, love hearts, that sort of stuff." He leaned back in his chair, smiling.

"Do you remember when an older person turned up? She would have been a woman of about thirty. But she wasn't a customer was she, Fraser, and she was threatening to take away your livelihood." Muir sat with his arms crossed, his face sternly set.

"In fact, this woman, as you well know, was a policewoman. A detective. And she'd seen you dealing to kids. And she was going to arrest you, wasn't she? You couldn't have that, could you? You took your knife out of your pocket and stuck her with it, didn't you?" He stood leaning on the table, staring down at Muir. "You stuck this 6-inch blade into her gut and ran off, leaving her to die. DIDN'T YOU?"

Angus paced around the room, then sat again, pausing before continuing in a softer tone. "You know, Fraser, it might have been better if you'd killed her because then she wouldn't be able to identify you as the attacker. You should have stayed and finished the job, you coward. But instead, you ran."

"I'm no coward. But I'm no murderer. I stuck her so I could get away. I did'nae mean to kill her."

"Thank you for confessing to the unlawful wounding of a police officer. Perhaps we can drop the attempted murder charge, now." Muir looked relieved at what Angus had just said but realised he'd just admitted to the stabbing. He slumped in his chair, his head on his chest, looking like a pup that had just been chastised for pooping in the corner – Its tail between its legs.

"But then again, perhaps I should leave the jury to decide whether it was attempted murder. Fraser Muir. I am charging you with..."

Chapter 69

Angus left the interview room and checked with Bob Graham. "Can you get the paperwork completed ASAP, so we can get up the road? I'm on a promise tonight."

"What? Does your missus only let you have sex once a month?"

"I'm not with Erika anymore. We never married. Just as well."

"I thought you two were together for life?"

"It seemed pretty good in the beginning, but she turned out to be a jealous psycho."

"And you gave her no reason to be jealous?"

"No way. But every time I was late home, she accused me of being with another woman. It was like being trapped in a Stephen King book. She even said I was shagging my sergeant."

"What, Caitlin? I'd give her one, given a chance..." He stopped speaking mid-sentence as the door that had stood ajar opened fully and Caitlin entered the office. Bob went red, then added, "If I wasn't happily married of course."

Caitlin had heard what he'd said just before she'd opened the door and grinned quietly to herself as she recognised his embarrassment at being caught out. She could have given him some lip about it but pretended she'd not heard his sexist comment. Some women would have been offended, but she saw it was a compliment – if a bit of a crude one. "Time we were hitting the road, boss."

"Aye. You're right. Let's get him processed and loaded into the car. I've a mind to put him in the boot. But I guess that would be frowned upon."

"I agree on both counts, boss." She smiled as she looked at her watch. Hen night still on then, unless something went wrong.

* * *

When Una opened her eyes, it was a hospital room she saw. Clinically clean, sparse, white, echoey. The dream world she'd been in faded away, and she looked around. A half-eaten punnet of grapes sat on the bedside locker. Flowers were wilting in a vase on the windowsill. She moved an arm, realising that she was hooked up to machines, so lay still again. How had she got here? She remembered the attack - the panic she felt when she'd been laying on the ground, her hand over the stomach wound, with blood pouring through her fingers. Una cautiously lifted the bedclothes to see clean dressings around her midriff.

There had been a tip-off that drugs were being dealt, and she had gone to investigate. She'd tried to call for backup but failed and took a risk. A risk that had resulted in bad consequences. What a fool she'd been. Una recalled how she'd tried to arrest the dealer, but with hindsight had been overconfident in her abilities and under-assessed his willingness to use a knife. She had felt a hard punch to her abdomen. She only felt the knife as he pulled it from her body and felt the pain deep within. Her eyes became wet as she realised her life could have ended that day.

She would be more careful in future... What if there were no future? What if her injuries resulted in her being declared unfit for duty - permanently? Oh, God! She hoped not. She loved her job. Tears rolled from her eyes, and she sobbed... Her mind wandered around the idea of her police career being ended. What would she do? She had no business skills. She drifted off to sleep again but was woken a few minutes later by the sound of a voice.

"Hello, Una. I'm Nurse Maureen. Good to see that you're back with us again."

Una opened her eyes and saw the smiling face of the woman in her cornflower-blue uniform. She still felt groggy, unable to think clearly. "Hello. Have you been looking after me?"

"Yes, dear."

"Thank you. What day is it?"

"Friday."

It took her a minute before she responded. "Oh, so I've been asleep for three *days*."

"No dear. You've been unconscious for two-and-a-half *weeks*." Una was shocked. "Should I inform your family and colleagues? They've been visiting regularly."

"Yes, please, and could I get a drink and something to eat?"

"Of course, dear. I'll be back in a minute." She left – the smell of antiseptic wafting behind her. Una drifted off again.

Chapter 70

The sun broke through the cloud and lightened the office as Suzanna walked in. "Angus. Have you finished processing Muir? If so, you may wish to come with me? Una has come out of her coma."

"Caitlin, you can finish off the last bits of admin, can't you?"

"Sure, boss. You go and see Una." Angus grabbed his coat and followed Suzanna out of the building.

* * *

Una smiled weakly as her two colleagues approached the hospital bed, Suzanna clutching a bouquet and Angus a fresh punnet of red grapes. She was propped up, watching TV, but picked up the controller and switched it off as they came closer.

"Una. So good to see you back in the land of the living. You had us worried. How are you feeling?" Suzanna asked.

"Sore. I can't change my position in bed without assistance. They say there's still a risk that I'll tear the wound open if I try shifting around by myself. And my head hurts. I bet I look like crap, don't I?"

"You'd find it difficult to pull a fella if you went nightclubbing, without doing your hair, but you look amazing, considering what you've been through."

"Yeah. Thanks, Angus. Really confidence-boosting words," she said, rolling her eyes.

"I have news that you'll wish to hear... The guy who attacked you is in custody. He's confessed to stabbing you."

Una's face brightened. "Good to hear that, Angus."

"For the record, then, was the man who stabbed you, Fraser Muir," Angus asked, showing her his mug shot.

"Who's Fraser Muir? That's not the guy who stabbed me."

Angus's face dropped. He'd spent the last couple of weeks chasing down the wrong man. And he'd confessed? Then he saw the corners of Una's mouth turn up. "Just teasing, Angus. Just teasing... Yes, for the record, I confirm that Fraser Muir was the man who stabbed me." She grinned. "Got yer."

Angus laughed, and Una couldn't help breaking into giggles. But she soon stopped herself, as pain in her gut told her that laughing was unwise. "I'm glad you're well enough to have some fun, Una," Suzanna commented. "Is there anything you need? Any supplies you'd like brought in – decent food, perhaps?"

"No thanks, boss. The food's okay here – well acceptable, anyway. I don't want any chocolate beside my bed, or my addiction will see me putting weight on again."

"There's no need to worry about that, Una. You were slim before you came into the hospital and you're even slimmer now."

"Are you saying I'm skinny?"

"No. Just extra slim – lean."

Una smiled. "I appreciate you coming to see me. But I'm sure you've more important things to be doing – it's a Friday night." Just then, a couple arrived. The 50-something woman was an older, greyer version of Una. The man had the look of a farmer: muscled, rugged, ruddy-faced, tousled hair. "Mum, Dad. Hi!" Una smiled, happy to see her parents.

"Hello, Mr and Mrs Wallace. We'll get out of your way," Suzanna said as she led Angus out of the room. She could hear tears of relief and nervous laughter, mixed with lots of chatting. She smiled. It was so good to know Una had pulled through.

* * *

As Suzanna and Angus arrived in the reception area, they heard shouting and screaming. A crowd of medical staff were trying to pull a man backwards. He appeared to be kicking out at something.

"Police. Out of the way. What's going on here?" Suzanna said as she pushed her way through the group.

On the floor was a man in a white dust-coat, curled into the foetal position, his arms covering his abdomen and his bloodied hands shielding his face. The angry man was still kicking out. "You negligent bastard. You won't even admit it. You took my son from me," he slurred.

Suzanna thought she recognised the man. She stepped in front of him, holding up her card. "Detective Chief Inspector McLeod. You're under arrest."

"You lot are as bad as him. You should arrest him for murder." The man threw off the arms that were trying to hold him back and took a swipe at Suzanna. She blocked his arm, grabbed his wrist, and twisted it, taking him off balance, then stepped forward, hooked a leg, and swept it from under him. He crashed to the floor on his back with a cry of pain as he hit the hard floor. Angus was by her side. He dropped to his knee, grabbed the man, and spun him onto his face, pulling his arms behind his back. Suzanna passed him her handcuffs, and he locked them in place.

"Does anyone know who this man is?" Suzanna asked.

The staff were unresponsive, but Angus spoke. "This fella is Billy Boyd's father. You know, the lad who stole your magnifying glass."

Now she knew why she recognised him. Billy's brother had been brought into this hospital following a road traffic accident. But why would the father be so angry?

One of the medical staff who'd stayed to give evidence spoke. "He was shouting about the doctor having murdered his son. About the doctor's negligence."

The nurse beside her added, "Doctor Wilson operated on this man's son. After he was released from hospital, he collapsed from a blood clot on the brain and died. That's what this is about. I know the man is drunk and must be dealt with for this assault, but he needs help as well – psychiatric help."

"You're probably right... Angus, get some uniform guys in here to take him in. We've got statements to gather." Angus took out his phone, but just as he hit the green button, he saw two officers walking towards them, so ended the call. Someone must have called it in.

Chapter 71

Alistair walked into Suzanna's office with a gentle tap on her door frame, then sat in the chair opposite her. "I just wanted to reiterate my thanks for a good result on the Bengali murder case."

"Thanks, Alistair. Having spent time in Kolkata before, when I was on my break from policing, certainly helped."

"Talking about breaks from policing, your time out was unusual. How did that come about?"

"I was a sergeant when I took my year out. I'd been working for Inspector Ferguson." Alistair's mouth opened a little, and he nodded, as if to say, I think I understand already.

"Ferguson was the worst boss anyone could wish for. He was a heavy drinker and smoker, let his private life overly influence his work, was irrational and treated his team awfully – me particularly. I don't know why, but he picked on me more than any others. Perhaps it was sex discrimination? Maybe he felt threatened by me? But whatever the reason, he made my life hell. He solved crimes but walked all over his team to take credit for the result, even though it had been a team effort. The team operated despite his poor leadership rather than because of it."

"Ferguson is rather infamous, for the reasons you've just mentioned. It's probably why he retired as a DI. Although he claimed the credit for his team's work, those who made decisions on promotion weren't blind to his methods."

"After working for him for two years I was so disillusioned I nearly resigned from the force. But my DCI persuaded me to try for unpaid leave."

"Well, I'm glad he did. Otherwise, the service would have lost you."

Suzanna was quiet, thinking back to that time, the humiliation when she made a mistake, the lack of praise when she succeeded, the acceptance of her ideas without acknowledgement, the sexual innuendos – he'd even touched her inappropriately once when he was drunk.

"By the way, don't worry about the cost of your trip. I've already talked it through with the Chief Super. He was his usual, huffing and puffing self," Alistair looked over his shoulder at the open doorway as if checking that he was not being overheard, "but he couldn't deny that it had been worth it, with the two culprits locked up and convictions certain... By the way, Ewan has given notice of early retirement. He'll be leaving in six months' time."

Suzanna's face brightened at the news. Her chief critic would be off her back. 'Just a few months to hang on. Brilliant.' She thought.

"We'll be heading down the bar after work today if you'd like to join us?"

"I think I will. It's been a while since I let my hair down and put away a couple of pints of heavy with the guys. I'll give Helen a ring and ask her if she wouldn't mind picking me up from the bar, so I can leave my car here."

"Oh, by the way, I just heard earlier that our search of the Forth near the Kincardine jetty was fruitful. The divers found the piece of sandstone that had been used to smash our victim's face. It had her blood on it and a trace of Mrs Mukherjee's DNA." Alistair gave a thumbs-up sign as he left the office, a smile on his face.

Chapter 72

The session in the bar was as jovial and noisy as ever. The team quizzed Zahir about his trip to his family's home country. They were all attentive as he recalled their time in Daulatdia, including their meeting of the mafia boss and fighting off the attack mounted by the humiliated pimps. It had been quite an eventful trip, Suzanna thought. She listened as Zahir enhanced all those occasions, dramatizing the danger, then went on to say how the scariest part of the trip was returning home and having to report to his mum that he'd not visited his uncle in Dhaka. They all laughed.

As usual, Suzanna was the first to leave the bar after a couple of non-alcoholic drinks. Alistair was enjoying himself as she said her goodbyes and headed off home. She parked her car outside her apartment and looked up at the Georgian building – at the bay window where just a few days ago she'd drawn the curtains and shortly afterwards made love with Callum. God! It had been good. He'd known exactly how to excite her, had pressed all the right buttons. It had been wonderful to lie with him afterwards, satisfied, content, and glowing. Just like old times.

But as she pictured the bed, her mind returned to two years ago when Callum had been on that bed straddled by a naked woman, riding him. Every detail of their intimacy had been open to her eyes. She remembered how his face had changed from ecstasy to shock as he saw her standing in the bedroom doorway, suitcase in hand, having returned early from a conference. Suzanna's eyes moistened, then flowed as she recalled the event. She wiped her wet cheeks with a tissue, got out of the car, then walked to her apartment, still pondering what to do. Distracted by her emotions, she stumbled on the entrance steps, only her instinctive agility saving her from skinned knees.

* * *

Suzanna unpacked and set the washing machine going, because it needed doing, and to distract her from the emotions that came with thinking about her dilemma. When she'd caught up on the chores, she made coffee and sat in her lounge. Her treasured heirloom sat on the table in its cloth bag, grabbing her attention. After removing it, she twizzled the magnifying glass, watching it glint as the lens caught the light. She recalled the distress of discovering it had been stolen from her home and later finding young Billy Boyd had been the thief.

Suzanna hadn't known that Billy's older brother Jimmy had died shortly after leaving the hospital. She'd learned that Jimmy had taken the lens from his younger brother, then ran across the road and been knocked down by a car. The last she'd heard, he was still in the hospital. It's no wonder that his dad was upset. Jimmy's death must have been a total shock. But that didn't excuse the drunken attack on the doctor, who'd no doubt done his best for the boy.

'Life isn't perfect, that's for sure,' she thought, 'and humans are fragile creatures. No one knew when they might meet their end or how. Only God!' She'd said it automatically, 'only God.' She wondered about that. Her parents had brought her up as a regular church-going Christian, but she'd lost faith in her teens and never got it back. Maybe she'd find time for one of those Alpha courses someday?

She replaced the magnifying glass into its bag and laid it on the table, then picked up her phone. A text to her sister, Charlie, was overdue. She asked if she could visit over the weekend, placed the phone down and looked around her apartment. It was good to be home. She was thankful that her great-great-uncle had put her to the test all those years ago. It had shaped her life, and she was happy – until she remembered her predicament and the action she must take.

She stared out of the window for a few minutes before picking up her phone and dialling. As the call was answered, she thought she saw the same man across the road on his phone that she'd seen a couple of weeks ago – strange. "Hi, James. I'm home and free to meet. Would you like to come round for a glass of something and a snack?"

"That'd be great. I can leave straight away if that suits?... I've missed you."

"Great. I'll see you in half an hour, then."

Time to come clean.

Epilogue

Three Weeks Later

She skipped breakfast and left the apartment early, trudging through the fresh snow, her new skis over her shoulder. Her whole body was glowing by the time she'd reached the base station. Two dozen skiers boarded the first cable car of the day and rode to the top of the mountain at 2400 metres. The sun rising from behind the mountain range warmed her face. The blue sky promised a glorious day ahead.

"What a fantastic day It's going to be," she said to her partner. "See you at the bottom."

She marched out of the station, dropped her skis onto the snow, then stepped into the bindings before skating off. As the slope dropped away, gravity took over, removing the need to skate, and she turned the skis parallel, facing straight down the slope. As the speed picked up, she transferred weight from one ski to the other, creating gentle rhythmic turns. The slope steepened, and the skis accelerated. Her body lowered, and she adopted the stance of a goalkeeper waiting to save a penalty kick – knees bent, arms slightly out from her sides, stomach sucked in, well-balanced and ready to pounce. She let the skis run, turning them onto their curved edges to let the sharp metal bite and carve turns in the snow.

The dawn patrol of Italian piste-bashing machines had packed down the overnight snowfall. The slope welcomed its first skier of the day. Devoid of ridges or piles of snow from other skiers, conditions were perfect for a downhill run. No obstacles, no unpredictable people weaving their way back and forth, closing off her path. She was free to let loose and feel the wind on her cheeks.

She flattened the skis and dropped lower, hands extended in front of her, reaching forward, her low centre of gravity enabling faster cornering and greater stability. The white, glistening surface rushed past her as she sped down the mountain. Her weight shifted from one ski to the other and her edges flipped over to take the next turn, paralleling the trees bordering the slope. Her speed continued to increase. She was flying down the slope, her legs instinctively moving to absorb bumps and change direction as she looked ahead. A ridge loomed, and she pre-jumped the rise to keep her feet on the snow.

The slope dropped away sharply as she hit the next ridge, her skis lifting off the snow, airborne for a few seconds. She landed with a thump and her legs absorbed the compression, her edges digging in to take the next turn. Now it was straight downhill to the base station and nothing in the way. Her skis pointed down the fall-line of the hill and she took off, adrenalin pumping through her excited body, the thrill of speed making her feel alive.

Nearing the base station, she straightened her legs, pushing upwards to create aerodynamic drag, then turned the skis sideways against the flow and sunk again, digging the sharp metal into the hardened snow. She skidded to a hall, ice particles shooting into the air, creating a glistening cloud, sparkling in the early sunlight.

As she looked back up the mountain, through the shining ice mist, she exclaimed, "Wow! That was *fantastic.*" Her breathing was heavy as she sucked in the chilled air, recovering from the exertion... She felt a buzz near her left breast. Then the phone broke into its ring tune.

She retrieved it as quickly as she could, answering before it stopped ringing. The screen declared the caller: Alistair.

"Hello, Alistair. What's up?" she said, still breathing heavily.

"Hi, Suzanna. Sorry to trouble you on your holiday, but we have a problem. There's been a murder."

"Surely Angus can handle that?"

"Yes. Yes. Of course, if he was able to. He went skiing over the weekend at Glenshee and took a fall on an icy patch. He's in hospital with his leg in plaster and with Una still out of play, recuperating, resources are tight. Rab has taken on the junior investigating officer role, but I need a senior on the ground to be SIO."

"What do we know so far?" He briefed her on the circumstances of the murder.

"Okay, Alistair. Look, I'll try to get home tonight and be in the office tomorrow. I take it the Force will cover my additional travel costs."

"Naturally. Although the Chief Super won't be happy, he'll have to accept that. He seems to spend most of his time scrutinizing budgets, nowadays."

"Okay, Alistair. Unless you hear from me again today, expect me to be at work in the morning, some time."

"See you tomorrow, Suzanna. And thanks."

Her partner came to a halt next to her. "I bet you've been here several minutes, going by the speed you set off at from the top. I saw you disappear over the first rise and that was the last time I saw you."

"Yes. It was fantastic letting the skis run. It brought back memories of racing the downhill when I was in the University Ski Team. Just wish I could do that more often." She looked her partner in the eye. "I've bad news, I'm afraid... You'll have likely noticed I was on the phone?"

"Yes?" He looked at her quizzically, expecting to hear something that would spoil their time together. He was already upset before she told him what the bad news was.

"Well, that was the Superintendent, Alistair Milne. He's asked me to return ASAP to take over a murder investigation. I've said I'll try to get a flight back tonight. I'm really sorry."

He rolled his eyes then looked at her disappointed "Work always comes first for you, doesn't it?"

"Crime is 24/7, 365. You know I have to respond when the call comes. It's the job. It's what I do." She looked sadly at him, wondering if she'd made the right choice.

* * *

Free book

Sign up for occasional updates from Harry (at www.harrynavinski.com) to **receive a** free gift.

Reviews

I hope you enjoyed reading this book. It would make me very happy if you could now leave a review on Amazon and Goodreads, so others may gain from your assessment and to help me build credibility as an author.

Acknowledgements

Although the NGOs, social enterprise, and characters mentioned in this novel are fictional, there are organisations working within India on anti-human trafficking, fulfilling similar roles to those described. All these entities are doing incredible work, and I encourage you to find out more about them and to consider supporting their work by following any or all of the links.

Freeset (www.freesetglobal.com) is the largest Freedom Business on the edge of Sonagachi and employs over 200 hundred people who would otherwise be caught up in the sex trade.

Justice Ventures International (JVI) is an NGO raising awareness of trafficking and helping repatriate victims (www.justiceventures.org).

International Justice Mission (IJM) works with the police within Indian cities and beyond, to assist victims to escape forced prostitution (www.ijm.org).

In Edinburgh, Shakti Women's Aid (named in this novel), is working hard to help abused women (www.shaktiedinburgh.co.uk).

Lastly, I'd just like to say a huge thank you to my supporters, who helped me get this book ready for publication. Keith Salmon, Monica and Pete Bennett, Annette Salmon, and Anastasia Woodcock, for their scrutiny of early draughts of the story. Jamie Salmon, for his great cover design, and all my beta readers, especially Gail Hunstone, for their feedback on later versions. I couldn't have done it without them.

About the Author

Harry spent most of his working life in the Royal Air Force, involved in aircraft maintenance, from hands-on work to senior management roles. During his career, he lived and worked on bases in England, Scotland, Germany, and Malta. He also travelled the world with the RAF.

During his time in the Air Force, he created and edited the RAF's magazine for sports and adventurous training, 'RAF Active'. Harry's articles, written from his experience of sports and adventurous activities, included skiing, sailing, judo, and scuba diving, to name a few.

After his time in the RAF, Harry spent 6 years on voluntary service in West Bengal (anti-human trafficking work) and it was whilst in India that he made his first attempt at writing fiction. On his return to the UK, he attended a creative writing course, at Cumbria's excellent Higham Hall, that inspired him to write his first novel – *The Glass.*

After his nomadic life, he has finally settled near the UK's beautiful Lake District National Park. His travels around the world have provided Harry with a tremendous source of knowledge and experiences for new books – yet to come – and he looks forward to sharing these.

For more information about Harry, visit his Author page on Amazon or visit Harry's website: www.harrynavinski.com.

You can also connect with Harry on Twitter and Facebook

You can connect with me on:

https://www.harrynavinski.com

https://twitter.com/HarryNavinski

https://www.facebook.com/harry.navinski.9

https://www.goodreads.com/author/show/20525174.Harry_Navinski

Subscribe to my newsletter:

https://mailchi.mp/f6237e815fa4/subscribe-to-mailing-list

Also by Harry Navinski

If you haven't yet read the first book in the DCI Suzanna McLeod series, check out The Glass now. In both The Glass and The Duty, there is mention of a test Suzanna sat to gain her inheritance. My novella, The Test, fills in that part of Suzanna's story if you would like to read it.

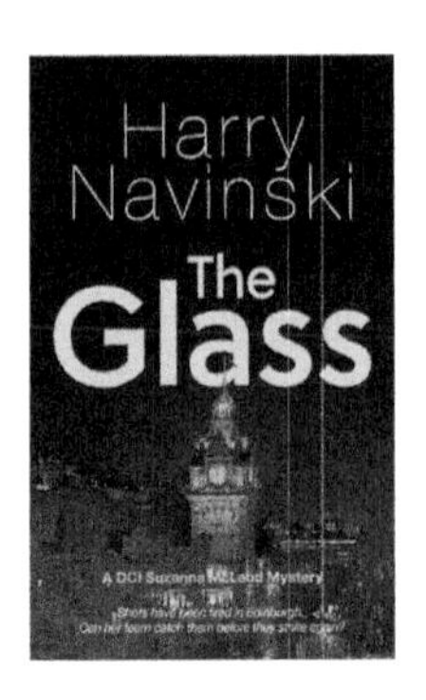

The Glass

DCI Suzanna McLeod's Edinburgh-based team has a reputation to live up to. But the Chief Superintendent is a by-the-book meddler and her team has personal problems that need her help.

Under pressure to catch armed robbers before they strike again, Suzanna's focus is challenged when her inherited magnifying glass is stolen – a cherished item that led to her becoming a detective. The young thief could never have known the impact its theft would have on him and his family.

As the chase is underway for the gunmen, Suzanna takes on the most dangerous of the criminals. But even after the case appears to be drawing to a close, something is nagging at Suzanna's gut. What could they have missed?

The Glass is the first book in the DCI Suzanna McLeod crime-fighting series. If you like fast-moving police investigations, engaging characters, action, and twists along the way, you'll love Harry Navinski's fresh crime novel.

'In many ways, this book is more than a good fictional story. There are gems within.'

'I can't wait for the next book to be released.'

'loved the way this book was written.'

'enjoyed this book from beginning to end, the pace picking as the book progressed.'

'I could easily see it made into a TV series.'

Buy *The Glass* today, to discover this exciting crime-fighting series.

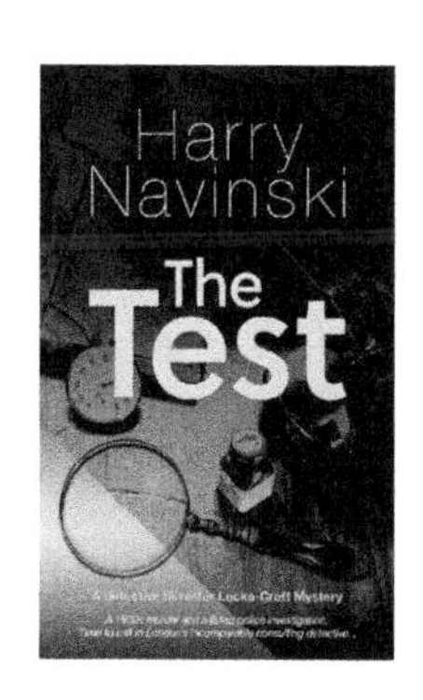

The Test

A dying man wishes his estate to be won by merit, not gained by undeserved inheritance. He creates a test – a Sherlock Holmes-style short crime story – to be taken by descendants as they turn eighteen.

Consulting detective, Silvester Locke-Croft, is called in to investigate the murder of a solicitor in 1920s London, uncovering hidden evidence and revealing the incompetence of Scotland Yard's detectives. His investigation concludes with dramatic exposure of the murderer, revealing corruption and collusion along the way.

The Test precedes the revelation in *The Glass*, of DCI Suzanna McLeod's inherence and career choice, followed up in *The Duty* – the second in this 21st Century police mystery series.

Get *The Test* today for an insight into 1920s London crime and Suzanna McLeod's backstory.

Reviewers Comments

'What a wonderful novella to set the scene [Suzanna's inheritance, in The Glass].' Holly J, UK Crime Fiction Book Club

'I really enjoyed it. I found it well-written and intriguing from the start. I learned some things about London in the 1920s and thought it was rather clever and interesting.' Julie B, UK Crime Fiction Book Club

'I'm very much "a picture the scene" kind of reader... I easily could see the story happening like watching a TV programme.' Gail H, UK Crime Fiction Book Club

‘I really liked the characters and also the fact that it wasn’t a straight-forward whodunnit.’ Cheryl N, UK Crime Fiction Book Club

‘I thoroughly enjoyed this short story... Great fun.’ Nick R, UK Crime Fiction Book Club

‘I liked how the solution kept building in tension until the very last minute to find out who the killer was.’ Anastasia W

Printed in Great Britain
by Amazon

42867265R00209